THE DISCOVERY

Also available from Eva Fischer-Dixon:

The Third Cloud

Hannah's Song

A Journey to Passion

For the Last Time

THE DISCOVERY

EVA FISCHER-DIXON

Library of Congress Control Number: 2005910010
ISBN :   Hardcover   1-4257-0237-6
                      Softcover   1-4257-0236-8

This book was printed in the United States of America.

To order additional copies of this book, contact:
Xlibris Corporation
1-888-795-4274
www.Xlibris.com
Orders@Xlibris.com
32069

TO MY MOTHER

PROLOGUE

"Are you alright?" she heard the voice of her friend sitting quietly next to her on the hard plastic seat in the lobby of the airport. Before replying, she glanced toward the direction of the gate only a few short steps from where they semi patiently waited, for the boarding call to their long flight.

"I am alright, as much as I can be," she replied although it was not entirely true and she suspected that Sandy sensed her increasing tension. Sandy reached out for her hand as it lay folded on the top of a leather bag that contained her treasured and much used lap top computer. She squeezed Chava's hand gently but assuring.

"It's not your first trip back, you shouldn't be nervous about it," Sandy said quietly.

"I suppose you are right, but it is my first trip to bury a relative, especially my mother," Chava whispered back to her. Sandy nodded, acknowledging that she could not argue about that fact, but deep down inside she felt concerned for her long time friend. She found it ironic that now it was her turn to consol Chava and she thought of that overused and old cliché "what are friends are for?"

CHAPTER ONE

O ne year, three months and seventeen days earlier Sandy was a total wreck; getting over a nasty divorce that left her financially in shambles and totally devastated emotionally. Her mind was family oriented, full of images of future children and seemingly happy times she spent with her handsome husband of eleven years; she neither could nor would accept the fact Dennis was a liar, a cheater and a thief. Even though an entire year passed since her divorce decree was granted, she was occasionally and unavoidably forced to think about him. She still had a difficult time believing that a man she so blindly trusted would secretly, slowly, deliberately and completely drain their joint savings and checking accounts, leaving her virtually penniless. He had full control over their finances ever since they were married and when she inquired from time to time about certain financial transactions, he would accuse her of not trusting him with such intensity that she always ended up apologizing to him.

Their making up was always passionate, although they seemed even more passionate than other times when they made love. She wanted to have children but Dennis always delayed the much desired event by explaining to her that he wanted children too, but not just yet. "Let's have a good time first, let's travel, let's have fun," he would say to her.

How ironic, Sandy thought, *that it was her friend Chava, sitting next her with her eyes closed, perhaps not sleeping just reflecting in the past happenings, just like she was now doing, that broke the now seeming inevitable truth to her.*

Chava was checking in with a receptionist at her gynecologist office to have her annual "well woman" examination when she noticed the name of a friend of hers and Sandy's, two lines above her own on the sign-in sheet. She turned around and noticed their mutual friend, Lorna sitting in the doctor's waiting room. She either did not notice Chava or tried not too as she had her head buried in a wrinkled much read "People Weekly", she held tightly with both of her hands.

After Chava signed her name, the time of her arrival and the time of her scheduled appointment on the list, she sat down next to Lorna and playfully tapped on the back of the magazine. Lorna looked up and she seemed almost embarrassed. She nervously smiled at Chava and they gave each other an almost not touching hug. "How are you?" asked Chava.

"I'm fine." Lorna replied. "How about you?" she asked in return.

"Doing great, just getting my annual checkup," Chava explained briefly. "We haven't seen you for a long time. As a matter of fact, Sandy and I were talking about you the other night that we miss our weekly "dinner and movie" gatherings. You certainly look great! What am I saying, you always look great," Chava said and laughed.

"I have been quite busy lately," replied Lorna in a tone of voice that made Chava look at her friend as a strange tingle ran through her mind. "You are not sick are you?" she asked her with concern.

She couldn't get an answer as the door that lead to a long, white hallway with small sanitized examination rooms on both sides opened. A nurse wearing white pants with a bright colored smock with a variety of babies printed on it and a stethoscope loosely hanging around her neck called Lorna's name. She abruptly got up dropping the magazine from her lap to the well walked on, but almost still clean floor and not even bothering to pick it up, she rushed to the open door just to disappear next to the nurse who promptly closed the door behind them. *What was that about?* Chava wondered.

She did not see Lorna after that strange encounter in her doctor's office for a few months, and by then, everything was out on the open. Her name was called shortly by another friendly nurse and by the time she finished with her routine examination, Lorna had already departed.

On her way out, as usual, she stopped by at the billing clerk's window and handed the person her insurance card so she could make a copy of it, and to make her co-payment. She was about to leave when the nurse who called Lorna inside tapped on her shoulder. "Excuse me Ms. Diamond," said the nurse stopping her. Chava turned around to face her. "I am sorry to trouble you but I was wondering if you would do us a favor?" Before Chava was able to respond, the nurse continued. "Lorna, I mean Mrs. King mentioned that you are friends, and I was just wondering if you wouldn't mind to take a couple of booklets for her that she forgot after she dressed."

"I'll be glad to," Chava responded. The nurse smiled back at Chava and she placed two magazine size booklets into Chava's obviously trustworthy hands. The nurse thanked her and let her go on her way. She didn't look at the booklets until she got into her car, after casually tossing them on the passenger seat.

One of the booklets, the shiny covered one was titled, "What you should know and expect during your first trimester," and the second one which had no picture on it's cover, as if it didn't want to advertise its inside contents simple read, "Women's Choices."

For several long moments, she was unable to take her eyes off the booklets while her hand idly rested on the key already pushed inside the ignition. *If Lorna was pregnant, why didn't she say so?* She wondered. They have been friends for several years and for the past two or three years, the three of them, Sandy, Lorna and herself got together religiously every Wednesday night for what they called "break the week in half night."

Most of the time they took turns to select a restaurant for the evening and after that they either ended up at the apartment or house of one of them to watch a movie, or just simply they went to a movie theater and made on the spot decisions what they wanted to see. Sandy and Chava had not seen Lorna for almost a month and their inquiring and concerned phone messages were left unanswered both at home and at her place of work, at a large local bank. What was even stranger is that when Sandy stopped by the high rise apartment building that Lorna called her "home, sweet home," the doorman not only prevented her passage as usual, but he quoted the strict instructions given to him and to his fellow colleagues by Lorna that nobody can disturb her, by calling up to her apartment or by letting anyone up. He put an emphasis on the word "nobody." Later on while she was still in awe, she recounted the short yet disturbing conversation between herself and the doorman to Chava who became equally surprised and shocked.

Still starring at the booklets that contained information on the wanted and unwanted pregnancies, Chava's lips parted, and as she later told Sandy, she felt as if a bolt of lightning that would have not killed her but instead jolted her to life or in that particular case to realization. The kind of realization that with some mighty power put those little pieces of puzzles into their places, the ones that occasionally gave the puzzle player the suspicion that perhaps those unruly pieces did not even belong to that particular puzzle board. "This just cannot be," whispered Chava and looked into the rear view mirror of her car as if she expected to see someone there.

She started her car and drove directly to Sandy's place, a twenty minute ride through the city's business district, the Embarcadero. Sandy and Dennis lived in the Marina area that Chava also loved but found outrageously expensive, not that she would complain about her own place. Living in Sausalito was not much cheaper, but Chava was lucky to find a "fixer upper" for half the price that a house would have cost in the Marina district. It was the very same house that she would turn into a luxurious home after her royalties began to flow in.

She parked her car in front of the garage and picked up the booklets from the passenger seat before locking her car. She pushed the doorbell impatiently more than once as she could hardly wait to see Sandy. It seemed like forever for the door to open. Chava began to wonder if anybody was home at all.

Sandy opened the door and Chava was stunned by her looks. Running mascara marks left zigzags on her smooth, wrinkle free face, her eyes were puffy from crying and her nose was red from wiping it often. She didn't say anything to Chava; she simply let the door open as a sign of invitation. She stepped into the immaculate, almost museum like house and for the first time in years, she hesitantly looked at her sobbing friend. Chava turned to her and asked the appropriate question of that moment. "What happened?"

Sandy did not respond, instead, she quietly handed Chava a ten page long document that was stapled together by the upper left corner. It was not the first time that Chava had seen a document like that, although those papers were not hers then either. It was a petition for a divorce proceeding with Dennis K. Johnston as the petitioner versus Sandy L. Johnston. She dropped the booklets to the abstract shaped coffee table's ceramic top and sunk into one of the most comfortable arm chairs, her favorite in Sandy's house, she had ever sat in. She carefully read each and every page while her friend went to the downstairs bathroom to clean up and reapply her barely visible makeup she always wore, at home or in public.

It was clear that Dennis wanted nothing to do with Sandy other than a divorce and even that, a quick one. Sandy went on to explain to Chava a short time later after she finished reading the documents drawn up by Dennis' lawyer who at one point of time in the past used to be Sandy's, that the document was hand delivered earlier that day and she immediately called her bank to close her accounts just to find out that they were already closed the previous day by Mr. Johnston, so she was told.

Chava got up and walked to her friend who began to weep again. "I have no money, I have no home, no car, and no job and most importantly, I have no marriage. I have lived with a man who just yesterday made plans for us to go to Catalina Island for a week next month, while all along he knew that it was all a lie."

They heard the door open at the end of the hallway that led to the outside. Chava couldn't believe her eyes when she saw Dennis walk in. He stopped for a moment and without uttering a single word to either of them, he proceeded to go upstairs to his home office. The two women looked at each other completely stunned about Dennis' arrogance, Chava didn't know what to say next and she pondered about getting a baseball bat and beating the crap out of Dennis for what he was doing to her friend.

Her thoughts were interrupted by the ringing of the phone and after the third ring, she motioned to Sandy that she should be picking up the phone but she just shook her head. Chava stepped to the phone at the end table and picked it up. Before she could say as much as a "hello" there were voices on the line.

"Dennis," she heard the familiar voice of Lorna.

"Hello sweetheart," he answered. Chava had to put her hand over the receiver for preventing herself from saying something. She supposed that Dennis thought that by letting the phone ring three times, Sandy didn't want to answer and Chava and he picked up the phone at the same time. "How are you feeling?" he asked her.

"Well, your child is misbehaving and I have been throwing up all morning. I am surprised that you went back to the house before she moved out, what are you doing there anyway?" She inquired.

"I have some business papers to gather together but I'll be there shortly. Chava is here with her," he explained.

"Chava probably suspects something," Lorna remarked.

"She is definitely smarter than Sandy," Dennis laughed.

"Hurry up Dennis, I miss you terribly," she purred into the phone. The sound made Chava's stomach turn and she ground her teeth in anger.

A little while later they both hang up the phone and Chava settled down next to Sandy. "Who was it?" she asked.

"I tell you later," Chava replied. Dennis came down the stairs with a stuffed briefcase and luggage. He left the same way as he arrived, silently, unashamed for what he was doing to his wife of eleven years.

After he left, Chava told her friend everything that transpired despite the fact that she was fully aware of the devastating affects of her words on Sandy. She knew that unloading the cruel reality, from Dennis's infidelity to Lorna's pregnancy by her best friend's husband was large potion of a bitter poison to swallow, but at the very same time, she was ready to offer a remedy to her devastated and disheveled friend.

"I have plenty of room in my house where you can stay as long as you want. I can loan you money until you are able to get a job. I even have a second car that you are able to use to commute," Chava offered without a moment of hesitation. She and Sandy both knew that it was much easier said than done but the bottom line was that it could be done.

CHAPTER TWO

F ifteen minutes before the scheduled departure time, their flight and gate number was announced over the intercom and promptly within minutes after the announcement, a line, two and at times three people deep began to form in front of the gate. The airline employee called the row numbers to be boarded first and they were clearly first class seats. Chava and Sandy got up and without having to wait in line, they walked up to the airline employee and handed her their boarding passes, which she quickly slid through the machine next to her. With a smile on her face that was either mandatory or voluntary, one can never be certain, she wished them a great trip as they began to walk down the tarmac.

As soon as they took their seats, one of the flight attendants offered them multiple choices of drinks; champagne, orange juice, wine, beer other alcoholic or refreshment beverages. They selected the orange juice, neither of them wanted to drink that early in the afternoon. Once all the passengers were accounted for, the flight attendants went through their motions; they made sure that all of the over head compartments were securely closed and that all passengers had their seatbelts on. And then, the inevitable showcase of presentation of what to do in case of an emergency was on.

Chava couldn't possibly recall just how many times she witnessed the same scene, yet she always held the illustrated instruction provided by the airlines to all passengers in her hand and she never failed to follow the flight attendant's demonstration on how to use the oxygen mask when it was dropped from its overhead hiding place if the airplane depressurized, how to follow the light on the floor if the plane plunged into darkness and so on.

She turned to her friend Sandy who was busy adjusting the air that she found was too much for her at that moment. "What?" she asked from Chava when she looked up seeing her watching what she was doing. "It's too much air," she commented.

"Pay attention," Chava pointed at the flight attendant who was about to finish the demonstration.

"Oh please," said Sandy and rolled her eyes. "If it's time to go, we go. No air mask or sliding down the emergency exit will help you if the plane explodes or ditches into the water."

"Your outlook is positively uplifting," Chava chuckled and placed the illustrated instruction back where she found it. The pilot announced they were cleared for take off and asked the flight attendants to take their seats.

Chava took a deep breath and she felt Sandy's hand on hers. "Are you still okay?" Sandy asked and while Chava wasn't sure if she was asking her about the flight taking off or about her mental state, either way, she nodded that she was alright. The plane took off and Chava closed her eyes as she recalled the conversation she had with one of the nurses at the hospice where her mother was a patient, as she was dying from cancer.

"Hi, this is Chava Diamond, Mrs. Diamond's daughter. I am calling from the United States," she introduced herself as she did each and every time she called religiously on every Saturday morning, not knowing which nurse she was talking to. It seemed to her that each time she called, there was someone new sitting at the nurse's station.

"Hello, this is Nurse Margit," replied the strange voice at the other end of the line.

"I was calling about my mother, how is she?" Chava asked.

"I am sorry to tell you, but your mother is gone," said the nurse, not convincingly enough for Chava to believe that her apology was sincere nor did Chava truly understand the real meaning of the information the nurse gave her that moment.

"Where did she go?" Chava asked and could not imagine why her terminally ill mother was allowed to leave the hospital.

"She passed away this morning," the nurse said bluntly.

"Oh," Chava mumbled, unable to think of anything to say at that very moment.

"Are you still there?" she heard the nurse's voice.

"Yes, yes I am still here." Chava switched hands holding the telephone. "What happened?" she was finally able to ask the simple yet important question.

"I shouldn't be telling you because I am not a doctor but because you are so far away, I am assuming that it is alright to tell you that Mrs. Diamond's cancer spread to her lungs and breasts. She passed away in her sleep during the early morning hours today," explained the nurse to Chava, who was listening intently although her mind was thousands of miles away.

"Would you please do me a favor and tell who ever is responsible for the funeral arrangements that I'll be there as soon as I can, possibly on Wednesday, and that I'll be paying for whatever expenses will occur. I would be very grateful if they put the funeral on hold, I don't want my mother to be buried in a common grave."

"Please consider it done," promised the nurse and after taking a few more quick notes, Chava pushed the button to disconnect the line. She remained sitting on the stool where she was while talking on the phone, finally letting her hand go of the receiver. "*What just happened?*" she wondered out loud. The realization that she just lost her only relative, her only family member in the entire world just wouldn't sink in. She picked up the receiver again and dialed the number of her closest friend, Sandy.

"What's up girl?" Sandy asked with her usual cheerful attitude. When Chava did not respond right away, she asked her again. "Did something happen, talk to me." Her cheerfulness was gone and her voice was becoming demanding.

"My mother passed away this morning," blurted out Chava.

"Oh my God," said Sandy with shock in her voice. "What are you going to do? Are you going back for the funeral?"

"I guess I better," commented Chava and than she asked her friend. "Would you like to see the country where I came from? My treat and first class all the way," she added.

"Honey, you don't have to pay for my trip, I'll go with you no matter who is paying," Sandy said without a moment of hesitation.

"I asked for a delay with the funeral but I think we can there by Wednesday. Would that be alright with you if we fly on Tuesday?" she asked Sandy.

"Sure thing Chava, I'll make arrangements with my neighbor to take care of my cat and I'll be ready. Would you like me to make the flight arrangements, I'll be glad too," she offered.

"No, it's okay. I can handle that." Chava replied, then she added. "Thanks anyway. I'll call you when I have the tickets and the itinerary.

It took less than an hour and their trip to her native country was set. She dreaded the trip as she dreaded all the trips she had ever taken back to her birth place, Hungary. She tried real hard not to think about the difficult and poverty stricken life she and her parents had to endure, but most of all, she hated the memory of the hopelessness she experienced while she was growing up. Things have changed there dramatically and even her books were translated into her native language and they were selling well. She thought about calling her Hungarian representative but she was not up to it. After all, it was not a joyous trip back to her old homeland.

She hated many things about her life in Hungary but she especially hated the hypocrisy that a great many people harbored and practiced. Just the thought that she might have to face her only living relative in Hungary, her despised cousin Pete, turned her stomach. She considered him nothing more than a leach who if he had a chance, would suck her bank account dry and once he satisfied himself he would still go for any leftovers that others might have left behind.

During her past visits, presents, money or material things, for instance, brand new clothing were never nice enough, nor was there ever enough for him or her aunt who already passed away before her mother did. Pete wanted to treat her, knowing that she was married to an "American," as a money pit, only if she would have let him to succeed. The situation and Pete's expectations after she became a successful writer was simply intolerable. He has not sent her as much as canned food when she was in a refugee camp waiting to immigrate to the United States of America, but he expected her to be his "sugar mommy." She plainly told him that if he didn't like what she gave him it was just "too bad", and she refused to give him American dollars which he wanted to sell on the black market, or send him clothing or other materialistic things he so bluntly asked for.

There was one point of time, Chava recalled, *that Pete tried to force Chava's parents to write the apartment over to his name.* Chava was sure that when that happened, her parents would have become homeless. She made threats to her parents that she would never go back, not even for a visit and that they would never see her again if they wrote their names on a contract he drew up with a shady attorney. Chava's mother knew that her daughter was serious with her threats and she refused to sign the document, she told Pete that Chava wanted to look at it first. He tore up the documents and tossed it into Chava's mother's face.

Chava was wondering if Pete, who claimed deep love for her parents would dare to show his face at the funeral, but she seriously doubted it. Still, she dreaded the thought that he just might attend his aunt's funeral.

Sandy looked at her and wondered what her friend was thinking about. She knew how Chava felt about going back to Hungary and even if Chava wouldn't have asked her to go with her, she would have offered it. She also knew that Chava was, to put it mildly, not a big fan of her native country's government or some of the people there. Chava never said it with so many words that she hated her native country, she just simply hated the life she was forced to live there.

Chava had a sad life, full of tragedies, Sandy thought. Her father passed away while she was a young girl, and it hurt her tremendously as she deeply loved her father. She was truly a daddy's girl. When her mother remarried, their life eased somewhat better but not much. She and her stepfather got along alright although "love" never was an emotion between them. Chava always felt that there was something, some sort of unsaid feelings between them, although he never told Chava that he loved her or even just liked her. Despite the fact that her stepfather never showed any emotion towards her, she always felt a high level of respect for him for helping her mother to raise her and for lifting them a touch above the poverty level.

Sandy had never encountered anyone who loved to tell stories as much as Chava did. Behind everything there was a story and Chava's love for writing was admirable. She could write virtually about any subject and Sandy loved to read her friend's writings. As far as she knew, writing was one of the two reasons why Chava left Hungary. One, she wanted to be a writer and the second was to leave poverty behind.

Their thoughts were interrupted by the flight attendant's question about the selection of their dinner entree. After the food was served and consumed, Sandy said to her friend; "I know that it sounds kind of silly, I was thinking that you and I should take a nice vacation somewhere after this trip. What do you think of that idea?" asked Sandy.

"Sounds good but let us first survive this one," Chava replied.

The male flight attendant returned and asked them what they would like to drink. "Some coffee would be nice," said Chava and Sandy wanted the same.

Sandy looked at the flight attendant who had a nice smile and it become evident that he took a liking to Chava. He brought the coffee to Chava on a tray with some cookies set at the side of the cup. "Thank you," said Chava. "By the way, my friend here also wanted some coffee as well."

"Yes, I know, but bringing them separately gives me an opportunity to come back," he said with a grin on his face. "By the way Ms. Diamond, I am great fan of yours, I love your stories, especially your suspense novel, The Third Cloud, and I hope that I don't have to wait too long for the next one."

Chava barely looked up at him as she replied briefly. "Let's hope not."

Sandy covered her mouth to hide a chuckle and Chava just played ignorant as she didn't "get" the flight attendants flirting words.

He indeed returned with another cup of coffee with sugar and crème but no cookies. "See," said Sandy. "He likes you best. Where is my cookie?" she asked jokingly. Chava smiled for the first time in days as she handed Sandy one of the cookies. "Honey, you missed the point," Sandy remarked.

"No I didn't, I'm just simply ignoring the "point," admitted Chava.

"I know that the timing is not exactly ideal, but you see, somehow deep inside, someday you and I will find the right man, the real love of our lives," said Sandy but she wasn't sure herself that she really believed in the encouraging words she spoke.

"Look who is trying to cheer me up now," remarked Chava, but she was glad that her friend was opening up to the possibility that she may date again someday, although she was not so sure about herself. *Will I ever able to love and trust again?* she wondered.

"I have never asked you this," said Sandy turning to her friend again. "Do you still have any friends or relatives left in Hungary?"

"Well, most of my friends left the country and some of them who still live in Hungary I have lost contact with a long time ago. I no longer have any living relatives I can brag about, unless we are still considering the "leach" among the human beings," explained Chava.

"Who is the "leach?" Sandy asked curiously but as she looked at Chava, she noticed a sprinkle of hatred in her eyes.

"The "leach" is my cousin Pete who would suck anyone's pocket book or wallet dry if he was given a chance."

"I hope we don't see that creep," remarked Sandy. She became quiet for a few moments then reached for Chava's hand and asked. "Honey, are you telling me that you have no living relatives at all left in Hungary?"

Chava nodded and looked up at the male flight attendant who was passing by them again. He stopped for a few moments and gave her a smile that gave a tingle she hasn't experienced for a very long time. It's not only that she had not been with a man since her separation and subsequent divorce from her husband Matthew, but she didn't even go out on a single date since then. She smiled back at the flight attendant whose nametag read Brandon, but she quickly turned her attention back to Sandy who followed her friend's eye movement and she couldn't help but to smile at her.

"I'm sorry," Chava shook her head. "I didn't mean to ignore your question. You are right; I have no one left in Hungary whom I could call a relative. There is nothing left that would draw me back to the place where my life was misery," she gave some thought what she was about to say to her friend. "Please don't misunderstand me, I do not hate my native country but I always despised hypocrisy and when I was growing up, it had one of the most oppressive government systems I had experienced. Hungary is a beautiful country with hills and mountains and there is Lake Balaton I always enjoyed. Hungary had a rich, eventful and tragic history and it used to have a very important part in the happenings of the world. I experienced a lot of bad things while I was growing up and I saw many injustices committed. Maybe someday I tell you about it."

"You know, many of our fellow Americans are taking their freedom and all what they have for granted, and you my friend had to suffer and endure extreme hardship to get where you are. I am forever grateful that I didn't have to go through hell like you did and yet, you are the only one who supported me and you were there for me when I was in a desperate situation. I hope that someday and somehow I can pay back your kindness," Sandy said and squeezed Chava's hand.

Chava shook her head. "Friends don't owe friends anything, don't you forget that. I am the one who should be grateful to you for coming with me in this difficult time of my life."

"I guess we are lucky to have each other for friends," remarked Sandy and smiled at her. Chava nodded in agreement and she thought, *indeed I am lucky to have good friends.*

CHAPTER THREE

Although it was a long flight, luckily it was an uneventful one. After a while the male flight attendant stopped flirting with Chava after Sandy jokingly told him that because she always had to ask him twice for everything that she wouldn't be leaving a tip. Chava looked at her friend when she said that, she didn't laugh at her friend's joke but Sandy noticed a twinkle of recognized humor in Chava's eyes.

Their flight landed in Frankfurt, Germany where they had to wait another two hours before their next connection with the Hungarian Airlines, MALEV took off. It was an old Russian airplane and Chava made a remark that she hoped that they would survive the couple of hours long flight.

To their pleasant surprise going through the Hungarian passport check and customs was a breeze unlike their fellow Hungarian national passengers who were stuck in long lines before the customs officer. A few minutes after passing through the customs area, they found themselves outside the relatively small airport. Chava looked around and Sandy asked her what she was looking for.

"It is certainly different to come back nowadays, unlike the first time I came back for a visit. When our plane landed, we were immediately surrounded by heavily armed soldiers and we had to board a bus to take us to the terminal. Now you can barely see any soldiers, I think I only noticed a couple of them inside the terminal and I also saw a few policeman, but the security is nothing like it used to be, which is a good thing."

A man wearing a beret walked up to them and asked if he could drive them to their destination. Chava made reservations at the Atrium Hyatt Hotel when she bought their airline tickets and before she agreed with the driver to take them, she asked which car was his. He pointed his car out to them and to their surprise it was an older model BMW, still in good shape with only a few dents on the doors and some chipped paint on the car's hood. "It doesn't have a taxi sign on," said Chava to the man suspiciously. She did notice that many of the cars outside the terminal had no taxi signs, yet the men waiting for passengers were hustling the arriving crowd.

"I am a private driver, you know, trying to make some money on the side. But I do have a license to carry passengers, do you want to see it?" he offered.

"Yes I do." Chava replied. The man pulled out his wallet from his pants back pocket and showed an ID to her. Satisfied with the license and after translating the brief conversation, he helped them with their luggage to his car and placed the two suitcases inside the trunk. "Please take us to the Atrium Hyatt Hotel," said Chava to the driver.

"Are you tired?" asked Sandy.

"Just a little bit, are you?" she asked in return.

"Actually not at all, snoozing a little bit on the plane helped."

"Once we check in, I need to call the nursing home where my mother passed away to see what I have to do to make the funeral arrangements," Chava said in a quiet voice.

"Excuse me," said the driver in Hungarian. "May I ask where you ladies are coming from?"

"California," Chava replied, not offering any further details.

"You speak good Hungarian, where did you learn?" asked the driver and it was obvious to both of them that he was either trying to initiate a conversation or was gathering information.

"I left this country a long time ago and I came back this one more time to bury my mother," replied Chava and she hoped that there wouldn't be anymore questions.

"I am very sorry to hear that," said the driver and that was all he said until they arrived at the hotel. He helped them with their suitcases again which were taken over by the doorman who readily stood outside the revolving door. Chava realized that she only had dollars so she turned to the driver.

"You have two options," she said to him after he told her how much they owed for the ride." I can give you twenty dollars which is a lot more than the ride cost or wait until I exchange money inside."

The driver smiled back at her as he replied. "The twenty dollars would do fine." He thanked her for the money and got back into his vehicle.

Their connecting rooms were pleasantly luxurious which Chava was certain that an average income Hungarian would never be able to experience. Leaving her suitcase on the luggage rack that stood next to the dresser where the bell boy left it, she went to the doors that separated her room from Sandy's and unlocked the door.

Her friend appeared several minutes later in a different outfit than she was wearing during their journey. She found Chava on the telephone talking in her native language. She could easily tell that the subject was Chava's late mother and very likely she was addressing the funeral arrangements. Sandy patiently sat down in one of the comfortable chairs by the small, yet stylish little desk that was stacked with leaflets and booklets bravely advertising the buzzing nightlife of the once so tight lipped city.

Sandy lifted her head up when she heard Chava raising her voice an octave higher when she answered apparently some issues that she was not too pleased to hear. Soon after she hung up the phone with a puzzled look on her face she turned to Sandy, but she didn't volunteer any comment or remark right away.

"What happened?" asked Sandy not able to hide her natural curiosity which seconds later turned into concern. Chava's face became white as the wall and Sandy was worried that her friend was perhaps close to passing out. "Chava, talk to me," she begged her. "Are you alright?"

Chava looked at her and as she shook her head and strange smile appeared on her face. "Something is not right and I won't be able to find out about it until tomorrow. I just talked to the nursing home's administrator who arranged my mother's funeral and without any further explanations, he said that my mother made three wishes before she passed away. He said that he already fulfilled one of her wishes, and then he added that to follow up on the remaining two wishes would be up to me. When I asked him what my mother's wishes were, he curtly replied that he will fill me in tomorrow, after the funeral services."

"That is indeed a little bit odd," remarked Sandy.

"The service is being held tomorrow at ten o'clock in one of the largest cemeteries in the city," announced Chava. "I don't like when people play games with me, especially in a situation such as this one. He could have met me tonight instead of keeping me in suspense. I hate when people do that," she said angrily but she knew that she had no choice other than to wait.

"Do you have any ideas what were her wishes?" asked Sandy.

"Not a single clue," replied Chava and went to the bathroom to wash her face and to freshen up.

"Oh well, there is another important thing in life and that is food," remarked Sandy when Chava returned to the room and changed clothes. Chava realized that actually she was rather hungry herself.

"Where do you want to eat?" asked Chava.

"This is your town, you decide," Sandy tossed the ball back to her friend's court.

"Let's eat here in the hotel tonight, I don't feel like going out, the funeral is going to take place tomorrow at ten," remarked Chava quietly and she looked at her friend who nodded in agreement.

The Atrium Hyatt Hotel's restaurant was exclusive and the food was just as good as Chava was able to recall. A gypsy band was playing and a strolling violinist walked between the tables offering to play favorite melodies to diners. Eventually he stopped by Chava and Sandy's table and asked them in Hungarian if they had a favorite song. Chava thought for a moment and then she looked at the man who must have been a good looking fellow in his youth. He was wearing dark trousers with crispy white shirt with a red, beautifully embroidered vest on the top it. His dark eyes suggested the earlier color of his now gray hair, he patiently looked at Chava. "Do you know the "Lark?" she asked the gypsy violinist. He politely smiled and replied.

"Excellent choice and actually that is also one of my favorites." Chava knew that he spoke the truth and then he began to play. Chava's eyes immediately became flooded with tears and very soon, Sandy understood why.

The music piece that Chava selected required great skill to play it properly and when it was done expertly, the listener could close his or her eyes and could hear a lark singing about freedom, about life, love and sadness. A good violinist, such as the one who played at the hotel's restaurant could make the violin cry as the bird, like the lark that was experiencing the pain of his lost love and freedom.

Sandy being a music lover herself understood perfectly why Chava would love that particular music. Within years both of them experienced happiness, freedom and great deal of sadness. She looked at her friend who just sat there concentrating on the beautiful sound of the violin, with her tears freely rolling down on her pretty but sad face, not caring who was seeing her emotions and she thought that she was one fortunate person to claim Chava as a friend. The emotionally devastating times Sandy so desperately wanted to forget and tried to leave behind was creeping back at her while she watched Chava's reaction to the music.

CHAPTER FOUR

The gentle yet steady knock on her door woke Chava. As usual, just like many other occasions when she traveled, she was momentarily confused for the first few seconds after waking up, not being sure where she was. The knocking came from the direction of the connecting door which led to Sandy's own hotel room. "Just a second," she yelled and pulled herself out of the bed. She glanced at the clock on the nightstand and she couldn't believe that it was already eight in the morning.

She unlocked the door and opened it. "How come you locked the door?" Sandy inquired but Chava just shrugged her shoulders, she didn't have a clue.

"You have to ask the wine bottle for that answer," she remarked as she slowly gathered her panties and bra and rushed into the bathroom. Sandy was fully dressed and ready to go but she soon realized that it would be a while before they could leave as Chava just turned the water on to take quick shower. A short time later the bathroom door opened and Chava stuck her head out. "Sandy, why don't you go downstairs and get us a table for breakfast," she suggested.

"Alrighty, see you downstairs and hurry up a little bit," she said urgently. "I am hungry."

"You are always hungry," remarked Chava and returned inside the bathroom from where Sandy was able to hear the sound of the hairdryer. She considered that a promising sign, she picked up her purse and left the room and headed to the Atrium Terrace where the breakfast buffet was served.

Chava finished her shower and drying her hair, she stood in front of the closet door debating what to wear. She reached for the stylish black dress and carefully removed it from the odd shaped hanger. She looked in the full mirror that also served as the closet door and tears swelled in her eyes. *I am going to bury my mother today,* she thought and an incredible sadness swept over her. The realization finally dawned on her after many days of denial that the inevitable happened, her mother, her only link to the family she used to know, and had, is gone. The painful thought that she will never, ever see her mother's sweet face and hear her voice gripped her heart and mind and she began to sob.

It took her several minutes to stop after she repeatedly had to remind herself that she must be strong and that she must go on. The telephone rang; it was Sandy checking on her, becoming very concerned because she didn't show up at the restaurant yet. "I'll be right there," she promised and went back to the bathroom to apply some makeup to cover up the redness and puffiness of her eyes.

She was alone in the glass elevator which she was grateful for and she slowly made her way toward the table when she noticed Sandy waiving at her direction. The restaurant, if someone may call it as such, was on the inside terrace of the Atrium Hyatt. Chava looked around as she walked and she glanced up at the small airplane hanging from the Atrium cupola. She took a liking to the hotel that lived up to its name with all those well cared for plants that were hanging from each and every level over the safety railing facing down the hotel's lobby. Sandy was seated by one of the tables set for two people by the railing. She already had one large and one smaller size plate in front of her, piled with food. Chava sat down, looked at her friend's food and smilingly shook her head.

She was hoping that the young waitress noticed her arrival, she craved the strong Hungarian coffee she was so used to when she lived in the country, coffee which she was never able to make the same way while she still lived there. She casually looked around and took a quick survey of her surroundings. In the middle of the restaurant were several tables with wicker cabana chairs and the one next to them were occupied by four Palestinians. It would have been more complicated to determine if they were just Arabs, but three of the men were wearing traditional headdresses.

She glanced from one to another and her eyes stalled on one of them and they made eye contact. Chava could not make out the look on his face as it was neither pleasant nor hateful, but he was steadily watching her. Another man at the table looked at her direction and leaned forward and whispered something to the one without the traditional Palestinian headdress. She turned away, back to Sandy who repeated her question for the second time. "What happened to you?" Sandy asked.

"I am okay, I just had a minor breakdown," confessed Chava.

"I know that it is going to be a very difficult day for you but you must hang in there. I am going to be right there with you every step of the way," said Sandy encouragingly, managing to squeeze a small smile out of Chava.

The waitress asked her if she wanted coffee or tea and she ordered a cappuccino. Sandy reminded Chava that it was a buffet but she shook her head. "I am too upset to eat, but you go ahead and help yourself, or as I see, you already have," she explained and placed a sugar cube into her steaming coffee that the young waitress quietly placed in front of her. She asked her politely if she could get anything else for her. Chava thanked her and declined the offer. She noticed that the young woman hesitated for a few moments before leaving. "Excuse me, are you Chava Diamond?" Chava nodded. "I love your books; I read all four of them that were translated into Hungarian. If it wouldn't be too much trouble, I have one of them with me; I like to read when I am on break, would you mind to sign it for me?" she asked Chava politely.

"It would be my pleasure," replied Chava in Hungarian and the waitress hurried away.

"It's a bitch to be famous isn't it?" Sandy said teasingly and dug into her food. Chava always admired Sandy who could virtually eat anything she wanted, and she wished that she had that kind of metabolism that her friend possessed. If she would have eaten half as much as Sandy was able consume, she would have gained weight after a few bites for sure. Sandy loved Hungarian food and Chava had to remind her that they had to leave in a short while as the cemetery was a long distance away.

Chava tried to avoid looking at the Palestinians at next table but she was curious to see if the man was still watching her. He did and his stare was extremely intense. He seemed tall, even as he sat on his cabana chair; his dark eyes matched the color of his hair. She guessed his age around mid or late thirties. He was well dressed and gave the impression of a business man. Chava wondered about what type of "business" was his specialty, and what was he doing on Hungary. Their eyes met and there was something in his eyes that Chava was unable to translate. Was it hate or just dislike? Was it curiosity of a man about a woman? She noticed a small scar above his left eyebrow and on his chin. Despite the scars, he was a handsome man and expressed a certain level of intelligence. Chava decided that he must have been a man of influence because of his mannerism and because of the way he carried himself. The men in his company were equally well dressed, with the exception of the traditional Palestinian headdress that did not quite match with their stylish suits. They were hanging on to every word he said and occasionally they glanced toward her direction when they noticed that he was staring at Chava.

Sandy looked at Chava at the same time as Chava was looking at the Palestinian man. She couldn't help noticing that man aroused Chava's attention or perhaps even her curiosity. "He is not bad looking being a rag head," remarked Sandy as she leaned forward to Chava.

She looked almost angrily at her friend. "Please don't talk like that," she asked her seriously.

"Sorry," apologized Sandy. "It just slipped out. It's just that those headdresses look like a Pizza Hut table cloth, that's all."

Chava once again turned her attention back to the young waitress who arrived back to their table a few minutes later with one of Chava's novels in hand. She handed a pen to Chava to autograph her book "Hannah's Song."

"What is your name?" Chava asked then she looked up and noticed the shiny golden plated name tag on the waitress' black vest over crispy white blouse.

"Agnes," said the waitress pointing at her nametag.

People's gratefulness always brought joy to Chava and seeing the girl's happy face, she felt a moment of satisfaction making someone happy even if only for a short time.

In the meantime Sandy managed to clear her plates as she made more than one trip to try all the various deliciously looking dishes on the buffet cart. She eventually declared that she was too full and she had to stop eating. They wrote their room number on their bill and headed back to their hotel room for one quick stop. Before they turned toward the elevator, Chava couldn't help herself, she just had to look around and yes, the Palestinian man was still watching her. She didn't know how she felt about that, but something inside her told her that it was not going to be the last time she would see him. She hushed that thought away as one of her intuitions, and they were not always right.

After a brief stop in their hotel rooms, the doorman of the hotel hailed a taxi for them and Chava gave the name of the cemetery to the taxi driver. Just as she recalled the cemetery was one of the largest in Budapest and it was divided into Christian and Jewish sections. She let Sandy take care of the cab fare while she slowly made her way to the administration office to get information about her mother's funeral.

Sandy joined her shortly just as a man dressed in a dark suit finished giving Chava directions to a chapel in the same large building the administration office was located. Sandy grabbed Chava's hand as they made their way to the room where the memorial service was to be held. Chava took a deep breath before she opened the door and with Sandy behind her, she stepped inside.

It was a fairly small chapel room with several pews and what she wouldn't exactly call an altar. On the right side of the altar which held a stand where the Bible or prayer book could be placed was another pew. On the side of the pew a small sign indicated that it was the place for family members. Sandy and Chava sat down there and looked at several older men, none familiar to Chava, who were sitting in the pews that were designated for guests.

There were no religious symbols in the small chapel other than the stand on the altar, on the left side was a small table standing on two narrow legs, covered by a white cloth with crochet edges.

Chava whispered to Sandy that she didn't know how Mr. Weiss, the man from the hospital who arranged her mother's funeral looked like and she was wondering where he was. A few minutes before ten o'clock, one of the doors opened, the opposite one from which Sandy and Chava entered earlier, and a dark gray suited man walked in wearing a black hat. He immediately noticed Chava and Sandy and he bowed towards them, and then took a seat in the first row of pews just in front of the strange men seated in the third and fourth pews.

Chava stared at him questioningly but he ignored her stare and once again, the same door opened two men walked in. The first man to step inside the chapel was tall and well dressed. Despite his almost jet black hair, the short and well trimmed beard were showing some gray but it was easy to determine that he was still a relatively young man. The man who followed him inside was an older man, perhaps in his sixties with white hair and beard. What caused Chava's jaw to drop was seeing that both of the men were wearing yarmulkes and prayer shawls. The second man carried a square marble box and placed it on the top of table by the altar.

Chava and Sandy exchanged looks and Chava was simply unable to hide her shock. She stepped off the pew and walked to the door motioning to the man Chava assumed was Mr. Weiss, to follow her and Sandy. The man hesitantly rose up but before joining Chava and Sandy outside the hallway, he stopped to talk to the men wearing yarmulkes. After few moments, Mr. Weiss and the two men also followed them out of the chapel.

"Are you Mr. Weiss?" asked Chava with an angry tone in her voice.

"Yes, I am Armin Weiss and this is Rabbi Goldstein and Cantor Roth, he will sing the Kaddish.

Chava stretched out her hand to shake hands with the Rabbi who smiled at her but he did not take the offered hand. It struck both women as a rude gesture but he sensed their thoughts and in a quiet voice he explained. "I am sorry; I cannot touch another woman other than my wife."

"I am sorry, I didn't know," apologized Chava and then she turned to Mr. Weiss.

"Why is my mother having a Jewish memorial service?" she asked staring at the man waiting for a reasonable explanation.

He nervously looked at Rabbi Goldstein who took the liberty to answer. "Mrs. Diamond, I am surprised that you were not aware of the fact that you were Jewish by faith."

"Excuse me Rabbi but I was baptized as Roman Catholic," replied Chava.

'Yes, I was informed about that. However; under the Jewish laws, if a child was born to a Jewish mother, that child, even if she or he becomes Christian or believer of other faiths, is a Jewish child. No matter what religion you may be following in the path of your life, you were born a Jew and you will pass this life as a Jew," said the Rabbi and looked at his watch and then he glanced at the Cantor.

Chava did not respond to the Rabbi's words, she turned to Mr. Weiss. "I wish to see my mother before the funeral."

Weiss was visibly nervous; there was no doubt about that. "Well, I am afraid that would be impossible," he exclaimed.

"Why is that? I would like to take a last look at my mother as I haven't seen her in the last two years," insisted Chava.

The man shook his head and he shot a pleading look towards the Rabbi. He stepped towards Chava but stopped two feet away from her as if he was afraid that she may touch him. "Your mother had three wishes which she was very specific about when she talked to me and Mr. Weiss. She wrote them down for you and one of her three wishes was to be cremated."

Chava was close to collapsing, she stumbled towards Sandy who grabbed and steadied her by her shoulders. Chava's heart was beating so fast and her breathing became hard, she was about to faint. Sandy dropped her own purse and grabbed Chava's and took out an inhaler, shook it rapidly and handed to her friend without letting her go. Chava took a deep breath, let it go and than she placed the opening of the inhaler between her lips and pushed on it, then she inhaled deeply. She could feel her lung and bronchial muscles relax and she managed to regain her composure.

"Excuse me Mrs. Diamond, I don't mean to be rude, but we have another funeral service to attend," said the Cantor who was quiet until that moment. Chava nodded and with Sandy still holding onto her arm, they returned to the chapel.

The Cantor sang a beautiful Kaddish, a song of the dead and as his genuinely beautiful voice filled the small chapel, Chava realized with surprise about the feeling she was experiencing. She felt angry at her mother for robbing her from the chance to see her one more time; for the last time. The biggest part of her anger focused on the fact that her mother did not tell her that she was born into a Jewish family and that it was the secret behind all those whispers in their neighborhood that she had to endure without getting any sort of explanation from her parents.

The more she thought about it, the angrier she became not only at her late mother but at herself as well. How could she not realize that they were Jewish? How could she be so blind not seeing any signs or hear any comments and discussions? But were there any? She was unable to recall a single incident from her childhood or from her teen years while growing up that would have given her an indication what religion was she born into. How could that be?

Although the Rabbi was praying and said some kind words about a woman whom he perhaps did not even know, how the departed lived for her family and for her faith. Chava could not clearly focus on what he was saying, her mind traveled back her childhood and she realized that she was unable to take her eyes from marble box resting on the small table on the altar.

The entire ceremony didn't take more than ten minutes and without saying as much as a goodbye, the Rabbi left in the company of the Cantor, leaving Mr. Weiss behind to conclude the ceremony by giving the marble box to Chava.

If Chava was speechless, Sandy was totally lost for words. Without saying a single word, they hailed a passing by taxi cab that turned around to pick them up. Later on she couldn't quite recall how they got back to the hotel, she didn't even remember paying for the cab fare although Sandy later told her that she did. She held on tight to the marble box as they entered the elevator and into their hotel rooms.

Chava was about to toss her purse on the dresser when she couldn't help noticing the somewhat unusual flower arrangement on the top of it. The flowers were colorful but she couldn't tell what kind they were, she hoped that perhaps Sandy would know. It really didn't matter; it was a small, yet beautiful flower arrangement made out of six unusual flowers, placed in a very nice glass vase. There were two Star Gazer Lilies which she eventually recognized, but the other four flowers, two long yellowish, one pink that looked like Jasmine, she wasn't sure about that and the sixth flower that had dark pink and white petals, she definitely didn't know. She also noticed that there was a card sticking out from between the flowers, she removed it from the envelope and read it. "I am sorry to hear about passing of your mother. You seem to be a remarkable woman I would very much like to know you better, unfortunately you are a . . . . Well, let's see how good of a suspense writer you are. Can you guess the last word?" The card was not signed, but there were three initials, "A-HH."

Chava wondered who might have sent her the flowers. At first she thought that perhaps it was her despised cousin Pete, who did not show up at her mother's memorial service after all, which was okay with her, but she didn't think that Pete wanted to know her better and she seriously doubted that Pete thought of her as being remarkable. Who was A-HH? She had to set that mystery aside, she picked up the box that contained her mother's ashes and placed the box on the top of her bed and lay down next to it. She wanted to wait until Sandy returned.

CHAPTER FIVE

S andy joined Chava a short while later and she also noticed the flowers. "Who sent you the flowers?" she asked, then she added. "I didn't think that too many people knew you were coming back here."

"Actually I don't know who sent them," she said and handed the card that came with the flower arrangement to Sandy. She silently read it and raised her eyebrows questioningly. "This is weird," she remarked. "What is the missing word, any ideas?" she asked.

"Maybe I can figure it out later," said Chava and motioned to Sandy to join her on the bed where she was already sitting. Chava hesitated at first but eventually she lifted the top of the box and placed the heavy lid on the bedspread. Inside the marble box was another box, Chava guessed it was made out of some sort of light weight marble. It contained her mother's ashes according to the note taped on the top. She carefully removed the container and placed it on the nightstand.

"Chava," said Sandy. "It has been one hell of a day for you. I am sorry that you didn't have a chance to say goodbye to you mom. I guess they did have to oblige her wishes to cremate her."

Chava nodded that she understood. "It hurts me that she didn't want me to see her," she said quietly.

"Sometimes people don't look the same after a long illness as we remember them. Perhaps, just perhaps," she softly touched Chava's unruly hair. "She didn't want you to see her in that stage of illness. You shouldn't be mad at her because of that."

"I could have lived with her wishes but it hurts me that she kept important things away from me, like the truth about my background," Chava sighed and gently touched the box that held her mother's ashes.

"I suppose you did not know that you were Jewish?" asked Sandy with a hint of doubtfulness.

"One time I asked my mother for my baptism paper and when she said that she didn't know where it was, I went to a priest and after taking some lessons in

Catholicism, I was baptized. I was sixteen years old at that time", she added and she stared at the painting on the wall showing a modern flower arrangement.

"Chava, even your name is Hebrew and I knew that fact all along and your maiden name was and it is again Diamond. How Jewish can you get?" Sandy acknowledged with a quiet laugh.

"Sandy, please," she said quietly wanting to stop her friend from being sarcastic with her. "I knew that Chava was a Hebrew name but it didn't mean anything. We had a lot of ethnic groups in Hungary and some kids had Greek names, some had Slavic names and so on," explained Chava. "Why could she not just come out and say it to me?" She wondered out loud as if she were alone in the room."

Sandy shook her head. "And there were no signs, no comments, nothing that would have given you a clue about your religious affiliation?" she asked her still seemingly disturb friend.

"My father was the member of the Communist Party and he was a known atheist. My mother never went to church or any religious place of gatherings. Please try to remember that I grew up in a Communist country where religion was almost not an option, especially in the cities where the Government had domestic spies all around and among the population. They would not stop you from going to church, but if you were a member of the Communist Party, you just simply could not attend religious services because it was the contrary of the Party's teachings," explained Chava, and as she was recalling some events from her youth, Sandy herself just began to comprehend the enormous emotional turmoil that her friend just began to experience.

"So you never went to church or a synagogue?" Sandy asked.

Chava smiled at her. "Well, that's not entirely true. When I went with my mother to the open market place during the hot summer months, we always passed a small Catholic church. I used to tell my mother that I will wait for her in there as it was so nice and cool inside the church. Once I found a Bible in one of the pews and I became fascinated with reading the stories of Abraham, Ruth, Rachel, David and of course, Jesus. A priest came by on my third visit in that church and asked me if I wanted to take the Bible home? I hesitated first but I said yes, and I began to read the Bible from the start to the very end," she stopped and she was still smiling as remembered her first encounter with the Bible.

"Did your parents know that you were reading the Bible?" asked Sandy.

"Of course, there was no place to hide anything in that tiny apartment we shared. When my father asked me why I was reading the Bible, I told him that I liked the stories. I still remember looking up at him and I was surprised to see that instead of him looking at me as I replied, he exchanged looks with my mother." Chava reached over to the nightstand next to the bed and pulled the top drawer open. She laughed softly and took out the Bible, then she flipped the pages. "Well I'll be, it's in English," she said and handed the Bible over to Sandy. "This is just to show you how this country has changed in seventeen years," she remarked.

"I am curious what your father said after discovering that you were reading the Bible," she asked Chava.

"He said, yes indeed, that is what exactly what they were, just stories. A month later when I finished reading it, I asked my parents during one supper that I wanted somebody to explain to me why is it that Mary and Joseph, Jesus' parents were Jewish and as you know, God's son, Jesus was also born Jewish, that Catholics don't like Jews? Unfortunately they had no answers and they had no desire to talk about the subject. I was very confused. My mother finally said that Christians blame the Jews for Jesus' crucifixion. Those statements disturb me because even the Bible said that the Romans crucified Jesus and not the Jews. My father told me that he didn't want to have any religious discussions in our home and if I wanted to be religious, I had to wait until I was old enough to leave their home and make a choice of my own," Chava recalled that disturbing night of questioning her parents.

"So what happened when your father passed away? What happened at his funeral?" Sandy asked curiously.

"Well, since my father was an atheist, a man from the Communist Party branch, where my father was a member came to the funeral and made a speech how great my father was and blah, blah, blah! He was a stupid man who knew nothing about my father and possibly they never even met. No matter how hard I try, I cannot remember a single event when my father participated any of their meetings or had done anything for the party. All I know is that he paid his membership fees and that he had a red book in which he pasted those little stamps he received each time he paid his membership dues. No one ever came to our apartment to talk about politics and a not single Comrade ever made an attempt to raise our lives above the poverty level. I was confused about many things when I was growing up, including what I learned in school and what I learned on my own," continued Chava's explanation.

"And from the Bible," Sandy interjected.

"From all directions," said Chava. "I began to read and read and read some more about life in America and in other countries. I wanted to learn about the lives of people in other countries who lived under Capitalism or under different government systems. I often wondered were those people satisfied and happy? I wanted to know if going to church meant that we could become better people and if so, why was it forbidden for a Communist to go to church? My mind was full of questions and I could not find an answer and there was nobody I could ask and nobody would volunteer to give me some explanation about the deep contradictions around us, and about the troubling feelings and questions I had. Most of all, I was afraid to ask, being concerned that my "strange" outlook and ideas would put my parents into danger."

"Give me an example?" asked Sandy.

"Well, let's see," Chava said while she pushed herself off the bed and walked to the window and then she turned around. "What Communism basically means is that everybody is equal and people as a whole, as we are saying it nowadays, we were supposed to be this one big team. My understanding of Communism was that the Government would share its profit with people, so there wouldn't be any rich or poor people, everybody would possess equal shares. Then I discovered that indeed there were very wealthy people in Hungary while others lived in poverty like my family did. So where was equality? I was about eleven years old when I realized that the society I was living in was not a Communist society, but it was a society of hypocrites. I had one single goal after that and it was to leave the country."

"How did you deal with the religion issue?" Sandy asked again.

"After my father died, I asked my mother if there was a difference between the Gods that the Jewish people prayed to versus the God that Catholics prayed to. She told me, and to tell you the truth, I live by those words to this day; that there was only one God and she also said that God was everywhere and that if I wanted to pray at home, God would listen to my prayers just as much as if I prayed in a church." Tears swelled in her eyes and the teardrops slowly began to roll down on her face. "That was the time when I asked her to show me my baptism papers and she denied knowing their whereabouts. I just assumed that if I was ever baptized, she must have hidden my baptism papers from my father. It's seems funny now how little did I know," Chava remarked bitterly. "And you know that the more I think about it now, deep down inside I knew that perhaps I was Jewish but I repressed that knowledge and since I was baptized, I didn't even think about that anymore," added Chava.

"Oh honey," Sandy said and rushed to comfort her. "I am so sorry that you still feel pain about your life here."

Chava wiped her face with the back of her hand and she said in a very quiet, almost whispering voice. "I hated my life here, I just hated it."

Sandy gently touched Chava's face. "You are a free person now, a free woman and you can do as you please. Your life experiences should be an example for those who live under oppression. You proved that a person can rise from poverty to become a successful and giving individual," said Sandy convincingly.

Chava turned around and looked out from the tenth floor hotel window that faced the old Chain Bridge that proudly stretched across the Danube River. The thousands of lights that lit up the Castle Hill allowed the public to enjoy the view of the buildings that stood on it. She could clearly see the Fisherman's Bastion from her hotel room window and she made a mental note to take Sandy there to see what was once one of her few favorite places in Budapest. She turned around and remained silent for a few moments, her face seemed troublingly serious. "There is one more thing that bothers me about my parent's secrecy and it is not telling me that we were Jewish. Were they trying to prevent me from being harassed in school? I must have suspected something because when I was in my early teens, I developed a fascination with the Holocaust and I used to take a bunch of books home on that subject from the library. I remember how upset my mother got and she said that she didn't care if I was reading it but she didn't want to hear anything about it. I did think at that time that why wouldn't anyone want to learn about the atrocities and now I am wondering if she had survived something she was trying to forget. Those books with pictures showing atrocities must have triggered something, some horrible memory in her." She stopped and took a deep breath. "The strangest thing about it is that no matter what church or synagogue I visited throughout my years of travel; I felt home in every one of them," she remarked.

"Chava, you are not having an identity crisis are you?" asked Sandy with raised eyebrows.

"I am not sure. I thought I knew who I was and where I have come from and now, I am wondering what else I don't know about my past. By the way, does it bother you that I turned out to be Jewish?" asked Chava from her friend in return.

Sandy's grimaced at her direction. "Are you out of your freaking mind? How can you possibly ask me that question? You are the best friend I ever had, and I could ever ask for. You are smart, you are talented and you were always helping others. You are one of the best and most successful writers in this decade and you went through hell just like I did when we both got divorced. So why would I care what your religion is? I cannot recall a single time when you have asked me what faith I belonged to." Her voice had a hint of hurt but she didn't move, she remained seated by the small desk.

"Please don't be mad at me," asked Chava and stretched her hands out toward her friend. Sandy made yet another face at her and got up to take her friend's hands.

"You can be a bitch sometimes," remarked Sandy. "Just one more thing; did Matthew ever ask you about your religion?" She asked curiously.

"You know, I have to give him credit for it, because when Matthew and I got married we had small ceremony in a non-domination chapel on the military post where we lived and that was it, the subject never came up," said Chava and walked back to the bed where the large marble like box, now opened and the second marble box with her mother's ashes removed from it, still held something that Chava had to deal with.

CHAPTER SIX

B oth of them returned to the bed and sat on the top of it, next to the box. Chava reached inside and removed a large white envelope with her name on it. She immediately recognized her mother's writing. Chava looked at Sandy who smiled at her. "You should open it," Sandy said to her encouragingly.

Chava's hand was shaking as she opened the envelope. Inside, there were pictures of her when she was a child, there were pictures of her graduating high school and there were pictures of her wedding to Matthew. She tossed the pictures on the top of her bed and focused on another envelope, a thick, long beige colored envelope with her nickname, "Edeskem," meaning "My Sweet" written on it.

She began to read it, at first to herself and then she began to translate the letter as it was written in Hungarian.

"My sweet child," Chava began to read her mother's long letter.

Knowing that you inherited your father's temper, I don't have to guess that you are probably experiencing a great amount of anger towards me, but by the time you finish reading what I felt I had to tell you in this letter, which I would rather call a testimonial of the love that I have always felt for you as a mother, and as your friend. By the time you finish reading this long letter, my testimonial, I am sure that you will understand and forgive your mother who loved you from the moment you were conceived until the last breath she took.

Before I go any further, it is an instruction from me to you, that once you read this letter, you must destroy it by burning it and then I want you to toss the ashes of this letter into the toilet and flush it. Do not wonder why, just do it!

So here we go! As you know I was born into a large family but some of my siblings died early in their lives and only six of us, four girls, including me and two boys lived to reach adult age. We were born into the Jewish faith and although we always believed in God's presence in our lives, we never quite made it inside a Synagogue. I don't know the reason for that, perhaps because we were even poorer than some of the other Jewish families around us, and just as I told you while you were growing up, my parents also told me that God was everywhere and no matter where you prayed, he heard your prayers, so as you see, that saying came from your grandparents and their parents before them.

Many things happened in our lives but I just want to explain to you some details that made us keep your Jewish heritage a secret from you and let you choose a religion of your choice, if that is what you wanted to do. I must admit, I cried for days when I found out that you converted to Catholicism, but you just wanted to confirm your faith as I was unable to give you documents to prove what religion you belonged to. Unlike the Catholic religion, parents don't get baptism papers when a Jewish child is born because there is no baptism in the Jewish faith, only Bar Mitzvahs for boys and Bat Mitzvahs for girls when they reach the early teen years.

Your late father also came from a large family and when he left his family's home, he married a young woman and had two children, a girl and a boy. I am sure that you still remember how much your father adored you, needless to say that he loved his first family as well, and he loved them very much indeed. During our fifteen years of marriage, until his death, he only talked about his first family once and it was then when he told me that he never wanted to talk about them again. Your grandparents and your fourteen aunts and uncles and their families and of course your father with his family were gathered up, just as I was forced with my sisters and brothers and their families to be squeezed into a cattle transport car without food and water and taken to Auschwitz. Of course it happened within a two month period and I did not know your father at the time.

I clearly remember when you were in your early teens, for a reason that was never clear to me, you developed a morbid curiosity about the Holocaust which not only frightened me but brought back some horrible memories. Have you ever wondered why I, and my surviving sister, Margit have never worn short sleeve blouses or sweaters? It was because we didn't want people to know that our left arm had a tattooed reminder that we were unwanted people." Chava stopped reading and stared in front of her. *That's right,* she recalled. *I have never seen my mother without her clothes, not even wearing anything with short sleeves.* After a few moments, she went back reading her mother's letter.

"Before I write any further, I have to tell you that what I am about to write is not a day to day account of my life and your father's life in the concentration camp, this is just an overall view what we and other six million people had to endure on a daily basis by the hands of the German Nazis who claimed to be the purest race in the world, but in reality, what they were the purest evil that human kind had ever seen walking on two legs. And now, back to what I have to tell and explain to you.

Just a few days after I celebrated my eighteenth birthday, our journey to horror began. It took us five days to arrive at Auschwitz and by the time our train pulled into Birkenau, there were many dead people among us, most of them old people and children. I am sure that you already know the conditions under which we were forced to travel, but just to confirm what you have already learned from books, interviews and movies, that we traveled without food, water and we could not sit or lay down, there were just too many of us squeezed in each of the many cattle cars. The smell, that stench we had to endure throughout our forced journey never left my nostrils and together with the sickly sweet smell of burning flesh that left through the chimneys of the crematoriums, remained with me for decades after liberation. You see, there was only one bucket to use as a "bathroom" for all those people in those cattle transfer cars and because even when the train stopped for short period of times, I assume to change engines, they would not always empty that bucket for us.

Arriving at the camp was almost a "blessing" after the horrible journey, but in reality arriving was also a chaotic event. It was very dark when we arrived late in the evening and we were confused, we didn't know what to do and many of us were crippled with fear not knowing what was about to happen. There were dogs barking, German soldiers were shouting while pointing weapons at us, meanwhile there were those people wearing striped pajama like outfits. We were forced into groups of five or six per line and there were some Nazi officers who pointed us left or right. Men and women were immediately separated and I was fortunate to remain with my sisters but it was the last time I have seen my brothers alive.

There were so many children, pregnant women, older people and they were sent to the left and we had no idea what was going to happen to them. We did not know anything about the gas chambers or about the crematorium just yet. We were sent to the right because we were young and we could work. We were marched into buildings with signs of "showers" painted on them in German and I was sure that there was some sort of trick, but actually we did get some quick cold showers after we had to remove everything, from clothing to jewelry. After the "shower" we were deloused with some awful smelling powder and forced into this other room where we were given some clothing and we had our hair shaved off completely. In another room, there were tables with two women sitting by each and we were told that we are going to get our numbers. We didn't realize that it not only meant placing our names into those large books in front of women but that we would also get our numbers crudely tattooed on our arms. They tried to stop us from feeling like human beings, they tried to turn us into something unspeakable, worse than animals, into disposable robots that could be easily programmed and destroyed when they were no longer needed. My tattoo number was B26721, you may recall this number later if you want, but I beg you that under no circumstances that you repeat that number to anyone, never ever, please remember that." Chava stopped translating just as she got to her mother's request about not mentioning her tattoo number to anyone.

"What is the matter?" asked Sandy.

"She wanted me to keep her tattoo number a secret," explained Chava.

"It's okay honey, you don't have to tell me," assured Sandy and urged her on to continue reading her mother's letter, so Chava continued.

"Many of the women in our group were crying and when were marched outside, there were female capos waiting for us with whips and they used it mercilessly on those who were crying or did not move quickly enough. We were finally taken to our barracks in Birkenau. I later learned that the female camp was originally inside the main camp in Auschwitz but a couple of years earlier they moved the female prisoners into Birkenau.

The inside of the barracks was shocking and yet, amazingly I can't recall any complaints, it was like a silent acceptance of a doomed future. I was fortunate to have my three sisters with me and it meant emotional support to one another. The sleeping areas were made out of brick and they were narrow. Two and many times three people had to sleep in one small place. There were some thin layers of burlap on the bottom and a thin blanket is all we got.

There were two things that were the hardest to accept for most of us. One was not knowing what happened to our loved ones whom were separated from us and it was the first time in many years when I was almost glad that my parents, your maternal grandparents were no longer alive so they didn't have to suffer like we did. We had no idea what happened to our brothers and women were wondering about the whereabouts of their children, their husbands, siblings and parents. It seemed so amazing later on that how naïve we were, how little we thought about the cruelty of the Germans and their allies. That naivety disappeared shortly after being in the camp only for a couple of days as rumors began to mingle among us. Rumors about the gas chambers begin to circulate but when we talked about it and we concluded that no matter how bad the Germans seemed to be, to imagine such magnitude of evil towards their fellow men was simply incomprehensible.

The second hardest thing that was difficult to deal with was hunger. We got coffee in the morning and I am using the term coffee very loosely here, sometimes with a thin slice of bread with nothing on it, then we got a watery soup made from either some sort of beets or potato scraps, nothing else in it. Sometimes it was what we believed, warm water. By the time evening came and we were herded back from whatever task they made us do that day, we were ready for our slice of bread which was about a quarter of an inch thick. How did they expect us to survive on such a ration of food? Well, the truth to the fact was that they did not want us to survive. We just grew weaker and weaker with every passing day and each day, there were bodies in the sleeping areas that were taken away by other prisoners.

Each morning around five or five thirty in the morning we were awaken and we had to line up outside our barracks to be accounted for, it was called in German "Appel." It was a brutal beginning to each day as sometimes we had to stand there for hours no matter what was the weather condition. It was the time when they checked the barracks to see if anyone of us was unable to get up and if somebody was unable to get up, it meant certain death. You know darling, in many ways, and it may sound strange, the Hungarian Jewish population were luckier than many others, if you can consider any of it luck. Some of the other nationality Jewish people were removed from their homes, like the Polish Jews or German Jews for instance, much earlier. That is true that we had to live in a ghetto in Budapest or other ghettos around Hungary but they only began to transfer and exterminate Hungarian Jews after the German occupation of the country in early 1944.

One morning a Nazi officer arrived to review our sorry looking group. He was well groomed and immaculately dressed with shiny boots on his feet as he walked up and down in front of us. He asked out loud if there were any twins among us. Two of my sisters, Lilly and Irene were twins and they wanted to step forward but I grabbed Lilly's hand, something told me that it was not a good idea for her and Irene to volunteer, but Irene stepped out of the line and Lilly followed her.

I found out later that the officer was Dr. Mengele, the "angel of death" himself. A truck came shortly after and they took them away and Margit, my other sister and I didn't even have a chance to say goodbye to them. I learned later on that they experimented on them and they were in such bad shape after the procedure that they were shot in the head on the following day. I also learned that those experiments were done on them and great many others without even as much as local anesthetics. I cannot imagine the horrific pain they had to endure and until death takes me away, I cannot forget the last look on their faces as the truck drove away with them. Their eyes told me that whatever was waiting for them it was going to end their suffering. I knew then that I have lost them forever and my fear and feelings were correct; we have never seen them again.

A few days later, on a freezing morning we were awakened as usual for our morning accountability. I was so cold and I can still recall how I had to blow my breath at my fingers to warm them up. I reached for Margit who was not moving and I gently shook her. She looked up at me and said. "You go ahead, I'll be right out there," but I didn't believe her; I have seen that happen far too many times. I shook her with all that little power that I have gathered together and screamed at her "you are going to get up and go outside with me right now." I could already hear the capo, a big boned Polish woman and another one, a German former prisoner who was arrested for murdering her family yelling outside. I could also hear the sound of whipping and I shook Margit again and yelled at her not to dare to leave me alone. Margit began to weep but there were no tears. She was shaking badly but I pulled her up to her feet and helped her out. I was praying real hard that it wouldn't be the morning when the Germans made their selection who would die that day or who could go on suffering yet another day.

God must have been heard my soundless chanting inside my head because by some miracle, they only took those away who didn't get up that morning and to this day, I don't know why, we were not forced to go work that particular day. I gave half of my daily ration to Margit to gain some strength and she felt slightly better on the following day. As you know, she survived Auschwitz as well to marry later to Steven and they had your cousin Pete. I know that later in life I gained a lot of weight but when Auschwitz was liberated, I weighted only 85 pounds.

But Chava, I must say that God did not close his eyes to our sufferings, at least not to mine. I am sure that you heard of a selection process called "tenth." You have always have been a history buff and I remember that you were reading about Roman times, one particular historical episode you were truly fascinated with was the story of Spartacus. Do you remember? I am only mentioning this to show you that particular story confirms that cruelty of man kind did not start with the Nazis or Germans, it goes back ever since man kind was created. Do you remember what Crassus did to his soldiers?" Chava stopped reading and translating and looked at Sandy.

"I don't know much about Roman times," Sandy admitted. Chava begin a brief explanation before she continued reading her mother's letter. "In ancient times, just like in the time of the Spartacus slave rebellion, Marcus Crassus, the Roman General and his soldiers failed to capture Spartacus at the beginning. Spartacus beat them and overpowered them twice. Marcus Crassus said that running away from a slave rebel was an unacceptable move from a Roman soldier and he decided that he would order an old disciplinary practice for his soldiers. He ordered every tenth Roman soldier to step forward and ordered his own comrades to slaughter them. He ordered to have over one hundred fifty of his own soldiers to be murdered to enforce discipline. That is what my mother was referring too," explained Chava to Sandy.

Sandy nodded that she understood. Chava picked up the letter and continued reading it and translating it. "On that particular morning as usual, we were all standing outside of our barracks for the morning Appel when Helga, one of the cruelest German female guards began to march up and down in front of us. A few minutes later a jeep arrived with three high ranked Nazi officers and not wanting to get out of the jeep, they begin to drive back and forth in front of us, trying to measure us up I suppose. Finally, after about ten or fifteen minutes, the jeep stopped and one of the officers began to tell us in a loud voice that one of the female prisoners had escaped and that we were going to be punished. My heart sunk as we knew that for every escaped prisoner there would be ten prisoners for each escapee going to be murdered. Something told me that it was going to be my last day on Earth and I silently began to pray as I always did before and after each inspection.

Helga walked up to the jeep and she and one of the officers briefly exchanged words. She hurried back and Helga began to walk in front of us and with her whip she pointed at every tenth person in each row. I could still hear the silent panic in each and every one of us, they decided upon a new type of punishment for us. I was close to collapsing when Helga finally reached me and pointed her whip at me, I was the tenth. She did not stop, once she selected me, she began to count once again starting with one and so on. There were about one hundred of us who were "tenth." I squeezed my sister's hand before stepping forward and I whispered to her, "I love you and please be strong."

I stood there with the others who were forced to step forward and I resigned to the fact that I would be joining my family in Heaven. I cannot describe to you how I felt. My fear was gone; I felt no hunger or thirst and the incredible feeling of inner peace came over me and then I did the most incredible thing, I begin to smile.

The officer's jeep began to move and one of the officers ordered the driver to stop the vehicle and then officer got out. He stepped directly in front of me. I thought that he was going to shoot me right there, but instead, he ordered me to show him my tattoo. He read it out loud, B26721 and then he lifted my face up with his whip and looked me in the eye. I couldn't help it, I just kept on smiling. He said to me, "Are you crazy? Why are you smiling when you are about to die?" I replied to him that I am looking forward to be with my family once again. He stared at me for a few moments and then he took out a small note book and wrote down my tattoo number. He curtly told me, "Step back." I couldn't believe it, he actually spared my life.

A few days later Helga and a Ukrainian female capo came into our barracks and yelled out my tattoo number, B26721 and once I crawled down from my bed, they ordered me to follow them. Margit, my sister and I hugged and once again, I began to pray in preparation to the unavoidable reality that I was going to be killed for certain. I considered myself lucky a few mornings earlier not being killed on the spot during the Appel and it was unimaginable to get lucky for the second time within days.

I was marched into Captain Schumann's private quarters and I was asked if I knew how to cook, clean and sew, all the tasks I knew how to do. Schumann was a career Nazi officer and no, he was not a nice person. He laid down ground rules of what he expected from me and he told me that breaking a single rule would mean certain death for me and to make a point, he ordered me to lower my raggedy dress. I was embarrassed and I hesitated but Helga, who was still there, ripped my clothes off from my skin and bone body. Schumann ordered me into the bathroom and for a brief moment I naively thought that he actually wanted me to take a shower or bath but as soon as I stepped into his bathroom, I felt a horrible pain on my back and again and again. He whipped me ten times that night just for good measure, and to understand that he meant business. I worked twenty hours a day, barely stopping to use the latrine because I was not allowed to use his bathroom.

I was actually somewhat fortunate because I was able to eat a little bit more and through a man who worked as a courier for the officers, and had access both to Birkenau and Auschwitz, I was able to smuggle a tiny bit of food for Margit whom I had not seen again until I arrived back to Budapest after the war. I thought that she was dead and she thought that I was dead. Schumann used to call me his "good luck charm Jew" because shortly after I began to work for him, he got promoted to Major and six months later to Colonel. Schumann was hung in Krakow after the war for ordering the murder of thousands of Jews and personally killing possibly hundreds according to eyewitness accounts.

In the meantime, your father's family was almost completely destroyed. From his fourteen siblings only a younger brother survived, the rest of his family was sent directly to the gas chambers as he learned later on. Although there were younger and healthy members in his family, for some reason the Germans sent them to die immediately. That is the reason why you never had any grandparents. He recounted one time, when we talked about his family, that as he was separated from his wife, his sixteen year old beautiful daughter and his fourteen year old son, his parents and his family, somehow he knew that he would never see them again.

You perhaps wonder how a once God fearing person could become an atheist, well, that was the time when your father became one. I am going to write this down, but by all means, this is not how I feel about God, but he said, "If there was a God, all those evil things would not have happened to good people just because they were born into the Jewish faith." I tried to tell him that it was not God who was doing those evil things, it was evil people doing those evil things, he wouldn't want to listen and he refused to discuss the issue any further.

Also the truth is that your father didn't want any children and he was not entirely happy when I found out that I was pregnant. However; his feelings changed immediately from the first moment he saw you. You were this beautiful creation, his and mine and he adored you with every breath he took. When we took you home from the hospital, he made me swear that we would not tell you that you were born to Jews. No, he was not ashamed of his religion but he didn't trust anyone and he couldn't bear even just a thought that he may lose you some day just because you were Jewish. He told me that if something was to happen to him and I had to raise you on my own, that I would let you choose if you wanted to worship God or not, and you, only you could decide if you wanted to follow Judaism or Catholicism or whatever religion you wished to believe in.

You are probably wondering, why he wanted to do that? The answer is basically very simple; because what we have experienced and what he and I observed around us. We have never trusted anyone who lived by us, across the yard or street. There was this unsettling feeling that we were just tolerated, we were almost resented for our survival of the holocaust and there was this feeling and sentiment, even during the 1956 revolution that someday, someone would finish the job of exterminating the Jewish population who survived the atrocities.

I cannot explain to you how I felt when you told me that you wanted to be baptized, but thinking of your late father, I have not objected. As I told you earlier, I cried for days after that day buts I loved you more than to judge you for leaving your faith. I figured, as long as you know where you belong and as long as you believe in God, I don't have to worry about your soul, and I don't. Many times I hoped that someday you would meet a nice Jewish boy and marry him but it also didn't happen. I must also confess that I liked Matthew, your ex-husband. He was always nice to me although I never quite figured out if he was aware of your Jewish heritage or not.

I also wanted you to know that it was difficult being away from you and not see your beautiful face every day, but I have always been very proud of you, how smart and how brave you are. Chava, I don't want you to feel guilty for not being with me during the last years of my life, it was my decision not to stay with you in your beautiful home in California. It was my decision not to accept your offer to take care of me for the rest of my life, but it was much appreciated. Last but not least about this subject, I also wish to thank you for the financial support you provided during the last years of my life. I have no regrets for returning to Hungary where I was born and where I wanted to die.

I hope that you are no longer angry with me and you will forgive me for wanting a Jewish memorial service. I never stopped being a Jew and I never stopped believing that God who spared my life for a reason, and that reason was to bring you into this world.

I have three wishes which I expressed and I am specifically asking for:

1. I want to be cremated.
2. I want you take my ashes to Auschwitz/Birkenau, find the seventh barracks from the entrance and set my urn down on the sixteenth "bed" on the left, on the lower lever, for a few short minutes.
3. My final wish is that you take my ashes to the land of my ancestors, to Israel, specifically to the Red Sea and scatter my ashes into the water.

I know in my heart that you will comply with my final wishes because you were always a good child of mine.

Well sweetheart, this is it. When you read this letter your mother is with God. I know that I have not sinned a single time in my life and believing in him will surely help me through the "Pearly Gates" so I can be with your beloved father. God is merciful and I know that he let him in too no matter if he believed in him or not.

Be strong my child and think of me as often as you can. I hope that I was a good mother to you, as I always tried to be one. I will pray until my last breath leaves my lips that someday soon you find true happiness and deep down inside, I know that you will. I'll be watching you and will be smiling down at you from above and don't forget, you must destroy this letter and you must never repeat my tattoo number to anyone.

I love you Chava.
Your mother, Helene."

It was a simple ending but Chava could barely finish reading her mother's writing, the last words were drowned in a quiet sob. She touched her mother's urn on the nightstand and gently stroked the top of it. She turned back to Sandy with tears streaming down her face and she noticed that her friend was also crying. "I have to take her ashes to Auschwitz and you are under no obligation to go there with me."

Sandy shook her head. "You have to physically remove me from your side if you don't want me to go with you. I am your friend and I always will be your friend. I am going with you to Poland and to Israel."

"Thank you," whispered Chava and gave Sandy a big hug. She went to the desk and looked for some matches but she was unable to find one, the room was a non-smoking room. Sandy left on a match searching mission and she returned shortly with two matches she got from one of the housekeepers. Chava went to the bathroom and page by page she burned her mother's letter and then she flushed the ashes down the toilet, just as her late mother instructed her to do so.

It took almost an hour before Chava finally was able to gather her thoughts together about what to do next. It was Sandy who returned to Chava's room after reapplying her makeup and asked the obvious question. "Are you hungry?"

CHAPTER SEVEN

ater that night when Sandy declared that she was exhausted and she could easily imagine how Chava must felt, they bid goodnight and she went to her room, straight to bed. Chava did the same but as she lay in her large and comfortable bed she experienced a feeling that she did not feel for a long time. She felt lonely and alone, despite her friend's presence next door. It was the type of loneliness that felt like being in the company of dozens of people who could not and would not care.

The feeling of emptiness of being down and out and the experience of loneliness was not new to Chava; it was more familiar to her than she cared to admit. She's been there before. Just three years earlier during a moody August evening her married life was abruptly ended when her husband, Colonel Matthew Roberts, a decorated Desert Storm veteran made his smooth move. During the candlelit dinner in their favorite Italian restaurant in San Francisco, he put his fork and knife down in the middle of the main entrée and asked her to pay attention to what he was about to say because he didn't wish to repeat himself. Chava dutifully placed her silverware down on the top of her plate where the food was arranged by the culinary artist, also known as the Great Chef of San Francisco, and she gave full attention to what her husband of twelve years had to say.

They had gone through similar, what she called "dramatic" scenes before and she could almost recite her husband's short but to the point speech. She smiled at him as she expected the usual apology from him when he was announcing to her that they have to move yet once again as they did many times during their marriage, and since the beginning of his flourishing Army carrier.

Each and every time they moved, Chava did not complain, she was fully aware of the demands of being married to a rising military officer and she let the packers and movers come and go, then she unpacked at the new installation and began yet another new life wherever they were stationed. She was easy going and living in a fantasy world of her own, wanting to become a writer was her dream since her childhood in the "old country." She knew that it was not easy for Matthew to get a security clearance after they got married because her relatives still resided in the then Communist country where she was born, but as if it was on cue, when her stepfather passed away several years later, somehow his promotions came much quicker.

He took her hands into his own over the table and looked into her eyes. She smiled at him assuring that whatever he was about to say she was surely going to support. What seemed a little bit different to her was that Matthew nervously moistened his lips before he spoke.

"Chava," he began. "You were always there to support me, you never complained, you were a picture perfect military wife, but I feel that the passion or something like that is just simply gone from our marriage and I don't love you anymore. I want a divorce."

She couldn't stop smiling in the same way as her brain was unable to compute what she was hearing. The cruel and unexpected words that left his lips controverted the casualness and the calmness of his voice as he spoke them to her. His voice sounded soothing even as he informed her that he no longer wanted to be part of her life.

He let her hands go but despite that, she didn't withdraw them from the table. "Say something," he demanded without raising his voice.

She looked at him calmly, no longer smiling; finally pulling her hands back, she lifted her wine glass. "Well then," she said to him. "Let's drink for the beginning of a new life."

She could tell that he was stunned, and for the first time in years, he was speechless. "You are not upset?" he finally asked her.

It took her only a few moments to think his question over and to her amazement, she realized that it was true; she didn't feel upset, at least not yet. In those particular moments the reality what was about to happen after she returned home didn't really sink in yet. She quietly got up and left the restaurant without saying as much as a "goodbye." She saw him one more time; actually she saw his picture to be exact in the newspaper, a few months later.

When she got home that evening, she walked around the empty house and walked into their bedroom. At first she just sat at the edge of the bed but later she lay down, touching his side of the bed gently and just then the tears began to fill her eyes. Twelve years of her married life went down the drain that evening. There were no warning signs, there were no clues and if there were any she most definitely missed them. She knew that somehow she needed to deal with the fact that twelve years worth of sacrifices and commitment to Matthew seemed to add up to nothing. They had no children and they didn't even have as much as a pet together. She lived for him, she catered for him, she waited for him and she prayed for him and in return she meant nothing to him. *Was there someone else in his life,* she wondered but it didn't really matter. He did not love her anymore and the questions began to linger, did he ever love her?

He was very clear with his short, yet to the point statement that he simply did not want to be married to her any longer and she knew that there wasn't anything she could have done to salvage their marriage. Nobody was ever able to negotiate with Matthew, she learned that early on and she could and would not do it, not even try it.

Chava left her country when she was only nineteen years old and she was building a brand new life for herself when she met Matthew on a blind date. After a brief courtship, on his insistence, they were married just before he received his orders for his first major assignment. Matthew was still just a young Captain then and their moving around the country and overseas began.

They settled into married life like many other young military couples did and she immediately realized that being alone was part of what she later called "a military spouse's job description." She dutifully attended officer's wife luncheons and other social gatherings, entertained Matthew's superiors and their families, and all along, she felt that something was missing. For a long time, she thought that perhaps a child would fill the lonely days and nights she spent alone in their small government quarters which eventually grew larger with each promotion Matthew was awarded.

Matthew was away on field duties a great many times and then he went overseas on missions he could not or would not talk about. Chava begin to write short stories, not mentioning to anyone about her love for the literary world or about her desire to become part of it. She wrote about her loneliness with such details that when she read what she finished writing, she sobbed and burned the labored pages until nothing was left of them other than black and gray ashes. But as usual, Matthew returned home and everything was alright once again, until the next time.

One thing and one thing only that kept her going was the love for her parents she left behind in her "old country." She hated her old life, the poverty she grew up in and the misery she felt with every passing day she had to spend in a society where hatred was hidden behind red flags and stars and hypocrisy that was called governmental power.

She had nightmares what people only saw in horror movies. The nightmares would not stop for years, but she never complained about them, perhaps only casually mentioning it to some friends of hers who experienced the same as she did in that certain notorious refugee camp. The nightmares began to vary after she married Matthew. At first, while she spent her fearful yet hopeful days in a rat infested refugee camp in Italy before immigrating to the United States, the nightmares were so frightening that she woke up in a cold sweat. She "dreamed" that she went back to her country and she was unable to leave again. After marrying Matthew the nightmares appeared in two versions. One version was the she went back to her old country with Matthew and they let him out but not her and the second version was that she went back alone and she couldn't get in touch with Matthew. It took over ten years before her nightmares began to fade and eventually go away without seeking any professional help. She could just imagine what prisoners of war had to go through, at least, other than been short of food and basic levels of sanitation, she was not tortured every day and there was always hope that her stay in the refugee camp would end eventually. She seldom talked about her every day life in the camp as she preferred not too, but she knew that someday she would write the story of her family and of herself.

Laying on the bed that she once shared with Matthew, she began to wonder if he ever truly loved her or if he just married her because she was different, because she was "European." Most people find her attractive; she noticed but ignored the approving and occasionally curious looks she received. She was pushing her early thirties but she could easily claim to be in her late twenties. Her shoulder length dark brown hair matched her dark brown eyes that could make any person nervous when she looked at the individual longer than a few seconds. Cheating on her husband was not an option or even a thought, she wasn't raised that way and she loved him despite the lonely hours she spent alone in his absence. *How strange it was,* she thought, *that it never occurred to me that perhaps he was seeing somebody else.* True, they treasured time together that was spent in the company of others, she simply assumed that he needed to unwind after the stressful missions he never talked about nor that she dared to ask about. It was just simply the way of life of a military spouse.

Without denying it, there were some "awkward" moments a few times. She recalled, when after a long mission he returned and then a few days later left again and between the times he spent home, he didn't even try to make love to her. She cuddled up to him a few times but he went to sleep, and she didn't dare to wake him up. She told herself that she cannot force herself on him and they would make love again after he was well rested after the next or the next and the next mission and now it was all over.

The following morning after Matthew's unexpected announcement, she called her lawyer just to be informed that he could not assist her because he was going to represent Matthew, after all, he said, Matthew and he were golfing partners. Her friend, Sandy's lawyer was more than willing to represent her after she told him about the circumstances of how Matthew concluded their marriage.

Matthew did not protest the financial settlement she requested and despite the fact that her lawyer wanted to ask for more, Chava didn't want to push the issue.

CHAPTER EIGHT

It was just about the most restless night in a long time that Chava could recall. She restlessly turned back and forth in the comfortable bed of her hotel room, until she finally decided that perhaps she could do something on her laptop, perhaps find out the mystery of the last word that the card that came with the flower arrangement excluded. *The stranger who's initials were A-HH was telling her that he was attracted to her but he could not get to know her better because she was a . . . what?"* she wondered.

She looked at the flowers and wondered why there were only six almost rare flowers in the very untraditional bouquet. She had never been familiar with the name of flowers and plants so she switched on her lap top and clicked on her Encarta file. She typed "list of flower names with pictures." Within seconds, several pages of listings of flowers appeared on the screen. She pulled a note pad and a pen from the small desk next to the computer and began to take notes. A short time later, she identified all of the flowers.

There was one Jasmine, two Eremurus, one Watsonia and two Star Gazer Lily. Once she wrote all of them down, she took the first initials of each of the flowers and started make out various words from them, most of them didn't make sense, but one of them finally did, she spelled out "Jewess". She immediately knew who sent her the flowers but the main question remained, how did he know about her mother's death?

She turned off her laptop computer and returned to bed. She succeeded to fall asleep, but once again, it was not a peaceful sleep. Chava woke up from the nightmare that was a combination of what she had read from her mother's letter or as she called it her testimonial and her own experiences while Chava waited for the immigration visa in the refugee camp in Italy. She stood under lukewarm shower for a long time just to wake up and clear her mind. By the time Chava finished with her shower, Sandy was already waiting for her in her room.

"I was about to send a posse after you," she said jokingly when Chava finally emerged from the bathroom still only wearing panties and bra. She smiled at her friend's joke and got dressed quickly. As if they were thinking about the same thing, without discussing where to go for breakfast, they walked down to the hotel's Atrium Terrace where they previously enjoyed the strong Hungarian coffee, and where Sandy was able to taste the variety of Hungarian pastries in large quantities.

"I was thinking that this morning we could stop by one of the travel agencies to make arrangements for our train ride to Poland and the flight to Israel. After that, perhaps I can show you around, what you think?" asked Chava from her friend who nodded with her mouth still full of food.

"That would be fine," Sandy said finally.

Chava was looking down into the lobby when her eyes stopped on a man whom she recognized as one of the Palestinian men who was giving her an almost hateful look the previous morning at breakfast. She turned her head and concentrated on her made to order omelet and asked the waitress for another cup of cappuccino.

They left the hotel an hour later and while they were waiting for a taxi in front of the hotel's entrance, something made Chava turn around. Her eyes met with the eyes of the man who stood behind her, it was the Palestinian man from the restaurant. She quickly turned back toward the street in front her and it seemed like forever getting a taxi. As they were standing there waiting, she heard the Palestinian's voice talking to another man. They stood so close to each other that Chava was able to smell tobacco on the man's breath. He was actually even more handsome up close, but the look in his eyes was troubling to Chava. She always prided herself to be able to read people's expressions through their eyes, at that particular instance, Chava could not decide what she was seeing in the Palestinian's dark brown eyes.

Still not noticing any taxi in the horizon, Chava decided that while they waited, she might as well face the man. She turned around and she was not disappointed, he was still standing there with his eyes nailed to Chava. "Thank you for the flowers," she said curtly. At first he didn't reply, he just looked at her with a stoic expression on his face. "Excuse me, you have some kind of problem with me?" asked Chava.

"I know who you are," said the man in a hateful voice.

"Good for you, just keep your distance and stay away from us," replied Chava in a low but forceful tone in her voice.

"What's going on?" inquired Sandy.

"This man thinks he knows me," Chava said and glanced at the man again. "He is the one who sent me the flowers, to a "Jewess.""

"You are writing bad things about my people," commented the man. "Be careful that you don't get hurt someday," he added.

"I am a romance and suspense novelist and not a political writer, I have no idea what you are talking about," Chava replied.

"I read your book, "For the Last Time." In that book you have portrayed my people as cold and heartless, not as we are in reality, freedom fighters," said the man and he sounded like a snake hissing his words instead of saying it.

"Get a grip," Sandy said to him and she pushed Chava in front of her to get into the taxi that stopped in front of them. "What a jerk," she said when the taxi left.

"A dangerous one," remarked Chava and turned around to see what the man was doing. He stood there and pointed his finger as if it was a weapon and made a motion as if he was firing a gun. *Asshole,* thought Chava but an uncomfortable and troubling feeling came over her. She somehow sensed that perhaps it was not the last time she would encounter that man. "I think he sent the flowers," Chava remarked. Sandy pulled back in surprise.

"Who the hell is he and how did he know about your mom?" she asked.

Chava shrugged her shoulders. "Not a clue," that's all she could say.

It was a few minutes drive and the taxi stopped on a busy street in front of a travel agency. Chava couldn't help smiling as it was the same agency that unintentionally helped her escape from the then Communist country. IBUSZ was a government controlled travel agency and despite that fact, it was somewhat reliable. The travel agent also turned out to be a friendly person and Chava purchased two first class train tickets to Krakow, Poland. She remembered that she also needed to buy seat tickets, not only train tickets as the latest one didn't assure seats, only transportation. She also made hotel arrangements in Krakow and once she finished with purchasing the train tickets, she asked the woman if she could also make flight arrangements from Krakow to Tel Aviv.

Thank God for technology, thought Chava as the ticket agent smiled and replied to her in perfect English, although Chava was speaking Hungarian to her. "Well of course." Fortunately El Al offered one daily flight from Krakow to Tel Aviv and Chava booked and purchased two tickets for herself and for Sandy on the flight as well.

Finished with making further travel arrangements, they managed to grab a taxi in front of the travel agency and Chava asked the driver to take them to Fisherman's Bastion, located in the Buda section of the city. Due to the heavy downtown traffic, it took them almost a half an hour to make it across the Chain Bridge into the older section of Budapest. The driver pulled over in front of the Hilton Hotel and he asked her if that was alright. He explained to them on their way toward their designation that no private vehicles other than the people who lived there were allowed to drive up to the tourist area, and of course, taxis and tour vehicles were also exceptions.

Chava paid the driver and they got out of the taxi. They walked up to the Trinity statue that stood on Holy Trinity Square, just outside Matthias Church and behind the Fisherman' Bastion. Entering the Matthias Church, the same old feeling came over Chava and her eyes filled with tears. When she entered the church, she dipped her fingers into the holy water that waited quietly in the heavy stone dish by the main entrance door and she made a sign of the cross on herself. Sandy watched her and silently followed her friend's movements.

"It's a beautiful church," whispered Sandy. Chava nodded and she quietly explained to her that it was built in the 13th Century in Gothic style and it was rebuilt again in the late 1800's. Chava guided her friend upward on a spiral staircase and once arriving to one of the upper levels, she showed her the replica of the heavily jeweled Hungarian Royal Crown with it's crooked cross on the top of it. Stories have it that an assassin tried to kill the king by hitting him on the head with a heavy object but cross on the top, although it became crooked, prevented the king from suffering a fatal head wound and he survived the attack.

After leaving the church, they walked up to the upper level of the Fisherman's Bastion. "What a great view," exclaimed Sandy and indeed it was. It was a clear, fogless morning, they could see quite far into the distance. Just across the Danube River, the Parliament building stood spaciously and victoriously, having survived two world wars and a revolution. "When was the Parliament House built?" asked Sandy.

"I think they finished it around the beginning of 1900. It's a huge place; I have been there on school outings when I was a child. You have to make reservations months ahead for a tour," Chava explained.

"Can't decide what style it was built in," wondered Sandy out loud, then she asked. "Was the Parliament built in a gothic style as well?"

"You are almost correct; it's a neo-gothic building with renaissance influence, although it is also noticeable that the base ground plan, reminiscing Baroque style, like many buildings around here, you'll see," she promised. Chava gave some time to Sandy to take some pictures while she walked along side of the bastion. Sandy caught up with her shortly.

"I noticed that this place, the Fisherman's Bastion has seven towers, do the towers have some sort of meaning to it?" she asked Chava with genuine curiosity.

"Good going Sandy," smiled Chava at her friend. "Indeed it does. It represents the seven tribes that came to this land."

"Very nice place," said Sandy in a pleased voice and then she pointed toward their hotel's direction. "I have to take a picture of that, I really like our hotel."

"I'm glad to hear that, but let's go, I have more things to show you," said Chava and she began to walk down the stairs to the ground level. They stopped for a few moments to take pictures, mostly Sandy, in front of Hungary's first Christian king, Saint Stephen and they began to walk around between medieval houses that were built next to the Baroque façade covered houses and neo-classic buildings.

"I hate to tell you this my friend, but I believe that I like this old area better than the new one," Sandy declared.

"You are not alone with that feeling," replied Chava and then she suddenly stopped and turned around.

"What's wrong?" asked Sandy noticing her friend's hesitation.

Chava shook her head. "I have this strange feeling as if we have been followed," she said and carefully looked around but was unable to determine if her intuition was correct or not.

"You think that the police are following us or do you think that your new friend does?" Sandy said and laughed.

"Oh please, spare me!" Chava said and made a face at her friend.

After walking around for a couple hours, they worked up a hunger and thirst. They returned to the Hilton Hotel to have lunch there. They both sat outside on the terrace so they could enjoy the view as much as the food they ordered.

Chava decided that she would take Sandy to see the Brave's Square next and perhaps, if her friend felt up to it, maybe they would check out the Museum of Fine Arts which was located on the left side of the Brave's Square. Although there was another museum to the right, Chava didn't quite favor that one much because of the type of exhibits they presented there. She told Sandy about her plan and when Sandy agreed, they once again took a taxi cab which they both agreed was a death trap. The driver was terrible and rude; he drove much too fast for the combination of circumstances, not kept up road pavements and far too many cars on the road.

They finally arrived to the Brave's Square and as Chava was paying for their fare, Sandy made a sign of the cross on herself and remarked, "Please thank him for me for not killing us."

"What did you friend say?" asked the driver catching the cross making and hearing but not understanding Sandy's remark.

"She said that you are going to kill someone one of these days because of the way you are driving," said Chava using her own words. The driver cursed them under his nose and sped away.

They spent the rest of the afternoon enjoying the beautiful paintings of world renowned masters exhibited in the Museum of Fine Arts. They also walked around the Brave's Square, then not having another choice; they hailed down yet another taxi and went back to their hotel. Luckily, the driver was more careful and he even asked Chava which direction she wanted him to take, the scenic or the quicker one. Chava told him to take his time. He drove them around a little bit then somehow they found themselves along the Danube River, soon after they were already in front of the hotel. Chava gave an extra tip to the driver for driving his cab carefully. He thanked her several times and then he welcomed a new passenger as soon as Sandy and Chava left his cab.

Both of them were very tired and they unanimously decided to take a short nap before going for dinner. Chava entered her room and she hoped that no more surprises were waiting but yet, there was another bouquet of flowers. This time it was a dozen red roses, her personal favorites with a note, "Until we meet again, AHH."

Her first reaction was to toss out the flowers, but she changed her mind and decided that she was going to leave them for the maid with a note that she could have them. They were leaving the following day and she was unable take neither the flower arrangement nor the red roses with her anyway. Chava didn't bother to change clothes, as she threw herself on the bed and within minutes, she was asleep.

CHAPTER NINE

Their evening was uneventful as they dined at the hotel's restaurant for the third straight night, trying different dishes each time. Chava knew all the various food creations and she welcomed the familiar and delicious flavors she missed. She often thought about some of the things she had missed after leaving Hungary, but there were not very many. She mostly missed her parents, her friends, who also moved away, and she missed the cultural events she often attended. She mostly missed the Hungarian culinary art and the culture scene that was pretty much it. She did not miss anything else.

They both packed up their luggage for the early morning start of their journey, Chava had asked for a wake up call from the front desk. Before turning in, she watched some television and she was amazed to discover that Hungary had more than just two channels, unlike when she still lived there. *Why am I surprised?* She asked herself. *This country is progressing at a faster pace than other former Communist countries, it always had,* she concluded to herself.

She slept relatively well but not without dreams. Every morning she woke up in amazement that she once again dreamed an entire event. She asked many people if they had dreams and most of her friends had negative responses, but not her, she just had to have a full story dream and sometimes even nightmares. During her last night in Hungary, she dreamt about her beloved mother, who looked healthy and beautiful in her dream. She spoke to Chava calmly, as always and she tried to convince her to find happiness. Chava woke up to find a tear soaked pillow underneath her face.

She took a quick shower and got dressed. Sandy had perfect timing, she was ready at the same time as Chava, and they decided on a quick breakfast before checking out of the hotel. Chava curiously looked around after settling down at their table, but the Palestinian man and his companions were nowhere in sight. She felt somewhat relieved not seeing him, as deep inside she harbored some unexplainable feelings towards that strange, yet handsome man. It was a feeling that she couldn't explain.

While Sandy got their luggage, Chava went to the front desk to check out. The young man behind the counter was very polite and he asked her if she and her friend were pleased with their accommodations. She answered yes, and when he asked again if there was anything else he could do for her, she thought of one. She opened her wallet and pulled out twenty dollars. "This is yours if you help me to solve a mystery," she said to the young man. He nodded.

"I'll be glad to, what is that you wish to find out?" He asked.

"You are probably not supposed to release the names of your hotel's guests, but I received some flowers, actually a couple of times, and the attached cards, both times only had the initials, A-HH. Would you make an exception and tell me if you had anybody staying here with those initials?" she asked. The young man hesitated and looked around, then glanced at her before he began to type on his computer keyboard. He pulled a page from a note pad and wrote something down then handed the paper to Chava. She looked at the paper and read the name, Abdul-Hafiz Hassan. She pushed the folded twenty dollars toward the young man, who smiled, and instead of taking it, he offered her his pen and put one of her first published books on the counter, it was "The Third Cloud."

"Your autograph would mean a lot more to me," he explained and blushed. Chava smiled at him, signed the book then placed the twenty dollars between the pages and pushed the book back to him. "Thank you," he said politely.

"It's always a pleasure, just keep on reading," answered Chava and turned around when Sandy tapped on her shoulder.

"Is everything alright?" she asked.

"Yes, I am ready when you are," responded Chava. She waved to the young man and began to pull her suitcase toward the hotel exit.

Because it was early in the morning they were in luck, there were taxis available and within minutes, they were on their way to the Western Railroad station. Their train was scheduled to depart for Poland in a couple of hours.

The train was already on the track and after checking the departure board, they made their way to the designated cabin. One of the conductors helped them lift up their luggage, and finding their seat numbers in the first class section of the train, they helped each other lifting their suitcases up to the overhead rack. Chava carefully placed the bag that Sandy bought earlier in the hotel's boutique and which was perfect to hold the urn next to her as she sat down. Sandy began to laugh when she took her seat.

"What so funny?" asked Chava.

"This is first class?"

Chava laughed too. The seats were hard but had cloth coverings on it, unlike the second class, where the seats were made out of hard wood. Chava pulled the curtains closed on their cabin's door for privacy and she watched as people hurried about outside the tracks. She couldn't help noticing people who were trying to sell some last minute souvenirs to the departing passengers.

Amazingly the train left on time and lucky for them, trains with international destinations only made a few stops, unlike commuter trains that made frequent stops. Chava looked at their train schedule and according to that, they were supposed to reach the border in about three hours. At one of the stops a young couple got on and took the seats next to Sandy. They eventually introduced themselves to Sandy and Chava and the young man told them in English that they just got married and they were on their way to Poland for their honeymoon. *Interesting choice for a honeymoon,* thought Chava. They were not very talkative at first but that changed later.

Chava knew that they were getting closer to the border because the passport and custom officers arrived and they went from cabin to cabin. She was hoping that there would not be any hassle, one could never know with former Communist officials. The officer who checked her passport asked her in Hungarian what was the purpose of her visit. She told him that her mother passed away and she came back for the funeral. He looked at her for a couple of long moments and without saying anything further, he stamped the passport and handed it back to her.

The custom officer was a jerk and he was trying to give Chava a hard time. He wanted to know what was in the bag next to her and when she told him, he said that he wanted to see it. Chava couldn't believe it but she had no choice, she carefully removed the urn from the bag and she was about to remove the top when the custom officer stopped her. It was easy to see that the urn was still sealed and he must have seen something like that before. He left without saying anything further to Sandy or Chava.

Sandy shook her head and quietly remarked. "What a jerk."

Chava glanced out the window and something caught her eyes. She motioned to Sandy who followed her finger to the direction of a train that was standing two tracks from theirs. In one of the open doors stood a young Hungarian soldier, Chava was unable to make out his grade or rank, but she was almost certain that he was just a private. On his right shoulder hang what Chava made out was a modified AK-47. There were a lot of things that Chava learned while she was married to a military officer, she learned to recognize uniforms, insignias and weapons. It was not the gun that caught her eyes but the dark wine bottle that the soldier was holding in his left hand drinking from it every couple of minutes, while occasionally he was looking around to see if anybody was watching. "Would you believe that?" Sandy exclaimed.

"I guess the Hungarian borders are safe enough," replied Chava and smiled, then turned from the window. They felt a jolt and it was a good sign, it meant that the new locomotive engine was finally attached to the front of the first car and the next part of their journey was about to begin. They heard a whistle and the train once again began to move. Chava was deep in thought when she heard her name called. "Chava, are you alright?" asked Sandy.

"Oh, I am sorry, I was just thinking about the time when I left this country during my big escape," she said, and a faint smile appeared on her lips.

"Excuse me," said the young man. "I couldn't help overhearing it, did you say that you escaped from Hungary?" he asked.

"Yes, I did many years ago when the government system was different," replied Chava.

"I cannot imagine living my life in another country," remarked the young man who called himself Miklos.

"But you are going to another country for your honeymoon," retorted Sandy not waiting for Chava to reply.

"Yes, but I am coming back. Don't you miss Hungary?" he asked with genuine curiosity.

"No, never!" Chava replied sternly.

Miklos translated her words to his equally young wife who asked Chava in Hungarian. "Why didn't you like it in Hungary, why did you want to leave?"

Chava remained silent for a few moments and she replied in English. "Miklos, would you please translate to Ildiko, I want to explain this in English so my friend can also understand it, would that be okay?" she asked.

The young man translated again and said, "Yes, that would be okay."

"I hated my life in Hungary," said Chava.

"You hated your own country?" asked Miklos. "I just cannot understand why?"

"I did not hate the country itself. I hated the poverty my parents and I were forced to live in, I hated the hopelessness and I hated the majority of the people because of their hypocrisy," explained Chava.

"But don't you think that people are making up the country itself?" Miklos argued.

"No, not in my way of thinking. A country is basically just a geographic word. A country is made of land, hills, mountains, forests and rivers, the people are the population, who in this case, called themselves Hungarians because the country's name is Hungary. Russians call themselves as such because they live in the land of Russia, just as we Americans call ourselves Americans because we are living in America, and so on," explained Chava.

"How about the government, what do you think of the government systems?" asked Miklos after translating Chava's words to his wife Ildiko.

"Government is people and people write policies, rules and laws, and they are the ones who are also enforcing it," added Chava.

"Interesting philosophy," said Miklos. "Don't you think that life is much better now in Hungary? Now we can travel freely, now we can go and work virtually in any country in the world and come back home, and most of all, now we have a freedom of speech."

"Oh, the freedom of speech," smiled Chava. "You know, actually it is difficult to tell what system was, or is better."

"I am not sure that I understand what you mean. How do you compare?" he asked.

"Well, both political systems, the old the Communist government and the new, a more Democratic government have good and bad effects. Let me explain," she said and smiled at Sandy. Her friend knew how much Chava enjoyed this sort of conversation being very political minded. "During the old Communist system, which I can still remember rather clearly, everybody had to work with the exceptions of housewives and students. If you didn't work, you went to jail. It's true, there was no freedom of speech, and I still remember when my mother raised hell when she caught me listening to Radio Free Europe. If the Police caught you or someone reported you, it meant an automatic six month jail sentence without trial. Okay, so we were oppressed, do you know what that word means?" she asked before she continued. When the young man nodded, Chava continued. "But in those days, we had free medical and dental care and I don't remember ever having to pay for medicine. The schools, the education system were also free, perhaps with a couple of exceptions. Nowadays, you have to pay for medical care, for medication, for education among other things. I grant it, you may travel freely and work in other countries but you have to pay high taxes on everything. Don't forget, we didn't have to pay taxes on anything under the Communist governmental system. I understand that now you have great many unemployment offices. While I lived in Hungary, almost one hundred percent of the population had some sort of roof above their heads and even just yesterday, I have seen people sleeping in parks and at railroad stations and so on. You may have freedom of speech now, but your country, Hungary also has high unemployment rates and a devastatingly high suicide rate as well. The freedom of speech is not cheap and it is my belief that Hungary's citizens paid and will pay for this freedom dearly," she stopped to allow Miklos to translate what she said.

"So do you think that we shouldn't have let all these changes happen?" asked Ildiko.

"On the contrary. I believe that change is good but perhaps it happened a little bit too fast. I think Hungary is doing great with all the new technology and all the new enterprising that I read on the Internet. It's fascinating to read about Hungarian millionaires and how privately owned companies are flourishing, but at the same time, I also learned about how retired people are forced out of their apartments because they were unable to pay their rents. I also heard that because of lack of housing, a lot of people froze to death on the streets during the cruel winter weather. It should give some concern to the new government system, don't you think?" asked Chava from Miklos.

"There are many unemployed and homeless people in America too," Miklos commented.

"I grant you that too, but we were talking about Hungary," Chava smiled at him. "You cannot compare the two countries because of the geographical sizes and the make up of the population. The United States is still the most desirable country in the world to immigrate too, no matter what you hear or read about. I would not live in any other country in this world," Chava concluded.

"May I ask what you do for a living?" asked Miklos.

"I am a writer," replied Chava.

Miklos expressed even more interest. "What do you write, stories?"

"I write romance and suspense novels."

"Are they popular?" he asked again.

"You better believe it," interrupted Sandy. "I am surprised that you have not heard of her because they are selling her books in Hungary too."

The door opened and the conductor stepped in. He was wearing a different kind of uniform and it dawned on Chava that they were already in the Slovak Republic. When the conductor handed back her ticket, she leaned back in her seat. "Are you sleepy?" asked Sandy. Chava nodded and closed her eyes. Sandy couldn't help noticing that Chava's left hand gently stroked the bag that contained her mother's ashes. The gesture brought tears into her eyes, she closed them in an attempt to catch some sleep. There was one more interruption when the Slovakian Customs Officer arrived, he just looked at their passports and asked what their destination were. Satisfied with their answer, he quietly closed the door and left.

CHAPTER TEN

A few hours later they reached the border crossing between the Slovak Republic and Poland. Once again, there was a new locomotive engine attached and after a thirty minute delay, they were on their way to Katowice where they were to change trains to Krakow.

Around five in the afternoon, Sandy turned to Chava. "I was wondering if there is dining car on this train?"

Miklos let her new bride's hand go and got up. "I am pretty sure, but I'll be glad to find it out for you," he offered. They took him up on his offer and when he returned, he had good news to report, there was a dining car and it was open for business. Sandy immediately declared that she was ready for some major food demolition and got up to lead the way. Chava turned to Miklos and Ildiko. "I would very much like to treat you both for dinner, how about joining us?" she asked them.

The two of them, obviously hungry, as Chava had not seen them consume food, just as Sandy and she didn't, other than a Diet Coke and some water, they looked at each other and hesitantly agreed. "Please don't be shy, it gives me great pleasure to do it," explained Chava.

As it was a tradition, many Europeans ate dinner in late hours of the night and Chava thought perhaps that was the reason why the dining car was not that busy yet. Their timing was good and the service and the food was efficient. All of them ate heartily and although some of the dishes were not familiar to Chava, they were tasty and there was not even a morsel left on their plates.

After dinner Chava and Sandy ordered coffee and the young couple had Cokes. They became less talkative; the long train ride was taking its toll even on them, despite their young ages. Returning into their cabin, Sandy moved over next to Chava so Ildiko could lay down on the hard seat with her head resting on Miklos lap. Both of them fell asleep almost immediately.

The train reached Katowice at seven thirty in the evening and they said goodbye to the young couple who continued their honeymoon trip to Warsaw. Chava and Sandy didn't have too much time to waste; their connection was leaving in thirty minutes. The Polish conductor was very helpful and in broken English he directed them to a track on the opposite side of the station, which meant that they had to take their suitcases down some steps and up again on the other side. The train was already on stand by and after they took their seats, they only had less then ten minutes to spare.

The train was a slower one and although it only made two stops within three hours, it was already very dark outside. Luckily, as in the front of all major railroad stations, there were taxis waiting and they took the first available one. Chava gave the address of the Hotel Alexander to the driver and he started the engine. "Are you from America," asked the driver.

"Yes, we are," replied Sandy.

"I like America, I was in Illinois two years ago visiting my cousins, and they are living in Skokie. Have you been there?" he asked again in a friendly tone.

"No, I am sorry. We live on the West coast," Sandy explained. The driver was a regular chatter box and spoke rather good English. They let him talk to them about what sites they should visit and how to get around. He told them some good information, such as the Hotel Alexander was in the very center of the city of Krakow and only a few minutes taxi ride from the railroad station where they had just arrived. True to his words, they arrived to their hotel in less than ten minutes. Sandy remarked that if she wasn't that tired and if she would have known the city better, they could have easily walked the distance.

After checking in to their hotel room, Chava felt totally exhausted. She briefly thought about the scenery they passed during the train ride as she opened her suitcase to take some clothes out. *I have seen enough poverty, I don't need to see anymore,* thought Chava. She came to that conclusion after seeing some run down buildings and beggars at railroad stations and along the railroad tracks as their train passed them by. She was saddened seeing hungry and raggedy looking people and it brought back bitter memories from her childhood.

Sandy felt very tired too and both of them bid goodnight and retired for the evening which was very unlike them.

The hotel room was very comfortable, they slept relatively well. In the morning, after taking a long hot shower, Chava was ready for breakfast before a short day of sight seeing and she was also planning to seek some guidance on how to get to the former concentration camp, Auschwitz-Birkenau the following day.

The restaurant was a pleasant surprise and the service was quick and prompt. They decided on the buffet instead ordering from the menu placed in front of them. Buffet was always Sandy's first choice, but they had to wait as a large group of tourists were already lined up around the buffet serving table.

The waiter placed two cups of steaming hot coffee in front of them and they both agreed that it smelled good. Chava watched the group walking around the buffet set up and tried to guess which country they were from, but she couldn't quite place the words she overheard when they talked.

Two tables away she noticed a man, dressed casually in Levy jeans with a white shirt and it came to her as a surprise that the man was already watching her. As they glanced at each other, she heard Sandy's voice, "Are we making a new friend?"

Chava smiled at Sandy as she retorted, "Are we being jealous?" they both laughed.

The man had curly jet black hair and the bluest eyes Chava could swear she had ever seen. He was still looking at her when she turned his way again and his lips curved into a gentle, almost embarrassed smile as he was caught doing something that he was not supposed to. Chava also smiled and turned back toward Sandy. "He is gorgeous," her friend remarked.

"And probably married," said Chava.

"How do you know that?" asked Sandy and looked at the man but he turned away.

"Honey, he is definitely not interested in just anyone," she remarked.

"And how do you know?" Chava asked teasingly.

"Well I was about to wink at him and he turned away," she explained.

Chava laughed and sipped from her still steaming coffee. She tried to do it as casually as possible to look at the man's direction but he was gone. She sighed and looked at the food line that was getting thinner. "I guess we might as well get in line too," she said and pushed her chair back to get up.

Sandy was in front of her in line when Chava felt a gentle touch on her arm. She turned around surprised by the touch and her heart almost jumped out of her chest. The man whom she exchanged looks was standing behind her. He was almost a head taller than her and she had to look up at him but it was worth all efforts. She had seen handsome men in her life, especially being around thousands of military personnel, but she had never seen anyone as handsome as the stranger was. They just sort of stood there and staring at each other without saying a single word. Chava thought that she could easily drown in his clear sky blue eyes and she bit her lips when she noticed that his lips were slightly parted. *If I was younger,* she thought, *I would kiss him right here and right now.* She tried to recall a single incident when she wanted to be kissed and embraced by anyone as much she wanted to be embraced by that total stranger but she was unable to recall any.

"Chava," she heard Sandy's voice. She turned back toward her friend and realized that the line was already way ahead of her. The man smiled at her and he said in perfect English.

"Here is a plate for you," and with that, he handed her a large white porcelain plate. Her hand was shaking when she reached for the plate and when her fingers brushed his hand still holding the plate, an electric jolt ran through her. Chava thought that her knees were giving out and that she was going to faint. "Are you alright?" he inquired.

"Yes, I am fine and thank you for the plate," mumbled Chava and taking a deep breath she began to place some food on her plate from the buffet table. A while later when she was picking on her food under Sandy's teasing glance, she couldn't quite recall how she made it back to their table.

"I have to admit," said Sandy, "that you are not only a good writer but you also have excellent taste in men. Even that Palestinian was a good looking man but he is no match for this guy. I wonder if he has a brother or cousin."

"Oh, please!" said Chava and rolled her eyes. "That is why I am a 35 year old divorced woman who has lived alone for over three years and traveling with a girlfriend instead of a husband or lover. Yeah, I really know how to pick them."

"Hey, I am older than you and I am not bitching," said Sandy in a mock protest. "Honey, I just know that you and I will find the right guy someday."

"And then are we going to share him?" Chava laughed. Her friend began to laugh so hard that she dropped her fork on her plate.

"You are full of . . . hot air," said Sandy and drank some of her cooling coffee.

The man was seated with seven others from the large, what appeared to be a tour group. Sandy leaned toward Chava. "Did he speak English?"

"Fluently, I could not detect any accent at all, maybe he is American," she replied.

"Chava," said Sandy and shook her head. "You were so out of it for a few seconds that I don't think that you could have detected a Chinese accent if your life was depended on it."

Chava did not reply, she quietly chewed on her food while she was exchanging glances with the man. A young woman was sitting next to him and talking to him, was she his wife? She thought that he didn't look like a day over thirty and the woman looked as if she was in her mid or late twenties. They talked and they laughed and it was quite obvious that they knew each other very well. Chava was unable to recall as she didn't pay much attention if the man was wearing a wedding band or not, then again, a lot of married man did not. They were not touching or kissing or showing any affection toward each other, but once again, many men did not show any affection in public.

The group finished with their breakfast and slowly began to leave the restaurant. The stranger and the young woman were just about the last ones to leave and when they headed towards the door, the man put his arm around the woman's shoulder. Chava's heart sank and her smiled disappeared from her face as she turned back and stared into her almost empty coffee cup, just missing the last look that the strange man gave her as he turned around before stepping out the door.

CHAPTER ELEVEN

The Concierge was a young and enthusiastic young man who was obviously very proud of his city; he also turned out to be very helpful. He gave Chava and Sandy all sorts of information where to go and what to see and most of all, how to get there. He also answered Chava's inquiry about what would be the best way to visit Auschwitz/Birkenau where she was planning to go on the following day. He suggested hiring a taxicab for a day which would cost her around fifty American dollars. That way, he explained, they didn't have to wait for a bus, the taxi would wait for her virtually all day. He offered to make the arrangements for her right after Chava slipped him a twenty dollar bill as a token of her appreciation for all the help he provided.

Sandy returned back to the lobby with her walking shoes on and she was ready to go. They were lucky in a sense that Hotel Alexander, just as the taxi driver told them, was located in the very center of the city of Krakow, only a few minutes walk from the city's Main Square or commonly called Grand Square. It was huge in size and according the brochure, the largest of European medieval cities. She couldn't confirm that as she had not seen all of it, but it was common for all country's to have the largest, the biggest and the tallest in the world whatever they wanted to designate as a tourist attraction.

The square was surrounded by over forty buildings, almost each of them demonstrating the particular construction style of their era, such as the Cloth Hall erected in the 16th century in Renaissance style while the Basilica of the Virgin Mary was built in Gothic style in the 14th century. The restaurants, cafes and clubs provided the latest additions to the old square. Sandy and Chava noticed a group of about thirty people with a tour guide who was holding a small British paper Union Jack. They looked at each other and quietly joined the group.

The group began to walk up on a scenic street called Kanonicza, which reminded both of them of Buda, the older but not the oldest part of Budapest. According to the tour guide, the street was used as a ceremonial route leading from the main city gate right into the Royal Castle, the Wawel. During the 14th century, the houses on both sides of the street were occupied by people and their families with nobility.

They slowly made their way up to the castle and they agreed that it was worth the effort to take the seemingly long walk. The castle had a magnificent courtyard and it was not difficult to imagine all the tournaments and events that might have taken place on its proportional premises. As they walked through the Royal Chambers, it was obvious, even to a non artistic person, that the royalty endorsed and employed many different nationality artists. It was very easy for Chava and Sandy to recognize Italian and Dutch paintings and tapestries.

In the Crown Treasury and Armory, Turkish and even Persian weaponry was displayed, not to mention the beautiful carpeting and oriental ceramics and pottery.

They entered the coolness of the Wawel Cathedral and it was undeniably one of the most breathtaking churches Chava had ever seen. The Cathedral not only served the purpose of worshipping but it was also where kings, queens, a number of bishops and many Polish heroes and artists were also buried in marble or other fine metal sarcophagus. Actually it was Sandy who pointed out to Chava that in the center of the nave, in a mausoleum, laid St. Stanislav, the patriot saint of Poland whose coffin was made out of silver. In return, Chava showed the brochure to Sandy that one of the kings, Vladislav II was buried in coffin carved out of red Hungarian marble.

They spent most of the morning at the castle and in the early afternoon, they made their way back to the Grand Square where Sandy said she wanted to vegetate. It basically meant that she wanted to sit down at one of the outdoor café's and watch people. Chava's feet began to hurt and she blamed herself for not bringing more comfortable shoes with her so she was ready to relax as well. Both of them knew that the following day was promising to be a difficult day for both of them, especially for Chava.

They had dinner at one of the restaurants located at the Grand Square and after that they walked back to the hotel where Chava wanted to do some writing before she retired for the evening. Sandy was always prepared for those times when Chava wanted to write, she honored her friend's desire to have a quiet surrounding when she wrote so she brought a few books with her that she always wanted to read, but otherwise she never had a chance.

The Concierge on duty stopped them and told them that a taxi is going to pick them up eight o'clock in the morning in front of the hotel to take them to Auschwitz. They thanked him and went upstairs to their rooms.

CHAPTER TWELVE

C hava worked late into the night on her new novel. It was not ambition or guilt for not writing for days that drove her, but it was the fear of nightmares that surely waited for her once she went to sleep. Eventually she couldn't concentrate any longer and forced herself to go to bed.

She woke up to the sound of knocking on her door, just to realize that she actually had a dreamless night. Sandy was ready to go and she was surprised to see that Chava was still in her tee shirt that she wore to bed. "I am so sorry, I forgot to set the alarm. Be a sweetheart and give me a few minutes," she asked. Sandy sat down at the edge of the bed and turned the television on while Chava took a quick shower.

It was only quarter after seven and the dining room was already rather busy with tourists getting ready either to leave the city, or to go for more sightseeing. They found a table set for two at the far side of the restaurant and asked the waiter for two strong coffees. Sandy looked toward the direction of the buffet cart and asked Chava if she wanted to wait until she got back or if she wanted to join her at the food serving. Chava shook her head. "No thanks sweetie, I don't think that I can eat, sorry. But you go ahead," she said encouragingly.

"Are you sure you don't want me to bring you something, maybe some cereal or fruit, anything?" Sandy insisted, but Chava motioned that she didn't want to eat.

She followed Sandy with her eyes as she went to the buffet cart but in reality, she wanted to see if that dark haired and blue eyed stranger was around. She didn't see him anywhere.

Chava slowly sipped the strong coffee and stared at the wall behind Sandy as they sat by their corner table. "Penny for your thoughts," she heard Sandy's voice.

"Not for those thoughts," she remarked then looked at her friend. "I am afraid."

Sandy placed her food back down on the plate. "Afraid of what honey?" she asked.

"What my mother is really trying to do to me, what her real purpose is behind her last three wishes," Chava said quietly. Sandy raised her eyebrows.

"I don't understand what you mean," she said.

"I'll tell you later. Right now I'm afraid that I have to face a part of my family's history that all these years I didn't know yet, and now I am forced to learn about." Chava motioned to the waiter who was walking by their table to refresh her coffee.

Sandy looked at her long and hard and reminded herself to be patient with Chava. She loved Chava so much for what she was, a good friend, a smart woman and being a sister to her that she never had. Chava was the most honest person Sandy could have ever met and she wanted nothing more for Chava than to have a joyful life that she had not experienced before, not even when she was married to Matthew. Sandy would have given up her own happiness just to see Chava come alive and be happy. She made that promise to herself in her darkest hours when nobody was there for her emotionally and financially, other than Chava.

"Hey," Sandy said to Chava cheerfully. "I haven't seen your blue eyed guy this morning." Just my luck, he was in the company of a young lady. I told you he was married," Chava said with a slightly bitter smile.

"You don't know who that woman is, she could have been his cousin, his sister . . . ," Sandy insisted.

"Well, she certainly wasn't his mother," said Chava and motioned with her hand to drop the subject that seemed hopeless at that moment. The waiter stopped by at their table and politely cleared his voice. "Excuse me madam, a taxi you ordered is waiting outside."

"Thank you," Chava replied and left a couple of dollars on the table for the waiter.

The taxi was a Polski Fiat and not a comfortable one for that matter, but they had no choice. The driver was a man in his early fifties and when Chava asked him if he spoke English, he said in Polish, "no." Chava asked him again if he spoke Russian and man said, "Yes." Chava inquired from him in Russian if he knew where they wanted to go and how much he wanted for the fare plus the time he would have to wait. The driver told them that he knew that they wanted to go Auschwitz/Birkenau, or as he referred to them in Polish, Oswiecim/Brezinka, and that it will cost her fifty dollars for the whole day.

Chava knew that it meant a lot of money for the service, but she also realized that convenience for not getting on a train and then getting a taxicab after that, fifty dollars was not really a high price to pay.

The driver told her that the former concentration camp was about 67 kilometers from Krakow and he expected them to arrive there in less than two hours. Chava translated the information from Russian to English to Sandy who just smiled and shook her head. "What?" asked Chava seeing Sandy's smile.

"Girl, you always manage to surprise me," Sandy remarked.

"I don't know, what do you mean?"

"I didn't know you speak Russian," Sandy said to Chava.

"Actually my Russian is very rusty. However; it's nothing unusual of my generation to speak Russian, it was mandatory to learn that language in schools," explained Chava.

They watched the small villages and towns passing by from the car's window, towns like Nowa Wies, Bulowice, and Leki with their wooden areas, rolling hills and fields where people were busy with planting or in some cases it seemed like harvesting. Sandy remarked quietly. "How could those people who lived around here claim, that they didn't know what was going on down the road not far from here."

Chava sighed before she replied. "They had to know about it. Although, before we judge them, you have to visualize their choices. What could they possibly do? They were an occupied nation and if they would have spoken out against what was going on, they would have ended up in the camp with their families themselves. On the other hand, there was no love lost towards Jews in those days."

Sandy didn't reply, there was not much she could have added to Chava's response, she knew that her friend was right. The driver turned around and said something in Russian. "What did he say?" inquired Sandy.

"He said that we are going to be there in a few minutes," translated Chava.

There was no mistake; they could see the camp from the distance as the car approached the entrance to the camp. There were already a few tour buses and several private cars and taxis lined up in the designated parking areas. The driver stopped and parked the car, then turned around and said something to Chava which sounded more like an explanation, and then Chava said something back to him. She finally turned to Sandy and translated. "He said that he will park here and if we want to go to Birkenau, it's 2 kilometers from here, he could drive us there too. I told him that I want to go there but I want to walk the distance. I also told him that we will meet him here later."

They got out of the car and Chava carefully took out the leather bag with her mother's ashes and held it close to her chest. They slowly began to walk toward the iron gate with the deceiving sign on the top that promised, "Arbeit Macht Frei," which translated from German, "Work will make you free."

Chava hesitantly stopped for a brief moment before stepped inside the camp and took a deep breath. Sandy reached for Chava's hand and they stepped in together. At first, they visited the museum where behind glass walls, tons of human hair, shoes, shawls, eyeglasses, piles of luggage were shown. They signed the visitor's register and a woman speaking English asked them if they wanted to join a tour with a guide. Chava thanked her and declined the offer. She bought a tour book, which sounded outrageous to her, nevertheless it pointed out the most notorious buildings.

Chava stopped in front of Block 10 and said to Sandy. "You don't have to come in if you don't want to. Cell Block 10 was the worst of all barracks, this is where all the inhumane experiments took place."

Sandy didn't reply, instead she walked right up to the door and entered, Chava right behind her. The walls on both sides of the hallway had pictures of victims, most of them did not survive the experiments for certain and yet, some of them had hope in their eyes. There were pictures of women who's breast bones were removed for whatever reason and it was hard for Sandy and Chava to imagine that such unnecessary surgeries were done without as much as local anesthetics.

Before entering one of the rooms where the actual experimentations took place, Chava was sure that she was going to hear the screaming of the victims, but there was just silence of the shocked tourists and sounds of weeping individuals coming from other rooms. Walking out of cell Block 10, Chava turned around and said. "So this was the place where two of my aunts, Lilly and Irene have perished."

Outside they heard English words and once again they sort of attached themselves to a group from England. It was interesting to Chava that most people did not utter a single word; only the tour guide's voice was audible. They visited barracks where people were actually starved to death, in other words, they remained there until they died. They noticed that there was a candle burning in front of one of the cells and they heard the explanation about a Catholic priest by the name of Alexander Kolbe, who volunteered to starve to death in the place of a younger man who was supposed to die but who cried out for his wife and children. The tour guide mentioned that Pope John Paul II awarded sainthood to the forty seven year old priest for his humanity and sacrifice.

They visited one cell block or barracks of horrors after another, the tour guide constantly reminded them of the barbed wired fences. Those fences were visible everywhere, positioned high above the ground, separating barracks and walkways with live electricity running through them during those horrific days when the camp was occupied with tens of thousands of prisoners of the Holocaust. They stopped in front of the wall where many of the executions took place and where blood stains were still visible. Entering the infamous "showers" gave goose bumps to Chava and when she looked up to see the small showerheads, it was not that hard to imagine how those thousands and thousand of people died suffocating from Cyclon B gas that was dropped through small holes through the ceiling.

She went outside and turned to Sandy. "I know that you don't want to leave me by myself, but I must do Birkenau on my own, I hope you understand."

Sandy nodded and hugged her. "I'll be waiting either in the museum or outside the gate, but I'll be waiting."

Chava began to walk toward Birkenau as she wanted to do that part of her mother's wishes by herself, ignoring the other people around her. She hoped that when she reached Birkenau, she would have a few minutes of privacy in the cell block her mother mentioned in her letter.

Arriving in Birkenau, in the distance she could see the railroad tracks where the transfers arrived from almost all corners of Europe and the gateway where the prisoners had to walk through towards their destinies. Chava stopped for a few minutes to read some explanation from her guide book and it made her realize that while it was very difficult for a man to survive in the camp, it had to be extremely difficult for a woman to do the same. According to her guide book the reason behind having less barracks assigned for females than males was because they did not expect women, who were not selected to die immediately upon their arrival, to survive for a long period of time.

Chava walked along the barracks and she finally noticed the barrack that housed her mother and her aunts in those days of horror. Chava knew that not all barracks were open for visitors and she soon realized that her mother's barrack was one of those that were not open for the public. She looked around and she noticed that the tourists were ignoring her as well, and as it appeared, Birkenau did not have as many visitors as the main camp, Auschwitz had.

She tried to open the door and it opened without any problem on her first try. The place was not as well preserved as the other barracks she had seen but it was not hard for her to imagine what was happening there during the days of war. She walked among the stone cubicles that once served as beds for the female prisoners and she wondered how those women who lived through their slavery survived the harsh Polish winters and the searing heat of the summers without any decent clothing.

She gently touched the brick walls that divided the sleeping areas into cubicles or squares where sometimes three or even four women were forced to share the space. Chava remembered that her mother mentioned the sixteenth row on the left, lower bed and she began to count them as she walked along. Arriving to the sixteenth bed, she stopped in the front of it and removed the marble urn from the leather carry case and placed the urn on the lower part of the "bed."

There was a small pile of bricks in the middle of the aisle and Chava guessed that during those days it might have served as some sort of small stove. She sat down on the top of it and just sat there taking in the smell and then she closed her eyes. "Mother, can you hear me?" She asked out loud. "Here you are again in this horrible place. Why did you want me to bring you back here? What is that you want me to discover? My sweet mother, please talk to me."

There was no answer and there were no sounds of any kind. There was no abolition of ghosts or spirits; there was only a small whistle of wind that crept through the cracks on the door. Chava stood up and stayed motionless for several moments as if she was frozen in time in the middle of the barracks. She slowly made a 360 degree turn; still slowly her eyes took in the sights of each row of beds as tears began to dwell in them. *Would I have survived this hell?* Chava asked herself.

She heard a sound, a weak, yet screeching sound that came from the doorway where she entered a half hour or so earlier. Chava turned around and she was stunned to see the person standing inside the barrack with the door closed behind him. The man slowly made his way towards her, his startling blue eyes locked in hers. "Are you okay?" he asked stopping only a few short steps away from her.

She didn't respond, just nodded. He studied her face and leaned against one of the beds. "You are not supposed to be in here," he said to her calmly, not scolding, just reminding.

"I know, but it goes for both of us," she replied. She bent down and removed the urn from the bed and gently placed it back into the leather case. "I had to come here, I had no choice. Why are you here?"

He studied her again, avoiding her question. "Are you American?" he asked.

"Yes, I am," she answered and tightened the leather strap under the handle.

"What are you doing here so far away from home?" he inquired.

"Just what do you think I am doing here?" she retorted with her question.

"Being a tourist or have you lost someone here?" he asked again.

"You are asking many questions for being a total stranger," she said and sat back down on the old brick stove.

He smiled and he stretched his hand out. "I am sorry. My name is Avraham Darom, just call me Avi," he said introducing himself.

"Chava Diamond," she said and they shook hands. He didn't let her hand go right away although she tried to pull it back. He finally let Chava's hand go but he didn't move he remained standing there, only a couple of feet away from her.

"I like the name Chava," he remarked. "It suits you."

"Thank you," she murmured, not knowing what to say. It was another first for her. She looked up at him. *Was he part of a group or was he following her? If so, how did he know how to find her?* she wondered. "So what are you doing here?" she finally asked breaking the silence.

"I am with a group of Israelis, mostly former Holocaust survivors. How about you?" he asked.

She placed her hand on the bag. "In this urn are my mother's ashes. One of her last wishes was to bring her ashes back here for a visit."

"That is an unusual request," he remarked.

She nodded. "Yes it is."

"So you are going to leave her ashes here?" he asked again.

"No, just visiting before I fulfill the last part of her final wishes," she explained briefly, not wanting to share too much information with a stranger she just met.

His eyes were glued on her and he wouldn't move, just stood there with his back against the warm brick wall that was once called a bed. Chava looked away as she was becoming increasingly uncomfortable being in his company, although she could not explain to herself the reason why she felt that way. She could smell his cologne, wasn't too strong but reminded her of Matthew. She used to love to smell his exclusive taste of cologne and how she loved to snuggle up next to him despite the fact that Matthew always remained reserved towards her.

The memory made her feel even sadder and tears dwelled in her eyes, not only from that particular memory, but from feeling lonely and from guilt for being in a place where thousands upon thousands of people lost their loved ones and she selfishly thought about her miserable love life. She got up and made an attempt to leave.

He reached out for her just as two tear drops rolled down on her face. They faced each other and Chava could smell fresh mint on his breath as he spoke. "You are so beautiful," he whispered. "I couldn't take my eyes off you in that restaurant and I hoped to see you again," he bent toward her and gently kissed her tears away but he did not attempt to kiss her on the lips.

Chava tried to pull away but he held her firmly. She gathered all her strength and pushed herself away from him and said calmly. "I am sorry, but this is neither the place nor the time to talk about private matters. Besides," she added. "What about your wife?"

"My wife," he looked baffled. "I have never been married."

"I thought that young lady you hugged as you walked out was your wife," she explained.

He smiled. "That's Ilana, my younger sister, I have another sister at home."

Chava looked down in front of her, feeling even more uncomfortable than before. "How did you find me here anyway?" she asked.

There was a moment of noticeable hesitation from his part before he replied. "I asked the concierge at the hotel if you were still registered and if he knew where you were heading today." It sounded like an acceptable explanation but something told her that it was not the entire story.

She looked around and attempted to take a mental picture of the sight of the miserable place, the very place where her mother and others had suffered immeasurable pain. She quietly said, "Excuse me, I have to leave, my friend is waiting."

"I'll walk with you," he offered. She did not reply which he translated as an agreement. He pushed the wooden door open for her and they stepped outside into the warm air. Chava made a full turn to see the watchtower, the railroad tracks and the long line of barracks that stood bravely, weathering the elements and the passing time, stubbornly enduring the sight and sounds of the suffering of its inhabitants so many years ago.

"If those walks could talk," she muttered the old cliché which was never more usable than a place where millions lost their lives. "Would we really want them to talk and tell us what happened here?"

"We know what happened here," he said quietly.

"Do we really know?" she asked and looked at him questioningly, then shook her head. "Not even close."

He stopped her. "What do you mean?" he asked.

It was now her turn to study his handsome face. His dark brown curly hair was cut short, in sort of a military fashion, his blue eyes were bright and intelligent and his lips were parted as he looked at her. She wanted to lean forward and kiss him so badly at that moment as he was questioningly looking at her. *Did he really want to know what she was thinking? Who was he and where did he come from? What did he want from her and where was he going?* "We know for over fifty years now what horrors and tortures the prisoners were subjected to at this place and many other similar camps. Yet, I have arrived to the questions millions of others asked before me. How could one human being subject another to such atrocities? How could a human being look at another human being, and not see a human being? They treated animals better than Jews, Gypsies or prisoners of war."

He did not reply because he knew that there were no answers to those questions and because he knew that she was aware of that fact too. He was fascinated by her and not just because he found her very attractive and smart, there was something else about her that he had not seen in any other women he dated in the past. Seeing her tears roll down her face made his heart ache and he wanted to take this strange woman who he did not know yet into his arms and ease the emotional pain she was experiencing. He wanted to know her better and he wanted to be with her, it was as simple as that. He finally replied. "Unfortunately hatred has always proved to be stronger than love or humanity, and all of us are capable to kill when feeling those emotions."

"Hatred has always proved to be stronger than love or humanity," she repeated his words. *I never thought of that but I must remember that,* she reminded herself and while she looked at him, she did not say anything further.

"Are you ready to leave?" he asked, bringing her back to reality. She nodded and they began to walk side by side back to Auschwitz.

"I was wondering why my twin aunts volunteered themselves for experiments when they must have suspected that they would have to suffer a great deal of pain," Chava said her thoughts out loud. "My mother said that perhaps they wanted to end their lives, mainly their suffering," she pointed to the barbed wire fence. "Why didn't they just throw themselves against the fence that had electricity running through it?"

"Actually that is a question easy to answer. Each time a prisoner electrocuted herself or himself by touching the fence, ten others were killed. I believe your aunts took upon the torturous experiments rather than killing themselves and others in the process. They were real heroes if you ask me," Avi explained.

"I think you are right," Chava agreed. She recalled that her mother mentioned that in her letter as well. They remained silent during their walk back to the museum that stood not far from the entrance gate and Chava noticed her friend Sandy standing there talking to a woman. "That's my friend," Chava said motioning toward the gate.

"Why don't you introduce me to her," suggested Avi.

Chava was somewhat taken aback by the request as she was certain that after that day, they probably would never see each other again. She tried to think realistically, but deep down inside Chava hoped that they would someday. Chava waived to Sandy who noticed her and Avi right away. She bid goodbye to the woman she was talking to, she walked over to them. "Sandy Johnston, this is Avi Darom," Chava introduced them to each other.

"Hello handsome," said Sandy and she shook hands with him. "How in the world did you two find each other?" she asked.

"Don't go there," said Chava and Sandy knew that she would not get an answer right then.

"It's good to meet you Sandy Johnston," smiled Avi.

"I hate to break up this party but we have to go," said Chava and grabbed Sandy's hand. "Our taxi is waiting."

"Hold on just a moment," said Avi grabbing her arm. "What's the hurry? I like to see you again."

"Sandy honey, why don't you wait for me at the cab," Chava said and handed the leather bag with her mother's ashes to her friend.

"Goodbye Avi, it was nice to meet you," said Sandy and walked out of the camp.

"Look Avi," started say Chava. "We are leaving tomorrow morning and you and I probably won't see each other again. Why don't we just say our goodbyes now," she suggested.

"Because you walked into my life and I can't just let you walk right out. I felt something very special the first time I saw you but I was not brave enough to tell you in that restaurant. I can't stop thinking about you ever since then and that is why we cannot say goodbye," he said in a very serious voice.

Chava laughed bitterly. "Look around Avi," she pointed with her right arm toward the barracks and the museum. "Here we are, possibly in one of the most horrific places on Earth and we talk about love."

"What are you afraid of?" asked Avi.

"You, to start with," blurted out Chava.

"I would never hurt you," Avi objected.

"Perhaps not in a physical sense, but you can easily hurt me emotionally. Besides, who are you and where did you come from? I don't know anything about you and you know what, that's okay. Goodbye Avi," said Chava and she began to walk away.

He didn't say anything; he just stood there looking after her. Chava could feel his eyes following her as she walked to the waiting taxi cab. Sandy was already sitting in the back seat, reading one of her Patricia Cornwell books she brought with her. "What happened?" she asked once the taxi began to return to Krakow.

"Nothing happened," Chava replied curtly.

"Chava, you need to snap out of this attitude, you are scaring men away," she said complaining. "Honey, you need to let some joy and happiness back into your life."

"Sandy, please," Chava made an attempt to stop her friend's preaching about her private life although she knew that it would be a loosing battle.

"He likes you and he seems like a nice and intelligent man," said Sandy. Chava took a deep breath and Sandy thought, *oh oh, here we come.*

"Let's look at the facts, shall we? Who is he? Okay, so we know his name. He never said where he was from and what is he doing for a living and why was he visiting Auschwitz? Did he lose relatives there as well? Okay, so I know that he is not married and that he has two sisters and besides, we are leaving tomorrow, and it's the end of that story," Chava declared.

"That is what I am talking about," said Sandy raising her voice. "You didn't give that man a chance to tell you about himself. You are so hot damn uptight when it comes to man that it pains me."

Chava pulled away from Sandy and then she looked at her. "What do you want from me Sandy? Fall into the arms of any man who shows the slightest interest in me? That is what you want?" she asked.

"No," said Sandy lowering her voice. "I want you to be happy for a change. However; to do that, you have to let a man to get a little bit closer to you. You don't realize it or you are just simply ignoring it when a man expresses interest in you. I don't know for sure but I am getting the feeling that you just don't want to let any man closer to you because you are afraid that you are going to get hurt again."

Chava thought about what her friend said and then she reached for Sandy's hand. "I am sorry and you are probably right. I am afraid to get hurt, aren't you?"

"Yes honey, I am very much afraid too, but . . ." she blinked at Chava. "I must give you a fair warning. When I find someone who expresses the slightest interest in me, I will grab that tiger by the tail, if you know what I mean. It's been way too long being alone," said Sandy.

"I agree and I promise you that I will be more patient the next time, if there will be one," Chava said and her thoughts wondered back to Avi's blue eyes as they watched her back at the barracks in Birkenau. She begin to feel regret for not giving him a chance to meet him in Krakow. *She should have at least given him her address and phone number,* she thought, but it was too late. The time of that opportunity has past and while it hurt her a little bit, she had to move on; she had to complete her mother's last wish.

CHAPTER THIRTEEN

I wish I was back home in my study and writing some blazing romance novel, thought Chava as they stood in the long line at the Krakow airport leading to the security checkpoint. There was no point to complain, the security was there for their protection and not to inconvenience the passengers.

The bus took them to their scheduled El AL flight that parked not too far from the main terminal. The flight attendants were polite and efficient and when they served the food with two sets of utensils, Sandy looked at Chava as if she didn't know why they got two forks, two knives and two forks. Chava whispered to her, "We are not supposed to use the same utensils for dairy and meat products," she explained.

Sandy nodded and whispered back, "Gotcha."

After landing in Lod at the Ben Gurion International Airport, under the watchful eyes of the security personnel they cleared through customs and walked outside the terminal. Chava looked around and noticed a man in a chauffeur uniform holding a sign with their names in English written on it. Pulling their suitcases behind them and Chava still carrying the leather bag and her purse, they walked up to the man who welcomed them warmly and directed them to a limousine parked a few feet away from the exit with "Dan Tel Aviv" written on it's side. He helped them with their suitcases and held the door open for them to get in.

The weather was hot, a typical summer day in the city Tel Aviv. The driver was talking to them in English and he informed them that choosing the Dan Tel Aviv Hotel couldn't have been a better choice because it was centrally located right on the beautiful white sandy beach. The view from a window looking at the Mediterranean Sea could easily take anyone's breath away. He told them that hotel was also a short walking distance from the main shopping district of Tel Aviv and also to the central entertainment section of the city. He reminded them the hotel also had superior cuisine that they just simply had to try and he especially emphasized the name of the restaurant which was La Regence Grill Room.

Sandy and Chava looked at each other and almost burst out laughing at the man's enthusiasm, but Chava bit her lips and gave a playful shove on Sandy's knee to behave.

The ride to the hotel was short and Chava couldn't believe how peaceful everything and everybody seemed. People were going about their business and young couples on the street were just like in any other metropolitan city and even in small towns perhaps, holding each others hand or hugging as they walked toward their destinations. Sandy looked at her and said as if she was reading her mind, "You didn't really expect terrorists running around did you?"

Arriving at their hotel, they stepped out of the limousine just in time to see a group of young men and women walking by them laughing and holding on to each other. Chava noticed with surprise that all of them carried M-16 rifles slung around their necks on a long leather strap. The limo driver noticed her stare and after he placed their luggage on the curb, he turned to Chava who was still staring after the group, "It is a common sight in Israel, you will see this all the time and everywhere. We have to be ready on a short notice," he smiled at her and pointed toward the direction of the entrance to the hotel. "Please," he said. "Follow me."

He carried their luggage inside the lobby of the hotel and Sandy gave him a few American dollars which he thanked her for and after wishing them a pleasant stay, he departed. Checking into the hotel only took a few minutes and in the company of the bellboy who insisted upon assisting with their suitcases. They were escorted to the fifth floor to their accommodations. Their rooms although not connected, were located next to each other looked identical inside. Chava was delighted when she noticed that her king size bed was actually facing the large glass door that led to the balcony. She was able to see out to the blue water that stretched as far as her eyes could see.

The air conditioning felt good but Chava pushed the sliding door aside and stepped outside to see the white sandy beach just below the hotel balconies. People were still out on the beach, despite the fact that it was late in the afternoon, perhaps waiting for the evening breeze to arrive. She thought she felt the breeze already it was still warm, yet pleasant. When she heard a knock on her door she returned inside her room and walking up to the door, she asked who it was.

"Give me a break," she heard Sandy's voice.

She opened the door and there stood Sandy, all dressed up. "Are you going somewhere?" she asked.

"We are going to have a nice dinner at the La Regence Grill Room," she said imitating a French accent. Chava laughed and motioned her inside. "Don't you just love your room?" asked Sandy.

"Yes I do but I need a shower and you will just have to wait," she said to Sandy who shook her head.

"Oh no, I'll be downstairs checking out the male population. You just hurry up, okay?" Sandy replied and walked out the door. Chava sighed and wondered where Sandy was getting her energy from. She took a quick shower and put on her favorite black dress and for accessories she placed a string of pearls around her neck with matching earrings. Although high heel shoes were not her favorites she always wore them when she dressed in her black dress. The dress itself was almost strapless and it gave the impression that only the two strips of black lace that crossed her shoulder from front to back held it up.

She placed some necessary items in her small black purse and checking herself in the mirror she winked. "You don't look too bad for an old broad," she said to herself and smiled. There was nobody in the hallway leading to the elevator.

When Chava got downstairs into the lobby, she was unable to see Sandy anywhere. She walked inside the restaurant, but Sandy wasn't there either. She turned around and walked into the bar. Yes, Sandy was there, indulged in conversation with a relatively handsome looking man in his forties who was wearing a military uniform. Chava was not quite familiar with the Israeli military insignias, but she was certain that the man was a high ranking officer. Sandy looked up and she noticed Chava, she pushed herself off from the barstool and walked up to her. "Come on Chava, let me introduce you to this guy, he seems very nice," she whispered to her.

Chava took a deep breath and followed her friend who was holding on to her hand as if she was afraid that Chava was about to run away. "Daniel, this is my best friend, Chava Diamond, Chava this is Daniel. Sorry, I didn't get your last name," she apologized.

Chava shook hands with the man who also stood up to welcome her. "I am Daniel Zehavi, it's good to meet you too," he said in a friendly voice and a smile on his face. Chava actually liked his mannerism and it was obvious that he took a liking to Sandy, which made Chava happy.

"You are welcome to join us for dinner," Chava said to him. As soon as he heard Chava's invitation, Daniel's smile became broader and he immediately nodded.

"Thank you for the invitation. I'll be honored to dine with two gorgeous ladies," he said and he lifted Sandy's hand to his lips and kissed it. A few minutes later the three of them walked into the restaurant where the maitre'd seated them by the window so they would have a chance to enjoy the scenery while they were enjoying their dinner.

"Would you be kind to help us out with ordering?" asked Sandy from Daniel.

"I'll be glad to," he said and he ordered dinner for all three of them. He also suggested red wine with Chava and Sandy's agreement.

The waiter left and Sandy's eyes rushed back to stare at Daniel who was very much doing the same. Chava just smiled, it was alright with her. Once the wine was poured, she slowly sipped from it and determining that although it was a little bit too sweet for her taste, it was a pleasant dinner wine. She stared out into the distance and she marveled at the clear water when she heard a somewhat familiar voice.

"May I have your autograph?" the man asked.

She looked up and almost spilled her wine. Avi stood next to their table holding one of her books titled "Hannah's Song." Her surprise was genuine and she just couldn't hide it. "What are you doing here?" she asked.

"I live here in Tel Aviv," he explained.

"Would you like to join us?" asked Sandy. Chava gave her what Sandy called an "evil eye" but forced herself back into a more polite mode.

"I would be happy too, if that was alright with Chava," Avi replied not moving as he waited for Chava's reaction.

"Sure, please, have seat," she said reluctantly and instead of looking at Avi, she gave a hard look at Sandy, then turned to him. "How is it that you are always able to find me?"

"Just by asking," replied Avi and ordered his food when the waiter approached him a few minutes later.

"You didn't tell me that you were from Israel," Chava said.

"Well, for one thing, you didn't ask me, and secondly, I just assumed that you figured it out from my Jewish name," he commented.

"You don't have an accent and there are a lot of Jewish people that live in the United States," replied Chava and once again, for some unexplainable reason she began to feel uncomfortable.

"I guess it's rude of us not introducing these two gentlemen to each other," said Sandy and she was about say Daniel's name to Avi when he got up and reached over the table to shake hand with the other man.

"Shalom Daniel, it's good to meet you," said Avi and the two men shook hands. Chava raised her eye brows but didn't say anything. The food arrived and Sandy and Chava shared half of each others as they always did when they were trying out new food specialties.

They consumed their food in relative silence, occasionally Daniel would asked them if they wanted some more wine, but Chava, not being a drinker, reached her limit as she already finished her small glass of red wine, Sandy wanted some more. She soon realized that she had not seen Sandy as cheerful for a long time as she seemed talking to Daniel. Avi on the other hand was even quieter than before, perhaps, just perhaps he felt just as uncomfortable as she did.

The waiter took their dishes away after inquiring if they were finished and asked them if they wanted to try some desserts, but all of them declined. When he left, Avi turned to Chava. "How long are you planning to stay in Israel?" he asked.

"I am not sure yet," replied Chava, and it was true. She wanted to look around in Tel Aviv and visit Jerusalem. She not only wanted to see the old city within the walls, but she also wanted to visit Yad Vashem, the Holocaust Museum. After Jerusalem she was planning to travel to Eilat by the Red Sea where she planned to rent a boat and take her mother's ashes out to the sea to oblige Helene's final last wish. There was no rush to go home and she was sad to admit, other than her work, there was nobody waiting either for her or for her friend, other than Sandy's cat. Chava could virtually stay and live anywhere, she could always write, no matter where her location was any given time.

"What are your further travel plans?" asked Avi. She didn't want to look at him or was she afraid to look at him, she was not certain. Her gut instinct told her that there was more to Avi then just about being one of the most handsome men she had ever seen. "Chava," she heard Avi's voice again. "Do you have any travel plans?"

Chava finally looked at him and her lips parted wanting to answer but his eyes penetrated hers so deeply that for a few moments she was unable to utter a single intelligible word. "Why so many questions?" she asked him in return.

"Excuse me," interrupted Sandy. "If you don't mind, Daniel and I are going to take off."

"No problem," Chava agreed. "Just be safe and not be sorry," she added. Sandy walked around the table and kissed her on the cheek. Chava managed to whisper to her. "Please be careful," Sandy nodded and smiled down at her.

Daniel shook hands with Chava and Avi. "Shalom, and I hope to see you soon," he said and put his arms around Sandy as if they have known each other for a long time.

"Your friend seems to be happy," commented Avi.

"She deserves to be happy," replied Chava.

"And you are not?" Avi asked.

"If you don't mind, I am rather tired. I really need to get some sleep," said Chava and signed her hotel number on the bill and gave it back to the waiter who was standing by. "You have a great night," said Chava and got up from the table.

"May I escort you to your room?" Avi asked.

"It won't be necessary," Chava replied and she wanted nothing more than just to run away and to be alone for a while. She needed to think clearly and she was not able to gather her thoughts for the past few days. Going back to her native land was disturbing enough, then her mother's funeral service and especially her mother's letter, or as she called it testimonial was ever more upsetting for her. A visit to Auschwitz and Birkenau could be easily upsetting to anyone who had even just a single cell of human emotion. For Chava, being there with her mother's ashes and to see what circumstances her mother had to endure and where most of her relatives perished was almost too much to comprehend all at once.

Her mind and emotions were running a marathon that was longer than twenty-six miles and she desperately needed some time alone, without Sandy, without anyone to sort her emotions out. She wanted to sit down by her laptop computer and write down her disturbing thoughts that were haunting her while they were still fresh in her mind.

She felt a touch on her arm, Avi gently placed his hand on her and that touch brought her back to reality. "You seemed lost in thoughts," he made a comment as if he read her mind.

"I am sorry, there were just so many things that have happened within a short period of time," she explained.

He walked with her to the elevator. She pushed the elevator button and impatiently kept looking up on the light to see which floor the elevator was approaching. Finally one of the four elevator doors opened, she walked inside and pushed the button to her floor. Before the door closed, Avi stopped it with his hand. "Chava," he said looking straight at her. "I would very much like to see you again and I would also like us to get to know each other."

Chava looked at him and her heart began to beat faster. Every inch of her being ached to be held by him, to feel his masculine arms around her body and to feel his warm breath on her neck and his soft lips pressed on hers. *Damn it,* she thought. *What is wrong with you? You want to have another heartbreak? You want another rejection? No way!* Chava forced herself to look at him. She tried not to get emotional, but regardless how hard she tried, tears still rushed into her eyes as she replied to him. "I survived one great disappointment in my life; I do not wish to experience another, not even if I have to live alone for the rest of my life. Shalom Avi," she said and pushed the "close door" button. As soon as Avi stepped back, the elevator door closed and began to climb.

She somehow made it into her room and stripping off her clothes, she let them fall to the floor. She climbed into bed and pulled the clean sheet and the blanket over herself, all the way up to her chin. Slowly her lips began to quiver and a river of tears began to flow. "What have you done to me mother?" she asked out loud. She felt alone before but she has never felt the immeasurable weight of her loneliness and unhappiness as she felt in that moment.

Chava didn't know how long she cried but she slowly drifted into sleep, into a wonderful dream. Avi was there and he was gently touching her forehead and was stroking her hair. He bent down to kiss her and her lips automatically opened up for his. It seemed so real that she could actually feel his tongue throbbing and searching for hers. She reached out and hugged him and she realized that he was still dressed. He wanted to pull away but Chava thought that this dream just simply cannot end, and then her eyes popped wide open.

It was not a dream, it was all too real. Avi was on the top of her, looking down at her with those bright blue eyes filled with desire for her. His face was only inches away from hers and he wanted to kiss her again. The reality of the situation was catching up with her and her fear was mixed with desire. Within seconds panic began to sweep over her troubled mind.

She could feel his hardness through his clothes and she could barely think straight. She pushed him back and tried to move from underneath him but he was much stronger and heavier than she was. No matter how hard she tried, she was not able to move as much as an inch. She turned her head when he tried to kiss her and she whispered to him as if there was someone else in the room. "How did you get in here?"

"I've got a key," he whispered back. "Chava," he said and bent over her again. "I am in love with you from the moment I first saw you in that restaurant in Krakow. The way you looked at me, your beautiful eyes told me stories of your unhappiness."

"You don't even know me," she said quietly.

"I know you better than you think," he said and without hesitation Avi pressed his lips on hers and while every brain cell, educated and nomadic objected to what was about to happen, her hands that were pushing him back just minutes earlier began to unbutton his shirt. She felt his warm skin pressing against hers and she shivered from the awakening of her long repressed wave of desires. *What is happening to me?* she wondered and for a few seconds she recalled how much she wanted to kiss him in that horrible place, in Birkenau. And now, he was right there with her holding her so tight that she could feel every single muscle in his body.

When his lips closed around her erect nipples, she just wanted to feel him inside her, for once, she didn't care about what her ex-husband used to call "warm up sessions." It has been so long since she has been with a man, not since Matthew left her and even before that. When he entered her gently but with undeniably impatient desire, a sigh left Chava's lips from sensational feeling having Avi inside her. She felt great joy as he filled her female being completely. He pushed her arms above her head and while he moved, his lips discovered and approved every inch of her body.

Chava came with such intensity; that for several moments she simply could not stop trembling. She bit her lips so hard that she was certain that they were bleeding. He was still hard inside her, throbbing and wanting to please her even more. He leaned over her, took face into his hands and kissed her hard and deep. She gasped for air and he let her head back down on her pillow as his tongue moved along from her ear down on her neck. She couldn't help it, she began to moan and she came for the second time, at that time simultaneously with him. The sudden realization, like an unexpected cold shower came over her, that the pleasure that Avi's erect body, not just his manhood but his firm and well built muscled body gave her was a new never experienced sensation. During her twelve years of marriage, as she was thinking back on those years, she had never experienced the pleasure she felt with Avi, who was virtually a total stranger to her. *How could this be?* Chava asked herself. *How could a man she hardly knew care about how she felt when they were making love, to whom her pleasure was more important than his own?*

He kissed her lips gently, then he leisurely kissed her breasts, running his tongue around her nipples, then he carefully slid down next to her. His arm still around her, he pulled her to his chest. She felt incredibly comfortable as she cuddled up next to him. There were no words exchanged, he just gently caressed her shoulder with his fingers. *Am I dreaming?* she wondered and with that thought, she fell asleep in his arms.

CHAPTER FOURTEEN

C hava was waking up, although her eyes were still closed. She realized that she did not dream nor had she any kind of nightmares for the first time in months. Chava smiled as she remembered the previous night with Avi and the unexpected pleasure she finally experienced, and not just wrote about nor read and dreamt about.

With her eyes still closed she turned toward Avi and then she finally opened them. He was awake and was watching her. When he noticed that she was awake, he bent to her and kissed her on the lips. She did not kiss him back, she felt somewhat confused about the mixed emotions she was feeling. On the one hand Avi was first man who truly made her blood pump and her heart beat faster when she looked at him. His touch was gentle as he caressed her and his soft lips were always ready to kiss her. He was passionate and patient with her when they made love as if he knew that it has been a long time since she was with a man. On the other hand he was still a total stranger to her.

She wanted to pull away but it wasn't meant to be. He was bending over her and while his lips pressed against hers and his tongue was searching for hers, his hands slowly, purposely with a mission of their own made their way between her legs. He gently pushed her legs apart and touched her where she had that certain "spot" which some of the modern women magazines were writing about and which she also thought was a myth or fiction. He stroked her steadily until she grabbed his hands and pulled them away. She looked at him and wanted to say, *take me now, right now,* but no words left her lips. It even surprised her when she reached down and touched him and guided him inside her with an unexplainable urgency. He smiled at her and slowly moved inside her. She couldn't help herself, the pleasure was just too great, and her tears began to shine in her eyes and ever slowly, rolled down on her flushed face. He looked at her questioningly and then kissed her tears away. "What is wrong?" he asked her whispering in her ear.

She pulled him down closer to her and whispered back to him. "Please don't stop," and then she kissed him with her arms around his neck, hugging him tightly. He knew that she was close to climax when her body tensed up and her fingers dug into his back and then it was over and she felt relaxed. He seemed to like to feel the inside of her moist body and he took his time to climax but when he did, just as she did, he exploded with great intensity.

They laid next to each other, her head once again resting on his chest. He drew her hand to his lips and kissed it, then he whispered to her. "I love you Chava." She didn't reply, she just continued caressing his chest. A few moments later, she fell asleep with the thought of how comfortable she felt with a man she knew virtually nothing about.

She woke up to the ringing of her telephone. Chava reached over to the nightstand to answer it. "Hello," said Chava sleepily.

"Hi Honey," she heard Sandy's voice. "Did you get some rest or were you as naughty as I was?" she joked with her friend.

Chava smiled and turned toward Avi but he was not in the bed. She heard water running in the bathroom and as she answered, "Yes, you can say that," the door opened and Avi walked out, already dressed. "Although I don't know the degree of your naughtiness comparing to mine."

He walked up to her and kissed her on the forehead and whispered to her, "I have to go now but I'll see you later." Chava nodded. Avi walked to the door where he turned around before opening it. He watched her silently for a few seconds, but he did not return her wave. There was no smile on his face which she found strange as he always smiled at her when they looked at each other. He opened the door and without saying a single word, he left.

"You want to grab some breakfast?" asked Sandy and then she added. "Don't say anything out loud but we need to talk about Avi."

Chava listened and they agreed that they would meet in a half an hour at the hotel restaurant. She pushed the bed sheet away and went to take shower. While she was drying her hair, she was wondering what Sandy wanted to discuss about Avi.

Sandy was already in the hotel's restaurant and Chava was surprised not seeing a pile of food in front of Sandy which would have been the usual sight. Instead, her friend's face was serious and she was slowly sipping her coffee, not stopping when Chava sat down. There was a cup of coffee already waiting for her which she thanked Sandy for ordering. "So what's up?" she asked.

Sandy put her cup down and before she said anything, she looked around them, then she leaned closer to her. "I am a little bit concerned about Avi," she said.

"You did say that you wanted to talk to me about him," Chava reminded her.

"Okay, so bear with me," said Sandy. "First of all, I think that Avi is a great looking guy and I remember what I told you about that I wanted you to be happy, but something happened here last night which you obviously didn't catch."

"I have no idea what you are talking about," said Chava and she tried to remember what was said last night in the restaurant.

"Please think back for a moment," Sandy asked her.

Chava took a careful sip from her still hot coffee and put it back down on the saucer. The scene with Daniel, Sandy, Avi and herself, like a videotaped production was replaying itself in her head. And then, she remembered something that she didn't catch at that time. Her eyes became wide as she looked at her friend sitting across the table from her. "Think Chava," said Sandy. "How did he know that we went to Auschwitz-Birkenau? How did he know which barracks you went inside? How did he know which hotel you were staying at? None of us said Daniel's name to Avi, yet, when they shook hands, Avi said, "Shalom Daniel, it's good to meet you." I asked Daniel later if he knew Avi and he said that it was the first time he ever met him and I believed him. I found this whole thing just a little bit too suspicious. Don't you?" she asked Chava.

Chava nodded that she did too. "He came into my room late last night and mind you, I had locked my door and the security chain was on," she looked toward the door which led to the lobby of the hotel and she noticed that a man and a woman were looking toward their direction and then they approached Sandy and Chava. When they stopped at their table and the woman spoke to Chava in fluent English.

"Excuse me, aren't you Chava Diamond, the writer?" she asked.

"Yes I am," Chava replied.

The woman stretched her hand out. "It's an honor to meet you, my name is Ruth Ashkenazi. I am a reporter with the Jerusalem Daily Star. Would you mind if I asked you some questions?"

Chava took a deep breath. "If you don't mind my asking, would you please show us some credentials?"

"I am sorry, I should have done it in the first place," apologized the woman and took an identification card on which information pertaining to her was printed in three languages, Hebrew, Arabic and English. This is my photographer, Benjamin Herzman." Chava shook hands with the man and after introducing Sandy to them, she asked them to join them.

"I love your books Ms. Diamond. They are suspenseful and some of them, especially your romance novels are so sexy. I truly enjoy reading them," said Ruth.

"Well thank you, it's always good to hear complements," replied Chava.

"Would it be possible to do a short interview with you?" inquired Ruth.

Sandy and Chava exchanged looks but then Chava changed her mind. "Sure, why not," she replied.

"Thank you so much," said Ruth and she took out a note pad. "Would I be pushing my luck if I ask you if we could take a couple of photographs as well?"

Chava smiled, "Why not?" she replied.

The photographer began to take pictures of Chava and Sandy, separately and together, with and without smiling. He eventually thanked them and left to develop the pictures. Ruth began to ask her questions. "How long are you planning to stay in Israel?" she addressed Chava with her first question.

"Probably a couple of weeks," answered Chava. "Unless my friend and traveling companion decide to leave early," she added.

"Is this a business or personal visit?" asked Ruth.

"Strictly personal," replied Chava.

"Is this your first trip to Israel?"

"Yes, yes it is," answered Chava and looked at Sandy who was motioning with her eyes for her to look toward the direction of the entrance of the restaurant. She turned her head and she noticed that Avi was standing in the door, watching them silently. Chava felt a cold chill rush through her body. He seemed like a movie star in a role that was frozen in a frame of a moving picture. Handsome beyond belief, yet his face did not show any sign of the passion that he expressed just the night before and early in that morning. His eyes, those strikingly blue eyes were nailed into hers as there was no one else around. He did not try to approach them and he did not make a single move, he just stood there watching them. Chava heard Ruth's voice and she turned back to her and again back towards the entrance but Avi was gone.

"Is there a new book in the horizon and if so, when can we have the pleasure of reading it? asked Ruth.

"I am working on my new book which is temporarily titled "The Wrath." If all goes well, I should be able to finish it real soon, perhaps in a couple of months," replied Chava.

"Back to your visit here," Ruth continued. "Do you have any relatives in Israel?"

"Not that I am aware of," confessed Chava and then she added. "But I believe that I have some family roots that possibly originated in the land of Israel."

"What are your plans while you are in Israel?"

Chava was not sure certain what to say but she decided to reveal the true reason beyond her visit to the Holy land. "Basically I am here to fulfill my beloved mother's last wish. She passed away recently and her last wish was to bring her ashes back to the land of her ancestors."

"I am sorry to hear about your loss," said Ruth and she sounded sincere. "How do you feel about the political situation in Israel?" she asked after a moment of silence.

"I try not to be involved in political issues if I can help it," replied Chava. Sandy smiled and bit her lips to muffle the sound of her giggle. She had never met another woman who enjoyed talking about politics as much as Chava did.

"Do you feel that the American media is fair towards the Israelis?"

"Are you trying to get me into trouble?" Chava asked instead of answering.

"Not at all," said Ruth. "I am just asking your opinion."

"But it would be printed in your newspaper, right?" Chava inquired.

Ruth laughed. "That's true. If you don't wish to answer that's fine."

"I do want to answer and trust me, I am the least concerned about criticism," Chava said and then she continued. "Not all media is fair, never was and never will be. Religion is a difficult issue and the motivator behind a great many wars. The ancient hatred against Jews is alive and well and there is no guarantee that another Holocaust could not or would happen. While this may sound ridiculous to our generation, Holocaust happen virtually almost everyday in various countries on our planet. Tutsis against Hutus, Croatians against Muslims or vice versa, Iraqis against Kurds, Hindus against Shiites, and the list go on and on. Holocaust is not only Christians or Muslims against Jews, it's religion against another religion. We just came from a visit in Auschwitz-Birkenau, a place that my beloved mother survived and visitors can only get a hazy picture about what horrible atrocities took place there. I thought that by visiting there I may gain some sort of understanding about those old and unanswered questions, such as, why did the Holocaust happen and could that happen again?"

She took a break and sipped from her refreshed coffee. "We, who care about the future, must teach everyone about what happened, so that the next generation could make the necessary steps to prevent another Holocaust. Who would have thought that a country, such as Germany whose culture was standing on high pedestals, where Goethe and Schiller was admired, where Bach and Handel composed beautiful music could turn again Jews with such depthless hatred that made them forget what the Bible taught and Christianity was all about? A great many of us are taking preventive measures to avoid getting sick, we use birth controls to prevent us from getting pregnant, why can't we use common sense and humanity to prevent discrimination and another Holocaust? But these things what I am telling you are not new subjects, questions and unfortunately I can not offer any real solutions."

"How do you feel about the Palestinian issue? You surely heard about the suicide bombings and killing of innocent people," asked Ruth for Chava's opinion.

"It breaks my heart each and every time I hear or read about the loss of innocent lives. I strongly believe that Palestinians should have their own homeland, but I believe that the issue is where to have that homeland? I am not a politician and I don't wish to get into a debate about territories. However; every single human being on this planet must have a place what they can call "my homeland." Although, on the same token, Israel must remain an independent country where Jews are able to come and live freely if that is what they wish to do. No other countries like Israel in this world where a Jew can freely admit his or her religion without a fear of retaliation or abuse. We must work real hard that Israel remains strong, healthy and free."

"Well, I think you gave me some valuable answers, thank you for your time," said Ruth and put her notepad away.

"Ruth," stated Chava. "Please remember what I said. I don't wish to read something in the paper tomorrow that you made up. Promise me?" asked Chava.

"Please Ms. Diamond," replied Ruth. "If for no other reason, out of respect for you and for what I believe is your love for my country, I will not distort anything from what you have told me. Please enjoy your stay and I wish you a safe return to America. And one more thing," she turned back to them as she was leaving. "Keep those books of yours coming."

"I will," promised Chava and they bid goodbye to Ruth.

"Wow," whistled Sandy. "You sure won't be popular around the Palestinians," she remarked.

"Why not?" asked Chava. "Didn't I say that they should have their own country?"

Sandy agreed with her and they began to eat the food they took from the buffet cart. Chava was deep in thoughts while she was eating and it didn't go unnoticed by Sandy. "Penny for your thoughts," she asked as usual when she saw her friend's facial expression, from which she read that her thoughts were drifting far, faraway.

Chava put her fork down and looked at Sandy. "I am so confused how I feel about Avi. He is a real mystery to me. Did you see him how he watched me from the doorway?"

"It was impossible not to," said Sandy. "There is something about him that I cannot put my finger on it."

"Tell me about Daniel," asked Chava. A smile spread over Sandy's face. "Oh my God, you are in love," exclaimed Chava. Sandy shook her head.

"I am not sure about love but I sure like him a great deal," she admitted. "It's been such a long time since I met anyone like Daniel. He is very charming, very intelligent and he is a great kisser," she said and giggled liked a schoolgirl.

"You are such a slut," Chava said and laughed seeing her friend's expression. "But so was I last night."

"You?" said Sandy loudly then she covered her mouth. "You gave in to Avi?"

"I know, I know, don't say it," replied Chava and to her friend's amusement, she blushed.

"Oh, no, no, no," protested Sandy. "Honey, no matter what we may think about Avi, you needed some heavy petting."

They both laughed and after finishing with their breakfast, they went for a short walk on the beach. The white sand was soft and the temperature was still pleasant, but it promised to be a hot day. They sat down on the sand to talk. "I don't know what to make out of Avi," said Chava. "Just as you said, I am also wondering how he keeps finding me, or us? It is becoming a concern to me too. He came into my room during the night and I did not invite him in you know."

"He didn't rape you did he?" asked Sandy in a concerned voice.

"No, nothing like that. Perhaps I even wanted him more than he wanted me, who knows? He told me that he fell in love with me in the moment he saw me in Krakow and that he loved me. Can I believe him? I don't know if I can or not. He was acting very strangely this morning when he left my room and when he stood in the entrance of the restaurant."

"The main question is how you do feel about him?" inquired Sandy from Chava.

"Other than confused? I like him and it was great being with him but I am not sure if I am in love with him. I honestly just don't know," Chava tried to explain.

"Well, perhaps you two can sit down and have a serious talk. That would be a good start," Sandy suggested.

"Of course, you are right. The next time I see him, that is exactly what I am going to do," said Chava in a determined voice. "If there is a next time," she added. "But what about you and Daniel?"

Sandy sighed. "He had to report to duty this morning but he gave me his cell phone and duty phone number to call in case we stay here in Tel Aviv. I told him that we didn't have specific plans. By the way what do you want to do next?" asked Sandy.

"Let's talk to the concierge, see what travel arrangements we have to make to go down to Eilat," said Chava and pushing herself up, she brushed off the fine sand from her dress and they headed back to the hotel.

CHAPTER FIFTEEN

Inside the hotel lobby the cool air felt good as they approached the Concierge. He suggested a tour in Jerusalem's Old City, an early morning trip to Massada, perhaps to the Dead Sea. He also recommended that while they were in Jerusalem perhaps they should pay a visit to Yad Vashem and upon their return to Tel Aviv; they can take a short flight from Tel Aviv to Eilat. Chava asked him if it was possible for him to make the arrangements and he gladly obliged. Chava was sure that a generous tip would also help, so she slipped two twenty dollar bills to the man behind the counter. He told them that he will ring up Chava in her room as soon as the reservations were arranged. Chava thanked him and walked over to the front desk to inquire if there were any messages for her, but there weren't any. She felt disappointed and she motioned to Sandy that she was ready to leave.

Chava informed her friend what the Concierge said and she suggested that they should pack their suitcases so they would be ready on a short notice. Chava also mentioned to Sandy that she wanted to work on her book from her laptop computer while they waited, and that she would let her know as soon as she heard anything in regards to their tour.

In her room everything looked the same and it was obvious from the unmade bed that the maids had not been there yet. She sat down by the desk and while she waited for her laptop computer to boot up, she turned around and looked at the bed. She closed her eyes for a moment and she could almost hear Avi's voice as he whispered to her *"I love you Chava"*.

She wanted to see him again; she knew and felt that for certain. She wanted to sit down with him and tell him everything about herself and ask him about his life. The thought that perhaps she would never see him again made her feel sad and she hoped that it was not the case. When he left her that morning, he didn't say how he was going to get in touch with her, despite the fact that she didn't tell him anything about her further itinerary. So how would he find her again? *He will find me again*, she thought. *Somehow he always finds me. Who was he and what was he doing for living?*

She turned back toward her computer screen and cued up one of her several email addresses. She stared at the screen and could not understand what she was seeing. She picked up the phone and asked Sandy to join her, she wanted to show her something. Chava opened the door when she heard Sandy's knock, she let her in.

"Wait until you see this," she said and pointed at her computer. Sandy followed her and she also looked at the screen. There were several emails, some from her agent in California, some personal mail from friends. "Do you see anything strange?" she asked.

"No, not really," admitted Sandy. "What am I looking at?"

"See the dates of the emails I received, they are dated yesterday," said Chava.

"So what's the problem?" asked Sandy still not understanding what her friend was getting at.

"Somebody accessed my mail and read it. I didn't have a chance to read any of my emails since we were in Budapest, that's the problem," explained Chava angrily.

"You think that the maid read your mail?" asked Sandy.

Chava pointed at the unmade bed. "She didn't come yet."

Sandy hesitated but she just had to ask. "You think that it was Avi?"

"Who else could have access to my computer? It's not that I was hiding it and he was here. He could have done it while I was asleep," said Chava and took a deep breath. Tears flooded her eyes and she bit her lips. Sandy placed her hands on Chava's shoulder.

"I am so sorry that you feel disappointed," she said.

"Oh I am not crying because of what happened," she nodded toward the bed. "I am crying because I am so angry that I let myself believe that maybe he was really in love with me."

She checked her other email addresses but all of them were read by someone. She turned off her computer and put it in its carry case. The phone rang and Chava picked up. She listened carefully and then she simply said, "Thank you, that would be fine."

After hanging up the phone, she explained to Sandy that it was the Concierge and he booked them on a tour bus that was leaving in two hours from the front of their hotel entrance. They would travel to Jerusalem and spend the night at the King David Hotel. Sandy asked her to wait for her in her room while she got her suitcase.

Chava was already packed; she just needed to put a few items away. She looked at the mirror and shook her head. "What is going on mother? Is this some kind of plot to destroy that little hope that I nursed that someday I would find someone who really loves me and maybe have his children? Please look down at me from Heaven and save me from more disappointments," she prayed out loud.

Sandy knocked again on her door and she opened it. She turned around from the door as she pulled her suitcase through the threshold. She could almost see Avi lay on the bed next to her with his arms around her shoulders.

In the lobby the Concierge had everything ready for them. Chava paid for the expenses and he gave them their itinerary, of their short, but scenic promising tour of old Jerusalem, Massada and the Dead Sea, just as Chava asked him to arrange. He also gave them a receipt that they could pick up their airline tickets at the counter at the airport in Tel Aviv upon their return from Jerusalem, so they could fly to Eilat directly.

They went to the hotel's bar while they waited and Sandy ordered beer while Chava sipped from the coffee that the bartender brought over from the restaurant for her. They spent their time discussing the upcoming short tour and Chava was pleased that Sandy was actually looking forward seeing those places that had so much history to offer.

The bellboy informed them that the tour bus arrived and they followed him outside. Chava asked Sandy to wait for a moment while she checked one more time for messages. Sandy crossed her fingers and wished that Avi sent or left a message for Chava, but once again, there were no messages waiting and she could easily read disappointment on her friend's face. She didn't say anything; she just gently squeezed Chava's hand and smiled at her sympathetically.

CHAPTER SIXTEEN

"The Yad Vashem Holocaust Memorial Authority is a state institution," began the introduction of the young tour guide who encouraged everyone in the tour bus to call him Alex. "It was first opened to the public in 1957 but ever since it has grown to its present size as more information, pictures and documents flow in. As you are going to see and walk through it, Yad Vashem is a collection of buildings. We have a huge Archive, a library and the in the Hall of Remembrance you can also find the Hall of Names. We also have an International School for Holocaust Studies and another building that houses the International Institute for Holocaust Research. I must also mention to you a very special building that is the home of an exhibition that is honoring those brave souls who placed themselves in danger by aiding and hiding Jews. The building is called the "Righteous Among the Nations.""

He took a short break as he looked at the passengers on the tour bus. "One of the most famous of those who are mentioned in that building is, and I am certain that you heard of him, was Oskar Schindler." He smiled at the tourists when he saw that they were nodding in recognition of the name. "We will arrive at our destination in a couple of minutes and there will be a short walk up to the Visitor's Entrance. Please stay together as a group as it is as huge complex, about 45 acres, and it would be difficult for me to track you down."

The bus stopped in the designated parking lot and Alex told them the place was called Mount of Remembrance, and they were just below Mt. Herzl and the Military Cemetery. Entering Yad Vashem they were warmly greeted by staff members of the Welcome Center, handing out different tour route maps and information about the complex written in various languages. They were also informed that an audio guide was also available for rent, but Alex told the group that if they wanted to stick with him and not go off on their own, it wouldn't be necessary to pay extra money, as he would provide information about the areas where they were about to visit.

The group was also given an option to participate in a two hour or four hour walking tour, and by the vote of raising their arms, they elected the two hour shorter version. Once they agreed on that, their group, which was about twenty people in size, also agreed that they would stay together. They exited the Visitor's Center by stepping out onto the Avenue of the Righteous Among the Nations. The road that led to their next stop was lined with trees that were planted in the honor of those who were not Jewish by religion but who followed their conscious and risked their lives to save Jews during the Holocaust.

Alex pointed out the first tree as they stepped outside and everyone recognized the name of Raoul Wallenberg. Sandy squeezed Chava's hand when she read the name of the Swedish diplomat who saved the lives of possibly thousands of Hungarian Jews in Budapest, Hungary. On the same side of the road, around the second row there was another tree pointed out with the name the tour guide mentioned earlier on the bus, Oskar Schindler and his wife Emily.

Walking along on the tree lined avenue they noticed a relatively new looking building, and according to the map they were given at the Visitor's Center, it was the new Holocaust History Museum. Where the group was standing they were able to observe the building from above. Slowly, their group made its way to the Warsaw Ghetto Square and the Memorial Wall. In the center of the square stood a two part monument whose creator none of them heard of before but they were certain that they would hear about him again. His name was Nathan Rapoport. The monuments were titled "The Last March" and it commemorated the hundreds of thousands of Jews who were deported from the Ghetto into death camps and of those who bravely fought the Germans during the Uprising, well knowing that it was a losing battle. They all felt that it was something they just had to do, to show the world that even a small group of people, not to mention the fact that not just any people but Jewish people who stood up against the evil giant, Nazi occupiers.

After several minutes of explanations from their tour guide Alex, everyone in the group engaged of picture taking, and then the group retraced their steps and began to walk toward the Historical Museum. The expertly assembled displays were arranged in chronological order supplemented with materials collected from all over the world, such as photos, documents and even artifacts.

The group began to follow multi language signs, not to mention Alex at the front who answered non-stop questions from his group that was assembled from various countries of the world. Chava and Sandy were most impressed that Alex was actually answering the questions in different languages and Chava even heard Russian as he talked to an elderly couple from Ukraine.

They were led up stairs to the Hall of Names, where according to the map and the attached information sheets, close to four million of Holocaust victim's names were entered and kept. The number was growing every day since it was established. Alex explained that it was very important to the Museum, as well as to Israel, that all six million Holocaust victim's names were collected, no matter how long it would take.

After the group visited the Hall of Names, they went downstairs to the Art Museum where various art works were exhibited from the holocaust era. Once they exited the Art Museum, they made their way to the Hall of Remembrance where they were able to pay their respects for those whose lives were taken during the Holocaust. The Eternal Flame was burning in the center of the Memorial and right next to it was a crypt that contained the ashes of victims. The ashes were gathered from various death camps from all over Europe.

They walked around the Hall of Remembrance and by following the same path, they noticed grey pillars reaching toward the sky and they were taller than any other building at Yad Vashem. Alex explained that they were called the Pillars of Heroism and that they were erected in the memory of those who fought against the Nazi war machine. They didn't have to walk too far to the last stop of their walking tour of Yad Vashem, when they reached the Children's Memorial. There were hundreds of candles burning all around in the dark space in the memory of over a million and a half murdered children. It was a very eerie place, where in the darkness names and birth places were read out loud from an audio tape.

As they selected the two hour walking tour, it ended at the Janusz Korczak Square. There was a statue of the Jewish Polish teacher who was caring for children in an orphanage in the Warsaw Ghetto. The statue projected his deep caring for the children and it showed him as protectively embracing them as they gathered around him.

Passing the statue their solemn group arrived back to the Visitor's Center. After looking around in the Visitor's Center for another twenty minutes, it appeared to Chava and she mentioned this to Sandy that people attempted to gather and focus their thoughts while they were trying to comprehend what they had just seen. From the modern new museum pictures that showed smiling faces, to looks of given up hope, one cannot but wonder what happened to humanity in those crazed days of World War Two. What could possibly cause an entire cultured nation such as Germany, and their allies to turn into bloodthirsty and power hungry barbarians?

Sandy would not let Chava's hand go throughout the two hour walking tour. Occasionally, when Chava glanced at the direction of her friend and their eyes met, she saw tears in Sandy's eyes. Many of the exhibit items were hard to look at without tears, especially the pictures of children as they lay on the ground in the Warsaw Ghetto, slowly starving to death, too weak to get up and knowing that their parents had already perished from starvation or disease. Seeing the children with their eyes big and wide in their sockets on their thin faces that were once chubby and well feed, there was only one question in those eyes, "why," was more than many people could handle.

Chava saw people in other groups openly crying and so were some of the people in her own group. Naturally, she was also deeply touched by the pictures and artifacts of the exhibits, but they were not all new to her. During her marriage to Matthew, she began to read upon country's histories before they moved there and one of those countries was Germany. She was not reading only about the present times, but she found books that took her back hundreds of years into the country's rich and at times bloody history. Once she was involved with that reading, she wanted to learn more about Germany's five "w-s", which were; who, when, why, what and where. The more she read the more disturbing thoughts came into her mind about the days and years of World War Two, especially the time frame of the Holocaust. Later, when she was on her own and her writing career began, she wrote a book about a Jewish girl who was hidden by a Nazi officer, and although the plot was somewhat impossible, it has become a best seller due to her expert explanation and her dedicated research into stories that she had read and followed up on.

The tour bus was extremely quiet on their return to Jerusalem's Central Bus Terminal. Upon arrival the people bid goodbye to each other, wishing pleasant and safe journeys in and around Israel. Chava and Sandy took a taxi back to their hotel and none of them were in the mood to eat, which they could have done at the cafeteria in Yad Vashem.

Sandy decided to take a nap and Chava wanted to enter what they had seen at Yad Vashem into her computer, in case she wanted to use the information later on. They both agreed to go for dinner around six thirty that evening and they both hoped for a quiet evening, just the two of them. Before Sandy entered her room next to Chava's, she held her back for a moment. "Thank you for coming with me. I know that it was a disturbing experience for you," said Chava to Sandy.

"Nothing is ever going to be as disturbing as Auschwitz was," replied Sandy and added. "You never have to thank me for anything, ever." Chava smiled at her friend and opened the door to her hotel room.

CHAPTER SEVENTEEN

"Alright, just don't break down the door," yelled Chava as she rushed to the door. She couldn't understand why Sandy couldn't wait for a few minutes longer until she was ready. She opened the door and was about to walk back toward the closet to put her shoes on when some unexplainable feeling or instinct, she wasn't sure about, stopped Chava in her tracks. She slowly turned around and she acknowledged with a fast pumping heart that it was not Sandy who stood inside her room with the door closed behind her, it was Avi.

They were two steps from each other and neither of them moved for several moments. Tears rushed into Chava's eyes as she stubbornly stared into Avi's blue eyes. She wasn't sure what she expected to see in those eyes that captivated her to the state of paralysis, but in those moments she couldn't feel anything else other than sheer desire and love. She wanted to say, *no more of those mysterious appearances and disappearances, no more looking at those moist lips that could penetrate her mouth and no more to those touches that wanted to discover her body,* but she said nothing of that sort. *I'll be strong and I will send him away right now,* but she did nothing of that kind.

He stepped toward her and he took her face between his hands and kissed her gently just once, lightly and tenderly and he looked at her as he confirmed what he had declared to her once before. "I love you Chava," and then kissed her with such passion that those tears that filled her eyes finally streamed down on her face and mingled with his sweet kisses. Her arms, as if they did not belong to the same stubborn mind that controlled her, wrapped around his neck as he picked her up and carried her to the bed. He gently laid her down on the top of the covers and began to take off his clothes, his eyes not leaving her for a single moment.

Chava pushed the bedspread down to the floor, but she did not get undressed. Chava admirably looked at his perfect body and for a moment, she wondered just how many hours he must have worked out to develop those muscles in his arms and chest. Her eyes wandered down his body and her lips parted when he saw him erect and that how perfect he was in every sense of the word.

Avi sat down next to her on the bed and began to undress her. Her dress came off first, than he unhooked her garter belt and slowly began to roll down her nylons. Her bra hooks were undone one by one, slowly and deliberately. When he pulled off the bra, at first he just marveled at her breasts and when he did that, she self consciously covered them with her arms. Avi gently pulled her arms away and pushed them above her head as he bent down to kiss her, then his lips moved down to her breasts and let his tongue circle her nipples.

Chava bit her lips and held her breath until she was forced to breath. It was somewhat disturbing for her that he was watching her, as he was taking an inventory of her likes and dislikes throughout his moves and touches. His eyes were so intense that she was able to conclude that his main goal was to completely please her any way he could.

Avi let her arms go and while with one hand he caressed her breasts; his other hand was busy removing her panties. His hand reached between her legs, and as his fingers were discovering her most private area, he looked at her with tenderness and then he kissed her with such passion that left her body trembling with desire.

Chava embraced his back as he bent over her and when he inserted his fingers inside her, a deep gasp escaped her parted lips so loud that he glanced at her to make certain that she was alright. Chava was shocked about her own high level of desire of wanting him so desperately, that she forgot her surroundings and the week's past events. She completely blocked out everything else other than the fact that she wanted to be with him no matter who he was or what he was doing outside her room. The words he spoke, *I love you Chava,* echoed in her mind and while she tried to deny it to herself, the reality of her love for Avi, a virtually total stranger to her was surfacing stronger by every passing, passion filled moment.

It was a complicated for her to deal with after a long and disappointing marriage, after which she vowed that she wouldn't be involved with just anyone. But there was no need to deny the truth any longer and the truth was that she didn't just want Avi physically; she wanted to be with him all the time as he was constantly on her mind.

When she didn't receive any messages from him in Tel Aviv, she concluded that perhaps she cared for him more than she cared to admit. She argued with herself that if she didn't care for him, it wouldn't hurt when she found out that there were no messages from him.

So let it be, she thought and she opened her eyes to find him staring at her. "You are so beautiful," he said and kissed her. He whispered to her over and over those words that she wanted to hear, the words she wanted to believe were true. "I love you Chava," he repeated them between kisses.

She raised her head so she could kiss him in return before she replied, "I love you too Avi," and she meant every little word. She was 35 years old with a twelve year long marriage behind her which she thought for great many years was a good, solid marriage. But now she clearly understood that it was not a passionate one. If it was love, she was sure she felt for Avi; she knew for certain that she did not love Matthew in the same way. She promised herself that she would never, ever compare men if she ever started to date another man after her divorce. It was the reason that she simply could not believe how she reacted to Avi's touch versus Matthew's. There was simply just no comparison. Even just her expectation of what Avi would do next, where his strong hands would touch her smooth skin was exciting. His lips could devour hers with desire, his tongue would dance with hers and his fingers that stroked her where she has never been touched by a man would cause her shiver with undeniable delight.

"Are you with me?" Avi asked with a smile.

She smiled back and whispered while kissing his neck, "more than you'll ever know." Her hand reached down to touch him and this time he began to tremble.

"What are you doing to me?" he asked her playfully but not expecting an answer and she did not offer one. She guided him inside her and he buried his head between her breasts before he moved, and moved he did. Much later on, while she was in the shower with her eyes closed and her lathered hands were washing away the invisible marking of his kisses, she almost felt him moving inside her, the way a tango dancer bent and twirled his partner to the rhythm of the music.

She lost sense of time between their love making. When they made love for the third time before sunrise and he was ready to climax he pushed himself up so they could face each other, he said to her, "I would love to have a child with you."

At first Chava thought that Avi was joking but what she saw in his eyes confirmed his seriousness. "A child needs both parents," she remarked breathlessly, unable to believe that they are having a conversation about something as delicate and sacred as creating a new life.

"He shall have both of his parents," he said assuring.

"I am not so sure," she replied and bit her lips together because he ever slowly moved inside her.

"I gave you my word," he said and the way he said that, Chava was convinced that he meant them.

"I am not even sure if I can conceive," she said quietly. "I have never been with a child."

He smiled and kissed her. "Because you have never been with the right man," he said and moved again. Chava hang on to him feeling that she was near to climax and when he sensed that, his movements became faster and they came together in perfect unison. He remained laying on the top of her, trying not to hurt her with his weight. Eventually, he lifted his head, kissed her and whispered to her. "It's going to be a boy." Chava giggled and caressed his thick hair. "What if it's a girl?"

"It's a boy," he said quietly and kissed her stomach. He slowly withdrew from her and laid down next to her with his arm across her chest. "I love you," he murmured as he drifted into a short and light sleep.

CHAPTER EIGHTEEN

The steady knock on her hotel room door woke her. She turned around but Avi was gone. She was confused for a moment about the knocking. She smiled of the thought that perhaps Avi got distraught by her and forgot the card that opened her door.

She pulled her knee long t-shirt on and went to the door. "Where did you disappear to?" she asked as she opened the door. It was not Avi who stood in the door, it was Daniel, wearing his military uniform. "I am sorry, I thought it was Avi," she explained and brushed her unruly hair back. Daniel looked just as surprised and puzzled. "Come on in," she said pointing inside her room.

"I am sorry to wake you Chava, I was hoping that perhaps Sandy was with you, in your room," he glanced around.

Chava looked at him questioningly, not understanding the situation. "What's going on?" she asked.

Daniel sat down on the couch and buried his head in his hands. "I am not sure, but something is not right," he said with worried look on his face. "You expected Avi, is he gone too?"

Chava took a deep breath and tried to think of any reasonable explanation. "Okay, let's back track to last night. I told Sandy that I'll let her know when I am ready as we were supposed to go to this restaurant we heard about. Avi showed up last night and he spent the night here. I didn't have a chance to let Sandy know that Avi arrived and to be totally honest, I didn't even think of it. I just woke up to your knocking on my door and Avi's gone. What is your side of the story?" she asked.

"I got two days off and I thought that I would surprise Sandy by showing up. She called me on my cell phone and told me that you guys were staying here at the King David Hotel. I arrived about half an hour earlier but she was not in her room. I hesitated before I knocked on your door, I thought that perhaps she already came to your room," explained Daniel and he was becoming increasingly upset.

Chava pulled herself together and said to him. "Daniel, I need to take a shower. Why don't you go downstairs and ask around in the lobby about Sandy. I'll meet you in the restaurant."

Daniel got up and nodded, but he turned around from the door before leaving. "It is not a good country to disappear in. I hope that we find her real soon."

"And Avi too," added Chava.

"Yes, him too," he agreed.

Chava was ready within twenty minutes. She grabbed her purse and she was just about to leave her room when her eyes wandered to her laptop computer. She walked back to the desk and booted up the computer. A few moments later she was logging onto her personal email address and among the dozens of email messages for that morning, she noticed one email with an Israeli email address and an attachment. After quickly checking the attachment for virus, she clicked on it. It was a short video tape titled "Who is your best friend?"

Chava covered her mouth for preventing herself from screaming. "Oh my dear God," she yelled out loud. On the screen Sandy appeared handcuffed and blindfolded. Behind her four Palestinian men stood with AK 47 rifles with their head covered so they couldn't be identified. Their eyes, that is all she was able to see, were dark either naturally or by anger, she couldn't tell. They told Sandy to speak, but she shook her head in protest. One of the men stepped forward and slapped Sandy across her face. Sobs were chocking Chava seeing her friend under those circumstances. Sandy lifted her head and a trickle of blood began to ooze down from the corner of her lip. She finally spoke. "Hi honey, it's Sandy," as she said that, the man stepped back next to the others. Chava wasn't sure if she was seeing it right, but it appeared that Sandy was about to smile. "Don't give the fuckers anything, do you understand me Chava? I'd rather die than these bastards get anything from me or from you. I had a good life and I don't care if I die. Tell Daniel that I am going to be okay. Do that for me honey, for the last time," she said and laughed. Another man stepped forward and hit Sandy on the head. Sandy fell off the chair and then the screen went dark.

She turned off her laptop, unplugged it and placed it in its carry case. Words couldn't possibly describe the way she felt and she knew that Daniel had to see the video for himself. She couldn't wait for the elevator to arrive, she used the staircase to rush downstairs. She found Daniel in the restaurant where he informed her that there was a change in shift of personal in the lobby during the time frame when both Avi and Sandy disappeared. Nobody had any recollection of noticing anything out of the ordinary.

Chava placed her laptop computer on the table and a short time later she replayed the video to Daniel. He angrily slammed his fist down on the table so hard, a couple of glasses fell over, and luckily they were still empty. "I need some coffee and maybe something to eat, it's going to be a long day," suggested Chava and incredible calmness came over her.

"You act like you have some sort of idea where to find her," said Daniel after ordering the food for both of them.

"As a matter of fact I do," said Chava and poured some cream into her coffee. "You are a Colonel right? I am not familiar with your insignias, but I was wondering if you or someone you know who would be able to run a background checks on Avi."

"You are kidding me, right?" asked Daniel.

"Do I look like I am kidding you?" retorted Chava but remained calm. "Avi seem to be able to find me and Sandy no matter where we go. I need to find out if he is involved with any special operations or perhaps he is working for the Mossad or perhaps some organizations, other than Israeli organizations," she suggested.

"I would probably able to get some information from Special Operations or Special Forces, but I doubt if the Mossad would give out any information. Besides, how do we know for sure if his real name was Avi. Do you know his last name?" he asked her.

"He said that his name was Avraham "Avi" Darom," Chava informed him.

"Did he say what he did for the living?" Daniel asked her again.

"We didn't get that far," said Chava and she noticed a surprised look on Daniel's face. "Daniel, it's more complicated than you can imagine, so let's not go there."

"It's really none of my business," he said. "He sure looked like he was really in love with you though," he remarked.

"Who says that he is not?" asked Chava. "We just don't know for certain who he is, where he is and what he is. But what about you and Sandy?" she inquired.

"I'd marry her the moment I see her again," declared Daniel with a smile.

"Have you ever been married?" she asked. Daniel nodded. "You don't have to talk about it if you don't want to," offered Chava noticing the sudden sadness that appeared on his face.

"No, it's not that. It's just too painful. You see, my wife and two daughters were killed on a bus four years ago when a Palestinian suicide bomber blew himself up. I was so devastated that I had to take leave from active duty. Then I thought, what would be the best way to pay back their untimely death than by going back to serve my country. And you see, I just met Sandy who is so full of life and who is ready for some happiness, just as I am," he explained and a faint smile appeared on his face. "She brought hope back to me you know."

Chava reached over and tapped on his hand. "We'll get her back, don't you worry. By the way, Sandy had it real hard too for a long time so I am glad that she met you. But you and I have a big mission ahead of us."

"What makes you so sure?" he asked.

"Sandy is a cleaver girl, she said something in that video tape that was a clue for me," said Chava.

"I didn't hear anything that would have given me a clue," admitted Daniel.

"Obviously you have not read any of my novels," she said. *"For the Last Time,"* is the title one of my books in which the heroine is being taken hostage by Palestinian terrorists. In the book she was taken to Hebron by her kidnappers. Sandy must have overheard the word "Hebron" and she was giving me a clue where they were planning to take her," explained Chava.

"They had a good head start," remarked Daniel. "The time on the email message was five in the morning, yet they already had a video sent to you in an email. It could only mean one thing," he said but he did not finish his sentence. He looked at Chava wondering if she knew what it was.

"That they shot the video locally and they are on the move," Chava finished his sentence. Daniel nodded in agreement, then he took out his cell phone and dialed. Before he talked, he looked around to see who was around them but the restaurant was not busy at all. Guests were sitting scarcely with empty tables between them. Chava couldn't understand a word he was saying as he was talking in Hebrew but two words, a name that caught her attention was, "Avraham Darom." It was obvious that Daniel was making an inquiry on the phone to find out more about the mysterious man who appeared and disappeared, but certainly making a deep impression in their lives, especially in Chava's.

While Daniel listened, he was looking back and forth between the door and Chava. He finally put his cell phone away and his fingers began to tap on the top of the table. Chava watched him patiently for a while, but after a few minutes, she could not stand it any longer. "Are you going to talk to me or what?" she asked.

Daniel took a deep breath. "There is no Avraham Darom anywhere in any database, none of them I can't tell you. I have some friends in certain places and they searched all of those databases without any success. He must be using an alias," he commented. Chava didn't look surprised, as she knew better than asking about Daniel's connections.

She concluded without saying anything out loud that Avi, no matter how her heart and every fiber in her body was objecting to the conclusion she was drawing, that perhaps Avi was working for a terrorist organization and maybe, just maybe he was not even Israeli. One of those guesses had to be right because of his actions, his sudden appearances and unexpected departures. She did not even want to mention her suspicion that Avi must have some sort of intelligence connection that he was able to gain information about her and

Sandy's whereabouts; therefore, he did not have any difficulties tracking and finding them.

The fact that Sandy and Avi disappeared virtually at the same time could not be a coincidence, she thought. She bit down on her lip in anger and embarrassment from the thought that perhaps he was ordered to seduce her and keep her "occupied" while they were kidnapping Sandy. *But that didn't quite make sense,* her mind objected to her thoughts and suspicions. If they wanted to get any information or secrets out of her, why didn't they just order Avi to kidnap her directly?

Chava had no answer to that question and what also bothered her was the fact she didn't know exactly what they were after. Did they want money? She was very wealthy and she made Forbes' 100 most upcoming and successful women list three years in a row or did they want something else? She harbored no secrets and newspapers and magazines already printed almost everything about her life, private and public in the past years. What did those kidnappers want from Sandy or from her?

Chava just couldn't help it, her thoughts wandered back to Avi. If he was a "bad guy" than she was not going to date anyone for the rest of her life, she made that promise to herself. If Avi was working with the terrorists, it was a thought she just simply could not and would not comprehend, yet she still had to take into consideration that she was in deeper trouble than she had ever been in her entire life.

She looked at Daniel and she could tell that there were some serious questions hanging over him which he wanted to ask from her badly. "Talk to me, ask me whatever you want Daniel," encouraged Chava.

He hesitated for a few moments and he blurted out. "Why her? What information could she have that they want? Is there something you are not telling me?" he finally asked her.

It was her time to measure the value of trust. Could she trust Daniel? She knew even less about Daniel than she knew about Avi, and that wasn't much. "Before I say anything further, I have to ask you a question Daniel."

"You can ask me just about anything," he assured her.

"Did you know Avi before we met?" she asked.

Daniel looked at her with surprise. "No," he replied and Chava believed him. "What made you think that I did?" he asked her curiously.

"When Sandy introduced you to Avi, you didn't say your name, neither did Sandy or I and when the two of you shook hands, Avi said, "Shalom Daniel, it's good to meet you." So how did he know your name?" inquired Chava.

Daniel appeared to be stunned. "You are right. I never gave a second thought to that," he admitted.

"Since I cannot read Hebrew, what does your name tag read on your uniform?" she asked Daniel again.

"Only our last name," he replied. "You know that you maybe on the right track with Avi, he . . ." he said and leaned toward her. "He may be working for the Mossad or he may be working for somebody else."

"And not even you, a decorated IDF Colonel could find that out?" she asked him.

He smiled and shook his head. "I already asked when I called and they said that information of that nature is guarded very closely, sorry."

"Okay," said Chava. "I want to show you something that is up in my room. Let's go," she said and got up. She turned around and as she did, she thought her imagination was playing tricks on her again. Chava was almost certain that was all it was, but she thought for a moment. For the second time since she arrived to Jerusalem, Chava saw the Palestinian man she first noticed in Budapest, Hungary, walking through the exit door of the hotel where she way staying. It most certainly could not have been a coincidence.

"Are you okay?" she heard Daniel's voice who noticed her expression of surprise or maybe confusion.

"Yes, I am okay," she replied and began to walk toward the elevator. The waiter ran after her and asked for her signature on the check so they would charge the breakfast to her room but Daniel pulled out his wallet and paid for their breakfast. "Thank you Daniel," said Chava as they got into the elevator. "I was so occupied with my thoughts that I forgot all about the bill."

"Don't mention it," he said and studied her face. *There was something she was holding back,* thought Daniel.

CHAPTER NINETEEN

The moment Chava walked into her room she noticed the flowers. The sight stopped her in the doorway making Daniel bump into her as he was following her inside. "What is the matter?" he asked and stepped in front of her, looking around in the already made up room.

Chava didn't say a word, she silently pointed towards the dresser. It was almost the identical flower arrangement that she received in her hotel room in Budapest. A little card tucked between the petals of one of the flowers. She carefully removed it and read the contents of the card out loud for Daniel. "Ahlan wa sahlan Jameela," and it was signed by the familiar initials A-HH. "It sounds Arabic, what does this mean in English?" she asked Daniel.

"It means welcome beautiful woman," he translated those words written on the card.

"He was in this room," said Chava almost scared.

"Who was in your room?" inquired Daniel.

"A total stranger who gave me an identical flower arrangement after my mother's funeral," explained Chava.

"Maybe the flowers were delivered," suggested Daniel.

"Maybe or maybe not," replied Chava. She offered Daniel one of the chairs to sit by the desk. From the nightstand, she removed the leather case that held her mother's ashes and gently set it down on the desk. Daniel looked at her questioningly. "These are my mother's ashes. She made three wishes shortly before she passed away. The first one was to be cremated and the second one was to take her ashes back to Auschwitz, the place where she suffered but survived," she stopped and looked through the window from which she could clearly see the old city of Jerusalem.

"What was her third wish if you don't mind my asking?"

"She wanted me to scatter her ashes into the Red Sea," replied Chava. "Abdul-Hafiz Hassan," she then murmured.

Daniel jumped to his feet so quickly that the chair fell over. "What did you just say?" he asked her with such a tone that Chava turned towards him.

"I began to believe that I am not just imagining it. I saw Abdul-Hafiz Hassan leaving this hotel before we came upstairs," she explained.

Daniel, without saying a single word to her, took out his cell phone and dialed. His voice expressed unhidden excitement and frustration at the same time. He was yelling part of the conversation he had with someone at the other end of the line and Chava cursed herself for not learning Hebrew, a language she never considered learning before. Finally Daniel became quiet and replied with measured answers to the person to whom he was talking. He looked at Chava and then turned away and walked to the window. It was obvious that someone put him on hold. He listened and answered to the person once again and a few minutes later, he put his cell phone away.

He turned back from the window to face her. "Chava, how do you know this Abdul-Hafiz Hassan? Where did you meet him?" he asked her.

Chava told him about their first encounter in the hotel restaurant in Budapest, Hungary and she informed Daniel about the flowers she received from him after her mother's memorial service. She finally told him about what she thought she saw during their walking tour of the old city. She also mentioned to Daniel about the brief note that was attached to the first flower arrangement Hassan sent to her. "Who is this Hassan person?" she asked him. It was obvious to her that hearing that name upset him.

"He is the mastermind behind many suicide bombings in Israel and responsible for the murder of innocent Israelis abroad. He is also one of the "ambassadors" if you call it as such, for one of the largest and better organized terrorist organizations in the Arab world," explained Daniel. "He has a nickname, they call him the "Ghost."

"The Ghost, but why?" Chava asked curiously.

"He can't be found anywhere. The Israeli intelligence has been looking for him for the past four years. Somehow he knows when the police or soldiers are getting close to him and he just simply disappears," said Daniel.

Chava laughed. "You could fool me. Maybe the Israeli intelligence is looking in all the wrong places. In Budapest, he didn't seem to worry about anything," she said to Daniel. "But what did you mean that he was one of the "ambassadors", ambassador of what?" she asked.

Daniel turned around to face her. "He is soliciting donations from all over the world to finance his and other terrorist organizations. He seems like a businessman, he always dresses well and he behaves as if he was in charge of a large corporation," he replied.

"That's definitely him," agreed Chava. "I am just surprised that he is able to come inside the hotel and have flowers sent to me and the Israeli intelligence is unable to catch him. I just don't understand what he wants from me?" she wondered out loud.

"Is there anything else I need to know?" Daniel asked her suspiciously.

"There is something, but I cannot tell you." Chava confessed to him. "I was told not to repeat and I won't repeat it to anyone under any circumstances."

"I am not going to ask you what it is but I want to know if Sandy knows the same thing?" asked Daniel.

"She does not know what I know, if that's what you mean. I learned something from my mother's letter she wrote to me before she died. She asked me to keep it to myself and I fully intend to follow my mother's instructions. Sandy only knows that my mother told me something in that letter, nothing else," she explained.

"So they may kill her for nothing, that is what you are telling me?" Daniel asked. He appeared to have tears in his eyes.

"They are not going to kill her," Chava said firmly. "If it takes me to give up my life, so be it, but I won't let them hurt Sandy."

"That is a very noble thing to say but how are you planning to accomplish that?" he asked.

Chava looked at him and when she spoke next, her voice was very serious. "Excuse me Daniel, but this is your country, yet, you have not offered or suggested any rescue ideas. I am going to report Sandy's disappearance to the Security Police and to the American Embassy and I will also request police assistance to find her with or without your help. It's up to you," said Chava almost angrily.

Daniel held out his hand as he wanted to stop her. "Just hold on," he protested. "The authorities are already aware of Sandy's disappearance and are organizing a search and rescue mission as we speak. I am going to join them shortly. What are you going to do? Are you going to stay here?" he asked.

Chava thought about his question for a few moments and then she replied. "If there is a military or police operation taking place, there is no point for me being there, I would just get in the way. I am going to fly to Eilat tomorrow and fulfill my mother's final wish. If Sandy is still not freed by then, I will return to Jerusalem and I will wait here."

Daniel's cell phone rang and he answered. He listened intensely and Chava heard the word, "okay" just before he put the cell phone back in his pocket. "I have to go," he said to Chava and headed toward the door. "Transfers have been arranged and an entire unit is ready to search for Sandy and her kidnappers. I want to bring her back alive. Have a safe trip and finish what you came here to do." He reached for the door but he turned around one more time before opening it. "Where are you staying in Eilat?" he asked.

"I am not sure, but the King Solomon Palace looked very nice on the Internet, I probably will stay there. Daniel," she said softly. "Please keep in touch."

He smiled at her and nodded. "Will do," and left Chava's room.

CHAPTER TWENTY

The plane ride was short and uneventful. A courtesy limousine sent by the King Solomon Palace Hotel was waiting to pick up Chava and two other passengers as soon their plane landed. After a fifteen minute ride the modern looking hotel came into sight. Chava was grateful for the accommodations provided to her after such a short notice. She soon realized after walking into the hotel lobby the possible reason for the extra effort the hotel made for her.

On the top of the check-in desk rested a small pile of the English language newspapers, the Jerusalem Daily Star. On the very first page with large letters it read, "Popular and much loved American writer arrived in Israel," and the article continued with the interview she had given at the hotel in Tel Aviv. Under the headline appeared her half page size color picture and Chava was pleased to realize that the picture was one of the better ones that was taken by journalists in a long time. She took a copy of the newspaper and tucked it under her arm while she was waiting for her hotel room key.

The Concierge walked up to Chava and asked her if he could be of any further assistance to her. She thanked the tall and well dressed man and after receiving her key, she began to follow the bellboy carrying her luggage toward the elevator.

Her surprise was complete the moment the door opened to her room which was not only a room, but it was a luxurious suite. At first she thought that it was a mistake, but the bellboy assured her that she got the suite for the same price as if it was a regular room, a complement from the hotel. After the bellboy placed her luggage onto the rack that stood next to her dresser, she reached into her purse and pulled out a five dollar bill. When he saw the money he smiled at her and pushed her money away. "Ms. Diamond," he said in perfect English. "It is a pleasure having you here. I have all of your books and instead of giving me a tip, if you could autograph at least one of them tomorrow or whenever you get a chance, it would mean more to me than any money."

Chava smiled at him. "That is a wonderful complement and I truly appreciated it. I'll be glad to sign any number of books for you, thank you."

The young man slightly bowed his head toward her and left her room after making her promise that she would call him right away if she needed anything, anything at all.

As soon as the door closed behind him, she tossed her purse on the bed and pushed the sliding door open that led to the balcony and she stepped outside. "So this is Eilat," she said out loud as if there was someone else there with her. "Why this place mother, why Eilat?" Chava asked. She stepped back inside into the coolness of her room and lay down on the bed. She stared at the ceiling and thought about her mother and her own life. She also thought about Sandy and she just could not help it, Avi also joined her thoughts. Where was he and who was he? He entered her life and then just as suddenly he departed from her life without a trace. She couldn't help it thinking about him every other moment of her waking hours. She could feel his sparkling blue eyes locked into hers, she could still feel his arms around her shoulders and when she closed her eyes, she could almost feel his soft lips pressing down on hers.

Tears rushed into her eyes and she felt so incredibly alone that it not only hurt her, it was crushing the evidently false sense of security blanket she built around her throughout the years following her divorce. *Was it some kind off curse cast on her for having such bad luck with men?* She wondered. Not that she had so many men in her life. Actually, she only confessed this to Sandy years ago, that her husband was the first man in her life and then there was Avi.

There was a knock on the door. She sighed and pushed herself off the bed. Before she opened the door she glanced in the mirror in the bathroom to see if she looked presentable. "Who is it?" she asked before opening the door. When there was no answer, she looked through the peephole but she was still unable to see anyone standing directly in front of the door. She became curious and unhooked the chair on the door and slowly opened it. Her heart jumped in her throat when she saw Avi standing next to the door.

"You should be more careful when opening that door," he said and not asking or waiting for Chava's permission, he stepped inside her room. Chava looked around, but there was nobody in the hallway. While she was closing the door, she didn't know how she felt. On one hand she was glad to see him, on the other hand, she knew that it was possibly the last time she was going to see him if he would not answer her questions.

She took a deep breath and tried to regain calmness before turning around from the door to face him. He stood right behind her and before she could make a move or say anything, he wrapped his arms around her tightly and his lips were separating hers without hesitation and with uncontrollable hunger. She gasped for air and everything she wanted to ask from him evaporated in that moment. She wanted nothing else but to be held by him and just to be with him.

He picked her up and carried her to the bed with her arms around his neck and her face buried in his shoulder. It only took a moment or two and she was out of her clothes and he was laying naked over her. She could not fathom the intensity of her desire for him and she could not comprehend how she could lose any logical thinking that she was so proud of harboring when it came to solving problem situations and finding solutions.

He entered her with a fury, with a borderless passion she had not known before. She wanted him as much as he wanted her and every inch of her body was throbbing from wanting more of him. She seemed to feel his hand and warm lips everywhere and she held onto him as if she was afraid that he would leave her.

She moved with his rhythm and then he finally slowed down and while still inside her, he pushed himself up to look at her flushed face. "Chava," he whispered to her. "I love you so much that if I die this moment, I would die a happiest man in the world."

A cliché, thought Chava. *He told me a cliché, that is all he could say to me?* It took every ounce of her will power to push him away and she rolled off the bed. She grabbed the blanket from the bed to cover herself. Chava stared at him with an incredible heartache and she suddenly found herself wondering what just happened.

Avi was shocked and he could not understand why Chava acted the way she did. "Chava," he said quietly. "What is the matter, what happened?" he asked.

"Who are you?" she asked while tears clouded her eyes. "Where have you come from? Who do you work for and what do you truly want from me?" she blurted out those questions that lingered through the past few days. "Do you have anything to do with Sandy's disappearance?"

Avi didn't reply, he just stared at her and then he buried his head between his knees in the bed sheet that he used to cover himself. "Chava," he said finally. "I don't want to lie to you, so please don't ask me those questions."

"What about just telling me the truth? Why can't you do that?" asked Chava and stepped back when she saw that Avi reached out towards her.

"Please come back to bed and we will talk about it tomorrow," he said almost begging her.

She shook her head. "No Avi," she said with a steady voice. "We should talk now and then I will decide if I wanted to go back to bed or not."

"It's not what you think," he said quietly.

"So what am I thinking or what am I supposed to think?" she asked him.

"The answers to your questions are not so simple, actually they are very complicated," he said but he knew that he did not sound convincing.

"Try me! I am a smart woman. I write mystery and suspense novels and I do a lot of research, so go ahead and try me," she said seriously. He looked at her and at that moment Chava knew that she was not going to find out anything from him or about him. "Just tell me one thing and I want to know the truth," Chava looked directly into his eyes.

"Did you have anything to do with Sandy's disappearance?" she repeated her question.

"I swear that I had nothing to do with her disappearance," said Avi but somehow Chava suspected that it was not true.

"Daniel, Sandy's friend checked you out through his military and police sources and nobody seems to know you in any of those circles. I pray to God that my suspicions about you are wrong," Chava said to Avi. She walked to the desk that stood a few feet from the window and placed her hand on the telephone.

"Chava," said Avi pleading with her. "Don't do this to us. You are destroying something very special I feel about you. I love you, I truly love you."

Chava swallowed her tears and tried to remain calm. She walked back to the bed but stopped a few feet from it. "Avi," she said and took a deep breath. "I love you with every bone, tissue and fiber in my body, but I cannot tolerate the menacing feeling of the suspicion I harbor towards you. You appeared in my life and I fell in love with you. We made wonderful love and then you disappeared. I hoped that you would come back and when you did, my hope for happiness returned with you. Then you were suddenly gone again and now, here you are for the third time. Just how I am supposed to explain these activities not only to myself but to my friend, to the police or to anyone? When you disappeared in Jerusalem, Sandy also disappeared the very same night. Coincidence? I don't think so, and neither does Daniel," she stopped for a moment. "So you see where I am coming from?"

Avi laughed and it was not a cheerful laugh, it was a laugh that came from desperation. "God, Chava I want to explain everything to you, but I just can't," he said and looked at her with a longing to touch her and to take her back into his arms. He could not possibly tell her anything about himself, at least, not just yet.

"Please leave," said Chava in a stern voice. Avi knew that he could not say or do anything that would change her mind; there was nothing else left for him to do, but to leave. He got up and while he was dressing, Chava turned her head away. She noticed that his jacket was on the floor just a step away from her, she bent down and tossed the jacket towards him on the top of the bed. When it landed, a Glock revolver fell out of his jacket's pocket. She stared at the gun and then she looked up at him with questions in her eyes but he offered no explanation. He put on his shirt and jacket, picked up the gun and put it inside his right pocket. They stood there looking at each other silently for another few seconds. Avi bit his lips together as he looked at her. Without uttering a single word, he turned around and with quick steps he walked to the door.

"Avi," Chava called after him. He stopped and turned around from the half open door. "If as much as a single hair bends on Sandy's head, I will hold you personally responsible."

Once again Avi did not respond, he stepped outside the hallway and quietly pulled the door closed behind him. Chava collapsed on the floor and an uncontrollable wave of tears began to stream down on her face and she sobbed herself to sleep just laying there.

CHAPTER TWENTY-ONE

She woke up in the middle of the night and it took her several seconds to recall what occurred hours earlier in the very same room. When she tried to get up, her shoulder ached from the hardness of the floor and from the position she fell asleep.

In the bathroom she let the hot water run down on her body as she stood in the shower with tears streaming down on her face, mixing with the water. *My whole life is falling apart,* she thought as her crying became ever more intense. "I lost my mother, I might have lost my friend and now, my last hope for happiness," Chava said out loud and then she looked up at the ceiling. She pressed her wet hands together in a prayer. "Please Lord," she prayed. "Do not abandon me now, you must help me out of this misery that I am feeling. Show me the way to rescue my friend and to find some inner peace."

She took a deep breath and finished showering. She went back to bed and hugged the second pillow as she slowly fell asleep again.

What is happening to me? It was the first thing that came to her mind when she woke up. She was laying in bed, tightly wrapped in a blanket she previously discarded to the floor. This almost panic like state of mind was so unlike her. Since her divorce from Matthew, she was always very much in control of all situations that required decision making, simple or complicated, it didn't matter at all. There were no other options; she had to deal with all aspects of her life, financial, emotional and personal as well as professional as well.

All of the sudden calmness swept over her and she sat up in bed. She knew exactly what she needed to do. She was going to treat the past couple of week's events as if they were part of one of her stories. She needed to write down the "story plot" in a chronological order to see where the plot took an unexpected turn. She had to make the important decision what her next move was going be. She quickly got dressed and sat down by the desk and began to write:

1. Mother's death
2. Trip to Hungary

3. Mother's funeral
4. Mother's testament
5. Meeting with the Palestinian man and receiving his flowers
6. Trip to Poland
7. Meeting with Avi
8. Visit to Auschwitz
9. Trip to Israel
10. Meeting Avi in Tel Aviv
11. Meeting with Daniel in Tel Aviv
12. Sandy disappear
13. Avi disappear
14. Sandy's message
15. Meeting with Avi in Jerusalem
16. Meeting with Daniel in Jerusalem
17. Seeing Hassan in Jerusalem and getting more flowers
18. Trip to Eilat
19. Breaking up with Avi in Eilat

Tears dwelled in her eyes as she wrote the last remark. *Was their meeting truly the very last time?* She wondered and that thought pained her a great deal. *No, no, no,* her mind feverishly objected to that thought. Chava closed her eyes so she could imagine and recall his strong hands stroking her hair. She could almost feel his hands touched her face as his fingers outlined her lips and when she kissed his fingers one by one. Chava recalled when his piercing blue eyes penetrated hers, or when Avi watched her so intensively that she was almost unable to bear looking at him without sensing his passionate desire for her. *That is the reason it just couldn't be over,* she decided, *I love him, no doubt about it.* She had no alternative, before she could sort out the feelings and emotions between Avi and herself, she had to find the way to rescue her kidnapped friend with or without any outside help.

She looked down on the sheet of paper in front of her and the feeling that something very important was missing came over her. Her thoughts were interrupted by a knock on her door. She yelled without getting up. "Who is it?" but there no response. She hesitantly got up and went to the door and looked through the peep hole but she was unable to see anyone. With the chain still in its place, she slowly opened the door and she noticed a bouquet of flowers in a crystal vase in front of her door. A chill dashed through her entire body as the flower arrangement looked identical to the ones she received in Budapest and in Jerusalem. Abdul-Hafiz Hassan has found her once again. She looked both ways down the long hallway, but there was no one to be seen along the corridor. She picked up the flowers and placed them on the desk where she sat down again.

At first she did not notice any card with the flowers, but eventually she found a tiny note hidden within the petals of one of them. The note was simple, and yet threatening, "We shall meet again soon, A-HH," she smiled. "Yes, you can count on that you son of a bitch and you will regret it. I can promise you that," she said out loud.

All of a sudden she felt very hungry. Chava once again studied the piece of paper with the chronologically listed events that happened to her. She folded the paper and put it in the pocket of her jeans. With the intent of leaving her room, she grabbed her purse and was about to open her room's door when the phone rang. She dashed back and grabbed the receiver. "Hello," she said into the receiver.

"This is Esther from the Concierge desk," said a woman on the other end of line. "Am I talking to Ms. Diamond?" she asked.

"Yes, I am Chava Diamond," replied Chava and wondered what was going on.

"Ms. Diamond, there is a gentleman by the name of Daniel Zehavi is waiting for you in our hotel's restaurant," explained the woman. "He asked me to tell you that he wished to talk to you in person."

"Please tell him to come up to my room," asked her Chava.

"I am sorry, but he was very persistent that you meet with him in the restaurant," insisted the woman.

Chava couldn't understand why Daniel didn't want to come up into her hotel room, but since she was on her way to the restaurant anyway, she told the woman that she'll be right down. She grabbed her purse again and hurried downstairs.

A few minutes later Chava walked into the restaurant and glanced around, but she was unable to locate Daniel anywhere inside. She turned around and made her way to the Concierge desk where a young man, wearing a suit with the hotel's logo embroiled on his jacket pocket was sitting behind it. "Excuse me," said Chava with a concerned voice. "I am looking for a friend of mine, Daniel Zehavi. Esther from this desk called me and she said that Daniel was waiting for me in the restaurant, yet my friend is not in there. Do you perhaps have another message waiting for me, my name is Chava Diamond?" she asked.

As soon as she finished her explanation and her question, she immediately sensed that something was wrong. The young man stood up after glancing at a small pile of notes in envelopes with names on neatly lined up on his desk, but found nothing for her. "I am terribly sorry Ms. Diamond, I am afraid I don't have any messages for you," he announced.

Chava nodded, thanked him and was about to walk away when she heard the Concierge voice. "Excuse me, Ms. Diamond," he called after her. She turned around and stepped back to his desk. "There is just one more thing. I am bit puzzled by your explanation about receiving a call from Esther," he said looking at her with concern.

"And why is that?" Chava inquired.

"Because we don't have any employees at this hotel by the name of Esther," he said quietly. Chava looked at him in silence. "I am sorry about this incident and I can assure you that our security officers will look into it if you wish to file a complaint," he offered.

Chava shook her head. "Thank you for the offer but I must decline at this time." As Chava walked back to the restaurant, she felt the Concierge's eyes following her.

As she once again walked inside the restaurant, she begin to wonder what was that phone call all about and how did the person who called her know Daniel's full name? Was there a connection between the caller and Daniel? She was also concerned where Daniel was. He promised her that he would keep her informed about Sandy's rescue mission, but she has not yet heard from him.

She was seated by the one of the waiters at the table of her request. She always liked to sit facing the door and watching the people entering and departing patrons, as she didn't like surprise visitors. Within a few minutes, a steaming cappuccino, a glass of ice water and a Caesar's salad was placed in front of her. Chava slowly consumed every bite of it. When the waiter asked her if she wanted anything else, she asked for the dessert menu. Although with some reservation, what would it taste like in Eilat, Israel; she selected her favorite, New York cheesecake.

While she was eating she took inventory of the restaurant patrons, mostly tourists and it seemed as always, there were some Americans among them. It was already too late for breakfast and not time for lunch yet, the restaurant had only a few late riser but hungry customers present. She could easily tell Americans apart from other tourists because for some reason, they were louder and the clothing they wore easily gave them away.

A few tables from hers several soldiers, male and female were enjoying coffee and desserts, their weapons casually swung around their shoulders towards their backs, they didn't seem threatening to her or to anyone else.

Her eyes stopped on at strikingly beautiful young blond woman sitting several tables away from hers, also drinking coffee and looking at the soldiers. When she turned her head, Chava and the woman's eyes met and the woman smiled at her. Chava returned the smile and looked toward the entrance where a young couple just entered. It was not hard to determine that they must have been on their honeymoon. *Eilat was certainly the right place*, thought Chava.

She took out the piece of paper from her pocket and studied it for a few short minutes. Questions began to develop about coincidental or perhaps planned meetings between her and some of the people who crossed paths with her. Everywhere she went, other than Hungary, Avi was present, but so was the Palestinian man, Abdul-Hafiz Hassan. According to Daniel, Hassan was a much wanted terrorist and he was almost everywhere where she went, except for Poland. What a good fortune that Sandy met Daniel who was able to help her or was he really helping? *There just has to be a connection,* she decided but the question still remained, who was the good guy and who was the bad? Who would gain the most from kidnapping Sandy? She simply had no answers yet, but an unexplainable feeling came over her and she sensed that something was going to happen real soon.

The waiter's voice interrupted her string of thoughts. He inquired if she wanted more coffee. When she declined, he gave her the bill for her signature. Chava signed her name and her room number and drinking one more gulp from her ice water, she got up to leave. She glanced toward the blond woman before leaving and Chava was surprised to notice that she was watching her as made her way toward the exit door.

CHAPTER TWENTY-TWO

I t only took a couple of minutes to boot up her computer. Among the dozens of messages she received, there was not a single message from Sandy's kidnappers, there were no messages with ransom demands or hints about her whereabouts. She heard a knock on the door and she yelled. "Who is it?"

"It's Esther, from Concierge desk," she heard the voice she recognized from the telephone call she received earlier. Her face darkened as she hesitantly made her way to the door. Looking through the peep hole her surprise was complete when she saw the blond woman from the restaurant standing in front of her door. With the security chain in place, she opened the door just a crack.

"What is that you want?" she asked.

"May I come in and talk to you Ms. Diamond?" she asked politely.

Chava hesitated and the woman noticed it. "Actually I would just like to talk to you about your book, I am a big fan of yours," she said and showed Chava a copy of one of her novels, "The Third Cloud." Despite the objection and the sound of alarm that went off in every brain cell in her head, Chava unhooked the chain, opening the door for the woman to enter. She slowly walked inside the room and looked around as if she wanted to be certain that they were alone.

"Have a seat," offered Chava.

"Thank you," said the woman and took a seat on left corner of the couch. Chava sat down opposite from her in an armchair and questioningly looked at the woman. Chava studied the woman's face for a couple minutes, while she thought that she must have been out of her mind letting a total stranger inside her hotel room. She might have been a terrorist for all she knew, after all, the woman already lied about who she was. Chava steadied her voice not to give away any fear she might have experienced. *Perhaps, just perhaps, this stranger knows more than I can imagine,* she thought. "So what is that I can do for you?" she asked the woman who called herself Esther.

"I am such a big fan of yours," explained the woman and opened the first page of the novel she was holding. "May I have your autograph please?" she asked politely.

"Where are you from?" Chava asked hearing a familiar accent as she reached for the book.

"You have good ears Ms. Diamond. Seldom anyone detects any accent when I speak English," the woman complemented Chava, and then she added. "I am from Germany."

"You are a long way from home as well," remarked Chava and took the pen that she left earlier on the top of the coffee table that stood between the couch and the armchair where she was sitting. "Who should I make this out to, Esther?" she put the emphasis on the name.

"You probably already suspect or even know that Esther is not my real name," admitted the woman.

"So tell me, whatever your name is," said Chava raising her voice. "Why this charade? Why did you trick me downstairs and how do you know about Daniel?"

The woman looked straight at her without any embarrassment or fear. "To start at the beginning, I couldn't give you my real name over the telephone. I wanted to make sure that you are by yourself and I also wanted to make certain that there wasn't anyone following you. I'll tell you about Daniel a little later on," she explained and she pointed at the book that Chava picked up from the table.

"Please sign the book, "to my niece, Hilde Schumann," said the woman calmly and it was her turn to study Chava's reaction. Chava had a surprised and puzzled look on her face and the pen slightly trembled in her hand as she was writing. Chava immediately recalled the name "Schumann" and the memory of that name gave her goose bumps.

"I don't understand," she said quietly and looked at the woman closely. She had hazel eyes, just like her own mother had, but the woman was naturally blond. She had what the Nazis called "Aryan" features.

"Forgive me for dropping such a big bombshell on you, but you are indeed my aunt," said the woman with a convincing smile.

Chava shook her head. "I don't think so."

"I suppose that an explanation is in order," suggested Hilde. "Shall we do it here or would you like to go someplace else?" she asked.

Chava's heart was racing so fast that she wasn't sure that she could get up. "Here would be fine," she replied.

"Very well then," said the woman and opened her handbag. She reached inside and pulled out a small photo album which she pushed in front of Chava. "Go ahead and open it," Hilde urged her, seeing Chava's hesitation.

Chava looked at her, then glanced down at the photo album that had seen better days. She steadied her shaking hand as she opened the album. She gasped out loud when she saw the first page of the album. In the middle of the page was an unmistakable picture of her late mother, Helene, emaciated with shaven head and in a striped prison uniform, the same one that all of the prisoners wore in Auschwitz. Her face was serious, more like sad, and in her arms was a baby, wrapped up, surprisingly in a beautiful, lacey blanket. Next to her mother stood, almost proudly Colonel Schumann, grinning into the camera with one of his fingers pointing at the baby.

"Who was the child?" asked Chava with her voice cracking.

"The child in your mother's arm was my mother, your half sister. She was named Waltraub. It was an old German name which my grandfather favored," Hilde explained.

Chava shook her head and pushed the album away. "This must be a computer generated picture. I was my mother's only child, she always told me that," objected Chava, but deep down inside somehow she knew that the picture was very real and her fear was that she was about to hear more bad news was creeping up her spine.

"I know that it must be a shock to you, but I am telling you the truth. Please continue to look at the other pictures," said Hilde and once again she pushed the album back into Chava's direction.

She stared at Hilde who did not turn away and stood Chava's probing stare. Without taking her eyes off from Hilde, she opened the album and then Chava looked at the following pages.

On the second page, it was her mother again in a somewhat smaller picture. She was sitting on the edge of an iron framed bed with a thin mattress visible on it. Next to the bed stood a beautiful, what seemed hand carved, painted baby's crib with nice, soft blankets hanging over on its side. Chava's mother was feeding the baby on her lap, but she was looking up at the camera with her big, sad hazel eyes. Chava thought that she could almost see the tears in her mother's eyes.

One of the pictures on the third page of the small photo album was Colonel Schumann holding the baby, his daughter, proudly in his arms, posing for the camera with a grin on his face. Chava didn't fully understand until that very moment what true evil really was. How could a man rape an emaciated woman and let her have his child? Evidently he was proud of the baby, Chava could tell from his pose in the picture and at the same time, he was responsible for the killing of thousands of other children and human beings. "How could this happen?" asked Chava looking up at Hilde.

She shrugged her shoulder. "I guess he liked grandmother," she replied with a sarcastic smile on her pretty face.

"Like?" Chava yelled at her angrily. "She was raped by your grandfather and forced to have his child for some sick reason. When contact was forbidden between Jews and Nazis, still, hundreds if not thousands of innocent women were raped and murdered after that. Colonel Schumann was a sick bastard."

"You can be mad at him, you should not be mad at your mother, my grandmother," said Hilde quietly.

"Me? Mad at my mother?" asked Chava fuming with anger. "My mother was an innocent person who just happened to be born into the Jewish faith. She was beaten, she was starved, she was raped and it appears that she was then separated from her child. She was a victim in that horrible situation and what made it worse was that she had to live with that secret for the rest of her life. Now more than ever I believe that until the day she died, she was raped every single day of her life by the memory of what she had survived."

Chava got up and she thought she was going to explode from the anger and disgust that she felt. She turned back and looked at the woman sitting on the couch, calling herself her niece. "How did your mother get out of that hellhole called Auschwitz?" she asked Hilde as she sat down again facing her.

"My grandfather, Colonel Karl Schumann, fell in love with the baby, who was my mother, and somehow he managed to get my mother out of the camp and sent her back to Germany to his parents. After my grandfather's execution in Poland at the end of the war, his parents raised my mother modestly, they just provided the necessities, like shelter, food, clothing and they even let her attend school. She told me later on that they never let her forget who her mother was, which basically meant that she was never fully accepted by my grandfather's family because she was a Jew."

"How did you come about?" asked Chava.

"My mother fell in love with a young man at the high school she attended and she got pregnant with me. My father wanted to marry her, but my grandparents told his family that my mother was a half Jew and she never saw him again, his entire family moved. We never found out where," she stopped and stared in front of her. "Eventually," she continued. "My mother left them and took me to Berlin where I lived until she died from an automobile accident. I was seven years old then."

"What happened to you after your mother's death?" inquired Chava.

"Amazingly, my grandparents took me back and despite the repeated reminders that I was part Jew, they actually treated me better than they treated my mother. They told me colorful stories about my grandfather, what a great man he was and what an enterprising person he was."

"Enterprising? What do you mean by that?" asked Chava suspiciously.

"It's a rather long, although intriguing story which I will fill you in some other time, but not just yet," she declared.

Chava knew that there was no point to force the issue. "It puzzles me that you did not seek me out any sooner. Why now? Why here in Israel?" asked Chava.

Hilde smiled at her and Chava did not like that smile. It was not a pleasant one, and the best way Chava could describe it to herself later, it was a vicious and borderline evil smile, almost like her grandfather, Colonel Schumann's on the pictures. "In the beginning, it was not you who we were are interested in, it was your mother. We searched high and low to find her and by just a stroke of luck we were able to locate her in that nursing home where she spent the last weeks of her life. Did you know that before your mother died, she would not talk about anything else but you?" she giggled as if what she said had a content of humor in it.

Chava did not respond, her mind was traveling with the speed of a bullet train, trying to decide what to make out of this entire mind boggling story she was hearing. She was wondering just how much she could believe from Hilde's description of her family.

It was very painful for Chava, but she had no choice other than to admit that her mother harbored some deep and devastating secrets which Helene fully intended to take with her into her grave. Chava wished that her mother shared those secrets with her, and Chava was certain that she would have easily understood what happened in those horrible circumstances where there were no options in methods how to survive. It needed not only strong will but also sheer luck from everyone who wanted to live through the horrors of the concentration camps.

Chava never heard of anyone who was willing to bear a mass murderer's child and she was certain that there was no willingness from her mother's part to have a murderer's child either. Unfortunately Helene's life depended upon just how much she was able to endure from what was forced upon her; such as having a baby and then taking that child away from her. Chava closed her eyes for a moment and tried to imagine how her mother must have felt, first being raped, then finding out that she was pregnant, having that baby and robbing her from her child. She was brutalized both physically and emotionally over and over again. She opened her eyes and looked at the German woman who claimed to be her niece.

"Why was so important to find my mother?" Chava asked.

"She had something that we wanted," declared Hilde.

"You mentioned more than once "we", who else was looking for my mother?" asked Chava again.

"Let's just say that there is another party involved," Hilde smiled and looked at her watch.

"Leaving or expecting someone?" Chava asked sarcastically.

Like on a cue, there was a knock on the door. "Ask who it is," ordered Hilde and removed her hand from handbag. Chava was not entirely shocked, yet caught her by surprise seeing a gun in Hilde's hand.

After a moment of hesitation, she yelled toward the door. "Who is it?"

"It's Daniel, please open the door," he asked in a hurried voice. Chava was at the edge of panic. Daniel was her only hope and now he was in danger as well.

Hilde got up from the couch and walked towards the door, keeping her eyes on Chava. She opened the door and that moment, Chava yelled, "Run Daniel, she has a gun," but it was too late. Daniel stepped inside her room.

Hilde motioned to him to put his hands where she could see them and Daniel obliged. Chava tried to act brave but her heart was filling up with fear. *I would never forgive myself if something happens to Daniel too,* she thought. "I am so sorry Daniel," she said to him.

"Shut up," Hilde yelled at Chava.

Fear gave away to anger and something snapped in Chava. She defiantly approached Hilde who pointed her gun at her blank range. "I swear I'll shoot you," she threatened Chava.

It came even as a surprise to Chava too when she laughed as she replied to the Hilde. "And what then? Who would give you the answer that you are looking for?" Chava causally walked back to the couch and sat down next to Daniel. Odd silence settled in the room and it seemed that Hilde wasn't sure about her next move. Chava's mind was working overtime, taking inventory of the situation. Avi's name that buzzed endlessly in her heart and mind; it came way ahead of anybody else's. She desperately tried to tell herself that it just couldn't be Avi's doing. Who was Hilde working with? Was it an organization or was she doing this for her own benefit? What were they after? Do they have anything to do with Sandy's kidnapping? There were so many questions that Chava was getting a headache.

She stared at Hilde who picked up the phone and to Chava's surprise began to speak Arabic with someone at the other end of the line. A cold chill dashed through Chava's body and she shook her head to the thought that occurred to her. Could it possible be that Hilde was working with Abdul-Hafiz Hassan? *No,* her brain screamed back at her. *Please God, don't let that be true,* Chava prayed.

She looked down at the small photo album which seemed abandoned on the coffee table. Her conversation with Hilde a short while earlier, like an instant replay rushed back into Chava's mind.

Hilde said that her grandfather was an enterprising man, she recalled. Hilde did not explain what she meant by that. Chava recanted what she learned from her mother's secret past. Evidently Colonel Schumann, a Captain when he first laid his eyes on Helene became a Major, and finally promoted to Colonel while Chava's mother was forced to be his own personal slave. He had a child with Helene and perhaps that child saved Helene's life. Schumann knew that once the truth came out about him fathering a child to a Jewess, both the child and the mother would have been destroyed and his fast accelerated career could have ended in a gutter. For some crazy notion, perhaps a fatherly feeling that he couldn't even explain to himself came over him and tried to save his daughter's life by somehow getting the child out of the camp, giving the baby a chance to live, to survive.

Schumann must have thought that Helene, Chava's mother brought him much needed luck. He was stuck in the rank of Captain for many years and once he selected Helene to be his housemaid, or better described as his own personal property, he got rapidly promoted twice. He possibly considered that keeping Helene alive was perhaps his way out of punishment for his monstrous deeds if the war did not end in his regime's favor.

Chava thought of her mother's long letter or as Helene called it, her "testimonial", and as if someone just turned on the light switch and brought light into the room, Chava knew exactly what the entire situation was all about. Being tracked by Avi and Abdul-Hafiz Hassan was not an accident. They both wanted that particular information that her mother entrusted in her and which was cremated with her mother and with her mother's testimonial that Chava destroyed in Budapest. It became obvious to Chava that she was the only person in the entire world who possessed the "key" to what others tracking her wanted.

Avi, just thinking about him made her face flush and her heart beat faster. She wondered what role Avi had played in Sandy's disappearance. On an even more personal level, did he seduce her in an attempt to get closer her late mother's secret? She hoped that it was not true because she loved him and desired him deeply. *Where are you Avi?* Chava wondered and sighed.

Daniel did not utter a single word ever since he stepped into Chava's hotel room. He just sat there and he didn't even try to get the gun away from Hilde. Chava couldn't imagine that a man with Daniel's military experience and being the member of the Israeli Defense Forces would give in to a woman with a gun so easily, almost voluntarily.

Hilde finally got off the phone and turned her full attention back to Chava and Daniel. "We are going for a short trip," she explained and motioned to them to walk toward the door. Before Chava opened the door, she felt the barrel of gun pressed against her back. "I would like to think that my aunt is a smart person. Please don't disappoint me by trying to do something foolish. Think about your friend, Ms. Johnston; her life is in your hands," she said as Chava pushed down the door handle.

As they walked toward the elevator, Hilde forced them to take the stairs instead. "Get going," she ordered them. Chava wanted to ask her where they were going but held her tongue. She thought that perhaps following Hilde's instructions, the woman would eventually lead her to Sandy.

"You are quiet Daniel," remarked Chava whispering to him.

"Your friend Avi Darom got us into this trouble," Daniel hissed at her direction.

"No talking," Hilde yelled at them as she closely followed them down the steps.

CHAPTER TWENTY-THREE

Shortly after arriving downstairs into the hotel garage, a large white van without side windows pulled up to them and they were forced to climb inside. There were two other men inside the van, and Chava didn't have to think about it, even for a second, if they were friend or foe.

Once in the van, the two strangers motioned to Daniel and Chava to sit in middle of the floor of the vehicle, while they stationed themselves by the van's back door. Chava looked at them not as much with fear, but with curiosity, although there was not much she could see. Both of the men were wearing masks, only their eyes showed and they blankly stared toward her and Daniel.

Chava hoped and prayed that they were taking them to the same place where Sandy was kept hostage for the past few days. She began to loose track of time as the van moved along the sometimes bumpy or smooth surfaced roads. Of course, Chava had no idea where they were taking them. She turned to Daniel who just set there with his eyes closed. Chava began to develop some serious concerns about him. When Chava first met Daniel after Sandy introduced them to each other, Daniel seemed like a perfect poster boy for the Israeli military with his bearings, his sureness of himself. Daniel's behavior in her hotel room, and the lack of any emotions, not to mention of his failure to initiate any counter actions began to develop some troubling thoughts to Chava.

What happened to the rescue mission? She ever so desperately wanted to ask Daniel but they were ordered not to exchange any words. Daniel, as he was sensing that Chava was looking at him, he finally glanced at her direction. At first she thought that she was hallucinating, but then Chava became certain that he was actually smiling at her.

Normally she would have thought that it was an encouraging or reassuring smile but under the circumstances, it has become even more disturbing. Did he smile at her because perhaps there were some new developments in Sandy's rescue mission and he was unable to tell her? If that was the case, she guessed, he was just acting the way he did, very passively not taking any actions against Hilde or the men who were keeping them hostage. Perhaps he hoped the same thing as she did, that their kidnappers were taking them to the same place where Sandy was kept hostage? She hoped so, although there were other troubling thoughts about Daniel, such as his remark that Avi got them into this mess. It still sounded rather strange to Chava.

She closed her eyes and visualized Avi, laying next to in bed after making love, cuddling up to her, holding her tight, talking about having his child. She smiled at that thought, she would have loved nothing better. Where did he disappear to? She still didn't know about just how much he was involved, if there was any involvement at all. *I love you Avi,* she thought, *come back and rescue me.*

She dozed off for a little while despite the bumpy ride and she was awakened by the jerky motion of the van's sudden stop. The two men finally moved as they approached them and one of them put a dark hood over her head and tied her hands behind her back. Chava was becoming increasingly dizzy from the dragging, pushing and shoving that followed. She had no idea where they were and where they were taking them, but she could smell salty air of nearby water.

Someone lifted her out of the van, and then she was dropped to the ground. Beneath her Chava could feel cement floor or pavement, when someone pulled her up to her feet and dragged her forward by her arm. She wished that her kidnappers would speak to each other so she could have tried to figure out what was going on, but no one spoke a single word.

When they stopped only a brief walk away, someone grabbed her arms and another man grabbed her legs and she was lifted onto something that was gently moving. She was roughly dropped again, and she felt pain in her left leg as she hit the floor. Chava did not complain as she did not want to give them the satisfaction by letting them know that she was hurting. Once again she was pushed by her shoulder to move forward, and finally someone told her in English to step down six steps and then stop. She heard the opening of a door in front of her and she was pushed inside. She quickly visualized a dark dungeon with filthy walls and a cot or not even that when one of her kidnappers untied her hands and pulled the hood from her head.

Chava gasped seeing her surroundings. She was inside a beautifully decorated spacious room that had classical cherry wood paneling from wall to wall up to the ceiling. In the middle of the room stood a handsomely made up king size bed with stylish, richly colored, shaded lamps that were attached to the wood paneling on each side. Even the nightstands that stood on both sides of the bed were made from cherry wood with small but exclusive statues standing on them. She walked to the cabinets that filled the opposite side of the room from the bed and opened them. Inside, she found various women's clothing, none of them she would have considered wearing anytime soon. She closed the cabinet doors and wandered to right side of the room where she noticed another door that led her to a large bathroom that not only had a shower and a bathtub, but also a hot tub that Chava wouldn't have mind trying out.

She went back to the room and sat down on the top of the bed when she heard noises that reminded her of what sounded like engines of race cars. Suddenly she felt a moving sensation. It was the first time that it dawned on her that she was on some sort of vessel. *Well that's just great,* she thought, *nobody is going to find me now for certain.*

She felt incredibly tired and stretched out on the top of the nicely made up bed and closed her eyes. Her intention was not to fall asleep just to rest, but her body reacted otherwise, she was sound asleep within seconds as if she was in her own bed back in California.

Chava didn't know how long she was asleep and she thought that she was dreaming when for several seconds she felt a warm breath on her neck and face. She smiled thinking that Avi finally found her. Soft lips were pressed on hers and her arms went around his neck, but something was wrong, she sensed that almost immediately. Her eyes popped wide open and her arms which seconds earlier embraced whom she thought was Avi, tried to push the man away. She couldn't believe her eyes when she recognized the man, it was Abdul-Hafiz Hassan, lying on the top of her and smiling down on her shocked and confused face. "I have been waiting for this moment for so long," he whispered to her.

She pressed the palms of her hands against his chest. "Get off from me," she demanded.

"A few moments ago you had your arms around me," he said and didn't move. He was much too strong for her to fight him off.

"I thought you were somebody else," she explained, still trying to roll out from underneath him.

"I wanted to kiss you ever since I saw you in Budapest at the Hyatt," he said still whispering. "I even forgave you for being a Jewess," he added.

"You are a sick bastard," said Chava and was about to slap his face when he grabbed her arms by her wrists and pinned them above her head.

"I am a much more of a man than your precious Avi," he said almost hissing at her and his lips attempted to kiss her again but she turned her head.

"I doubt that very seriously," Chava replied and laughed.

Hassan with his knees pushed Chava's legs apart and she was almost certain that she was going to be raped when she heard a voice coming from the direction of the cabin door.

"Get off from her right now," said the man standing in the doorway with a gun in his hand.

Hassan turned around and without letting Chava go, he replied. "It is not your affair, leave us," his words echoed anger and frustration.

"Thank God you are here, Daniel, get this monster off me," said Chava.

"And a good looking and wealthy monster he is," said Hilde stepping inside. She was watching the scene from behind Daniel's back.

Hassan released Chava from his strong grip and rolled off from the bed. Chava was totally confused. She sat up and looked directly at Daniel who was still standing at the doorway with an M-16 automatic rifle in hand. Realization struck her like lightning and she was so angry, that tears dwelled up in her eyes. He didn't say anything to her, he turned around and walked out of her cabin. Hilde pointed toward direction of the door and said to Chava who was still sitting on the top of the bed, and to Hassan who was standing next to it. "We have business to discuss, follow me to the Saloon," she said and walked out from the cabin, followed by Chava with Hassan right behind her.

Before entering the so called Saloon, Hassan grabbed Chava's arm, forcing her to turn around. "You and I will finish our private business real soon," he said and reached out to touch her face but she pulled back.

"I'd rather die," she said looking him straight into his eyes.

"That could be easily arranged," he said calmly and Chava knew that it was not an empty promise.

CHAPTER TWENTY-FOUR

T he area that Hilde called the Saloon was another classical cherry wood paneled large cabin on the yacht. Comfortable beige colored couches and armchairs surrounded a large square coffee table that was also made from cherry wood and it had several dishes filled with fruits and various nuts. Chava noticed a large Plasma television screen attached to the wood paneling and various original paintings that were hanging on the remaining walls. One of the paintings, an original Dali showing an extorted figure that could have been symbolically identified or compared with the situation in the Saloon, it seemed like an appropriate addition to the place.

Daniel was standing by the bar looking at Hilde questioningly as if he was waiting for her to say what she wanted to drink. He lifted a bottle of expensive Napoleon cognac from the well stocked bar and poured some into several glasses. He placed the glasses with the cognac in front of Hilde and of the rest of the people present. Finished acting as a bartender, he sat down in a beige armchair across from Chava who wouldn't take her accusing eyes off from him. Hilde's voice sounded like a sharp whip when she spoke. "The gloves are off dear Auntie Chava," said Hilde addressing her words directly to Chava. "I want that number and I want it now," she demanded.

"What in the hell are you talking about?" asked Chava and at that very moment her guesses about the reason behind everything that has happened became clear.

"I want to know the number that was tattooed on your mother's arm," said Hilde almost angrily.

"I have never seen her tattoo," said Chava and actually that was the truth.

"You are telling me that you have never seen your mother's arm?" asked Hilde and it was obvious to Chava that the woman did not believe her.

"It maybe difficult for you to believe but I have never seen my mother without any clothing and she always wore long sleeves, year round," explained Chava.

"You are a lying bitch," said Hilde and reached for a remote control that was on the corner table between two couches. She pushed several buttons and the Plasma television screen lit up. Chava realized that there must have been a VCR somewhere because to her surprise and sadness, Armin Weiss, her mother's nursing home administrator appeared on the screen. The elderly man's face was bruised and his eye lids were almost completely swollen shut. A thin line of blood was trickling down from the corner of his lips.

"Tell us about the letter," Chava heard Hilde's voice from the video tape.

"Mrs. Diamond wrote a letter to her daughter Chava, and I gave that letter to her during her mother's memorial service," explained Mr. Weiss and fear was clearly visible in his eyes.

"What was in that letter?" Hilde asked Armin Weiss again.

"I don't know," said Mr. Weiss. "I am telling you the truth. I don't know the content of that letter. The only thing I know is that according to one of her nurses, she wrote that letter for several days," he explained.

"Have you ever seen a tattoo on Mrs. Diamond's arm?" Hilde asked.

"No, she always wore a long sleeve gown. Besides, why would I look for any tattoos, most of us have one," he added quietly.

"Yes, that's true," said Hilde with an annoyed smile.

"Please let me go," pleaded Mr. Weiss. "You really have no use for me."

"You are right about that," replied Hilde and placed a gun to Mr. Weiss' forehead and fired a shot. Chava's body jerked backwards in horror and she looked towards Daniel who just sat there watching the video. His face was a solid mask that would not reflect any emotions one way or another.

"Daniel," Chava called out to him. "How could you possibly side with these animals? How could you?" she asked him with tears in her eyes.

He looked at her coldly, then after a few moments of hesitation he took out his wallet and tossed his late wife and his children's picture across the table towards her. "My government killed my family. My government sold out my family and my people by refusing to cooperate with the Palestinians. They were forcing them to put a bomb on the bus that my family used to come home from school and shopping. I have begged my government for more secure transportation methods, for putting guards or preventing devices on buses but nobody listened," Daniel nodded as he remembered. "After I lost my family, I found the way to revenge their deaths."

"You out of your fricking mind?" Chava yelled at him. "You did nothing less than sell out your own people. You are an officer in the Israeli Defense Forces, still wearing your country's military uniform; you were trusted by thousands of people for the love of God," she looked at him in despise. "I hope you rot in hell for what you have done."

"Shut up," Hilde yelled at her and raised her weapon at Chava. "That's enough of this bullshit. Do you think that I personally care about the Palestinian causes or the Israeli causes? Not in a million years," she said and laughed, then her face became serious. "But I do care about what is rightfully mine."

Chava was still furious from what she had learned about Daniel's betrayal of his country, but instead of Hilde, she turned her attention to Abdul-Hafiz Hassan. "And what is your part of this despicable charade?"

"You don't have to answer any of her questions," Hilde said to the Palestinian. Hassan didn't listen to her. He got up from the armchair and stepped in front of Chava.

"You wrote about my people in your book The Third Cloud, but just how much do you really know about them?" he asked her almost humanely.

Chava looked up at him as she answered. "I know about the suicide bombings and about killing innocent civilians indiscriminately. I know that you are coming from a wealthy family and I know that many Arabian countries are pumping money into Palestinian terrorist organizations to buy weapons so they can terrorize more Israelis."

He laughed hearing her words. "Do you like my yacht?" he asked.

"What?" Chava asked not understanding the sudden change of course of their discussion.

"This my yacht, it is called, "Abdul-Mu'id", it means the "Servant of the Restorer." I believe that Allah will help us to win our battle against our oppressors and I will use all means that are available to me to provide for my people and assist them to get their own country."

Chava shook her head. "No, you are not helping your people. If you want to help your people, instead of pumping millions of dollars that flows into Palestinian terrorist organizations to buy weapons, you should be using that money to build better schools, hospitals and enrich people's lives. You are nothing but a two bit terrorist who is on a power trip. The way you acted in Hungary and the way you conduct your affairs, by sending me flowers with threatening notes in the form of a puzzle, you are nothing but a pitiful terrorist who keeps on telling himself that you are a freedom fighter. The quote "that one country's terrorist is another country's freedom fighter" does not apply in your case," said Chava passionately. As soon as she said the last word, Hassan slapped her face hard, leaving his palm print on it. The sudden pain rushed tears in her eyes.

"Don't touch her again," she heard Daniel's warning.

Hilde pointed her weapon once again at Chava and yelled at them with great agitation in her voice. "Stop it, all of you! What in the world do you think you are doing? Did you forget the objective of our plan?"

There was a momentary silence in the Saloon. Chava took the cool glass of cognac and pressed it against her burning face where Hassan struck her. She glanced at Hassan's direction who already went back to sit in his armchair. Their eyes met and Chava seldom, if ever had seen so much hatred as she noticed in his dark, almost black eyes. She could read his lips as he silently mattered. "We have not finished yet."

She was not afraid of him before and she was not afraid of him right then. She realized that while sitting in that Saloon of the yacht that Hassan claimed as his own, slowly but surely a mystery was beginning to unfold right in front of her. There was one more important question that Chava wanted and needed to find out the answer to. Why did Hilde go through so much trouble to find out about Chava's mother, Helene's tattoo number which was so crudely written on her left arm while she was enslaved in the Auschwitz concentration camp in Poland? Hilde must have spent a great deal of time trying to track down Chava's mother and to search for allies to fulfill her plan. Some things still remained a mystery, such as how did Hilde, Hassan and Daniel hook up to form a small band of terrorists?

"Where is my friend Sandy Johnston?" asked Chava turning her attention to Hilde.

"She will be freed as soon as you tell me what we want to hear," remarked the woman.

"I don't have the information that you want," said Chava calmly and her eyes stood Hilde's cold stare.

"On the contrary," Hilde retorted. "I believe you do."

"So what is it going to be, a stand off between who is telling the truth and who is not?" Chava asked and smiled.

It was Hilde's smile that sent a chill down on Chava's spine. The German woman reached for her glass of cognac and lifted her glass. "May the strongest willed win," and with that, she swallowed her drink with one gulp. Chava looked at her and she slowly lifted the glass to her lips and drank down the velvety colored Napoleon cognac. She set her glass down on the big square table and looked at Hassan who did not touch his drink.

"What about you, why don't you drink your fine cognac?" asked Chava teasingly, knowing full well that Muslims were not supposed to drink alcohol. Hassan lifted his glass and while staring at Chava, he drank his brandy. She smiled at him acknowledging that Hassan, that particular Muslim was not following all the rules that were laid down in the Koran.

Chava looked around and soon she realized that Hilde, Hassan and Daniel were all staring at her. Suddenly she wasn't feeling well, she felt faint and she felt that her heart was slowing down. It was the first time since her kidnapping that she experienced fear. *What is happening to me?* She asked herself as she lay back on the couch, unable to sit up. *All of them were drinking, so why am I the only one who looks and feels sick?* She wondered. "What did you put in drink?" she asked weakly.

"Nothing that will kill you," she heard Hilde's voice. "You refused to give us an answer so we gave you Sodium Pentothal; it was in your drink."

"You bastards, you gave me truth serum," Chava hissed at them and like a crazy person, she laughed as she helplessly lay on the couch. "Go ahead and ask me anything," she childishly dared them.

Hilde went to the couch where Chava was sitting and pushed her in an upward position and then sat down next to her. "So tell me Auntie Chava, what was tattooed on your mother's arm?" she asked Chava.

Chava looked at her funny, as she if she was drunk. "I love Avi," she said and smiled at the direction of Hassan while she tried to focus her eyes on the Palestinian. Her vision was becoming blurrier by the minute.

"What was tattooed on your mother's arm?" Hilde repeated her question with a raised voice.

"I love to write stories. Do you know that I am a popular writer?" asked Chava and clumsily pointed at herself.

Hilde slapped Chava's face on both sides. "I am going to ask you one more time. What was the number tattooed on your mother's arm?"

Chava's lips began to form the letter "B" but her mind worked overtime. *NO,* her mind screamed at her inside her brain. *You must NOT give them what they want to know. You have the power to prevent them from getting the number. Your mother asked you, no, told you NOT to give out that number under any circumstances. You must remain strong and defy them,* you *cannot betray your own mother's wishes,* she reminded herself.

Hilde leaned towards her and slapped her again. "Talk to me you bitch! You must tell me the number on your Jewish bitch of a mother's arm," she yelled at Chava. She didn't reply, she tried to concentrate at Hilde who's face was inches away from hers but she just couldn't see her clearly.

"Maybe in the next life time," she whispered and she slumped back on the couch and was about to lose consciousness. She could no longer even see imagines or outlines of the people around her but before she was completely overcome by the powerful serum that was also used as sedative by some doctors, she heard Daniel's voice.

"It shouldn't have been mixed with alcohol, it was much more potent than with water," he remarked. *As if you care,* was the last thought on Chava's mind as she slipped into unconsciousness where she didn't have to worry about pain, fear or terrorists.

CHAPTER TWENTY-FIVE

C hava desperately tried to open her eyes but she was not succeeding. She felt a throbbing pain in her temples and tasted bitterness in her mouth. She made an unfruitful attempt to concentrate on the sounds around her as it was quiet, there were no audible noises for her to detect. Chava reached out and touched her immediate area assuming that she was placed on the same bed where she had been before. She felt incredibly sleepy. Because she was not feeling well anyway, she turned over and fell asleep once again while rubbing her temples to ease the pain.

"Wake up Jewess," Chava heard the unwelcome voice, and at the same time, she felt warm breath on her face, hands and on her breasts. She felt light headed and sick in her stomach, not to mention the fact that she was unable to move.

"Get off me," Chava whispered. Her throat was dry and she wanted nothing more than a glass of water to drink.

"Listen to me Chava," Hassan said to her. "Don't be mistaken, you only have two options here and now. You either cooperate with us or you die. It's as simple as that. You are not only beautiful but are also very smart, so it shouldn't be a hard decision for you to make."

"Take your hands off me," Chava asked him again but he didn't listen. Hassan touched her face and stroked her hair, not forcefully, more like with a gentle intimacy.

"I don't want to hurt you," he said very calmly. Chava tried to turn her head but he held her face between his hands. "I can't believe this feeling myself, but I fell in love with you. If you just give Hilde that cursed tattoo numbers your mother had on her arm, she would let you go and I can take you to wonderful places," Hassan pleaded with Chava.

For the first time since she drank the tainted Napoleon cognac, she managed to open her eyes, looking directly into Hassan's. *How funny,* she thought. *He was actually a handsome man, who happened to be a real bastard. Hassan in great many ways was betraying his own people.* "Give it up," she said to him calmly.

"You and I as a couple? It's never going to happen. You are much stronger than me, but you are never really going to have me."

He bent down and kissed her. She didn't protest, and she did not react to his kiss. She just laid there not moving. He took off his shirt and unzipped his pants, then he slowly began to unbutton her blouse. She did not say a single word to him, she just watched him, not taking her eyes off from him. He was watching her too and Chava knew from the look in his eyes that he was indeed in love with her. The coldness in his eyes was gone, and Chava thought that she noticed genuine desire, and even gentleness in his dark eyes.

He was about pull off her skirt when shots rang out and the sounds of hurrying footsteps were audible outside her cabin. The door swung open and two men dressed in solid green military outfits with black hoods that only had two holes for the eyes and one for the mouth, rushed in. Hassan reached underneath the mattress and pulled out a gun. A shot was fired and Hassan, mortally wounded, fell over Chava who pushed him aside and rolled off the bed to the floor.

One of the black hooded men approached her and reached out in her direction. Chava screamed at him. "Stay away from me." The man stopped and kneeled down in front of her. She didn't want to look at him, she didn't want to think that she fell from one terrorist group hands into another.

"You are safe, we are Israeli Commandos," he said and reached out to help her up. She buttoned up her blouse and rearranged her skirt, and then slowly she began to follow the two men out of the cabin. Before she stepped out to the short walkway, she turned around to take one more look at Hassan who was laying dead on the bed. "May your God help you to go to hell where you belong," she murmured.

She was taken to the Saloon where she found herself surrounded by at least a dozen heavily armed men wearing the same uniform with black hoods, just as her two rescuers wore. The only other person she knew from group of strangers was Hilde, she was seated in one of the armchairs with her hands tied behind her back. To her right and left sat two armed man with their rifles, which Chava recognized as IMI Uzi SMG was pointed at the German woman. Daniel was nowhere to be seen. *He either escaped or was killed in the shootout I heard,* Chava thought. The crew of the yacht that was mainly made up from the men who actually kidnapped her, and faked Daniel's kidnapping were also gone.

One of the hooded men who escorted her to the Saloon pulled Chava aside. "What was going on in that cabin?" he asked her.

Chava thought that it was a strange and personal question coming from the man who claimed to be an Israeli Commando. She suspiciously looked at him, and then she shook her head and smiled. While she didn't immediately recognize the voice as he was speaking in a low tone, those startling blue eyes she could see through the holes of the hood gave him away. "Avi?" she asked him.

"What was going on in there?" he asked again.

"Nothing was going on," she explained. "I was drugged. They gave me Sodium Pentothal and when I came to, he was about to rape me. I was very weak and I couldn't fight him off." He gently touched her face and she pressed it against his strong hands.

"Commander," one of the man called out towards him as he walked inside the Saloon. Avi turned around to look at him.

"I'll be right there," he said and motioned to Chava to sit down. He walked up to the man who called out for him. Chava tried unsuccessfully to hear what was said between them but they were speaking in Hebrew. She noticed that Avi turned and glanced around the Saloon before he issued his order. "Everybody, get out of here, right now," then he rushed back to Chava. "One of my men found explosives in the engine room with a timer and he is trying to defuse them. The timer is set to explode in fifteen minutes, we have to evacuate this yacht in case he is not going to succeed."

"Did you find Daniel?" Chava asked.

"He was here on this yacht?" Avi asked her with surprise. She nodded as a response.

No further conversation taken place as she was ushered quietly but firmly out of the cabin. Closely behind her, surrounded by Israeli Commandos a defiant Hilde was also rushed off the yacht. There was an Israeli Coast Guard boat standing by, and a couple minutes later it stopped next to the yacht after seeing Avi's signal. She was helped down the steps that were attached to the side of the yacht and within short period of time, the entire yacht was evacuated.

The Israeli Coast Guard boat sped away from the yacht and just in time because the yacht, the once beautiful floating mini palace exploded into millions of tiny pieces. "That was a close call," remarked Chava standing next to the still hooded Avi, who did not reply. He silently pulled her closer and locked his arms around Chava.

CHAPTER TWENTY-SIX

The flight from Eilat to Jerusalem was a short one. During the flight, Avi would not release Chava's hand, he held on to her like a magnet. Hilde quietly sat between two of her captors on the large transport helicopter, but her eyes said more than Chava cared to acknowledge.

Arriving in Jerusalem, they were taken to an Israeli controlled police station where Avi changed clothes from his Commando outfit to a comfortable levy jeans and t-shirt. On his back, hanging from a long shoulder strap was his Uzi that he would not leave behind. He drove Chava in an unmarked police car to the Hyatt Regency Jerusalem Hotel. The first sight of the building almost took Chava's breath away with its architectural style and the beauty of its surroundings.

The hotel was located in a terrace architectural design on the slopes of the famous Mount Scopus that was a part of the Judean Mountain Range. Avi asked Chava if she was up for a short history lesson of the area. She wanted to hear Avi's voice, no matter what the subject was, although she was also genuinely interested in learning more about the place.

Avi explained to her that Mount Scopus not only had the Hyatt Regency Jerusalem Hotel built on it, but it was also the place where Israel faced one of it's first struggles defending itself as a Jewish State of Israel, after it was declared a country, independent from any others back in 1948. Mount Scopus was also the home of the first campus of the Hebrew University, Avi went on saying, where just recently, Hamas terrorist infiltrated the university's cafeteria during the lunch hour and killed many innocent students, including foreign students, not only Israelis.

He proudly mentioned that the first Hadassah Hospital was also built there and then his voice chocked up when he told her the story of the seventy-seven doctors, nurses and medical students who were killed in cold blood on April 13, 1948, when their humanitarian convoy was attacked by rebellious Arabs who declined recognition of the newly established Israeli state.

As the road curved around, the Hyatt Regency Jerusalem Hotel came in full view. It was a truly breathtaking sight. Arriving at the hotel, Avi parked the car himself, not letting the valet do it for them. They found a parking place not far from the main entrance and a couple of minutes later they walked into the hotel's lobby. Chava took an instant liking to the place.

The lobby reminded her of stories in which she read about the hanging gardens of Babylon. Although it was already in the late afternoon, the sun still brightly shined through the pyramid shaped glass windows on the ceiling. The hanging gardens were the signature touches of the Hyatt hotel chain, she supposed, like the hotel she and Sandy stayed in Budapest, at the Attrium Hyatt. That was built in a similar way, although that one was not as lavishly decorated comparing to the one she entered in Jerusalem.

While she stood there, looking around, Avi had a brief talk with a check in clerk, who without a moment of hesitation got on the computer. A few minutes later, Avi touched Chava's elbow as a sign that they were ready to go to their room. Entering their "room," Chava smiled with pleasure. The luxurious suite had windows that overlooked parts of both the Old and New Jerusalem. She tried to soak in the view, the beauty, the history and the sadness that was Jerusalem.

Avi gently touched her shoulders and made her turn around to face him. "I missed you," he said touching her face. With one finger he outlined the curve of her lips. Just like before, she kissed his fingers and she ever so desperately wanted to be kissed by him. He leaned towards her and his soft lips melted into hers, parting it slowly so his tongue could enter her mouth to search for hers. She felt weak again and he grabbed her just in time before she collapsed.

"I am sorry," she apologized. "For some reason I felt faint. Probably because I am hungry and thirsty and I need a bath in a worst way."

"Hmm," Avi said with a very serious face. "And which of these necessities do you wish to satisfy first madam?"

"Well, let's see," said Chava and put her finger on her cheek. "Let's take a shower while room service could bring the food and drink?" she suggested.

"Normally I would be glad to agree with you, but you haven't seen the shower yet," said Avi and carried her to the bathroom. The private Jacuzzi was up and running and Chava knew exactly what he meant.

"I believe that your order of events is the most practicable," she agreed and they went back to the dayroom part of their hotel suite. Avi picked up the menu from one of the desks and once they made the selection, he placed the orders. He put the receiver down and took a seat on the couch, next to her. She put her feet up on his lap so she could face him, and without hearing any request from Chava, Avi took it upon himself to massage them. Chava looked at him and Avi knew that Chava was about to do the obvious, she was going to ask him questions.

"What?" said Avi seeing the wondering look in her eyes. "Go ahead and ask whatever you want."

"How did you know about the bathroom in this place? Am I not the first woman you brought here?" she asked him with a raised eyebrow.

Avi rolled his eyes. He couldn't believe that Chava's first question was a personal one in nature, but in a way, he was also glad of that. "Oh, Chava," he said and smiled. "I live in this country and advertisements are everywhere. I saw the commercial about this place and ever since then I wanted to stay here with you in this suite."

"Sorry," said Chava apologetically. "I might as well tell you how sorry I am about having doubts about your honesty earlier when we met in Tel Aviv, and here in Jerusalem."

Avi looked somewhat surprised. "What made you think that I was not honest? You thought that I was dishonest because I couldn't tell you my real identity and what I was doing?" he asked.

"Well, you need to look at the situations from my point of view. You disappeared more than once without as much as giving me a hint that you had to leave, or without leaving any messages. You have never called me, and on the night when Sandy disappeared, once again you were gone as well. It gave me the impression that perhaps you had something to do with her disappearance."

Avi thought about it for a moment before he replied. "I suppose you are right, it does seem that way doesn't it?" he said. "I actually witnessed the last stages of Sandy's kidnapping, when they placed her into their vehicle. I believe that she was not conscious from the way they situated her in their van. There was not much I could have done as I didn't even have my car keys and I left my cell phone and my gun in my car. It was the first time that I felt that I failed to help another human being and I blamed myself for not being able to stop her kidnapping."

"Did you have a chance to look at her kidnappers?" Chava inquired.

"There were three of them and I immediately recognized one of them. He is a noted troublemaker, but he is not ranked high in his organization. I recognized the second man; he is a member of Hamas. Once again, according to our sources he is not in any decision making position. I did not recognize the third man. I got information that the van was reported stolen earlier in the day and someone else reported a stolen license plate that was taken from a car parked in one of the shopping areas," Avi explained.

"Avi," said Chava quietly. "Will you ever forgive me for what I said and the way I behaved at the other hotel?" she asked.

"I can't recall a thing," answered Avi and smiled at her slyly. "I should apologize to you Chava. You must believe me that I just couldn't reveal anything to you about the ongoing investigations and who I really am and who I am really working for," he said apologetically.

"Avi, I still don't know anything about you," she said seriously. "Can you tell me now? Are you able to talk to me about what you do and who you really are?" she asked.

He smiled and nodded. "Okay," he said finally. "My real name is Avraham Ben-Yishan, Avi for friend, family and for my future wife," he remarked.

"Aha," said Chava and raised her eyebrows. "Please, continue."

"I am a Colonel in the Israeli Special Forces, with the Sayeret Duvdevan Unit," he explained. "I also served in the Golani Brigade for a few years when I was a young Lieutenant and later Captain."

"I heard of the Golani Brigade," remarked Chava. "Isn't that the famous brigade who was always sent to the areas where the fighting was the most dangerous?" she asked.

"Yeah, something like that," he agreed and smiled at her.

"How long have you been working with the Special Forces?" she inquired with genuine curiosity.

"For many, many years," he admitted but did mention any specific length of time.

"So tell me Avi," she said. "How did you get involved in my particular case?"

He took a deep breath before he continued. "First, a confession, okay?"

Chava looked at him surprised. "There is more to confess?"

Avi nodded. "Before I met you, I read everything you ever wrote, books that is. When I saw your picture on the back of your books, I truly believed that you were, and you are still one of the most beautiful and intelligent woman I have ever seen."

It was one of those rare moments in Chava's life when she did not know what to say. Her lips curled into a big smile and poked him with her foot. "I love when you talk like that."

"No Chava," protested Avi. "I am dead serious. I tried to find television interviews with you and I watched them over and over, so many times, that even my sisters began to tease me that you were not even a real person," he stopped and leaned forward to kiss her. She wrapped her arms around his neck and pulled him down on the top of her. "I guess I was in love with you long before I actually met you."

"Why did you wait this long?" she asked and offered her lips. He was just about to kiss her when there was a discreet knock on the door.

"Room Service," said the person on the other side of the door. Avi got up and picked up his gun from the middle of the coffee table and made his way to the door.

He looked through the peep hole and he said loudly. "Just a minute please."

He quickly picked up the phone in the entry way and called room service. Chava couldn't understand what he was saying because he was speaking in Hebrew. A few moments later when he was evidently satisfied with what he was hearing, he went back to the door and opened it.

A young man, wearing the hotel's uniform entered pushing a cart with food and drinks on the top of it, with plates, silverware and napkins on the shelf beneath. He nodded towards Chava who was still sitting on the couch and then he quietly set up the table in the dining room. Finished with the task, he asked something from Avi. He shook his head and after giving him what seemed like a generous tip, the young man left their suite.

"The food and drinks are served," he announced and pointed to the table.

"Who did you call before you let him in?" she asked.

"I called the room service and asked them for description of the delivery person," he explained. Chava admitted to herself that she wouldn't have thought of that.

While they ate, Chava restarted their previous conversation by saying, "I am still curious how you got involved with my case."

"Actually I first become involved with tracking Hassan's activities. We suspected for a long time that he was involved with smuggling weapons, but we just could not catch him no matter how hard we tried. It seemed that he was always one step ahead of us."

"I'll bet that this is where Daniel comes into the picture," Chava remarked. Avi nodded in agreement.

"As you probably know, Abdul-Hafiz Hassan came from a very wealthy family. His parents still live in Saudi Arabia. They originally lived in Gaza City, where Hassan spent his early years while his parents made their fortune in the oil business in Saudi Arabia. He liked to dress well and spend money lavishly in many European countries. His favorite country where he spent a great deal of time and money was Germany. Our sources said that there is where he hooked up with Hilde, who was and we believe still is a member of a neo Nazi organization in Frankfurt."

"And how did Daniel get involved with them? It's not like he was going to advertise himself in the newspaper," Chava wondered out loud.

"Well, believe it or not, it's almost exactly what happened. We began to monitor some heavy internet email traffic between a certain German neo-Nazi website and someone in Daniel Zehavi's unit. It took us a couple of weeks when finally our computer experts succeeded in narrowing down the internet addresses and identified who was behind all of those emails that came out of the Daniel's unit. Zehavi had access to some of our information, and that is how he managed to warn Hassan every time we got close to him and his gun running operation for various terrorist organizations."

"Okay, that makes sense. But what about me? What about my mother and why is the number tattooed on my mother's arm is so important to Hilde and to the others?" inquired Chava.

"It all began during World Ward Two when fortunes were confiscated from Jewish people who were destined to die in gas chambers or be killed in so many ways that it hurts just to think about it. Some of those Nazis still live comfortable lives in South America from the fortunes they stole from their murdered victims. Colonel Schumann, who kept your mother as his slave, was not any different from the others. He collected and smuggled out possibly hundreds of thousand of dollars worth of jewelry, art work and cash in various dominations to Switzerland. Because it appeared to him that your mother brought him good fortune, he humored her by choosing her concentration camp identification tattoo number as the number for his safe deposit box number. Of course, he was executed for war crimes in Poland at the end of the war and other than your mother, who for some reason was let onto his secret by him, only his parents knew about the importance of those numbers on your mother's arm," he explained.

"Oh my God," whispered Chava and covered her mouth in shock. Then a thought occurred to her. "The only thing I don't understand is that they knew about the tattoo, why they had to look for my mother and go through all of this that just happened?" she asked from Avi.

Avi nodded that it was a good question. "There was one important thing that Colonel Schumann either failed or purposely did not mention or reveal to his parents about the tattoo and it was the actual tattoo number. In other words; they knew about the tattoo, but they did not know the actual number."

"What about Hilde? What do you know about her?" asked Chava.

"It also appears that there was no love lost between Hilde's mother and her grandparents. For some unknown reason, after Hilde's mother died, the elder Schumann's took Hilde back. Just before Colonel Schumann's father died, he mentioned to Hilde about the tattoo number and Swiss safe deposit box. I am assuming that was that time frame when she began to search for your mother in Hungary. By the time Hilde found her, I am sorry to say, she passed away and you arrived back to Budapest. Mr. Weiss gave you the letter from your mother in which I assume she told you the numbers of her tattoo."

Chava remained silent as she tried to comprehend Avi's explanation. "So Hassan came to Hungary to get in touch with me?" she finally asked.

"More likely to keep an eye on you," said Avi. "But apparently I was not the only one who developed feelings for you."

"Avi," she said quietly. "I decided to release that tattoo number to the Holocaust Research Center in Los Angeles when I return home to the United States. If it's possible, I want them to investigate what is in that Swiss bank account and who they belong to. I want those things to be returned to the survivors or their relatives."

"That would be the right thing to do," agreed Avi. "I will never ask you for that number, I hope you know that," he remarked.

"It never crossed my mind that you would," Chava said and finished with her meal.

"Good," said Avi and put his napkins on his plate. For a few short moments he looked at her with such love that she was tempted to jump into his arms with or without an invitation. He got up and pulled her up to her feet, he led her into the bathroom where the Jacuzzi was foaming from the aromatic oils and minerals that were even favored by Queen Cleopatra herself, and which where the Hyatt Regency Jerusalem Hotel's specialties.

They gazed into each others eyes as they slowly began to remove each other's clothes, piece by piece, letting them fall on the marble floor of the bathroom. The water temperature was perfect, but their body temperature was burning from desire. Avi pulled her to him and kissed her neck as she bent her head backwards. His hands, soft from the wonderfully smelling bath oil was smooth, so was the feeling of Chava's skin when he touched her gently. He caressed her breasts, her back and her shoulder and everywhere he could reach.

Chava had great difficulties holding onto him because she wanted to touch and feel him with her hands too. She wanted to be certain that it was not just a dream, and that Avi was really there with her, holding her, touching and kissing her.

With a soft sponge he gently washed her and she let herself go, she placed herself under his total control. Her mind was at ease, and the conclusion she drew from that moment was the undeniable fact that she was totally and unconditionally in love with Avi. The long years of what she realized, as if it were only part of a bad memory, were years of an unhappy marriage and just then she was certain that for first time in her life she was truly loved by a real man who was willing to give up his life for her. She snapped back to reality when his hands reached between her legs and he even washed her there with his eyes resting on her face, searching for her reaction. And react she did by biting her tongue as a deep sigh left her lips. She was more than ready for him, but to her surprise, he stopped.

"It's your turn," he said with a sheepish smile on his face and handed her the sponge.

"You'll be sorry," she whispered. He just smiled at her and she knew that he was ready for any challenge that she was about to impose on him. She couldn't help it but to smile as she washed his back, his chest and his strong arms. And then, she reached down and touched him. He was erect and just as she was ready for him, he was also very much ready to take her, but she unexpectedly got up out of the tub and turned to him. "It's your turn," then she dashed back toward the spacious bedroom.

She heard him laugh as he ran after her, not covering himself to her delight. Avi jumped on the bed and immediately got on the top of her. He just lay there, stroking her hair and kissing her playfully. "How did I get so lucky?" he asked her after a long and passionate kiss that for a few seconds forced her to gasp for air.

"About what?" she asked although she suspected what Avi meant.

"Of finding you and for you loving me?" he said very seriously.

"I think that it goes both ways, don't you think?" she asked him.

"Chava," he said to her as she gazed into his blue eyes. "I want you to be my wife," Avi proposed.

She took a deep breath but remained silent. Avi's smile was quickly fading away and a concerned look took over his face. Chava looked at him still silently, not because she didn't know the answer she wanted to give, she was just simply overcome of that very special moment that only comes once in a lifetime.

"Chava," he called in a concerned voice.

"When?" she said to him with all the seriousness she could master.

The worried look disappeared in an instant from his handsome face and his eyes that moments ago were reflecting concern lit up and shined down on her. He kissed her gently, not hard, and then he kissed her eyes, her nose and her lips over and over again. He slowly made the trek down on all the valleys and hills of her firm body. His hands followed his lips and he reached down to stroke her while his lips discovered the curves of her legs all the way down to her toes.

"Avi, please," she begged him and pulled him closer so she could see his face. He kissed her nipples and ran his tongue around them when she couldn't stand it any longer and reached down and guided him inside herself. He completed her perfectly and she gasped when he began to move.

He leaned down to her and whispered. "I love you Chava, now and forever."

"I . . . love . . . you . . . too," she mumbled, gasping for air between each word.

They made love with great passion and when it was over, their exhaustion level only measured up to the satisfaction and happiness they felt. Chava fell asleep with his arms tightly wrapped around her.

Avi wouldn't move, he just wanted to lay next to her, forever like that if it was up to him. Deep down inside he felt that holding onto her in the next few days would be a hard, if not an impossible task. Avi knew Chava and he suspected that not mentioning her missing friend before they made love was intentional; she wanted to keep the rest of the evening only for themselves. It's not that he blamed her for wanting to find her close friend, Sandy Johnston. He would have done the very same thing, search and search some more until all rocks were turned over and looked under.

Each year Avi told himself, that particular year with the Special Forces is going to be the last one, unfortunately terrorists had other plans for him. He could and would not leave his comrades in his Special Forces Unit behind because they were not only his comrades; they were also his brothers in arm.

He trained many of them and lost some of them throughout the years. Their jobs were always done, yet never finished, no matter what sacrifices they had to make either professionally or personally.

Perhaps, just perhaps, he thought. *Chava is a good reason to return to civilian life. I have to introduce her to my family as soon as possible,* and with that thought in mind, he finally drifted to sleep.

CHAPTER TWENTY-SEVEN

The sound of running water in the shower woke him. A short time later Chava returned to the bedroom where Avi was still in bed with a blue thin satin sheet covering him so tightly that it had left nothing for imagination. Chava shook her head. "You are being a bad boy," she said and laughed.

He petted the bed next to him, inviting her back. "I guess it's time for you to straightened me out," Avi replied and blinked at her.

Chava dropped the white monogrammed hotel bathrobe from her body and jumped in the bed. She lay down next to Avi and while he turned to kiss her, without hesitation she reached down and touched him. "Hmm," murmured Avi. "Are you being a bad girl?" he asked her jokingly and his lips came down hard on hers with his throbbing tongue opening them to enter her mouth.

They were breathing heavily and no part of their body went without touching or kissing when the telephone's sharp ring stopped them as if ice water were dumped on them. Avi knew, and Chava suspected that only a couple of people were aware of their whereabouts, and whatever the caller had to say could not wait.

Avi sat up in bed and with his right arm he held onto Chava, but his left hand reached for the telephone receiver. Avi didn't say anything, he did not introduce himself, he just listened intensely. A few minutes later, he said one word. "Okay," and hung up the phone.

Chava looked at him with questions in her eyes. Avi thought for a moment about what he just heard, then he turned to Chava. "In one of your novels, "For the Last Time," a writer was kidnapped and was taken to Hebron, is that correct?" he asked her.

Chava nodded. "I received a video email from Sandy's kidnappers and she also mentioned that book. Do you think that she is in Hebron? Isn't that city under Palestinian jurisdiction?" she asked.

"I was told that one of our informers in Hebron saw your friend in a car that he was passing. She appears to be okay," he explained.

"How long ago was she spotted?" inquired Chava.

"Yesterday afternoon," Avi replied.

"That is not exactly a good sign," said Chava sitting up on the bed. "It means that she was seen after the arrest of Hilde and the death of Hassan. They are going to kill her to revenge his death," she said and turned to Avi. "You must do something, and do it right now."

"I believe you are correct," Avi agreed with her. "We don't have any time to waste. I will drive you back to the Police Headquarters where you will be safe," he told her while he was getting dressed.

"No can do," Chava said to him firmly. "I am either going with you or I am going back to Eilat."

Avi stopped and looked at her. "What for?"

Chava smiled and leaned to him for a kiss. "I have left my mother's ashes in my hotel room," she explained. "I must fulfill her final wish."

"I want to have someone with you when you are in Eilat," suggested Avi with concern, although he suspected that Chava would not agree with him, and he was right.

"If you could make a flight arrangement for me, that would be great," she said, and then she added. "Perhaps we can meet there after Sandy has been rescued," she suggested.

Avi did not answer as he went to the bathroom taking his clothing with him. Moments later Chava heard the shower running and within minutes, he returned freshly showered and dressed. In the meantime Chava also got ready and they left the hotel suite with heavy hearts for more than one reason.

Avi was silent as he drove back to the Police Headquarters in Jerusalem. Leaving Chava in a small office, he went to talk to the members of his Special Forces Unit. On his way to their quarters where they were set up temporarily the previous night, Avi stopped by one of the secretary's desk, and asked her to make arrangements for a flight that would take Chava back to Eilat.

He was genuinely concerned about letting her go on her own but he had no choice, he needed all of his men to participate in Sandy's rescue mission. A few minutes later the secretary was able to give him Chava's confirmed flight information. Avi continued his way down the hall to meet his waiting Special Rescue Unit, a few doors down from the office where he left Chava.

She was impatient; she was never good at waiting for anything for a long period of time. When Avi did not return for fifteen minutes, Chava left the small office. She slowly made her way down the long hallway, unknown to her in the direction where Avi was holding his briefing about the rescue mission. Chava was about to open the door where she heard the voices were coming from, when she felt a hand on her shoulder. She turned around from the sudden touch just to face a young woman in police uniform. She asked Chava some questions which she was unable to understand.

"I am sorry," Chava explained. "I don't speak Hebrew."

The young woman glanced down on Chava's temporary pass that was hanging from her neck on a thin silver chain. "Oh my goodness," she said in perfect English. "Are you Chava Diamond, the writer?"

"Yes, that's me," she smiled at the young woman.

"I tremendously enjoy reading your books. You must really love Israel because you always write about my country in your books," she said with unhidden joy.

"Well, not always," Chava objected playfully. "If you say that, you are giving me the impression that you have not read all of my books after all."

The young woman blushed. "By the way, my name is Rima Lehman," she introduced herself to Chava. "It's an honor to meet you."

"Well Rima, it is always a pleasure to meet someone who likes my writing," Chava replied and shook hands with her. "It's encourages me to write more stories," she added.

"Oh, I really envy you for the ability to write a whole book length stories. I have difficulties just writing a short letter," said Rima as she walked along side with Chava back to the office where Avi left her.

"You obviously didn't want me in there," said Chava stopping and pointing back at the door.

"I am sorry about that," replied Rima. "Not even we are allowed to go in there when they having their briefings, unless we are invited to assist them, which is seldom if ever," she explained.

"What's with those hoods?" Chava asked curiously.

"They always wear hoods when they are getting ready for a mission," Rima explained. "I have never seen anyone else's face from that unit with the exception of the Commander's."

"I like his face a lot," remarked Chava with a big smile on her face.

Rima sighed as she answered. "We all do, but evidently he is off the market."

"What do you mean?" asked Chava.

"He told a few people that he was getting married soon, and they told to the rest us," she stopped as she said that and took a deep breath. "Lucky lady, whoever she is," Rima remarked.

"You speak very good English," Chava complimented her just as they arrived back to the small office.

"I grew up in the States but my parents wanted to live in Israel. They said that all Jewish people should be moving to Israel because this is the only country where nobody discriminates against us just because we are Jews," Rima explained.

Chava sat down and looked at Rima with a serious face. The young woman returned her gaze. "Did I say something wrong?" she asked Chava.

"No, you said nothing wrong Rima," Chava replied. "Although I can only partially agree with your parent's opinion. I think Jewish people should be able to live anywhere in the world in peace and without fear of pogroms, inquisitions or extermination," she said as they sat down. Rima held on to every word Chava was saying. She continued. "On the same philosophy of your parents, do you think that all black people in the world should move back to Africa, because the majority of the blacks in this world live in Africa? The whole idea is ridicules and senseless. We are living in the twenty-first century for heaven's sake," she said almost feverishly. "We shouldn't have to talk about this subject and we still do, because we are forced to. Look at this wonderful country of yours! There are only a very few countries in this world that are able to claim such tremendous history, culture and survival as Israel. And yet," she stopped and thought for a second. "Just a few days ago there was a teenager who was captured wearing a suicide jacket with explosives. What is this world coming too?" she asked not expecting a reasonable explanation.

"It's take off time," said Avi standing in the doorway catching her last words. "What are you two ladies are talking about?" he asked with curiosity as she reached out to help Chava up from her chair.

Rima looked back and forth at them and at that very moment she realized who the mysterious woman was who captured Colonel Avi Ben-Yisan's heart. She immediately noticed the connection and the gentleness between Chava and Avi as they touched and as they so lovingly looked at each other.

"It was great talking to you Rima," said Chava and shook hands with the young woman. "And please don't forget, as the old saying goes, your home is where your heart is. Good bye for now."

Rima was smiling as they left the office. Avi put his arm around Chava's shoulder, looking very comfortable with her. While as a woman she was jealous of Chava, as a human being she was happy that Avi found a good person to love and who loved him back. *That could be a good story to write*, she thought as she walked back to her own office.

CHAPTER TWENTY-EIGHT

A vi drove Chava back to Tel Aviv to catch her flight to Eilat. They spent most of the forty minute drive in silence, each of them in thought about various scenarios that were waiting for them. "I would really like to introduce you to my family," said Avi breaking the silence.

"I would like that very much too," she replied and squeezed his right hand on the steering wheel.

"How do you feel about getting married when it's all over?" he asked her. Chava smiled and she thought that he was actually very cute as he acted like he was fully concentrating on driving, when in reality, he was probably concerned of getting a negative answer from her.

"I feel very strongly," she said and she just couldn't help it, she had to laugh.

He was quiet for a few more minutes and then he began to laugh too. "You make me feel like a young kid asking his parents permission to drive their new car," he remarked.

"Avi," Chava's voice turned serious. "Have you thought about where we are going to live?" she asked him.

Avi was taken aback by her question. "Here, in Israel of course," he said with certainty. Chava pulled her hand back and brushed her hair out of her face.

"I am an American," she said to Avi. "I love the United States and what it stands for. America gave me liberty, freedom and a brand new life. I can't just throw everything away, give up everything and move here," she took a deep breath. "You surely can't expect that from me," she remarked.

The smile disappeared from Avi's face and he did not respond to her words, he remained silent for the rest of their journey. At the airport after going through several security checkpoints, he put a police sign on his windshield when he stopped in front of the terminal. He escorted Chava to the ticket counter and he showed an identification card to the agent. The two of them spoke briefly while the person keyed and printed Chava's airline ticket.

Chava was torn emotionally and she wasn't feeling well which she did not want to mention to Avi. She was having dizzy spells and she blamed the pastry that she consumed at the police station for the nausea she was experiencing. That was only the physical aspects of her inner struggle. On the one hand she was concerned about Avi's mission to rescue her longtime friend Sandy, but on the other hand, she was concerned that Avi and his men may arrive too late to find her friend alive. Of course, there was the sudden obstacle that none of them thought about earlier, where would they live after they got married. While Chava liked Israel, she was not certain that she wanted to spend the rest of her life there.

She immigrated to the United States to be an American, which was her only childhood dream. Although she lived in other countries when her Army officer husband was stationed overseas, she always knew that her home was back in California. She did not want to lose Avi because she loved him, and she wanted to be with him. Unfortunately Chava could not think of any permanent solution to their situation, she needed to hear or come up with some reasonable suggestion, but it seemed that both of them stubbornly held their stand, and were not willing to compromise.

Still without talking to her, Avi guided Chava into the direction of the departure gate as her flight was scheduled to leave a half an hour later. The small plane was already parked near by the gate and the airline employees were preparing to board the passengers. "I have to go," Avi said abruptly. "Perhaps I'll see you in Eilat," he remarked and tried to avoid looking at Chava.

She looked at him sadly and leaned to him. "Avi, please let's not part this way. I love you and I want to be with you."

"Then you will move here to Israel," he replied stubbornly.

"It's not that simple," Chava shook her head. "I told you, I am an American and I am not convinced that I belong here."

"And I am an Israeli and this is my country," replied Avi and finally looked directly at her. "I suppose we have to make a big decision about our future together when we meet again," he said with sadness on his face and Chava could have sworn that there were tears in his blue eyes.

The boarding call sounded and Chava reached out for Avi but he pulled away. "Avi," Chava pleaded with him. "Don't let me go feeling like this."

Avi looked back at her as he was walking away without giving a reply or kissing her goodbye. Chava turned back towards the gate and wiped her tears away. After her ticket was confirmed, she walked to the door that led to the tarmac where the plane was waiting for departure to the seaport city of Eilat. Once on board, Chava took her seat and buckled up her seat belt. She hoped that nobody was going to sit next to her. Chava turned her face toward the window not as much to look outside, but to hide the tears that were streaming down on her face.

She felt a hand on her shoulder and for a second she thought that the flight attendant wanted to say something to her. To her surprise, it was Avi standing there. He bent down to kiss her and he whispered to her. "I am so sorry about my behavior. I love you Chava, we will work something out, I promise."

She managed to squeeze a little smile on her face after she kissed him back. One of the flight attendants said something to Avi in Hebrew, and Chava, although she did not understand the words, she knew that the plane was about to depart and Avi had to leave. "Please be very careful," Chava said to him, and then she added. "I would love to have Sandy as my maid of honor at our wedding."

Avi's face was very serious as he left the plane, turning around one more time from the door before stepping out from the airplane. Chava could not explain why, but she was simply unable to stop crying. The passengers on the opposite side of the aisle from her seat glanced at her curiously, but once again she turned toward the window and silently sobbed into her Kleenex tissues. She felt emotionally and physically exhausted.

The plane was cleared for departure and Chava was on her way to fulfill her mother's final wish to have her ashes scattered into the Red Sea.

CHAPTER TWENTY-NINE

Hebron with its ancient history, and its violent present one fell under a joint jurisdiction of Israelis and Palestinians. It was a fact that the military action planners had difficulty to ignore if they wanted to avoid an international incident. The city was located less than 90 kilometers from Tel Aviv and about the half of that from Jerusalem, yet the cities were worlds apart. Within the city lived over one hundred thousand Arabs, but the surrounding areas also had Jewish settlers, whom were met not only with disapproval from the Arabs, but they were forced to deal with their deep resentment and hatred.

Hebron's history was both fascinating and tragic. The city was founded by Hittites, and was later liked by King David with such a high degree that he actually made Hebron his capital city. Unfortunately, like many other countries of that era, Hebron was not exempt from Roman invasion and destruction by fire, just to be rebuilt some time later. Of course, eventually the city of Hebron once again fell under the occupation of Muslims. The Crusades also reached the city and the long string of musical chairs of occupants of Hebron began in the 1100s.

Many centuries later, in 1917, it was the British troops turn to capture the city and they remained there until Israel was announced as an independent state. Although some British troops were present, they were unable to prevent the riots between the Arabs and the Jew. By the time 1936 arrived, there were no Jewish families left in Hebron due to the constant threats to the life of the Jewish community.

As a result of the 1967 Six-Day War, Hebron fell under the Israeli government control, and Jewish families began to move back into the city decades after the notorious riots that took place there. A few years later, authorized by the Knesset, settlements began to appear east of Hebron, an action that met the disapproval of Hebron's Arab population. Needless to say, the newly established Jewish community immediately became a subject for of harassments and target by terrorists.

Hebron was also considered a Holy city both by the Arabs and the Jews. According to the Bible, in the Book of Genesis, Abraham purchased property in Hebron where the Tomb of the Patriarch was built, and where he was buried along side with his wife Sarah. It is also said that even Isaac, Jacob and their wives, Rebekah and Leah were also buried there.

Avi faced many hurdles in planning his unit's rescue mission of the kidnapped American woman, Sandy Johnston, Chava's longtime friend. Whoever was Chava's friend was a friend of his as well. The information he received by the eyewitness, who also happened to be an informer was that Sandy was seen in a car that was headed toward the direction of the recently opened Arab market.

Hebron was situated in the Judean hills and while the city was dominantly Arab, over seven thousand Jewish people lived in the adjacent community called Kiryat Arba, that happened to be the most frequently quoted explanation for the presence of the soldiers of the Israeli Defense Forces, or IDF for short.

On the main road toward the city the travelers must passed through an Israeli check point to enter the city, which was divided into H1 an H2 sections according to the established so called "Hebron Protocol". It meant that the H1 area, the larger of the two was under full control of the Palestinian Security Forces, while in the H2 section the Israeli military maintained control over several aspects of daily life of the Palestinians who lived there. It included several restrictions imposed on Palestinian businesses and other activities inside the city. Among the several restricting imposed by the "Hebron Protocol," the IDF was restricted from entering the H1 section unless the Palestinian Security Forces were also present.

And that was Avi's major dilemma. From intelligence gathering he knew the exact location of the particular house where Sandy Johnston was kept in the H1 section, and it was right off the Arab market. Of course, it meant the presence of people during the daylight hours. Despite that fact, it was still easily approachable if the timing was right.

Avi was one of those people in the Israeli Special Forces community who was not willing to share information with any other branches before their missions, unless it was absolutely necessary and only if it was a joint maneuver. Trusting anyone was a big issue with him and by tracking and meeting with such person as Daniel Zehavi, whom he considered a traitor by every sense of the word, just re-enforced his view on sharing as limited information as possible with others outside his unit. It was difficult for him to make the call, but he had no choice, he had to contact the IDF officer in charge at the IDF outpost outside Hebron. He introduced himself as Major Shlomi Osman.

The officer was cooperative with him and he suggested that perhaps they could talk to a person in the Palestinian Security Force whom he fairly trusted as they shared a common goal, to prevent terrorist activities on both sides. He hoped that perhaps talking to the Palestinian officer would give them easier access, and perhaps even manpower. Avi told him to hold on to that thought for a few minutes so he could think the suggestion over and that he would get back to him.

Within a few minutes after his telephone conversation with Major Osman, he assembled his most trusted eleven member team and he asked their opinion on what they thought of the IDF officer's suggestion. There were several minutes of silence in the room, filled with hesitation which Avi sensed right away. "They that the answer had to be a "yes" or a "no," there were no place for a "maybe." We either try to work with the Palestinians on this case or we do it ourselves. I have to say that it's my opinion that it could easily backfire if we let them into our plans and if someone notifies the hostage takers or it could work if they want to get rid of those terrorists themselves. I must also remind you that there aren't many good examples of tangible cooperation between us, the Israelis and the Palestinians. I want to hear your input and then I will make my decision," said Avi, and he looked at each of his men while he rested his eyes on his closest and longtime friend, Captain Tomer Gadir. Tomer was sitting on the floor with his long legs crossed with his mouth steadily chewing the ever present gum.

Avi trusted everyone in his Special Forces Unit, especially within that in his Elite Hostage Rescue Team that counted up to twelve members, including him, but Tomer was very special soldier with his nerves of steel. Avi had never seen him lose his patience and he always remained calm even under some hair raising situations the team encountered during some of their missions.

Tomer was tall, and his dark hair was cut in a military fashion. His dark brown eyes were always full of life, at any given moment he was always ready to smile. Despite his easy going temperament, he was extremely protective over his family and his friends, or anyone he served with him. He was the type of man and comrade whom people wanted to be around because he gave them the sense of safety and security. Everyone who knew Tomer was certain that he would sacrifice his life to save innocent people from demise.

As one could imagine, Tomer was liked by everyone, especially by his teammates who endlessly teased him for being brave and fearless in deadly situations, yet he was extremely shy when it came to meeting women in general. Perhaps that was the reason why at age thirty-four he remained unmarried; no matter how good looking he was and had an easy going nature.

Off duty Avi and Tomer hung out together and even their families socialized. Often they spoke among each other about what they expected from a woman whom they were destined to meet, fall in love and they would marry. Avi met that person in Chava, and when he told Tomer about her, and only Tomer in his unit, he was genuinely happy for his friend Avi. He jokingly asked him if Chava had any sisters or friends. When Avi told him that as a matter of fact she did have a very nice friend named Sandy, Tomer got excited and he began to demand a description of Sandy Johnston from Avi.

He intensely listened as Avi told him about Sandy's cheerful personality, and he also mentioned that far as he knew Sandy got divorced because of her husband's unfaithfulness which was only briefly mentioned to him by her during their short encounter in Tel Aviv. He added that Daniel Zehavi, the Israeli Colonel who betrayed his country, also expressed interest in Sandy, whom he met at the hotel's bar while she was waiting for Chava to come downstairs. He wasn't sure how far their relationship developed, if there was a relationship at all. Avi confirmed to Tomer that Sandy was an innocent person who fell into the hands of a traitor, who sold her out to his terrorist friends.

When he finished talking about Sandy and Chava, Avi noticed that his friend's hands turned into a fist and all Avi could do is smile. He knew that Tomer was ready to take any action necessary to rescue Sandy. That conversation took place a couple of days earlier before they rescued Chava from Hassan's yacht. Tomer became convinced more than ever that it was God's will for him to be among those who rescue Sandy, and that she was sent his way to meet the love of his life. Avi tried to bring down Tomer's enthusiasm, not knowing if Sandy would even like his friend, but it was an impossible task. Once Tomer made up his mind about something, there was not a single person who could change his mind, so Avi gave up trying after just one time. Avi decided that he would just let destiny take over, whatever was meant to be will happen no matter what they do. He had one major concern, and it was the fact they didn't even know if Sandy Johnston was still alive or became an innocent victim of an incredible conspiracy.

Sitting there he once again looked at each of his teammates, and his eyes remained on Tomer. He was waiting for a response to his questions regarding the possibility of a joint rescue maneuver. "What do you think Tomer?" Avi asked him. Tomer shrugged his shoulder and glanced at the others sitting and some of them standing around him.

"It could work, but as you said, we would be taking a great risk. Of course, we wouldn't have to tell them the exact location of the house until we get close enough to our target and ready for the assault." He stopped for a moment. "I think we should do it," he said finally and pulled his Uzi from behind his back to the front on his chest.

Avi looked around and it seemed that everybody agreed with Tomer. He smiled at the Captain and nodded. "So be it," he agreed. "If it works, we may be used as an example for a good neighbor policy, and if not," he stopped in mid sentence. "No, it's going to work. Get ready, we meet up in fifteen minutes at the MPC in the back of this building. Check and double check your weapons, ammunition and your gear," Avi instructed his team as he took out his cell phone.

Major Shlomi Osman picked up the phone at the first ring and quickly introduced himself. Avi briefly talked to him and he explained that he didn't wish to give all details to the Palestinians ahead of time to prevent a possible leak of information to the kidnappers. Major Osman agreed that it was probably a good idea. He told Avi that the Palestinian security officer's name was Captain Ahmed Rabbani whom he knew from previous joined search encounters. He thought that Rabbani was a decent human being who tried to protect his own people from the terrorist's influence knowing that they were hiding among them. Avi informed him that they would be on the road within minutes, and that they would discuss the details once they met up at the checkpoint, rather than discussing it over unsecured telephone lines.

The Military Personnel Carrier, MPC for short, was ready to leave and Avi was the last one to climb on board. All of them were wearing their usual mission outfits, green uniform, but at this particular time, instead of wearing the usual black hood, their faces were marked with camouflage paint to protect their identities from potential revenge seekers as much as possible.

CHAPTER THIRTY

Hebron was located a little over thirty-eight miles from Jerusalem. Within a half an hour when they reached the IDF outpost and check point, Major Shlomi Osman was waiting for them outside the building. As the MPC arrived and Avi got out, he noticed the Major right away, but he also noticed the tall Palestinian talking to Osman as he leaned against a blue Toyota truck with blue license plates with POLICE written in Arabic, Hebrew and in English on its side.

After walking up to them, Avi saluted and introduced himself. They all shook hands in a friendly, yet professional matter. Avi asked Osman if there was a relatively secure place where the three of them could talk. Major Osman showed him a small building behind them, it served as his command center, as he smilingly explained. They quickly walked inside. It was getting dark already and Avi wanted to get the "show" on the road.

Captain Rabbani intensely listened as Avi talked and he took notes. "I want you to understand that if you are cooperating with us you may make some enemies among your people and you may also loose some of your men during the rescue mission."

Rabbani nodded and answered him in English, their common language. "We are never going to have peace if terrorists use our city as a safe haven. After Major Osman called me, I talked to several of my rescue squad team members who are specially trained for hostage rescue missions and they all agreed to help. I must admit some of them were a little bit surprised at first when I told them that IDF Special Forces was also going to be involved, but they would not question my authority. Also, there is a general understanding that an innocent life is in danger and something must be done to free her," he answered to Avi.

"Very well then," said Avi and looked around in the room. "I have a map but I would prefer a detailed street map around the Arab market," he inquired from them.

Rabbani opened the small brief case he was carrying and pulled out a map. "I thought you may need it," he said and smiled at Avi.

164

"Thanks," replied Avi and returned his smile. He looked at the map closely and pointed at the house on the detailed map. "If the information we received is correct," he explained. "Sandy Johnston is held hostage in this house."

"I know the area very well," said Rabbani. "Actually my parents live a few blocks from it. What we need is a diversion so we can block off the street. There is also a back street, right behind the house. As you know most of our streets are rather narrow and winding, but that particular backstreet is a dead end so that could be helpful."

"What kind of diversion you have in mind?" asked Avi.

"A car accident where nobody gets hurt, but argument would ensue and the police would have to block off the street as a diversion," Rabbani said and smiled again.

Avi laughed. "Good idea," he agreed and looked at his watch. "How long would it take for you to organize all this and get your people ready?" he asked from the Police Captain.

Rabbani also checked his watch before he replied. "If I make the call now, we could be action ready in less than an hour," he replied.

"How many of your personnel are going to be involved?" inquired Avi from him.

"Fifteen," he responded and he asked Avi return. "And how many did you bring?"

"Twelve, including myself," he answered. "That makes twenty-seven against an unknown number of terrorists," he remarked.

"That is true, so we must be entering, rescue and leave within a few minutes before others could be alarmed," said Rabbani.

"I could spare some people," suggested the Major but after Avi thanked him, he turned Osman's offer down. "Your people need to secure the entrances and exits, and you already have a handful with the problems with the settlers. Thanks anyway," he said to the Major.

"I was also thinking about private vehicles," suggested Rabbani. "If your MPC is noticed on a street of Hebron's H1 section, it could cause an immediate alert."

Avi looked at him with pleasant surprise. "Excellent idea Captain," he admitted. "How would you get the cars out here?"

"That shouldn't be a problem. I have a couple of vans only a few minutes from the city's entrance and they could be here in ten minutes after I make a couple of calls," he explained. "We can pick up your people while mine stage the car accident and block off the road. At the same time my hostage rescue team could take their position around the back of the house, unless you want to do that part," he inquired.

"Your plan sounds great," Avi agreed and looked at the map closely one more time. "Let's get on with it," he said.

Captain Rabbani took out a cell phone and made three phone calls while Osman who spoke Arabic listened in. Avi looked at him questioningly and after Rabbani finished his calls, Major Osman gave thumbs up to Avi.

They went outside and Rabbani shook hands with Avi. Before he got into his truck, Avi asked him to check his watch and coordinate it with his, but both of them showed the correct time. Avi saluted him as Rabbani drove off and he walked back to the MPC to brief his team about the plan the three of them had worked out. There were some concerned looks exchanged between them and it didn't go without Avi's notice. "Look guys," he said. "I will not hold it against you if you don't want to participate, I never had. If I have to go by myself with the Palestinians, so be it."

"What have you been smoking Colonel?" Tomer asked from Avi.

"What?" Avi asked him in return, but than he heard his team break out in laughter. He looked at them and he laughed too, his man would never let him go by himself, they were ready to die for him if he asked them to. "Alright guys," said Avi when the laughing died down. "In about ten minutes, two Palestinian vans will be arriving to transfer us inside H1 sector and to our position and then let's do our job that we were trained to do," Avi said and looked around. Every one of them saluted him as he climbed out of MPC to wait for the vans promised to them by the Palestinian Police Captain Ahmed Rabbani.

CHAPTER THIRTY-ONE

The next hour and a half passed as quickly as an unexpected lightning. The two unmarked vans arrived and Avi's Special Forces team was transferred inside the city. They parked a short distance apart on the street in front of the house they suspected Sandy Johnston was held hostage. Avi hoped that despite the fact that the houses were built adjacent to each other that would not turn out to be a problem. On his headset he heard Captain Rabbani's voice as he told him that his men were in position, but it was also heard by all of Avi's team members as well.

There was no traffic on the street from either direction. Rabbani's traffic accident plan was working perfectly. The police managed to barricade off both end of the street leading to the direction of the area where the rescue mission was about to take place. Avi told Rabbani that his team will enter the house from the front in two minutes, and then his men should enter the house from the back two minutes after that. He warned Rabbani to use precaution; he didn't want his men to die from friendly fire. Rabbani expressed the same concern for his personnel.

The house had some lights on the upper level, the first floor was in darkness. Avi suspected that perhaps there was a basement to the house as well, and where possibly Sandy was held, or at least he hoped that she was still alive.

Two minutes after his brief conversation with Rabbani, Avi signaled to his men to leave the vans and approach the house. He led one part of the team and his friend, Captain Tomer Gadir led the other from the second van. Just as they approached the house and ran up on the front steps, an older Palestinian man stepped outside from his house next door. The time frame while he stopped in shock and was virtually paralyzed with fear seeing the camouflage Israeli commanders was enough for the Palestinian policemen who drove the Israelis inside Hebron, to walk up to him, and coerced him to sit in one of the vans for the duration of the rescue attempt.

Avi tried to open the front door and to his amazement it was not locked. He motioned to his team who were standing by and stooping on the steps towards the front door and both sides of the door. He pushed the door handle down carefully, hoping that it was not booby trapped. They were in luck, it opened noiselessly, not giving as much as a squeaking sound. Avi entered first and he was closely followed by the others. They carefully surveyed and silently searched the first floor, room by room on the long hallway, but they encountered no one. There were items laying around which gave them the impression that the house was lived in and had more than one occupant. Captain Rabbani and part of his team entered through the back door and they were also unable to locate anyone.

Noises of moving about reached them from the floor above and as they carefully looked around with their night vision goggles attached to their helmets, Avi motioned with his hand upward. The staircase was old but made out of cement which quieted their movements. Tomer was the first one going up and just as he approached the top of the stairs, he found himself face to face with a Palestinian wearing a traditional headdress, a keffiyeh. Before he could say a word, Tomer's Glock handgun ended the terrorist's troubled life. His lifeless body tumbled down the steps as the team members stepped aside to let the body roll all the way to the first floor.

Noise of glass breaking on the floor above gave a cue to Avi and his men that Captain Rabbani's men entered the second floor through three windows from the back by rappelling down from the roof on robes. Kicking the windows in with their feet, they tried to spread out on the hallway which was very similar to the ground floor's hallway with six rooms altogether, three on each side.

Rabbani confirmed into his headphone to Avi and his team, that they were in the building and Avi's team also rushed forward. Within minutes a chaotic firefight broke out between the terrorists and the two teams and three of Avi's men fell wounded to the floor and so did four of the Palestinian policemen. The terrorists were cornered and they were determined to die rather than become prisoners. They had nothing but their lives to loose and with that in mind, they wanted to take as many Israelis and Palestinian policemen with them as possible.

Avi carefully and very quickly looked inside the furthest room that remained the only terrorist controlled area of the house. His eyes fell on one of the Palestinians who was holding a cell phone, attempting to make a call perhaps to either alert his terrorist comrades or call for back up. Either way, he was unable to make the phone call due to Avi's quick action. Another Palestinian, the last one alive, tried to make a run for it and jumped out from the second story window to the street below. While he survived the fall, he was immediately arrested and despite his broken ankle, he was not taken to the hospital as he demanded while cursing the Palestinian rescue team members, who remained behind to cover the back street in case of another escape attempt by the terrorists.

Within minutes, six Palestinian terrorists were dead and yet, the room by room search proved to be fruitless, they came up with nothing, and without Sandy. There was no sign of the kidnapped American woman anywhere.

Captain Rabbani noticed the look of disappointment on Avi and his men's face as they were attending to their wounded comrades just as his men did with the fallen policemen. "What about basements, do these houses have basements?" Avi asked him. The Palestinian Police Captain nodded and motioned to his men to follow him. Avi gave orders to have his wounded soldiers taken downstairs and the rest of them to follow him and the Palestinian policemen.

It took them several minutes to locate the basement door as it was covered with heavy Bedouin rugs, obviously with the intent to hide it from undesired visitors. Avi ordered the bomb expert from his team to check if the door leading to the basement was booby trapped or not. Once again luck was on their side, they were able to venture down to the impressively large, dungeon like basement without any interference by anyone particular.

They took each step very carefully, not knowing what they may find. Rabbani quietly said it in his headset what Avi also noticed, that there was a ray of light visible around the corner, as the basement curved around huge cement beams underneath the entire house.

Avi motioned with his fingers who would go forward and who would stay behind to guard the entrance and to cover them. Tomer, Captain Rabbani and Avi at the front with three of their team members covering them, slowly scanned the other areas of the basement for possible hidden rooms or passages.

The sight that welcomed them was terrifying. A Palestinian stood almost at the end of the corner with a gun pointing at Sandy's head. She was kneeling facing the arriving commandos with her hands tied behind her back. Tomer's lips parted when he saw her and Sandy's eyes met with his. It was a scene straight out of a Western movie in which the enemies pointed their guns at each other, and when both of them could be dead within seconds. The commandos were pointing their Uzis at the terrorist and he had a handgun pointing at Sandy's head.

Without looking at Tomer's direction, Avi could sense that something incredible just happened between Tomer and Sandy. It was impossible not to notice the stare between the two and sudden panic grabbed Avi by his heart. He knew Tomer way to well, and he knew that his friend may try to do something that he would not be able to prevent.

The Palestinian yelled in their direction in Arabic, and Captain Rabbani responded with a pleading voice which seemingly angered the terrorist. "What is he saying?" Avi whispered to Rabbani.

"He said that if we don't leave within the next five minutes, he is going to kill Ms. Johnston and he does not care if he dies afterwards," he translated.

Avi glanced at Tomer and he could see that his friend had great difficulty controlling his temper. Just as he turned back toward Sandy, Tomer with his Glock in hand leaped forward, and that very same moment the Palestinian terrorist hand with the gun changed direction and fired two shots at Tomer's way, hitting him in the chest. Sandy's scream was bone chilling. "No . . . ," and then she quickly leaped to her feet and bit into the terrorist's gun holding hand. At the very same instant, Avi fired a single shot and the bullet from his handgun hit the terrorist exactly between his eyes. He was dead in that second.

Sandy dashed toward Tomer and kneeled down next to him on the floor, as Captain Rabbani was untying her hands. "Who are you?" she asked whispering while touching Tomer's smooth face. "Please don't die on me," she pleaded with him. Avi and the team's medic also kneeled down to the seemingly unconscious soldier. Tomer's eyes opened and the first person he saw was Sandy's tear soaked face. "Are you alright?" asked Sandy.

"Yeah," said Tomer and tried to sit up, than he changed his mind and let Sandy hold him. "But I think I'll swallow my gum," he said and smiled.

"What?" asked Sandy not being sure if she heard him correctly.

There was laughter by the rest of the commandos who surrounded them. The medic pulled off the flack jacket that Tomer was wearing over his fatigue and pulled two bullets from the front. He unbuttoned Tomer's shirt, and other than some deep redness in the area where the bullets hit the flack jacket, there was no physical injury to Tomer.

"That's enough fun for one day, don't you think?" Avi asked as he grabbed Tomer's arm, pulling him up to his feet. Tomer turned around and looked at the dead terrorist. "We have to get out here," Avi stated the obvious and as if it was a direct order, his team and the Palestinian hostage rescue team left the house. Captain Rabbani told Avi outside before they parted that he will file a complete report on the rescue mission and wished Avi and his team a safe journey back to Jerusalem.

They boarded the two vans waiting outside and they released the older Palestinian man who was confused of what was going on to say the least. Avi joined two of his team members, and the three soldiers who were hurt, fortunately none of them seriously, in the second van. Once they arrived back to the IDF outpost, a medical helicopter was called in to airlift the three injured soldiers for medical treatments.

In the first van, Tomer and Sandy were sitting next to each other as they traveled back to Jerusalem. Fellow team members began to smile among each other seeing that every time Sandy looked at Tomer, his face would turn red. Sandy reached out and took his hand that was resting on his stretched out leg and held it until they arrived back to the biblical city.

"I don't know how to thank you," said Sandy and she just couldn't take her eyes off Tomer. He felt an incredible sensation each time he glanced or looked at her and he just couldn't get over the feeling that struck him when he saw her for the first time, kneeling in that basement with a gun pointing at her head. *If there is such thing as love at first sight, then I am in love,* he thought.

Avi walked up to them as they stood in a small office in the Jerusalem police station and he couldn't help smiling. *So finally Tomer found someone who caught his interest,* Avi thought and he felt hopeful for the two of them. At the same time, he couldn't help thinking about the person he was missing the most, of course, it was Chava. And then, just then he finally realized what he had to do.

CHAPTER THIRTY-TWO

C hava never got sick flying on an airplane before, but she just couldn't help it on her flight to Eilat. She barely had enough time to grab the bag from the back of the seat in front of when she lost what little food she had in her stomach. She could not imagine why she got sick. She guessed that her light headedness and nausea was caused by stress that rattled her nerves. Her mother's death, the visit to Auschwitz, the situation with Avi, Sandy's and even her own kidnapping was enough to cause a breakdown to anyone. She couldn't help thinking that by scattering her mother's ashes into the Red Sea would sever any physical contact with the last family member she knew. Of course, there was still Hilde, a name that gave her cold chills. She could never, ever consider her as a real relative. Hilde was a side product of a monster, and nothing more. Chava was certain that Hilde would get the punishment that she so rightfully deserved.

The flight attendant brought her a cool wet towel and she pressed it against her burning forehead. *Maybe I am coming down with something,* she thought, although she had no idea what was causing her physical illness. The mental part was not that hard to figure out. "I have some airsickness pills if you like," offered the flight attendant but Chava didn't want any and she politely turned down the offer.

Arriving in Eilat she was glad to see that the courtesy limousine was once again waiting for her, just like when she arrived there at the first time. Back at the hotel she was informed that her belongings were still in the same room where she stayed before and the Concierge also informed her that there would be no charges for the hotel room while she was forced to be away under the most disturbing circumstances. She thanked the young man and grabbed the card that opened her door.

She let the water run in her bathtub until it was almost full and she poured some bath oil into the water. She lowered herself into the water and soaked what seemed like hours, although it was only a short time, when the ringing of the telephone woke her up. She tried to get out of the water but she became very dizzy. By the time she managed to make it to the phone, it stopped ringing. Chava was angry with herself. There she was buck naked and dripping all over the place and she couldn't even make it to the lousy telephone. She wanted Avi there and suddenly she felt very alone as if she was abandoned.

She slowly made it back to the bathtub where she let the bath water drain while she dried herself. Chava looked in the mirror and she didn't like what she saw. She looked very tired, and her face was very pale. *I need to eat and drink something;* she thought and went back inside to call for room service. In the small refrigerator she found a bottle of mineral water which she drank almost at once. She glanced at the clock on the nightstand and she decided to lay down on the bed that had not been touched by anyone for days.

The knock on the door woke her up. "Who is it?" she asked.

"Room Service," she heard an unfamiliar voice. She looked through the peep hole and indeed it was the room service. She opened the door. The young man in the hotel's uniform placed her food at the table, and after she gave him a few dollars, he left her room. Chava was so hungry that she devoured both main entrees she ordered, not being sure which one she wanted, and when she finished, she felt full and not so light headed.

Her mind wandered back to Avi and restless thoughts began to bother her again. What if Sandy was already dead? What if Avi got killed during the rescue mission? Tears clouded her eyes and she couldn't think straight when another thought occurred to her. What was she going to do if Avi dies? She regretted every word she told him about not wanting to move to Israel. There just had to be a solution for their situation because she didn't want to be apart from him.

She went out to the balcony of her hotel room and her heart became full with the beauty of the scenery in view. The sun was settling over the Bay of Aqaba or as it was also known as the Bay of Eilat. The city was a resort town that bordered the Red Sea and the nearby desert, located in the southernmost tip of Israel. It was a favorite destination for vacationers, honeymooners and most of all, foreign tourists. The borders to Jordan and Egypt were only a few minutes drive away which made Eilat an even more attractive destination. Chava could see the bay or so called inlet of the Red Sea from her hotel's balcony, and as she leaned on the balcony's railing, she could feel the wafting of the warm, yet most welcomed evening breeze.

She finally felt better than she had been feeling all day, and while she didn't know for certain what caused the sudden change in her physical wellness, she was glad that her nausea stopped and her dizziness was gone. By feeling better, her emotional state also improved and everything seemed somewhat brighter than earlier on that particular day.

Chava returned to her room and rang the Concierge desk. A couple of moments later a pleasant voice answered and she recognized it from an earlier time. She asked the Concierge if he would be kind enough to arrange a boat ride for her for the following morning. He asked her to give him a few minutes, and he assured Chava that he would get back to her as soon as possible. She agreed and hung up the telephone.

She booted up her computer and not surprisingly she found virtually hundreds of messages from various people and organizations. Chava scrolled down and reviewed the subjects of pages and pages of emails and she came across a message from her literary agent that she knew she couldn't possibly ignore. She clicked on the reply button and wrote to her agent, Angela that she needed to contact her publisher to tell them that she would have to delay the upcoming signing tour for a later day because of circumstances beyond her control. She did not elaborate any further on the subject.

She read some more email, mostly from people who were concerned about her whereabouts for various reasons. She left the messages in her inbox to be answered at a later time. As she sat there, a smile appeared on her face as an idea of a new story began to shape up in her mind, the story of her mother. "You will live on after all my sweet mother," she blurted out loud and touched the urn that contained her mother's ashes. "I will title the book "Once Upon a Time . . ."

Her thoughts were interrupted by the ringing of the telephone. The Concierge informed her that he secured a boat ride for her on the following morning. The Captain of the boat was willing to take her further out to the actual sea and not just around the bay. Chava thanked him and hung up the telephone.

CHAPTER THIRTY-THREE

The hotel's restaurant was not crowded at all when she walked in and she asked the Maitre'd if it was possible for her to sit at the terrace. He gladly obliged and she was seated at possibly the best table that overlooked the bay. The morning breeze was still present; but the sun was determined to show its daily routine, it promised to be another hot day. The waiter who spoke English told her that the expected temperature for that day was going to be over 100 degrees. She thanked him for the information and began to eat her breakfast that she selected from the buffet style serving.

She could barely make it up to her floor of her hotel room where she staggered into the bathroom and threw up. She pushed a cold towel to her forehead and stared in the mirror. *It just can't be true,* she thought suspiciously. The telephone rang and she angrily yelled out, "What now?" she picked up the telephone and asked. "Yes?"

"Excuse Ms. Diamond, your ride is here to take you to the harbor for your boat ride," said the seemingly ever present Concierge.

"Okay, thank you. I'll be right down," replied Chava and went back to the bathroom to freshen up. She changed into light pants and a short sleeved blouse, then pulled out a scarf from her dresser drawer and tied it around her neck. She took out the leather carrier case from the closet and placed her mother's urn inside. Chava slowly zipped up the bag and made her way downstairs.

In the middle of the car door that picked her up in front of the hotel's entrance had a large round blue marking on the driver's side with "Beer Sheba" written with small black letters inside of a circle. "Shalom," said the young man and asked her something in Hebrew. Chava informed him that she didn't speak his language. He apologized and he asked her in English if she preferred to sit in the front or in the back seat of the car.

Without giving an answer she got in on the passenger side, next to the driver. He started up the car's engine right away and drove quietly for a while. His curiosity got the best of him and he asked her politely where she was from?

Chava told him that she was from California and in return she asked him if he had ever been there.

"Are the beaches as nice as here?" he asked.

She smiled at him and assured him that they were. "And where are you from?" asked Chava.

"I was born and raised in Beer Sheba, but I always wanted to live by water. After the Army I moved here and bought a boat, taking tourists to fish or just for a boat ride, such as yourself," he explained. "By the way, my name is Ro'i," he said and reached over with his left hand, switching the wheel into his right hand to shake hands with her.

It was a short ride from the hotel to harbor where his fishing boat was docked. "Let me guess," Chava smiled at him. "The name of your boat is Beer Sheba?"

He laughed looking at the direction of his tied up boat with "Beer Sheba" painted with large letters on one side in English and Hebrew on the other. "You're good," he laughed.

He helped her to step over the rail onto his boat. "It's a 275 Explorer," he explained proudly. "I wouldn't trade this boat with any other boats out on the market."

"I don't know much about boats but this one is very nice," Chava paid him a complement after looking around.

In the harbor there were dozens of smaller and larger boats docked either waiting for tourists who wanted to enjoy deep sea fishing or just docked there waiting for their owners to take them out for a joyous short or longer voyage of the bluest water Chava had ever seen.

He showed her around the boat and gave her the option to go down below and wait there in comfort or stay with him as he steered the boat out to open water. She sat down on the side seat, next to the pilot's seat still holding on to the leather case. "You can put it down, it won't go overboard," he suggested.

"No thanks, although that is the original idea," remarked Chava.

"Excuse me?" said Ro'i.

"The purpose of this short trip is to scatter my mother's ashes into the Red Sea," she explained.

"Wow," was the only response from the young man. A few minutes later he turned to Chava once again. "Was she from Israel?" he asked her.

"No," replied Chava. "She was a Holocaust survivor who just wanted to be cremated and have her ashes brought back to the land of her ancestors."

"Actually from a Jewish person that is not an unreasonable wish," said Ro'i and began to concentrate on maneuvering his boat out of the harbor. It was not an easy task and required sailing skills because of the virtually dozens of various size boats around them that also headed out to the open sea.

The water around the harbor was smooth and Chava prayed that the Red Sea around the bay wouldn't be too choppy either. There was no wind and the two quiet engines happily hummed as they powered the boat toward their master's destination. "I'll go as far as you want me to go, to but how far do you have in mind?" Ro'i asked her.

She shrugged. "Just go and we will see," she said not being sure of the distance. She sat back and placed the leather case between her feet. He was standing as he steered the boat and occasionally he looked at her, pointing out various race boats and telling her about their owners and the races they have won.

Chava closed her eyes and enjoyed the speed generated breeze hissing at her and by her. "Look, dolphins," she heard Ro'i's voice. She got up and looked over the side of the boat where several dolphins were swimming fast next to the boat as if it was some kind of competition. She smiled seeing the dolphins as they were one of her favorite sea creatures, yet she had never seen them in their natural habitat. Chava admired the dolphins trusting nature swimming along with boats and ships not thinking about the deadly harm humans could cast upon them.

She looked around and the shores of Jordan and Israel already looked like thin lines in the distance. Chava realized with surprise that most of the boats around them took different directions and with the exception a couple of sail boats, they were very much alone. "Ro'i," she called out the young man's name. "I think this place would be fine."

By her request, Ro'i began to slow the boat down and a few minutes later he turned off the engines. Chava reached down and placed the leather case on the pilot's seat and unzipped the bag. The marble like box didn't seem heavy at all and she was careful loosening up the top. She stepped back toward the edge of the boat and turned around. "Ro'i," she said. "I have a favor to ask"

"Yes," he said and stepped to her.

"You wouldn't happen to know any prayers in Hebrew would you?" she asked almost embarrassed.

"I think I can come up with a couple," he smiled at her. "Would you like me to say a prayer for your mother?" he asked Chava.

"I would appreciate that," she said gratefully.

Ro'i was about to go down to the sleeping quarters, but as he walked he touched the back pocket of his jeans and turned back around stepping next to her again pulling out a yarmulke. "Here it is," he exclaimed and placed it on the top of his head. "Are you ready?" he asked Chava. She nodded and removed the top from the urn.

Ro'i gently began to rock back and forth and with his eyes closed he began to pray. Chava didn't speak Hebrew but she recognized the word "Adonai" which meant "My Lord". She slowly turned the urn on its side and began to scatter her mother's ashes into the water of the Red Sea. She finished doing so at the same time Ro'i finished his prayer.

"Thank you," Chava said to him in a quiet and somber voice.

"No extra charge," Ro'i said smiling. "Would you like something to drink?" he asked her. "I have some sodas in the cooler," he offered.

"That would be nice, Diet Coke if you have any," she replied.

"You've got it," he said and went down below leaving Chava alone with her thoughts.

Chava could almost hear her mother's voice as Helene told her what one of her teachers said to her during one of those teacher and parent meetings. "Mrs. Diamond, I am sorry to tell you this, but someday you will shed a lot of tears because of Chava," said the teacher to Helene. Her mother was stunned and asked the teacher to clarify what he meant. He replied, "This country (Hungary) will not be big enough for your daughter and she will take every step possible to leave it. Chava is one of my brightest and most talented students I ever had the pleasure of teaching. She is more interested learning about world affairs than about chemistry or physics. But don't be alarmed, she will succeed no matter what she sets her mind to."

"Goodbye sweet mother," she said and turned around to the steps that led down to the sleeping quarters wondering what took Ro'i so long. She saw a man standing there, but it was not Ro'i. Her hands grabbed the railing and the recognition of the man sent shock waves through her entire body. He turned around to face her and in his hands he was holding a gun.

"Might as well say another prayer before you join your mother," he said to her.

Chava remained still and for some reason, she felt no fear. "Daniel," she said calmly. "I wish I can say that I am happy to see you but I would be lying." She glanced around. "There aren't any boats near by, how did you find me?" she asked curiously.

"I staked out the hotel and when I saw the car with "Beer Sheba" on it I went inside your hotel. I overhead the Concierge calling you to tell you that your ride has arrived and the rest was easy. I recalled why you came here in the first place. I came to the harbor, found this boat and hid downstairs," he explained calmly.

Chava's heart sank at the thought what Daniel might have done to Ro'i. "Did you kill him?" she asked quietly with her eyes showing flames of anger. Daniel shrugged his shoulders.

Chava felt immeasurable hatred toward Daniel. "You know," she said while she took a couple of steps towards him. "I have seen some people in my life time who I would consider cold blooded and sociopath, but this is my first and perhaps the last time in my life when I will look at someone and would consider him less than human."

"You are not helping yourself talking like that," he remarked without moving or lowering his gun.

"I hope that you don't expect me to beg for my life," remarked Chava without any fear. "I refuse to do that because your family didn't do it either when a Palestinian terrorist blew them into pieces," she said calmly.

"Shut up," Daniel shouted at Chava. "You did not know my family and you have no idea what they were about," he said to her angrily. Chava noticed that Daniel's hand was trembling as he pointed his gun at her.

"I know that they were Jewish, and I know that they were innocent," said Chava and stopped a couple of feet from him. "Do you think that they would have approved of you selling out the very country that gave shelter to millions of persecuted Jews from all over the world? I doubt that," Chava looked at him, but Daniel's eyes didn't even flinch. "I have no doubt that you loved your wife and children very much, but betraying your country by collaborating with their enemy is appalling," she continued.

Daniel shook his head and like a maniac he laughed out loud. "You don't have a clue what you are talking about," he yelled at Chava. "I sent my superiors dozens of messages and I virtually begged them to increase security on buses and on public transportation in general but my begging went unanswered."

"So let me understand this Daniel," Chava paused before she continued. "You didn't honestly believe that your collaboration with the Palestinians was going to stop those suicide bombings did you? Moreover, I strongly believe that because of your actions, there will be even more attacks, and what then? Other innocent victim's husbands, wives or children began to collaborate with those who believe that by killing themselves in the name of Allah would go to Paradise straight away and there will be seventy virgins waiting for them?" She shook her head disbelieving. She softened her voice as she added. "Daniel! Please just think about what you have done and what you have been doing?"

Daniel stared at her without saying anything for a while, then he slowly lowered his handgun to his side. "You know, you are probably right and I always knew that what I was doing was wrong, but I just had to do something that would hurt those too who choose to ignore my pleading. I loved my wife and children as I have never loved anything or anybody in this world. One day without warning, without having a chance to say goodbye to them, they were gone," he closed his eyes for a moment and then he looked directly at Chava. "It is life's irony that I was coming from our Headquarters where I dropped off yet another proposal about how to prevent carrying bombs onto passenger buses, when I heard the explosion just a few blocks from where I was," Daniel stopped and looked over at the quiet waters that surrounded the boat's area. "I knew right then that they were on that bus; my gut feeling told me that they took that earlier bus home. I ran like a crazed animal to the direction of the explosion, and then I saw this head on the sidewalk. It was a child's head with long blond hair with a big white ribbon still intact on the top of the head, where her hair from the sides of her face were pulled up into a bundle. My first thought, that it was a little bit funny, because the child's tongue was sort of sticking out of her mouth, you know, like a puppy's tongue when they are sleeping. Well, I just stood there for a moment when the realization struck me like lightning that was not just any child's head, but that head once belonged to my beloved daughter."

"Oh dear God," whispered Chava. Tears flooded her eyes and began to stream down her face. She covered her mouth with her hands.

Daniel stared at her and then he took a deep breath. "They were never quite able to put my wife, my son and my daughter together, no matter how hard they tried, you know, bits and pieces all over the place. Did you know that there is a bunch of Hassidic Jews who actually search and crawl around inch by inch to find all human remains?" he shook his head convincingly. "That is true; yet, there were just so many pieces to put back together. Apparently they stood right next to the suicide bomber," said Daniel in a matter of fact voice.

"Oh Daniel," said Chava. "I am so sorry."

"Yeah," nodded Daniel. "Everybody is so hot damn sorry about everything, yet nobody lifted a little finger to try to prevent what happened."

Chava did not reply right away, she just silently looked at Daniel. He seemed like a totally different person whom she first met in Tel Aviv. "Are you going to kill me?" she asked quietly.

Daniel looked up at her and he shook his head. "You are a good person Chava. No, I am not going to kill you. You don't deserve to die, but I do," he said and before Chava could say or do anything, Daniel lifted his handgun to his temple and shot himself in the forehead. He was already dead by the time his body landed on the floor of the boat. Chava screamed and kneeled down next to the dead man, but there was nothing she could have done.

She heard a weak voice from below and rushed downstairs to find Ro'i, laying on the ground holding his head, blood still dripping down on his t-shirt. "Are you alright?" he asked her.

"I am alright, how about you?" she asked him.

"I was so concerned when I heard the gunshot," he explained. "I prayed that he didn't hurt you."

"Thank you Ro'i," she said and she pressed a wet cloth on his bleeding head. "You think you can get up and go upstairs?" she asked him.

"I guess so," he replied and tried to get up.

"Maybe you better lay down," Chava suggested. "We have to get you to a doctor."

"He hit me so hard that I must have passed out right away," said Ro'i pushing the cloth tightly on his wound and he reached for Chava to help him to get up. He put his arms around her shoulder and taking one step at a time, they managed to go up to the deck.

Ro'i looked at Daniel's dead body lay at the end of his boat and he spit in his direction, then he turned his attention back to Chava. "Here is the key to the ignition," said Ro'i and he handed her several keys on a chain, singling out one of them.

"I have never driven a boat before," she said hesitantly.

"It's not much different from driving a car," he said encouragingly. "I will help you to steer once we get back to the busiest area of the harbor," Ro'i promised her and tried to get comfortable in the seat next to the pilot's. His head was throbbing from pain and he knew that he had a concussion because he had difficulty focusing from time to time.

Chava started up the engines and rolled the wheel slowly to make the boat turn around, back toward the Bay of Eilat. "You are doing great," Ro'i complemented her as they were nearing the harbor. Chava heard a sound of what appeared to be coming from the direction of the harbor and a couple of seconds later an Israeli military helicopter became visible in the distance.

Within minutes the chopper was nearly above them, but not wanting to stir up waves, it stayed a safe distance in the air. Chava recognized Avi right away he was hanging out on the helicopter's open door, waving at her. She waved back and she pointed at the direction of the harbor. The helicopter made one more circle above them then headed back to Port of Eilat.

Ro'i helped Chava to steer his boat back to the place where he usually docked and by the time they arrived back, Avi and an ambulance were waiting. The medic took a look at Ro'i's injury and he determined that he was certain that Ro'i indeed had suffered a concussion. Despite his objection, they loaded him up in the ambulance and took him to the hospital in Eilat.

Avi and the policemen in his company checked on Daniel's body and after Avi talked to the officials, they took the rest of the matter into their own hands, letting Avi take Chava back to the hotel.

"It's finally over," Avi said to her, walking next to each other, his arm around her shoulder. Chava had never felt so tired in her entire life as she felt then. Her nausea was returning and she was grateful that she didn't get sick during the boat ride. She tried to be strong, but as soon as she was safely in Avi's arms, she felt that all of her energy and strength suddenly abandoning her.

"What about Hilde? What is going to happen to her?" Chava inquired quietly.

Avi hesitated with his response but Chava was persistent. "Alright," he finally said. "Hilde is no longer with us."

"Did she escape?" Chava stopped him for moment.

"She didn't," replied Avi. "She was found dead in her jail cell. At this point of time, we are not certain of the cause of her death, but apparently she committed suicide."

Chava sighed. "I guess it is truly over."

"The case is, but you and I have some unfinished business to attend to," he said as he pushed the hotel door open for her to enter.

CHAPTER THIRTY-FOUR

She wasn't quite sure how she made it up to her hotel room, but there she was, standing in the middle of the room, trying to cope with the day's events. *It's just getting to be way too much to bear and comprehend,* Chava thought. At first she sat down on the couch, but soon she became restless and went to the desk to boot up her computer, then she lost patience once again. She turned to Avi. "I am so tired that I don't know what to do with myself," she said to him.

Avi stood there watching her for a few moments. "I know just exactly what you need," he said and went inside the bathroom, letting warm water run into the bathtub. On the bathroom counter he found some lilac bath oil and he poured a generous portion under the running water.

Avi returned inside the room and he found Chava sitting on the edge of the bed deep in thoughts. "What are you thinking about?" he asked while he took off her shoes and began to undress her. She did not reply and he didn't want to force her into a conversation that she didn't feel like having. Chava felt totally exhausted and she let him undress her down to her bra and panties, then she gently pushed his hesitating hands away, she took them off herself.

His heart was aching seeing her so emotionally and physically drained and he tried to find the way to refresh her mind and body. Avi returned to the bathroom to turn off the water, then he poked his head out. "The water is ready, come on." She was naked and too tired to feel embarrassed, besides, she felt comfortable in the presence of Avi.

She slowly made her way into the bathroom thinking that Avi was going to join her in the bathtub, but he just sat on the closed top of the toilet waiting for her. He smiled at her as she first tested the water temperature and then she stepped inside the fragranced water. She lowered herself in the tub and the water gently splashed around her, surrounding her and caressing her like a lover. "It's wonderful," she said to him thankfully and closed her eyes.

She could have easily fallen asleep if not for Avi, who kneeled down next to the bathtub and with a soft sponge loaded with liquid smoothing soap he slowly and gently began to wash her shoulders and her breasts. While with one arm he pulled her forward in the tub, he soaped and washed her back, then let her lay back once again. Chava didn't move when he began to wash her lower half. When she opened her eyes, tears rushed into them from what she witnessed.

Avi was not looking at her face, instead he was completely indulged in what he was doing. He concentrated on every move he made as he wanted to make absolutely certain that his touch was soft and gentle. When he finished washing her feet, he looked at her with so much love and admiration that those built up teardrops rolled down on Chava's face. She almost missed seeing it that Avi also had tears in his eyes. "I love you Avi," Chava whispered to him. He nodded that he knew, and then he reached for the towels he placed next to the tub and pushed it on his face. "What's wrong Avi?" she asked him not understanding the presence of his tears.

He took a deep breath and placed the sponge on the side of the bathtub. "For the first time in my life I was terrified earlier today because I thought that I lost you," he said softly and looked at her again. She lifted her arm out of the water and touched his face. "I have never been so scared in my life when I heard that someone spotted Daniel in Eilat. I knew that he was coming after you and I was not here to protect you."

"You can't be in two places at the same time and I choose to come back here by myself, remember?" Chava asked him.

He didn't reply. He reached inside the bathtub to check the water's temperature. "You better get out, the water is getting too cool," he suggested and offered his arms for Chava to get up. As she was getting up, Chava felt light headed, right away Avi's arms went around Chava to steady her. He wrapped her in a large bath towel and began to dry her, and then, as if she was a child, he combed her hair. When he was satisfied with what he was doing, he picked her up into his arms and carried her back to the bed.

"Can I get you anything before I take a shower?" he asked her.

"A glass of cold water perhaps," replied Chava.

From the small refrigerator in the room he removed a bottle of Evian water and poured it into a glass and gave it to her. Chava slowly sipped from it and when she drank enough, Avi took the glass back from her. "I'll be right back," he said and went to take a shower.

Chava laid back on the comfortable bed and stretched out under the soft comforter. As if she was watching a replay, the day's events rushed through her mind and when she closed her eyes, she thought that perhaps everything was just a nightmare. Chava imagined that she was back in her house in Sausalito, California and she was working on a suspense book where the heroine's mother dies, and after the funeral her friend gets kidnapped. As the story line continued, the heroine meets a devastatingly handsome stranger and falls in love. She smiled at what a great plot that story would make and with that thought, she fell asleep.

About ten minutes later Avi returned to the bed and smiled down at Chava, seemingly sleeping peacefully. Although the circumstances of their actual meeting was less than desirable, he did tell the truth when he confessed to Chava that he was falling in love with her long before they eventually met. He never dreamt that they would ever meet in person; however, he set the standards for his future wife with Chava's caliber. It was hard to fathom for him that she was not only in his life, but she actually loved him.

Avi felt that there were changes taking place in her too. When they first met he immediately felt an intimate connection with her, just like he once dreamed about. Now since he got to know her better, she seemed a lot more vulnerable and softer in real life. Of course, he couldn't deny it from himself that what happened to her in the past two weeks would have shaken up even him who was trained to bear hardships of any kind. Losing a parent was hard enough, and then meeting a terrorist leader, a traitor and a murderous niece while fulfilling her mother's last wishes was enough to disturb anyone's inner peace to the core.

He carefully lay down next to her not wanting to interrupt her sleep knowing what a difficult day she survived. Avi thanked God a great many times for looking after Chava and giving her back to him. He gently put his arm over her and she turned as she slept facing him. Avi kissed her forehead and looking at her he knew that there was some major decision making ahead of him if he wanted Chava by his side forever. Avi dozed off thinking about how his family was going to react when he introduced Chava to them. He prayed, and for a good reason that she would be liked by his parents and his sisters.

CHAPTER THIRTY-FIVE

Chava looked at the gun pointing at her and her heart was pounding so fast that she thought that she was going to faint. Her assailant's eyes were dark and cold and she knew that he had no soul, he was a merciless killer. "I am not Daniel," he said to her and put the gun to Chava's forehead. She could actually see his fingers pulling the trigger.

She screamed out so loud that she woke herself up. "Chava, darling, you were having a nightmare," she heard Avi's calming voice as she glanced around in her hotel room. She told Avi about her nightmare and she was shaking so badly that Avi had to turn the light on and hold her tight.

"I am sorry," said Chava apologetically and took a deep breath. "I am so happy that you are here with me," she whispered to him and leaned over to kiss him. His lips were soft as always, yet when he kissed her back they forced her lips apart to make a way to his tongue that searched for hers.

He rolled her over on her back and his hands cupped her breasts, and then his lips closed around her hardening nipples. "Avi," she whispered and her hands stroked his back. He began to kiss her smooth skin around her belly and while one hand caressed her breast, his other hand made its way inside her thighs, parting it gently. His fingers stroked her where she was most sensitive and he moved them inside her until she began to moan. He entered her slowly, taking his time to explore, to feel every inch of her.

"I love you Chava," he whispered as he lowered his head to kiss her. "I want to be with you always."

"Me too," were the only words she could muster. She had to be dreaming, she told herself. He was a skillful lover, considerate, gentle and yet very passionate who knew exactly how to please her. His top priority was to give her pleasure, placing himself second when it came to giving and receiving joy. Where and how he learned all that, she never wanted to find out, she knew that for sure.

He withdrew from her and turned on his back pulling Chava on the top of him. She lowered herself on him slowly, wanting to feel the sensation of him being inside of her. She thought that if there was a perfect match sexually that this was the one. While she moved, her hand caressed his chest when she bent over him. Feeling his fullness inside her and his tongue dancing in her mouth was enough for her to block everything out that was outside of that room.

He wanted to switch positions and when she was on her back again, his fingers touched her moist inside and her back arched from the pleasure of his touch. Like the other occasions when they made love, she couldn't help but moan in a low but steady voice that only matched his movements. Chava never could imagine that a man could give her so much pleasure as Avi did, and she knew that no matter what the future would bring, the memories of their lovemaking would remain with her forever. She was also certain of fact that there wouldn't be any other men in her life if she could not have Avi. She loved him with every pore of her body and having him is what she hoped for the rest of her life would be a gift from God.

She felt electricity building up in her body, Avi either sensed it or felt it, she was not certain, but he began moving faster until she cried out from the wave of pleasure, and then he came with her, becoming one, united at the end of a joy filled journey.

They rested in each other's arms, exchanging soft and gentle kisses. Chava felt relaxed for the first time in weeks, and the hope that there was still a possibility for happiness once again seemed promising.

CHAPTER THIRTY-SIX

C hava opened her eyes and the first image that she saw was Avi's blue eyes watching her. She smiled at him and he leaned forward to kiss her. "Marry me," he said quietly, yet very seriously.

"I said yes before, you remember?" Chava replied.

"I remember, but I want you marry me now, today," he replied.

"Avi," said Chava sitting up. "We have a lot of unsolved issues to discuss before we make that one big important step for the rest of our lives."

He knew that she was going to bring that up, yet he didn't have anything prepared to say to her or to offer her. "Alright, let's meet my family first and I also have a surprise for you later on."

"I don't like surprises," remarked Chava shaking her head.

"This one you are going to like," Avi assured her and got out of the bed. "Unfortunately it won't get here until later tonight," he said and reached for the telephone on the nightstand.

"I am going to take a quick shower," said Chava.

She heard him talking in Hebrew on the phone and he was still on the phone when she returned and began to dress. Avi turned around and smiled at her and he motioned to her to stop. He quickly finished with his phone calls and rushed to her, forcing her to lay down.

"What do you have in mind?" she asked him teasingly. He smiled at her sheepishly and took her hand and pulled it to his erection. "Hmmm," Chava laughed and bit her lips. "Is this breakfast?" she asked.

Avi bent down and kissed her so long that she had to gasp for air. "God, Avi," she managed to say. "You are really taking my breath away."

Chava couldn't explain what it was about Avi, but she just couldn't get enough of him, she was simply unable to resist him. His eyes spoke when his lips were silent, and they told her that he wanted her, that he desired her in the worst way. Avi began to explore her once again with gentle kisses and Chava felt his hands almost everywhere. He gently pushed her legs apart and his lips and tongue began to dance around her inner thigh. "Avi, please no," she

187

whispered but she was not sure if she really wanted him to stop. It was a brand new experience for her and while she knew all about oral sex, she had never known the feeling of sensation of what she was about to receive.

Avi didn't stop until she began to beg him, she wanted to feel him inside her and he obliged. He kissed her breasts and ran his tongue around her nipples, and then, just then Chava realized that she lost every bit of will power had when it came to Avi. Years passed after her divorce from Matthew and although it was not due to lack of volunteers to have sexual relationships with her, she was the one who choose to be celibate until she found the right person. She smiled at that thought as evidently Avi was worth the waiting for.

"What are you smiling about," he teased her, slowly moving inside her.

She was breathing hard and had difficulty talking. "You wouldn't believe if I told you," she finally managed to say.

"I would like to know," he said but he was breathing harder too.

"Not now," she begged him and he knew why. "I think I am coming," she moaned and her fingers dug into Avi's back. He smiled at her again and his lips pressed down hard on hers. He remained inside her, resting and enjoying the feeling that they were one, conjoined by their mutual desire for each other.

Chava caressed his back while his tongue made its way down on her neck and breasts. The telephone rang but they tried to ignore it. She looked at him as he shrugged his shoulder. He was kissing her over and over again, and Chava felt elated. She was more important to him than anyone else. His movements were slow and deliberate for a while, and then she knew that he was ready to climax when his movements became faster and his arms embraced her tightly and then she felt him exploding inside her.

He remained on the top of her still holding onto her as if he didn't want to let her go. He finally moved to her side, burying his head in the curve of her neck. There was no need to make small talk, they knew exactly how and what they felt for each other. Avi dozed off and so did Chava when the relentless ring of the telephone scared them awake. Avi sighed and reached for the telephone on the nightstand.

Chava noticed that Avi never introduced himself on telephone when he answered, he just simply always said "ken" which meant "yes" in Hebrew. He listened intensely and then he said, "Todah" which she learned meant "thank you."

"Is everything alright?" Chava asked when she saw a somewhat troubled look on his face. Avi tried to smile at her, but Chava immediately knew that it was a forced smile. "Can you tell me about it?" she asked again.

He bent over to kiss her. "Perhaps later on," said Avi and then he got up and went to the bathroom. Chava heard the running of the water in the shower and she got up as well. She put on her bathrobe and booted up her computer to check her email while Avi finished showering. She didn't find anything interesting other than her publicist and agent were asking her where she was and what was happening. "I'd like to know that too," she murmured and glanced toward the bathroom. *Why wasn't he talking to her about the phone call he received?* She wondered. *At least he could have told me if it was work related, he just simply brushed me off,* she thought. *What sort of secret was he still keeping from her? He doesn't trust her yet?* Those questions were troublesome to her as she wanted to be trusted by him, especially if he planned to spend the rest of his life with her.

When he came out of the bathroom he was freshly shaved and he apologized to her. "I hope you don't mind that I used one of your razors?" She shook her head. "Are you hungry?" he asked Chava.

"I am famished," she replied.

"Well it is too late for breakfast, but would you mind if you have lunch right here instead of going out?" he asked.

"What's going on Avi? Why can't we go to the restaurant downstairs?" asked Chava.

Avi didn't respond right away and when he did, Chava became even more puzzled than before. "I would like you to stay in this room until I return," said Avi.

Chava frowned. "Where are you going?" she asked.

"I have some business to attend to, but I'll be back in a few hours," Avi promised. "What would you like to eat?" Avi asked Chava handing her the menu for Room Service.

She felt hurt, but she hid her disappointment. "I think I will have a roast beef sandwich and some fresh fruit, and perhaps some orange juice to drink."

Avi picked up the phone and placed the order. He walked to the coffee table and put his shoulder holster on with the Glock handgun he always carried and picked up his ever present Uzi with the long shoulder strap and put it around his back.

"Avi," said Chava stepping next to him. "Why don't you trust me?" she asked.

He stopped and took a deep breath. "Chava, I trust you but I cannot talk about my business with you. I am sure that you can understand why," he tried to explain.

"Alright," said Chava and walked back to the desk her feelings clearly hurt.

Avi didn't say anything he just followed her with his eyes. He loved her so much, but he was a soldier first and foremost. He couldn't possibly tell her about his Special Forces activities. "I'll be back in a few hours," he promised and wanted to kiss her, but she turned her head. "I love you Chava," Avi said before closing the door behind him.

She felt disappointed and Avi's behavior brought back bad memories of Matthew. He never shared anything with her other than few words now and then, and even in those days she felt that Matthew was treating her like a dog that was thrown bits and pieces of food to keep the dog from whining. She was fully aware that there was information that Matthew or Avi could not share with her due the nature of their business, both of them were military men, but she felt left out of their lives by not knowing where they were going. Avi at least could have told her where his business was taking him, not the nature of it.

Chava sat back down by her computer and found the last chapter of her latest novel she was working on. She had to re-read some of the pages and it occurred to her that it had been days since she wrote a single paragraph. There was a knock on the door; it was room service, her lunch arrived.

She picked on her food and ate only a small portion of the sandwich and drank the whole glass of orange juice. It only took several minutes before she had to rush into the bathroom and throw up what she just ate. Her nausea was in full swing and she stayed in the bathroom for almost an hour throwing up until her stomach was completely empty, and then she became dizzy again. She scattered back to the bed and laid down, curling up under the comforter. *Maybe I should tell Avi that I have been feeling ill lately,* she thought, but she hushed that idea away. *If he can keep secret from me then I will keep this secret from him.*

CHAPTER THIRTY-SEVEN

C hava tossed and turned until she finally fell asleep for a few hours. When she woke, she glanced at the clock and she was surprised to learn that it was already six o'clock in the evening. Although there was some daylight left outside, it has become evident the Avi did not keep his word on returning in a few hours. "Where are you Avi?" she asked out loud.

She got up and got dressed. After brushing her hair, Chava looked in the mirror. She made an assessment that she looked somewhat more presentable then she did a few hours earlier. Her stomach didn't bother her, the nausea and the dizziness were gone, and she actually felt much better. The telephone rang and she rushed to answer it. "Hello," said Chava answering the phone.

"Is this Ms. Diamond?" asked the unfamiliar voice.

"Yes it is," Chava replied.

"There has been an incident involving Colonel Ben-Yishan," said the stranger.

"Who are you?" Chava asked suspiciously while her heart was gripped by fear for Avi.

"I am sorry Ms. Diamond, I am Lieutenant Elad Hayat, I serve under Avi's command," he explained.

"Where is he now?" asked Chava and reached for her purse. *This just cannot be happening*, she thought.

"He asked for you Ms. Diamond, and I have an instruction to take you to him. I am downstairs in the lobby," he offered.

"I am on my way," Chava said and slammed the phone down.

She impatiently waited for the elevator. "Come on, come on," she mumbled. The elevator finally arrived and she stepped inside and hurriedly pushed the first floor button several times, making the two elderly people in the elevator to glance at each other. "Hello," she said quietly towards them.

Chava didn't want to act rude and she waited until the elderly couple left the elevator. She dashed out and her eyes immediately began to search for Lieutenant Hayat who she assumed was wearing a uniform. She noticed him almost right away as he was leaning against one of the marble pillars in the lobby. He saw her too and began to walk towards her. "Ms. Diamond?" he asked. She nodded.

"How is Avi?" she asked him barely able to keep her anxiety under control.

"You have to see it for yourself Ms. Diamond," he said very seriously and his voice was giving her even more concern.

"Where is he?" she asked again.

"Please follow me," said the Lieutenant and began to walk towards the restaurant.

"Where are you going?" Chava asked.

"I want to take the short cut to where I parked my jeep, it's just at the back of the restaurant," he explained.

She thought that the explanation was awkward and not being familiar with the hotel's layout, she had no choice but to follow him, to take his word that he knew where he was going.

The restaurant was becoming busy because as usual, they began to serve dinner right on time at six in the evening. She noticed a long table on the right side of the establishment, and then she saw him sitting at the table. Avi noticed her too and with a big grin on his face, he got up and rushed to her. "Thank you Elad," he said to the Lieutenant. "You did well." Avi shook hands with him and the Lieutenant, who was grinning too, walked to the table to join the others.

Chava did not think that what just happened was funny and she turned her back to the table with full intention that she was going to leave the place. She was angry at Avi for causing her additional fear that she did not need after what she had to go through in the previous morning, not to mention the past week's events. *Avi should have been more considerate*, she thought. He grabbed Chava by her arm and turned her around to face him. "Chava I am sorry that I got you worried," he said and kissed her on the forehead. "I promised you a surprise, didn't I?" he asked.

"And I told you that I don't like surprises," she said angrily. She pulled her arms from his grip and headed towards the door. Once outside she broke down in tears and hurried towards the woman's restroom with Avi right behind her.

Avi knocked on the bathroom door and asked her to come out. There was only another woman inside the restroom and when she left, she shot a dirty look at Avi, but he didn't care. He pushed the door open and entered. She looked at him accusingly. "Chava I am so sorry," Avi tried to approach her but she backed off against the wall.

"Avi," Chava shook her head with tears rolling down on her face. "Have you given some thought of what you have just done to me?" His face became serious and he stared on the floor in front of him in silence.

"I shouldn't have to remind you what I have gone through," said Chava. "I still don't know what happened to my friend Sandy, so I am worried about her too. Then I get this phone call that there was an incident involving you. How do you think I felt?"

"I am sorry," repeated Avi.

"I have buckets full of sorries at home worth nothing," she said and wiped the tears off from her face.

"Chava, you are right," he said apologetically. "It was an insensitive thing from me to do, and if I can change it back I would, but I cannot. So please forgive me. I love you and I don't want to lose you because of some stupid mistake I made."

Chava looked at him and she knew that he was sincerely regretful. "Alright," she said quietly. "But no more surprises," she reminded him.

"Just a couple of more," he said and made a funny face at her.

"Avi," she shook her head. "Aren't you listening to me?" she asked.

"They are pleasant ones, I promise," he said convincingly.

Chava took a deep breath and she let some cold water run on her hand to wash her face. There were some fresh clean towels at the end of the counter, he handed her one of them. Before they stepped outside, Chava stopped him. "Avi, I was scared to death just from the thought that I lost you," she said to him.

"I know," he replied. "I felt the same way yesterday morning about you," he kissed her on the cheek and walked her back to the restaurant.

CHAPTER THIRTY-EIGHT

"You must be hungry," Avi said and without waiting for Chava's response, he guided her through the hotel restaurant's door and pointed at the direction of the long table. "You may know someone else at that table," he said leaning towards her.

Chava glanced at the people who sat around the long table, and at first she did not recognize anyone. There was one young woman seated facing the door looking at their direction as they entered, Chava thought that she might have known or seen her somewhere. Next to her was another young woman, a look alike of the first one although she seemed a little bit older. Next to them sat a couple whose age Chava guessed in the mid sixties. Six uniformed soldiers were sitting on both sides of the young women and the couple, and a few other soldiers, also in uniform occupied some chairs at the other side of the table.

On the opposite side of the table, sitting next to his comrades sat a soldier, taller than the others were, but that is not what captured Chava's attention. Next to the tall soldier was a woman who turned around with a radiant looking face and a big broad smile. Sandy screamed out Chava's name out loud, and as she jumped off from her seat, her chair flipped over. She almost tripped as she hurried towards her friend Chava.

Chava broke down in tears and she hugged Sandy so tight that she thought her arms were going to fall off. Both were crying from joy seeing each other alive and well and free most of all. "Are you alright?" asked Chava.

Sandy nodded and whispered to her. "I am better then fine and I am in love."

Chava raised her eyebrows and looked back at the table from where a tall soldier was getting up and began to walk toward their direction. Avi and Tomer shook hands and briefly hugged, than Avi introduced them to each other. "Captain Tomer Gadir," said Avi. "May I introduce you to my future wife, Chava Diamond, the world famous novelist."

"It's truly a pleasure to meet you Chava," said Tomer and also shook hands with Chava. "I heard so much about you and it's easy to see and tell that Avi did not exaggerate."

"Well thank you for your kind words," replied Chava to his complement. She turned to Sandy and she couldn't help smiling. Her friend's eyes were glued on Tomer and Chava could easily tell that he was in love with Sandy as well. "So, tell me, how did you kids met?" she asked teasingly, already suspecting the answer.

"Someday you can write a book about it my friend," laughed Sandy. "I have so much to tell you, but in a nutshell, he and Avi and the others came for my rescue and here I am," said Sandy and locked her arms into Tomer's.

Chava felt an incredible relief seeing her friend right there and she was about to ask Avi how long did he know that Sandy was free, when she heard his voice whispering to her. "Those civilian people sitting at the table are my family," said Avi.

She almost panicked hearing that, she was not prepared for anything like that. He escorted her to the table and introduced his sisters to Chava. It was then that she realized why one of the young women looked familiar; she recalled seeing her with Avi in Krakow, Poland. "This is my mother, Sa'ada," Avi introduced her to Chava. "This is my father Rabbi Yisrael Ben-Yishan, my youngest sister Ilana, you saw her with me in Poland," Avi confirmed her recognition of the young woman. "And my other sister, Moran," said Avi then turned to the soldiers sitting on the other side of the table and introduced them to her one by one. "Everyone, this is Ms. Chava Diamond, my future wife," said Avi as a final introduction. Chava noticed that everyone with the exception of Avi's mother was smiling. It came to her as a shock that Avi's father was a Rabbi, but she did not make a comment about it.

They took a seat across from Avi's parents and Chava was glad that Sandy was sitting next to her. Two waiters arrived to their table and began to take orders. Chava looked at Avi's mother Sa'ada and smiled at the woman. It was almost painful for Chava to see that it was not enough that Avi's mother did not return her smile; instead, she whispered something to her husband. The Rabbi gently motioned to her to remain quiet. Chava turned to Avi. "I don't think that your mother approves of me," she said quietly.

"She is not the one who is marrying you," he said to Chava, and then Avi turned to his mother who shook her head. Sa'ada looked long and hard at Chava who stood her stare, still smiling at Avi mother. Sa'ada said something to Avi loud enough to make his sisters and his friends became unexpectedly quiet. Avi's face turned red at what Chava guessed from anger, or embarrassment, but he didn't talk back to his mother. Chava looked at him, not understanding what was happening, then she glanced at the Rabbi whose head was bowed to his chest.

"Avi," said Chava. "What is going on?"

"Chava," said Avi with a sigh. "My mother is a very traditional woman or you may call her an old fashioned person who wants me to marry a sabra," he explained nervously.

"It means that someone who was born in this country, right?" Chava asked. Avi nodded. "Please let me understand this," said Chava. "You are a Colonel in IDF's Special Forces, you are thirty-four years old, and yet you are asking your parents blessing so that you can marry me? That is what you are trying to tell me?" Chava asked fighting back tears.

"It's not that simple," he tried to explain. "My parents are Orthodox Jews. While they are liberal about certain things, they follow the traditions when it comes to family issues. Yes, it is very important to me that I have their blessings, but it doesn't mean that I don't want to marry you. Chava, I love you, and you mean the world to me," Avi said and reached for her hand, Chava pulled it away. She felt an arm around her shoulder and it was Sandy's.

"Maybe I am naïve," Chava replied and stood up. "Where I came from, when two people love each other, they get married and hopefully live happily ever after no matter what their families want." She felt tightness in her chest and it was difficult for her to breath. She felt incredibly betrayed by Avi. *What happened with the passionate and uncontrollable desire he felt for me? What happened to the feeling that he could not live without me? Isn't that what he was telling me all along?* Chava thought.

Chava opened her purse and pulled out her wallet with her mother's picture in it and took it out. She leaned over the table and pushed the picture in front of Avi's father, the Rabbi. "I know that you speak English because I noticed that you understood what I was saying. So now hear this Rabbi," said Chava with her voice crackling with emotion. "My mother survived the Auschwitz concentration camp not only because of her faith in God, but because of her will to survive. She believed that there were only two kinds of people in this world, good and bad, and that a Jew can be just as bad as a Christian or Muslim. She believed in God, but lost her faith in the religious world."

She looked at Sa'ada and back again at the Rabbi. "I respect your beliefs and I would never challenge your religion, or anybody else's. It is most unfortunate that your wife does not care about her son's happiness. She thinks that I am not good enough for your son because I am not sabra? Is that it?" Chava turned to Avi who was staring down at the table in front of him. "Avi," she called out his name but he did not respond, and he did not look at her.

The Rabbi looked at Chava straight in the eye and then he slowly turned to Avi. "Son, I believe Chava truly loves you. I'll be glad to give my blessing and I'll be happy to perform your wedding ceremony, if that is what you want." His wife said something to him, but with a movement of his hands he hushed her up.

Avi didn't move or say anything; instead he lifted his head up and looked at his mother. Chava felt that her heart was sinking faster than the Titanic after hitting an iceberg. Sandy got up as well and hugged her. The area where they were sitting became so quit that it was easy to hear what the other guests were talking about at the far side of the restaurant. Chava looked at Avi's friends and she could tell that they were stunned silent.

"Rabbi," said Chava in a soft voice. "Thank you for your kindness, but you see, you could not marry me to Avi because I am not Jewish. Although I was born into the Jewish faith, I choose to be a Christian. I hope that you forgive me for this most unpleasant encounter, and thank you for coming to meet me."

She turned around and in the company of Sandy and Tomer, she left the restaurant. The elevator could not come fast enough as they stood there waiting. Avi came out of the restaurant and slowly walked up to them. Sandy and Tomer wanted to leave but Chava stopped them. Tomer's face expressed anger and disappointment as he said to Avi. "I don't understand you man," and he shook his head.

Chava forced a smile on her pale face and looked into those eyes that captivated her so many times. "When I first saw you, the entire world around me disappeared and the only person I could see was you, Avi. I didn't know who you were, and where you came from, but I sensed then that my life was never going to be the same again. You appeared to be larger than life, a brave soldier, and passionate lover. And now I am seeing is a coward standing in front of me."

Tears gathered in Avi's eyes as he stood there staring at Chava, yet he has not spoken a single word. The elevator door opened and people departed from it. Tomer held the door open as Sandy put her hand on Chava's shoulder. She followed Sandy inside the elevator and as the door was closing, Chava shook her head and whispered one single word towards Avi, "Why?"

The elevator door closed and began to ascend towards Chava's floor. She began to shake so badly in the elevator that both of them had to hold her by her arms. Once they reached her room, Tomer told Sandy that he would see her later and left the two women alone.

Inside her room Chava broke down and sobbed uncontrollably. "This is not happening," she kept on repeating and there was nothing Sandy could say or do to make her feel better. An hour later when her tears were still streaming down on her face, she became physically ill and began to throw up, barely making it into the bathroom. As she was sitting at the edge of the bathtub, a violent stabbing pain ravished through her body. She screamed for Sandy who rushed into the bathroom to find Chava on the bathroom floor, bending over in agony. Around her legs was a pool of blood and Chava was trembling from pain and panic.

Sandy ran back to the room and called the front desk. She asked them to send medical assistance or an ambulance immediately. Less then ten minutes passed by when they finally heard a knock on the door and two men hurried inside. Sandy immediately showed them where Chava was still laying on the bathroom floor, unable to move. A third man arrived a short time later. "What's wrong with her?" Sandy asked one of the two men who turned out to be a doctor hoping that he spoke English.

"I believe that Ms. Diamond may have suffered a miscarriage," he commented. "I am going to start an IV now and then we will transfer her to the hospital for further treatment," he announced and within seconds he inserted an IV line into Chava's left arm, then he motioned to the men standing there waiting for his instructions. The men carefully placed Chava on a stretcher and secured her with two belts to prevent her from falling off. They rolled her out from the room with Sandy walking beside the stretcher holding onto Chava's hand.

"Chava, I am so sorry, I didn't know . . . ," Sandy mumbled to Chava.

She shook her head. "I suspected but I wasn't sure myself," and once again tears rushed down on Chava face.

People were staring as the ambulance personnel pushed the stretcher through the lobby and they were just about at the exit door, when Avi noticed Sandy and the doctor who was holding the IV bag as they walked along side of the stretcher. He rushed towards them and he stepped to the ambulance door. "Chava," he yelled. "What's wrong?"

Chava lifted her tear soaked face and said to him on a weak voice. "Please go away."

After Sandy and the doctor got inside the ambulance with Chava, the two men closed the ambulance door, got inside the front of the vehicle and drove away. Avi stood there, unable to move. "What have I done?" he asked himself out loud. "Oh my God, what have I done?"

CHAPTER THIRTY-NINE

The flight home from Israel was a long and mostly silent. Sandy and Chava barely spoke of the past weeks events and Chava preferred it that way. She spent four days in a hospital in Eilat and then she was released with a clean bill of health. The female gynecologist, who performed a minor surgery on her, assured Chava that she was perfectly capable of having children and when they left, she asked Chava for her autograph as she was a fan of hers.

Chava was glad to be back in California and within a few days her daily routine returned. She asked Sandy to stay with her for the first couple of days, and then she realized that she must pick up her life where she left it before her faithful trip to Europe and to Israel. It was a life she built for herself and it was a life that she thought she enjoyed before. While her life was returning to what she called "fairly normal", no matter how hard she tried, there was an important element missing. Although she never admitted openly, she knew exactly what was missing. It was Avi Ben-Yishan.

It had been two months since her return from Israel, but sleepless nights and tearful days did not lessen or shorten, but she managed to keep it a secret from everyone. Not even Sandy knew about the emotional turmoil Chava was going through. Writing was not going well and despite frequent reminder phone calls and emails from her agent, Chava could not make herself to sit down and write. She spent entire days just laying in bed and her lips kept on repeating the same words, "how could this all happen?" or "what went wrong?"

Finding out that she was pregnant in the worst way was even more heartbreaking than she would have ever imagined, and the circumstances bordered with anyone's worst nightmare. She felt life slipping out of her and she was not able to stop the event, nor was Chava able to stop Avi's mother from taking him away from her.

What had she done to a total stranger like Sa'ada was to her, who did not know anything about her other than she was a writer? What so terrible about Chava that Sa'ada didn't want her son to marry her? What had she done wrong? Avi and she made passionate love that morning as if it was their very first time.

She would have never imagined in a million years that it was their last. How could a mother hold such a grip over a son's life as Avi's did? But it was true and it did happen to her.

Chava could not understand any of it, most of all, she was unable to comprehend how could someone declare everlasting love and then, within a few hours, turn away from her and from what they had together?

Chava looked at the lovely flowers Sandy brought for her a few days earlier and memories of other flowers flashed back into her mind. While she was laying in her hospital bed in Eilat, Sandy became her guardian angel, not leaving her bedside, giving up her chances to be with Tomer. On an occasion while Sandy was in the bathroom, one of her nurses stopped by at her bed and informed her that she had a visitor. Chava was surprised, as other than Sandy and Tomer, nobody stopped by to visit her. Tomer had to leave for Jerusalem so she knew that it was not him who came to see her.

"What is his or her name?" Chava asked the nurse.

"He said his name is Avi," the nurse informed her.

"Please tell him to go away," Chava responded and turned her head.

"He has been here almost all day Ms. Diamond, are you sure that you don't want to see him?" she asked Chava.

"Yes, I am sure," replied Chava and closed her eyes.

Sandy returned and had a large bouquet of flowers in her hands. "It's for you honey," she said smiling.

"Oh Sandy, you didn't have to do that," said Chava admiring the colorful flower arrangement.

"Well, actually it's from him," said Sandy quietly.

"Him as Avi?" asked Chava and her face turned serious. Sandy nodded. "Please take the flowers away or give it to some other patient," said Chava and Sandy knew that Chava would not rest until those flowers disappeared from her sight, so she gave it to one of the nurses entering the room.

Avi went to the hospital every single day until his duty forced him to join his team in Jerusalem. He begged the nurses to speak in his behalf, to try to convince Chava to see him. Chava was not in any shape or form to change her mind. Her heart was broken and her mind was clouded with a combination of anger, sadness but mostly with disappointment.

It was still very painful to remember back on those days what she considered "days of betrayal" of her love and so hard to come by trust. She touched the flower petals in front of her and bitterly smiled. "I was loved once, so I thought," she mumbled to herself and if she was waking up from a deep sleep, she smiled and went to her computer that was dormant for weeks. She booted up the computer and clicked on Microsoft Word. In the middle of the first page she typed with large letters,

"ONCE UPON A TIME . . ."
A novel by
CHAVA DIAMOND"

The second page was momentarily blank until words began to appear one by one and the pages were filling up almost as fast as her mind was producing them. She typed fast and furious, and she wrote through that evening and night.

It was six o'clock in the next morning and despite the fact that she had not slept all night Chava was wide awake. She stretched and cued up her printer to print over two hundred pages of her newest novel. While the printer was humming away, she took a shower and made an omelet for herself, nothing fancy just ham and cheese. Her usual two pieces of toast accompanied the omelet to her desk to check on the prints and to place more paper into the printer.

By the time she was done it was eight thirty and she was ready to call her agent. Angela was delighted to hear from her, but when she heard the news that Chava wrote a book overnight, her excitement died down somewhat. Nevertheless, she encouraged Chava to drop off the manuscript so she could read it over.

It took her less then an hour to arrive at San Francisco's Embarcadero Square where Angela's agency's was located. The secretary smiled at Chava and told her that Angela was expecting her; it should be only a moment or two before she was able to get her. The door opened and the ever well dressed Angela stepped out of her office and gave Chava a big hug. As usual, she was dressed in her business attire. Once Chava asked her if she ever dressed in casual to go to work, she replied that she always wore business attire because she never knew when the next Donald Trump look alike would stop by.

Angela asked her secretary if she would be kind enough to bring two cappuccinos for them and then she ushered Chava inside her office decorated with leather furniture and dark brown wood paneling. Chava sat down and without a moment of hesitation, she took out her two hundred and forty-nine page manuscript titled, "Once upon a time . . . ," and placed it in front of Angela. She looked down at the manuscript and raised her eyebrows.

"You wrote this overnight?" Angela asked, having difficulty believing it.

"Yep," she replied. "Go ahead and read it."

"Alright," agreed Angela and began to turn the pages. One of the best things she ever invested earlier in her career was taking speed reading classes. She turned page after page until three quarters into reading she stopped and looked at Chava. She was staring at her agent with questions in her eyes but Angela just looked at her, and then reached for the Kleenex box she kept inside her top desk drawer. She pulled out several and blew her nose while went back to reading. Very shortly tears began to roll down on her face and she had to take out more Kleenex tissues to wipe the tears away so she could continue reading.

Almost an hour and two more cappuccinos later, Angela finally read the last page. Her tears were unstoppable and without saying a word, she got up and stepped to Chava to hug her again. "So what do you think?" asked Chava.

"It is going to be the best seller of the year," Angela said finally and kissed Chava on her cheek. "Chava, you are my dearest friend and long time client, so I am not exaggerating about what I am about to say to you."

"Alright, I am listening," said Chava and embraced herself for a possibly criticism.

"Chava," Angela began, but before she continued, she took a deep breath. "This is by far the best book you have ever written."

"Wow," Chava smiled bitterly. "I guess all I have to do is fall apart each time before I need to write a new book."

Angela hugged her yet again and assured her that "Once upon a time . . . ," has just become a top priority publishing project on her list. They said goodbye, and after Chava left her agent's office, she drove to one of her favorite places in San Francisco, to the Museum of Fine Arts where she spent the rest of the day.

CHAPTER FORTY

A ngela's voice sounded excited when Chava answered the phone on a lazy Tuesday morning, almost five months to the day when Sandy and Chava returned home from Israel. "Chava," she said into the phone. "I have great news to tell you. Your book is coming out in two weeks. It has been a record in your publisher's history and not surprisingly, they loved your book as much as I did. Congratulations Chava, you have another hit, perhaps the biggest one yet."

Great, thought Chava. *Isn't that sad that I have almost no one to share this news?* That thought made her even sadder and brought her to tears. There was not a single day that passed by when she did not think of the handsome Israeli officer, Avi Ben-Yishan, whom she fell in love and who so cold heartedly abandoned her. It was true that he wanted to see her in the hospital, for what reason, she will never know. Did he want to apologize for not standing up to his mother who didn't want Chava to join their family or did he want to explain what transpired during the few hours when they were apart? *It does not matter now,* she thought. *It's over.* She needed to say that to herself over and over, although she obviously failed to convince herself. *If it was over, why did it still hurt when I think about him,* she wondered. When she closed her eyes, she was still able to recall his kisses and his touch. Chava could almost feel his strong hands as they softly wandered around her body and she more than ever ached to be loved by him. In her dream, when she managed to sleep, she could almost feel him inside her, moving with her. Chava would still tremble when she recalled their lovemaking. Had she not lost their child, she could at least have some part of him living with her now, but obviously it was not meant to be.

Chava frequently thought about her mother, Helene, especially on Sundays when she usually wrote to her in the past. Chava compared her urge to write to Helene to those people who felt the needs to worship on every Sunday. She always felt the need to write to her mother on every single Sunday since her departure from Hungary, even when she had virtually nothing new to say. Chava knew how much her mother loved to read the letters she wrote about her life, about what she was working on. Helene always felt great job from seeing her daughter's picture on the back cover of a new book, even if she was unable to read them because they were written in English. Chava sent her mother newspaper clippings and articles if there were pictures of her because Chava knew how happy those things made her mother feel.

Chava often wished that her mother lived with her in the United States, but Helene refuse to leave her native country permanently. She joined Chava in California for brief periods of time until she got sick with cancer. Chava also often wondered about her mother's real reason behind sending her to Auschwitz, and to Israel to scatter her ashes in the Red Sea. Ever since she read her mother's "testimonial" she wanted to figure out those questions, but so far she failed to do so.

Angela's phone call once again reminded Chava that she wanted to tell her mother about the news of the release of her latest book. Sadness returned back into Chava's heart when as usual it dawned on Chava that her mother was no longer among the living. She didn't want to be alone that day; she wanted to be in the company of someone who loved her. Chava picked up the phone and dialed Sandy's number and asked her if she was free for lunch.

As soon as her friend answered the phone, Chava knew right away that something must have happened as Sandy's voice sounded very excited. "Oh yes, I'll be glad to meet you," Sandy agreed.

"Where would you like to go for lunch?" she asked Chava.

"Why don't we meet in the atrium lobby of the Hyatt Regency, how does that sound?" suggested Chava and then she added. "By the way, it's my treat."

"Sounds great, but would you mind if I bring someone with me?" inquired Sandy.

Chava was somewhat surprised by the question, but any friend of Sandy's she would consider her own, of course she immediately agreed. Driving through traffic was not fun but she had no choice, it was midday and everybody in the Embarcadero business district, it seemed like to Chava, decided to take their lunches at the same time.

Arriving in front of the Hyatt Regency she stopped at the front and let the valet take care of her parking. She always loved the atrium lobby with those tall trees and trellises that surrounded the Eclipse Café. Chava spotted a table that seated four and settled down at the table where she was immediately approached by a waiter asking her if she was waiting for others, or was she ready to order something to drink. She ordered ice tea and informed the waiter that she would order when the rest of her party arrived.

The place was filling up mostly with business attired people, coming in pairs or even in larger groups. Chava was glad that she got there a little bit earlier. She loved people watching and that not only made the time go faster for her, but some of the people gave her ideas for characters for her future books. In later years when her popularity grew into fame, her face became easily recognizable as the effect of numerous talk show appearances, book signings, television, newspapers and magazine interviews. It seemed that some people still got enchanted by the fact, that when Chava arrived to America she did not speak the language and through her then husband, Matthew, she mastered the English language, establishing herself as a notable, well liked and read writer. On more occasions than Chava was able to recall, her lunch or dinner was interrupted by autograph seekers, it was something she didn't mind most of the time, she was grateful that people appreciated what she liked to do best, which was writing.

It took a long time to get used to people's stares when she arrived somewhere, like stores or eateries, but eventually she learned to ignore those looks that tried to figure out who she was and why did she look familiar. She began to study the menu in front of her, and then she looked around as she was unable to shake the feeling that someone was watching her. There were some people who took a second look to her, recognizing who she was, but it was a different feeling, not the usual looks she received.

Chava strained her eyes to see anyone she might find familiar in the growing crowd. The large trees in the atrium lobby could easily hide anyone from plain view, so she gave up her visual search and returned her attention to the menu when she felt a hand on her shoulder. When Chava turned around she saw Sandy standing there, she couldn't believe her eyes. Next to Sandy in civilian clothes stood Captain Tomer Gadir, Avi's friend and one of Sandy's rescuers. He looked even more handsome when he was not wearing a uniform. Chava got up to give a big hug to both of them, and then she showed them the seats opposite from her. "I want to feast my eyes on both of you," she said smiling. Tomer was holding Sandy's hand and he was jumpy, unable to hide his happiness. "I have something to tell you," said Chava.

"Me too," Sandy replied to her and Chava knew that whatever her friend had to say was good news. It was easy to tell from Sandy's face.

"You go first," suggested Chava.

"Alright," agreed Sandy and before she continued, she looked at Tomer and took a deep breath. "We are getting married."

Chava got up from her seat and walked around the table to hug them once again. "I am so incredibly happy for you two," she said with tears in her eyes. "Oh, don't be mistaken, these are tears of happiness, nothing more than that."

Sandy also wiped her tears when Tomer pulled her to him and kissed her forehead. The gesture made Chava both happy and yet, her heart was tearing apart. "So when is the big date?" she asked.

"We wanted to have it on next Saturday but it's a Sabbath, so instead, we are getting married on Sunday. It's going to be a small wedding, that is what we both want," explained Sandy with excitement. "Of course, if nobody else, you are going to be there."

"I wouldn't miss it for the world," said Chava and squeezed their hands over the table, and just then she noticed some sort of hesitation on their faces. "What is it; do you want to tell me something else?"

They nervously looked at each other before Tomer spoke. "The thing is, I asked Avi to be my best man. He is also going to be there."

Chava let their hands go and sat back in her chair. She cannot go to their wedding, she cannot face Avi again, ever. As if Sandy was reading her mind, she shook her head. "No Chava," she said to her friend. "You have to be there. You are my family as I am yours. I cannot go through without you being there, your presence at our wedding means the world to me and Tomer."

Tomer nodded in agreement. "And to me as well Chava," he said softly and reached for her hand. "Please, I am begging you, don't back out. You are very important to both of us."

Chava took a deep breath as she looked at their faces. She knew that no matter what her mind and heart was saying, she couldn't possibly refuse her friend's request. *How can I face Avi again?* She wondered. All of her emotional wounds will be reopened, and the sleepless nights and her painful memories would resurface ever more powerfully. She sighed. "Alright," she said finally and noticed the immediate relief on her friend's faces.

The waiter arrived and took their orders for their food and drinks. "And what is that you wanted to tell us?" inquired Sandy.

"Most definitely not as exciting as the news that the two of you are getting married. My little news is that my new book is going to be released in two weeks," Chava informed them.

"That's wonderful Chava," said Sandy and she was genuinely glad to hear that Chava was writing again.

"So Tomer, how long have you been here?" Chava asked and with all her might, she desperately tried to avoid asking him about Avi.

"We got here late last night," answered Tomer. "I tell you, it has been a long flight. I got so restless that I began to pace back and forth until one of the passengers began to complain that I was making him dizzy." They laughed at his words. Chava could not avoid replaying his first word "we," and suspicion arose.

"What is going to happen after the wedding? You are not going to take my friend away from me are you?" Chava said jokingly.

"Actually I am here to stay," said Tomer to Chava's surprise. "I got out of the IDF a couple of weeks ago and I already have a job with an Israeli security firm that is located right here in San Francisco," explained Tomer and he casually added. "And so did Avi," the moment he said the name he immediately regretted it, but it was out there and he could not take it back.

"Now that is truly wonderful," said Chava lifting her ice tea and ignoring Tomer's remark about Avi. "To your happiness." They clinked their glasses and although they were not drinking alcoholic beverages, it didn't really matter.

CHAPTER FORTY-ONE

C hava dressed slowly, full of concerns and regrets about agreeing to be at her friend's wedding after finding it out that Avi was actually going to be Tomer's best man. The problem was that it was impossible to turn Sandy down, not just because she was her best and closest friend, but simply because they stood by each other no matter what.

Arriving at the San Francisco City Hall she felt lucky finding a parking place right away close to the entrance, although it took her a long time to get out of her car knowing what was waiting for her. Chava walked up the wide marble steps and headed towards the office, where the Justice of the Peace held scheduled wedding ceremonies. She walked inside and she immediately noticed Sandy. She looked absolutely gorgeous in her peach color gown with a tiny peach color rose in her hair as she stood next to Tomer, who was wearing a dark suit on that Sunday morning. This was clearly Sandy's happiest day of her life. There were only two other people whom she was able to see, one was Jack, Sandy's cousin, who drove down with his wife Joan, from Sacramento. She was hopeful that perhaps for some reason Avi was not able to make it, but as she turned around back toward the entrance, she saw him.

Avi was leaning against the wood paneling of the room and was watching her. It wasn't the first time she saw him in civilian clothes, and it really didn't quite matter what he was wearing, he looked even more handsome as she dared to recall in the loneliness of her luxurious Sausalito home. His suit was navy blue and his shirt pale blue, almost as if he coordinated his outfit with Chava's dress. Avi was wearing a tie and the pose he projected he could have been easily mistaken for a model. His lips parted when their eyes met but no sound escaped.

Chava froze where she stood, she was unable to make as much as a single step. He pushed himself away from the wall and walked up to her. She could feel her entire body tremble as their eyes locked into each others. "Shalom Chava," said Avi softly and pushed his right hand forward for a handshake.

She didn't take the offered hand, and Chava had difficulties moving her lips to reply. "Hello," she managed to mumble.

"You look beautiful," he said with a frail smile.

Chava did not reply, and what she felt was overpowering. She always thought that if someday she would see Avi again she would collapse, or she would fall apart, instead, her trembling stopped and an incredible calmness came over her. She managed to break her stare from him and not caring if he found her rude or not, she turned her back to him and calmly walked to Tomer and Sandy. She hugged and kissed them both, and managed to make a small conversation.

The Justice of the Peace, a man in his early sixties entered and warmly welcomed everyone in the room. Sandy was glowing as she stood in front of the judge's desk. On her right stood Chava wearing a light blue dress, her face pale and without any make up, she still looked radiant despite the fact that she was up most of the night worrying about seeing Avi again.

The ceremony was simple and very private, the way Sandy and Tomer wanted it. After the paperwork was signed and congratulations were said, they left the City Hall. Chava was driving Tomer and Sandy, while the rest of the party drove with Jack, Sandy's cousin. They all headed toward Scala's Bistro that was adjacent to the historic Sir Francis Drake Hotel, located a half a block from Union Square. Chava insisted on making the arrangements and to cover the expenses as a wedding token to her friend, when Sandy mentioned to Chava that they did not have any special plans for lunch that would have served as their reception.

The place was one of Sandy's favorite from all the places they used to hang out. The high ceilings still had original murals, dark mahogany, gilt mirrors and richly colored floor tile coverings that gave an impression of an old world atmosphere and the feel of classic eateries in Europe. The tables were covered with white linen cloths that gave a touch of extra elegance to the always busy restaurant.

They were seated shortly after their arrival. Chava made sure that she was not seated next to Avi, although she could not avoid sitting across the table from him. She did not order the food or drinks ahead of time, she thought that it would be the best that everybody ordered whatever they liked.

The pink champagne Sandy ordered was cooled to perfection, and it was Chava who initiated a short speech. "Sandy, you are the best friend a human being could ever ask for. You were there in my brightest, and in my darkest hours," she looked at Avi, and then she turned back to the couple. "I always considered you more than just a friend; instead, you are more like a sister to me. And you Tomer," she smiled at the glowing young man. "What I learned about you, brought you up to a level of gaining a brother and not a friend. I wish both of you a lifetime worth of happiness in peace and harmony. To you my friends," she said and lifted her champagne glass in the honor of Sandy and Tomer."

"If I may say something too please," said Avi and stood up. "Tomer, I have known you since we were little kids. I always honored and admired your bravery, and I continue to do so until I die. We went through hell and back together, and I have not known a man who was a better friend then you are to me. Like Chava, I am too wishing both of you long life and everlasting happiness," he said and nodded towards Sandy and Tomer. "And just one more thing Tomer," he said and instead of looking at Tomer, he looked directly at Chava. "Treasure your bride's love and trust, and hold on to her tightly, don't let some stupid mistake drive you away from her."

Tomer and Sandy looked at each other well knowing what Avi meant. Sandy glanced at Chava's direction and she noticed that her friend's face was turning very serious as she stared toward the direction of the entrance. She glanced that way too and murmured into her napkin. "Oh, no!"

A tall, handsome man with dark blondish hair and green eyes, wearing a military uniform stopped by their table. "Hello Chava," he said in a firm, direct voice, and then he turned to the rest of the people sitting around the table. "Good evening everyone."

"Matthew," replied Chava acknowledging her ex-husband. She had to admit to herself that he didn't change, he still carried himself well due to his military training.

"You haven't changed, you still look beautiful," Matthew complemented her.

"What do you want Matthew?" Chava asked calmly taking a deep breath.

"May I have a word with you?" he asked her.

"She is busy," said Avi unexpectedly. Chava looked at him with a very serious face as if she was forbidding him from getting involved.

"I'll give you a couple of minutes," replied Chava and got up. Matthew, always a gentleman helped her with the chair. "If you excuse me, I'll be right back," said Chava and followed Matthew out to the lobby. She didn't have to turn around, she could feel Avi's watchful eyes following them. "What do you want Matthew?" she asked him again once they were by themselves. He looked her up and down, as if he was taking inventory of her stylish and expensive outfit, or simply his memory was taking him back to times when he told her what and what not to wear as an officer's wife. Chava really didn't care.

He found her more attractive than ever, and Chava surprisingly felt the same way about him. Of course, there was that certain way that she found him attractive and it was not the way of a desperately lovesick person. Before their divorce, she would have followed him just about everywhere, but as she looked at him standing there, still extremely handsome in his uniform, she felt absolutely no emotion in her heart for him. The way he treated her on the last day of their marriage when she still thought that she loved him, sent cold chills down on Chava's spine.

"I have been thinking about you lately and wanted to look you up. I walked in here and you were sitting right there, it's a lucky coincidence, don't you think? As if it was some sort of sign," he said and touched her face with his hand. She pulled back.

"The only sign I am seeing is exit," Chava remarked sarcastically.

He ignored it and pulled her closer to him. "You can't forget all the nice times we had, for Christ sake; we were married for a long time. Surely you still have some feelings for me?" he asked her. Chava began to laugh which came as a surprise to him.

"You are right about that Matthew! Those special feelings that I still harbor for you are the ones you should try to avoid at all costs," she replied and with quick steps she walked to the ladies room, leaving her stunned ex-husband standing there.

This is just too much to take, Chava thought as she looked in the mirror. It was bad enough that she was spending the day in the company of the man who was possibly the love of her life and who abandoned her because of his mother, and then there was the unexpected appearance of her ex-husband Matthew, a miserable man who was only capable of loving himself and no one else.

Why did Avi have to come back into my life? she asked herself the question. Matthew didn't mean anything anymore, but Avi? Just how long was she able to keep up her cool appearance and deny the fact that she was still, if not more than ever in love with him. Tears rushed into her eyes and she took a tissue out of her small purse to wipe them away.

The door to the ladies room opened and Sandy walked in. "Oh thank God," she said and hugged her. "I was worried that perhaps that idiot kidnapped you or hurt you," she looked Chava up and down and then she smiled. "If about nothing else, Matthew was right about you. Chava, you are beautiful."

Chava playfully pushed Sandy on her shoulder. "I am not, but you are. And you are married to a great guy," she shook her head smiling. "I am so happy for you Sandy, so happy," she repeated and her tears began to stream down on her face again.

Sandy understood Chava completely. Chava was a perfect example of a strong willed person who could accomplish virtually anything she wanted in life, but even the strongest person would buckle under the pressure that her friend went through. She knew that Chava loved Avi, and she also knew that if Avi wanted to win Chava back, it would be an uphill battle all the way. What happened to Chava during a two weeks time frame was like watching a suspense movie, full of surprises, romances and tragedies, but without an end. "What can I do for you Chava?" she asked her.

"I am so sorry for ruining your wedding day," apologized Chava and rinsed her face from the cold water running into the marble sink.

"You haven't ruined anything," objected Sandy. "I want you to be happy too," she said and handed Chava a clean towel from the stack on the small table that stood at the end of the counter. "You do know that Avi loves you don't you?" she asked Chava.

She looked at Sandy as she replied. "Maybe he does, but he choose his mother over me and destroyed the trust I built for him," her tears rushed back into her eyes. "Sandy, I lost my baby because of him," Chava said accusingly.

Sandy shook her head. "You don't know that for sure," she argued. "Maybe that baby just wasn't meant to be born Chava. It happens sometimes," she said and rubbed Chava's back. "You know, perhaps the blame shouldn't be just placed on Avi alone. It was not a stranger who influenced him, it was his own mother. Why she didn't want you in their family, I have no idea. Although it is not an excuse for his behavior, the saying that "blood is thicker than water" was certainly true in your case. What can he possibly do to make it up to you?" she asked.

"I don't know, I just don't know," whispered Chava.

"Do you feel like going back to have dinner?" asked Sandy.

"Look at me, I am a mess," said Chava. "My face is puffy from crying."

Sandy laughed. "Honey, you look better on your worst day than the way I look on my best."

Chava laughed and hugged her friend again. Sandy put her arm into Chava's and they slowly made their way back to the restaurant where the food was just placed on their table. Nobody said a word about what happened, the dinner was consumed quietly. Afterward, to everyone's surprise, except Chava's who ordered it, a large cake was brought in. Sandy clapped her hands with joy, and after they cut the cake, they asked the waiter to offer the rest of the cake to the other patrons as well.

During the dinner Avi wouldn't take her eyes off Chava, but she made all efforts to avoid his stare. Each time their eyes met, the more she became convinced that her life was not going to be easy from then on, especially that Avi was not only visiting San Francisco, but he actually moved to live and work there. Sausalito, where Chava lived, was just on the other side of the Golden Gate Bridge, a short driving distance away. Just that knowledge itself that he was so nearby was becoming an increasingly disturbing fact of reality for Chava.

A couple of hours later as they were leaving the restaurant, Sandy and Tomer said goodbye to Sandy's cousin Jack and his wife who were returning to their home in Sacramento. They thanked Chava for making arrangements for them and for Avi for being the best man. A taxi was called and the newlyweds left for Sandy's home and from there to a short honeymoon in Carmel by the Sea.

While the valet was getting Chava's car, Avi stepped to her and touched her arm. "Chava," he said softly. "I would like to spend some time with you. I would like you to know me, the real me," he pleaded.

Chava turned around to face him. She reached out and touched his face with her hand. "A few months ago, if you would have asked me to die for you, I would have asked you what method should I use," her eyes filled up with tears as she continued. "Now, as I am standing here in front of you, I can confess to you Avi, that I love you more than I ever did. But my heart and my mind is devastated from what you have done to me. I can not imagine my life with you, at least not right now, and I am not sure if I could imagine it again." When she finished, it was not her eyes that became clouded with tears, it was Avi's.

Her car arrived and the valet left the door open for her to get in. "You killed all the hard earned trust that I built up for you," she said and leaving Avi standing there, she got in her car. Avi ran down on the steps and tapped on her car's window. She pushed the button and window rolled down.

"Chava," he said fighting back his emotions. "I love you so much that it hurts me. Please, I am begging you, tell me how I can make it up to you?" he pleaded with her.

Chava thought for a moment, biting her lips before she replied. "You just have to find the way to take back what happened," she pushed the button again and the window closed. She put the gear into drive and left for home.

CHAPTER FORTY-TWO

Someone is following me? Chava wondered. It was not the first time that she had a distinct feeling that someone was either watching her or following her. Chava thought that someone was watching her before and during the lunch with Sandy and Tomer at the Hyatt Regency Hotel's atrium lobby's restaurant, and after that on almost every occasion when she made short excursions from her home in Sausalito. She always looked around and tried to identify some familiar or not so familiar faces in her surroundings that looked suspicious, but she could not identify or put a finger on anyone specifically.

Angela, her agent called Chava a week after the release of her latest book, and her excitement was evident from her voice. "Well Chava, have you seen this morning's Chronicle?" she asked Chava.

"No, I haven't touched the paper yet," replied Chava and glanced at the paper that was still on top of her curio cabinet in the entrance way of her house, rolled up with a rubber band around it. "Is anything worth reading?" she asked Angela teasingly.

"Mr. Gabriel Smith, the so called "Author's Executioner" who, as you know one of the top book critics in the country gave your book five stars. Five stars Chava," she repeated. "He said that during his career that spanned over twenty-eight years, he only gave five stars seven times and Chava, you are one of those rare people who actually were able to please Mr. Smith."

"That's great, I think," said Chava but her enthusiasm was not at the same level as Angela's.

"There is more," said Angela. "I have received invitations for you to appear on the ever popular "Lillian Walker's Daily Show". Also, all major magazines were calling, wanting to interview you and have photos taken. Do you have any plans for the next two weeks?" she asked from Chava.

"Hmmm, let me see my busy social calendar," laughed Chava. "No, I believe I am free for the next few years."

"Okay funny girl," answered Angela herself laughing. "I'll be in touch once I make your appearance schedules so we can compare notes if you are available on those days. Chava, please don't forget that in two weeks, you have a big book signing coming up at B & N in the city," she reminded Chava.

"Okay, talk to you later," said Chava and hung up the phone. She remained seated there staring at the calendar on her kitchen wall. Just a year ago she would have jumped from joy hearing that one of the most popular talk show hosts was inviting her so soon after her new book hit the number one slot on the Best Seller's List, but her heart was not into any kind of celebration.

She was about to get up from her table when the telephone rang again. "Yes," she answered as always. It was Sandy at the other end of the line, making her routine daily check in with Chava. "Are you alright?" asked her Sandy.

"Yes, I am fine," replied Chava, but she knew that her voice sounded depressed and she was certain that she could not fool Sandy.

"No, you are not," declared Sandy just as Chava suspected. "What is the matter or should I guess?" she asked.

"Don't go there," Chava warned her.

"Okay, but you know he is here at my house everyday and I have never seen a grown man as lovesick as he is, well, you know, other than you," confessed Sandy.

"Gee thanks," replied Chava. "You think that he is following me?" she asked Sandy.

"You mean Avi? Oh, I don't think so, why? Is somebody following you?" inquired Sandy with concern.

"It's just a feeling," said Chava.

"But how do you know? I mean what makes you think that? Ever since you became popular people recognize you and some may even follow you to see what you are doing or what you are buying, you know, that sort of stuff," said Sandy, wondering who would follow Chava as she was certain that Avi was not.

"Trust me on this, I can tell the difference when a "fan" is following or watching. This feeling is different," she tried to explain to her friend.

"When did you start noticing this?" Sandy asked her.

"That day when you brought Tomer with you to the Hyatt Regency was the first time that I felt that I was followed, but I couldn't see anybody who would stand out," she replied.

"Do you have your security alarm on around your house and inside too?" inquired Sandy.

"Of course," answered Chava.

"Maybe you should notify the police," suggested Sandy with genuine concern. "There are a lot of weirdoes out there," she warned Chava although she knew that it was not necessary.

"I'll think about it," she promised.

"I meant to ask you," said Sandy after a few moments of hesitation. "Have you contacted the Holocaust Survivors Research Center yet? I was just wondering?"

"I am sorry, I should have told you," Chava said apologetically. "I am no longer the sole keeper of my mother's secret. It's out of my hands, thank God," she added.

"You did the right thing," Sandy agreed with her. "Let's hope that even if those poor people are not alive, at least any of their surviving relatives will be able to get their rightful belongings back."

"That is exactly what I am hoping for," replied Chava.

"Why don't you come over for dinner tonight, we can talk some more?" suggested Sandy.

"Is Avi going to be there?" asked Chava.

"Well yes, I can't just get rid of him, he virtually spends all his free time here," explained Sandy.

"Sorry sweetheart, I have to turn you down," said Chava. "I'll call you later okay?"

"Okay, talk to you later," they said their goodbyes and hung up the telephone.

CHAPTER FORTY-THREE

For some unexplainable reason Chava always managed to remain calm under circumstances that would have made another person perspire from nervousness. She calmly sat in the make-up room that was designated for guests, and when the Lillian Walker's Daily Show producer arrived to escort her inside the studio, she calmly walked next to her.

Lillian Walker was a somewhat liked, yet controversial person and one of the most watched talk show hostesses on air any given day. Her popularity stemmed from the fact that she was an outspoken person, who didn't shy away from troubling issues and was brutally honest on air, allowing no mercy for her guests who by her judgment didn't deserve it. Many times lawsuits followed her programs, and on the majority of those occasions those lawsuits were won by her guests or were settled out of court.

Lillian and Chava met an hour earlier before the show began and although it was a live show, it was being taped for future reruns. They had a nice chat which was by all means not a clue just how she was going to behave towards Chava once the cameras began to roll. Seated in a dark red armchair next to Lillian's oval shape desk, Chava looked around to see the live audience and it came to her as a shock that the studio was jam packed with people of various ages.

The sign was given, "five, four, three, two, one and you are on," motioned the lead cameraman. Lillian turned straight toward the camera with the red light on its top. "Ladies and Gentlemen welcome to the Lillian Walker Daily Show Book Corner," she began. "I would also like to welcome today's guest, a popular novelist who's suspense novels kept us sitting on the edge of our seats and who's romance novels wanted us to fall in love all over again. Please give a warm welcome to Ms. Chava Diamond," she asked from the audience.

To Chava's surprise, the audience rose to their feet and gave her a long and loud applause. She got up as well and bowed toward them, then sat down again.

"First and foremost Chava, I wish to congratulate you on your latest novel, "Once upon a time . . ." Trust me when I tell you this, and I must admit that I seldom say something like this because I am not a cry baby, but when I finished reading your novel, my husband had to make a trip to our Kleenex box to bring me the entire box, not only a few tissues," she said and held up Chava's book so the camera could zoom in on it.

"I am sorry, "said Chava regretfully.

"No apology is necessary. When I was reading your novel, it appeared to me that you perhaps not only created this main character, but perhaps you wrote about a real person. How right am I? Was your book's heroine a real person?" inquired Lillian with what seemed like a genuine respect.

"You are absolutely right. Helene, one of the main characters in my book was my mother and that part of the story was based on her life; and about her will to survive at all costs" explained Chava and she added. "All cost as long as it was honorable."

"Was this book a partial autobiography of what happened to you after your mother's passing?" she asked the straight shooting question from Chava.

Chava smiled as she replied. "I am a writer and as a writer I create stories. The story of Helene and my family's demise at the hands of the Nazis was true."

"You are not getting away that easy," said Lillian and shook a finger at Chava who was still smiling. "Tell me Chava," she continued. "The part about the main character, your heroine named Maya, when she meets this dashing Israeli officer who becomes the love of her life was that about you perhaps?"

Chava remained calm as she replied. "I have never discussed my private life in public as it belongs to me. Most of the magazines and newspapers already told the public about my humble beginnings in my native country and dug out some things that didn't even belong to me," she said and she turned to the audience. "My book is about a person's struggle of self discovery nothing more than that. I combined my mother's story with a fictional."

Lillian Walker looked at her with a certain smile that sent a chill up on Chava's spine. "Can you tell us about your mother's tattoo?" her question stunned Chava and for a few short moments her smile froze on her face, then her face became serious and offensive.

"All prisoners, Jewish, political and even gypsies were tattooed upon their arrival to Auschwitz and for that matter, the same thing happened in almost all major concentration camps, there is no secret about that," explained Chava forcing her voice to sound calm.

"Well now, now Chava, you are holding back something," Lillian pressured her. "It came to our attention that your mother's tattoo symbolized a lot more than just an identification number," said Lillian and with her hand she pointed at the camera to focus on Chava instead on her. "It also came into our attention that your mother was favored by one of the Nazi officers, was that true?"

That was the last straw, Chava was about to snap. Her calmness was gone, her old self was back, and she felt stronger than ever. "What kind of person are you

Ms. Walker?" Chava stood up and stepped toward the talk show hostess. "What gives you the right to disturb a law obeying citizen's most painful memories? Have you ever lost a relative to starvation, to illness or to just plain and simple uncontrollable brutality? Have you?" her voice sounded threatening. "How dare you to disgrace my mother's suffering and her memory?"

Lillian Walker's face was turning red. "Sit down," she hissed toward Chava who backed toward her seat and slowly sat down. "I didn't intend to disgrace your mother's memory or any other Jewish persons, especially women who find the way to survive," she tried to explain with another forced smile on her face.

"You don't deserve to mention my mother's name out loud," Chava said to her. "And don't you dare to think and repeat that Jewish women found their way to survive by the way you insinuating it. They were given no choices. If a Nazi soldier wanted to rape a female prisoner, the only option that woman had was to choose to die then or die later. On a great many occasions, both happened at once, they were raped and killed right after they were brutalized," Chava explained more to the audience than to Lillian. The people were hanging onto every word she was saying.

"There must have been a way to resist. As a person of strong confidence," tried to say Lillian. "I do believe that I would have resisted in some ways. My family always had been very strong and they have always been survivors during harsh circumstances."

Chava laughed out loud unexpectedly. "Oh, please forgive me, I am not laughing at the subject because it's way too serious to be laughing matter," she said and her face once again became serious. "But I am laughing because it is not I, but it is you who are hiding something," she said and reached inside her purse and pulled out a folded yellow envelope. "You see Ms. Walker, as a writer, I do a lot of research for my books, because as always, I am trying to be very thorough when I mention places and various facts. So what I did," Chava continued and removed several pieces of copied documents and lifted them up towards one of the cameras. Before she was able to continue, Lillian smiled and waived into the direction of the cameramen, but the lead cameraman focused his camera on Chava instead of her.

"I believe we should go on a commercial break at this time," said Lillian and looked around, her eyes searching for her show's producer and showed her to cut, but she just smiled back at her and the show went on without the usual commercial break. The camera was still focused on Chava and zoomed in on the documents which she held up one by one.

"This particular document here which I was fortunate to obtain from the Holocaust Survivors Research Center shows that your father's original name, Ms. Walker was actually Udo Waltheim who immigrated to the United States in 1946 from Germany. Although he was granted a visa to enter the US, two years after his arrival he was investigated by the Immigration and Naturalization

Services because of his involvement with guarding concentration camps," she once again lifted the document toward the camera then tossed it into the direction of Lillian whose face was ashen white. "Furthermore, I have information that the investigation lasted for five years during which time, your father met and married your mother, also a German immigrant," she continued.

"What are you trying to do Chava?" asked Lillian and her eyes showed tears of anger. "Don't you know that we are live on camera?"

"Ms. Walker," said Chava standing up. "You were trying to force me to reveal some of my family's most disturbing inner and social struggles. My mother and father had a hard life to begin with and then the Hungarian and German Nazis forced them to live in unspeakable circumstances and do despicable acts to survive. I don't ever let anyone, including you, or the media, to smear my family and other concentration camp victim's memories, and try to distort the fact, that human beings just like all of us her, were forced to live under circumstances that would not be fit even for an animal."

"That's enough," Lillian hissed at her.

"It's never going to be enough and it will never end because of people like you," she turned away from Lillian. She got up and walked toward the audience. She stopped in front of the first row and looked at the people's faces in front of her. The camera was eating her up, her movements, her facial impressions and her words. "I apologize to all of you for what you just witnessed. Deep in my heart I know that all of you are decent working or retired people and perhaps we have some students here as well today," she smiled and nodded as recognition toward some young people a few rows up. "Please look at the person next to you, yes, please do it," she urged the audience.

In the control room, the vice president of the network, George Prescott would not hear anyone speaking to him, although several of them were talking to him at once. He raised his hand to hush them up and then he picked up one of the headsets with a microphone. "Wendy," he called out for the show's producer.

Wendy glanced up to the control room where she was able to see Mr. Prescott. She turned around and looked at the head cameraman and lipped to him "we are toasted," when she heard her name called again. "Yes Mr. Prescott, this is Wendy," she said and crossed her fingers.

"What is going on down there, you do know that this is a live show, don't you?" he asked.

"Yes sir, I apologize for what is happening but it seems that the audience loves her, so we thought that . . . ," Wendy tried to explain but Prescott cut her off.

"No apology is needed, you guys are doing a fantastic job. Don't let Ms. Diamond leave, I may have a job offer for her," he said and put the head phone on and turned up the speaker.

"You are wondering why I asked you to look at the person next to you, right?" she smiled at the audience. There were sounds of three hundred "yes" in the audience. Chava continued. "Some of us are white, some of us black, some of us Hispanics and let's face it, some of us are mutts," she said and everyone in audience laughed. "But the fact is that you are all sitting here in peace and harmony, listening to one person who is trying to disgrace the memory of family, and the other one is trying to keep those memories sacred. I am not angry at Ms. Walker's distasteful approach of my beloved mother's suffering, I am angry at that we allow people like her go on the air and we make her popular by watching her with fascination as she is trying to challenge history."

She shook her head. "I love the United States of America," she said and placed her right hand above her heart. "There is no other country in the world like ours. This is a country where basically all of us are able to enjoy of the freedom of many things. We can say what we want, and vote as we want, criticize politicians if we want and we can fall in love and marry whomever we want. Sure, there are problems in our country and perhaps at times we are not treated as equally as the Declaration of Independence suggested the way we should be treated. But today, we, all of us have the possibilities, and the willpower to make changes, to make our lives better. You show me a country in this world that is always willing to offer immediate assistance to other countries in need on the same day that other country declared our country evil and infidel. This country of ours turns the other cheek when it comes to help countries whose population suffered from earthquakes and other natural disasters. Our country provides more humanitarian aid to starving and poverty stricken nations than any other country is willing or capable to give."

Not a single person in the audience moved, all eyes and ears were focused on Chava. "Do you know why?" she asked but did not expect an answer. "We do that not just because our country is one of the most powerful and richest nations on this planet, we aid people because we are Americans and we know our place in God's eyes. You don't have to be a Christian, a Jew, and a Baptist or Muslim to give, you have to be a human being to give, to aid your fellow man and that is we are all about. But there is a danger," she said lowering her voice. "We are in danger because we are trying to forget what happened yesterday, a week ago or years ago. We can't do that, and we can not afford to do that," she shook her head. "We are simply not allowed to do that because we have way too many Lillian Walkers out there who are trying to tear apart people's background, their families and you know what? I was just doing the very same thing today, and I do apologize for it. As you may guess, my defense mechanism kicked in."

She began to walk toward the stage where Lillian Walker disappeared from several minutes earlier. Chava didn't sit down, she turned once again toward the audience. "This is a quite unusual day for me, as you might have guessed," she said and there was light laughter among the audience members. "I am not a politician and other than that I vote every four years, my political ambition ends right there. However; if you are a reader of my books, which I suspect you are, than you probably noticed that in my suspense books I always bring the criminals to justice and in my romance novels, there is always a happy ending. Unfortunately, in real life those things do not always work out that way. However, I am a firm believer that better things will come our way, everyone's way but first, we must do some important things. Such as; we must believe in God, in our country, in our families and most of all, we must always believe in ourselves."

The clapping of the hands echoed like thunder from the audience and people were giving her a standing in ovation. Chava stepped forward and bowed. "God Bless you all," she said and was about to leave the studio stage when Wendy rushed up to her and stopped her. "Ms. Diamond, would you like or mind to have a Q & A session?" she asked with flashed face.

"Well, I don't know," said Chava hesitantly. "I was under the impression that I have outlived my welcome here."

"Oh no, you are most welcome to continue. We have about fifteen minutes air time left and our vice president, Mr. Prescott wishes to speak to you before you leave. I believe he was very impressed how you, well, you know, took over the show," she said with a big grin on her face. "We are on commercial now, and we only have two more minutes left before we come back live on the air."

Chava looked at the audience and she realized that nobody moved, apparently they were waiting for something else to happen. "Why don't you ask them if they want a Q & A session," she said to Wendy who ran back to the audience section. Chava heard applause and saw Wendy waving at her to return to the stage. She turned back and took a seat on stage, picking up a hand held microphone from Lillian Walker's desk.

"Five, four, three, two, one, you are on," Chava heard the sound of the lead cameraman.

"I was asked if I would mind to do a short Question and Answer session and I'll be glad to do so. Please raise your hand if you have a question," she asked from the audience and dozens of arms were raised in the air. Wendy with her headphone and a hand held microphone motioned to the person to walk down the stairs for a better camera view. It was an elderly man.

"My name is Arthur and I am also a Holocaust survivor, just like your late mother was Ms. Diamond. I was taken from Romania by the Germans and I immigrated here after the liberation of Mauthausen. I can tell you that I have witnessed many horrible things in that camp. I also know that your mother was a very brave woman, I loved reading about her. My question is to you, how you, who became a Christian, feel about the Germans who murdered your family. Do you hate them?"

Chava nodded that she understood the question. "Thank you for being here and I am happy that you also had the will power and courage to go on under despicable circumstances, that some people nowadays believe that they were fictional. To answer your question, I always believe that hate is a very strong word. If I tell you that I hated the Nazis for what they have done to my family, I would go down to their level. Technically the Nazis hated anybody who was not German and pure Aryan by birth, as they were called then. I have not lived then, so today, I cannot say that I hate all Germans because of what another generation had done during World War Two. There were, although not very many Germans, who actually helped sheltering Jews and some even assisted the escapes of Jews out of Germany or other occupied countries. I try not to speak in general terms when I say this. I hate what the Nazis did to millions of innocent people and to humanity, but I do not hate Germany as a nation or on a larger scale."

A younger man wearing the U of Berkeley T-shirt stepped down to Wendy and took the microphone. "Ms. Diamond, first I want to say that I really like your suspense novels, I am not much for romance novels though," he said and smiled seeing that Chava was smiling at him. "However, I did read your latest book and I have become curious if you have any explanation what made German Nazis commit those atrocities?" he asked.

Chava got up with her microphone and she slowly made her way to where the audience was seated. "I wish I can answer your question with specific details on how and why a human being able to commit brutal torture, or kill a fellow human being without a blink of an eye or without a social conscious, but I cannot. I visited Auschwitz a few months ago and I was inside the very same barracks where my mother and her sisters endured beatings, starvation, the harsh weather conditions and the uncertainty. While I was visiting there, I asked myself the question would I have survived? I could not answer my own question then and I cannot answer it now. Many times in my life, especially right there where all those horrible things happened but I have fortunately only read about it, I tried to understand how one person looked at another and not see a fellow human being? What unimaginable force took over millions of German's minds overnight to turn on their Jewish neighbors and threat them like pariahs. In the morning, a Jewish child who was growing up right next door to the Christian child went to school together, studied together and played together and during the dinner in both homes that night, the Christian child's parent told the child that he or she could not study or play with the dirty Jew child next door. Never again, they told the child," she stopped at looked at the young man. He bowed his head. "In the home of the Jewish child, the parents told the child that he or she could never again go to school, study or play with the Christian child. The child asked the parents but why not? They told the child, "because you are Jewish," she stopped and looked at the faces in the front row. She saw tears in some eyes and she noticed just plain "could not understand why that happened" look on others.

"Thank you so much," said the young man and stepped aside to give the microphone to the next person, a young woman.

"Hi, Ms. Diamond, I am pleased to meet you in person," she said. "My name is Gertrud, but everyone calls me Gertie," she introduced herself.

"It is also my pleasure to meet you Gertie," Chava replied. "What is your question?"

"As you might have guessed from my name, I am also of a German descent and I just want your opinion. Do you think that all Germans hated Jews during World War Two?" she asked from Chava.

Chava smiled. "I was hoping that this Q & A won't turn into a World War Two debate, but I will answer your question," said Chava and she continued. "Actually I always believed that not all Germans felt the same way. I also always believed that the Nazi propaganda machine did a great job scaring people with exaggerated and made up stories about, for example, that Jewish people sacrifice Christian babies during High Holy Holidays and so on. They terrorized their own people with putting their own citizens into concentration camps for minor violations so they could experience what was waiting for them if they resisted their regime. Hitler was the most hated person in the world in those days, the symbol of ultimate evil. But let's not forget that he was only one person who could not possibly have done all those horrible things all by himself, he had to have a large support group which he found in people like Himmler, Goering, Eichmann and in the majority of the German population."

Wendy motioned to her that she only had eight minutes left. An older lady stepped took the microphone next. "Ms. Diamond, I just love your name, is your name real?" she asked.

Chava laughed. "Yes, it is real," she replied. "Chava means Eva in English but my parents named me in Hebrew."

"I love your romance novels and I have read them more than once and some of them I have read several times. In your last novel, and that is why I made this trip to the studio, you described the scene where Maya and the Israeli officer, Yaniv met the first time, and I must admit, as old as I am, I have read the love scenes over and over," she said and the audience laughed. "Basically I don't have a question for you, but I just wanted you to know I fell in love with Yaniv and if I was just twenty years younger, I would travel to Israel to find him." The audience laughed and applauded and so did Chava.

She smiled and looked up at the next person. He was a tall young man with blue eyes and something about his eyes made Chava very uncomfortable.

"I am Helmut," he said introducing himself with a strong German accent. "I am glad to hear that you don't hate Germans, we are not all bad people you know."

Chava did not reply, but she could not take her eyes off from him and he stared back at her. "Do you have a question?" she finally asked.

"Ja, I want to know who killed Hilde?" he asked from Chava.

"Excuse me?" she asked being startled by hearing Hilde's name. "There was no such character mentioned in my book," she replied to him.

"Ja, I do know that," he replied. "But she was a very pretty, headstrong girl who died in an Israeli prison, do you know how?" he asked Chava again.

The studio became deadly silent. People around them sensed that they were about to witness something unusual and at the same time they were wondering why Chava looked so shocked and why she didn't reply right away as she did to other questions. Wendy whispered into her microphone to call security immediately.

"I was told that Hilde killed herself, she hung herself in jail while she was waiting to be questioned," she said and people in the audience couldn't understand what they were talking about.

"No, I don't believe you. I believe that you and that your Jew friend killed her," said Helmut and he calmly pulled out a twenty-two caliber revolver from his back pocket and pointed at Chava who was standing only eight feet from him. "She was my girlfriend and true comrade who believed that we can bring back the glory of German values, like our fathers and grandfathers had."

"Helmut, you are wrong about her. Hilde was not who you thought she was. She did not care about any causes, she cared about how to get a hold of those possibly millions of dollars worth of confiscated goods that the Nazis took away from Jews arriving to Auschwitz," Chava said calmly and as she looked passed Helmut, she made out a figure of a familiar person. *No, it just can't be him,* she thought. Avi was standing there with a gun in his hand, pointing at the back of Helmut's head while he placed a finger on his lips, as if he was telling people to remain quiet.

Wendy also motioned to her to stay calm and that security was on their way. Chava knew that it could be as little as split second and her life would be over if Helmut pulled the trigger. He didn't move and he didn't care who was around him, he focused all his attention on Chava standing right in front of him. He was stalking her for weeks and he couldn't believe his fortune when he found out that Chava was about to appear on Lillian Walker's controversial show.

When he found out that Hilde, his girlfriend of three years died, he immediately suspected that Israelis tortured and killed her. He had no solid evidence if that was the truth or not, but he decided that it just had to be the truth because Jews wanted to take revenge on her when they found out that her grandfather served in the German army during World War Two. Somehow in his twisted mind, he connected all the imagined torture of Hilde to Chava, as his girlfriend told him that she was going to Israel to find her, because Chava wanted to rip her off from some rightful inheritance from her grandfather.

Chava couldn't help it; she was no longer focusing on Helmut's face. Her eyes remained locked on his finger that rested on gun's trigger. When she saw in slow motion that Helmut's finger began to move, Chava closed her eyes. In that brief moment, an incredible peace came over her, then she heard the unmistakable sound of a gun shot and then another. Chava felt a sharp pain, but she didn't have a chance to open her eyes to see the shooter, as she collapsed in front of the steps that led to the audience stand.

There was a lot of screaming in the audience and a full scale panic was about to break out when the police arrived and escorted everyone into the studio's lobby. The ambulance arrived minutes later and the medical technician immediately began to work on Chava's wound. A policeman had to force Avi to let Chava's hand go and in the first time in his life, Avi openly wept.

CHAPTER FORTY-FOUR

C hava opened her eyes and she tried to focus on the person sitting on a chair next to her bed. It took great effort to finally clear her vision, but once she did, Chava recognized her ever faithful friend Sandy, dozed off just sitting there. Chava's lips were incredibly dry and she looked at the table next to her bed if there was any water there.

Her shoulder was aching when she tried to move and she realized that she was probably shot in her left shoulder. She had an IV tube inserted into her right arm and the tube was interlocked with three other tubes and they all led all the way up on an IV stand that stood next to her bed.

The door opened and a nurse walked in carrying a fresh bag of IV fluid to replace the one that was almost empty, hooked up on the modern IV stand with a fancy monitor. Sandy immediately snapped awake and when she noticed that Chava was awake, she made a sign of a cross on her chest. The nurse smiled at Chava. "How are you feeling?" she asked.

"I honestly don't know," replied Chava in a raspy voice. "Can I get some water or ice cubes please," she asked from the nurse.

"Let me take your vital signs and I will bring you some ice chips, okay?" she asked and Chava nodded that it would be fine. "The doctor should be in shortly to check on you and to talk to you about your injury and the therapy that you will need."

As soon as the nurse was gone, Sandy sat down on the edge of Chava's bed and took her friend's hand into hers. "Welcome back," she said with tears shining in her eyes.

"I guess it's good to be back," whispered Chava and looked around in her hospital room. There were several huge bouquet of flowers placed on an extra end table someone brought in to make room for the incoming flow of beautiful flowers. Chava turned her head back toward Sandy and took a deep breath. "So what happened?" she inquired from Sandy.

"You remember that you told me that you thought that someone was stalking you?" Sandy asked. Chava nodded that she did. "You were right. That German guy was watching your house and your movements. I mentioned to Tomer and Avi what you told me and they began to watch you and anyone who might have followed you. They noticed that the German guy was always there wherever you went and they began to monitor his movements as well."

"And he found me and shot me," concluded Chava.

"Actually, Avi shot him first and as he was falling to the ground, he fired into your direction. God must have been watching over you. You were very lucky that your injury was minor considering the fact that if Avi didn't shot that guy, he would have probably killed you," explained Sandy.

Chava closed her eyes and she recalled the last thing she remembered before the shots rang out. She remembered that peaceful feeling she was experiencing for that brief moment and the sudden pain she felt a second later. "Was he here?" she asked.

"He held your hand throughout the ambulance ride to this hospital," replied Sandy. "He loves you very much you know," she added. Chava turned her head and tears flooded her eyes. *Yes I know, and I love him too,* she thought.

"Where is he now?" Chava asked.

Sandy's face became very serious and pointed at a huge bouquet of red roses in a large vase. "That is from him," she said and squeezed Chava's hand.

"You didn't answer my question," she reminded her friend.

"He went back to Israel," Sandy confessed to her.

Chava couldn't hold her tears back any longer. "Did he say anything to you?" she asked.

Sandy hesitated before she replied. "He said that he finally realized what he had to do and he flew back to Tel Aviv the following day."

The door opened once again, the nurse returned in the company of a doctor who introduced himself as Dr. Shapiro. The nurse walked around the bed and placed a cup with ice cubes on the table next to it. The doctor looked at Chava's chart and handed it back to the nurse. "How are you feeling?" he asked Chava while looking in her eyes with a thin flashlight, pointed straight into them.

"I guess I am okay," she replied. "What can you tell me about my injury?" she asked Dr. Shapiro.

"You were very fortunate because the bullet went through clearly without causing damage to any major bone structure. Of course, there was a serious damage to your rotator cuff. It was reparable and it will heal perfectly if you are sticking to your therapy regimen. Although you suffered a shot injury, not a dislocation, the therapy will be the just same. You should be able to regain your arm movement completely in a few weeks," he explained.

"When would I'll be able to leave the hospital?" asked Chava.

"Why, you don't like our Jell-O?" he asked her in return and smiled at Chava.

"I wouldn't know and I am not sure I want to stay that long to find out," she replied.

"You should be able to leave in about a week," he said and patted her feet, ready to leave. "I'll be seeing you tomorrow morning, good night," he promised and left Chava's room.

Chava sighed and looked at the cup of ice. Sandy immediately placed a teaspoon of ice cubes between Chava's lips, and Chava thought that they tasted heavenly. The nurse checked the IV drip and the bag of antibiotics and she told Chava that she would be back in a half an hour to bring a new bag of that as well.

When she left, Chava turned to Sandy. "I guess it's all over between Avi and me," she said with great sadness in her voice. Sandy did not reply as she didn't know what to say to make her friend feel better, but deep down inside she hoped that it was not the case.

CHAPTER FORTY-FIVE

What happened on the Lillian Walker Daily Show between the hostess and Chava and the German man's attempt to kill Chava, her shooting and survival became the topic of every single newspaper and television media in the country. Avi's heroism was mentioned and the media was openly wondering who he was and where he came from to save Chava's life.

Her stay in the hospital was only a week long and she left the hospital during the late night hours through a side door where no media was waiting, unlike the front where they camped out ever since the studio incident. Chava didn't return to her home, Sandy thought that it would be a better idea if Chava stayed with her and Tomer for a while, in which Chava agreed.

Although Chava never openly asked about Avi, Tomer mentioned briefly during their dinner one night that he had not heard anything from Avi. It was a very rare thing, as they always kept constant contact. Sandy gave him a look to be quiet, they didn't need to upset Chava any further.

Angela, her literary agent called Chava, and asked her if she felt up to doing the already scheduled signing session in a couple of days, or she wanted to cancel it? Chava gladly agreed. She wanted to get out of the house and do something useful. Her shoulder, although it was healing quickly, was still very sensitive to the touch. She was getting physical therapy every other day and it helped her to make her arm move better and less painfully.

She was shocked to see the long line of people that wrapped around the corner from the door of the midtown bookstore when she arrived in Sandy's car, an hour before her book signing session began. People in the front clapped in joy seeing her getting out of the car and she waved at them with her right arm and showed them several pens in her hand. "Do you believe this?" she asked from Sandy nodding towards the patiently waiting crowd.

"Of course, and I am very proud of you," replied Sandy and helped Chava to take off her light coat which she placed around the chair, behind the wide table that was covered with a huge poster of the cover of her latest book, "Once upon a time . . ."

Inside the large book store her enlarged picture and large posters of the cover of her book were everywhere. They hung from the ceiling and they were posted on stands by each book aisle. Angela also arrived a short while later bringing them two large cups of Starbucks cappuccino and a six pack of Schweppes soda water, which was Chava's favorite soft drink. The store manager walked up them and excitedly assured Chava, that it had been a great pleasure for her to have Chava on her store's premises. She remarked that she have not seen such a long line of enthusiastic, yet patient people already waiting for a few hours to buy Chava's book, and to get her signature.

The doors finally opened right on time at ten o'clock and people dashed in to grab Chava's book, at times taking several copies. Once they paid for the books they had to get in line again to get her autograph. "How do you feel?" she heard Sandy's voice next to her. She volunteered to assist her to take the book from the fans so she didn't have to reach out for them.

"I am alright," Chava assured her, but Sandy knew that it was not entirely true. She caught Chava crying several times, and she confessed to Sandy that she might have made a mistake when she pushed Avi away when he tried to gain her forgiveness. Sandy felt sad for both of them, because she knew that people who loved each other that much as Avi and Chava did, shouldn't be separated by pride or stubbornness.

CHAPTER FORTY-SIX

The line was so long waiting to purchase her book and obtain her autograph that it seemed endless. The store's manager, Mrs. Martin stopped by at the signing table and asked Chava what time did she want to stop signing as the agreed four hours was fast approaching. Angela put her hand on Chava's arm. "Chava, it's up to you. How do you feel? Are you still okay?" she asked her.

Chava pointed at the direction of the door and smiled. "Since I don't have any plans for the rest of the day, I will stay here as long as it takes to please everyone. These people have been waiting in line for hours; I cannot possibly turn them away. How is the book supply?" she asked from Mrs. Martin.

"We ordered four thousand copies and I believe that we are doing fine," she reported.

"Well then," said Chava. "I will take a break in a half an hour and you may want to get something to eat," she replied and turning her attention back towards the line of people. She smiled at the person who stepped up to the front of the table with four copies of her latest novel. "Who would you like me to dedicate these?" Chava asked the person who began to give her the first names of her relatives.

The Subway sandwiches were fresh and Chava hungrily ate hers and washed the food down with a Schweppes soda water. She stretched her legs out and Angela touched her shoulders to massage them. Chava almost fell of the chair from the sharp pain when Angela squeezed her left shoulder. "Oh my God, Chava," she said genuinely scared. "Please forgive me, I completely forgot about your surgery."

Chava gathered up her strength and hushed her up. "It's easy to forget about it when I don't moan all the time from the pain. I know that you didn't mean to hurt me," she told Angela, who for the next ten minutes repeatedly apologized to Chava.

After that seemingly quick half an hour break, they returned inside the book store and Chava began to sign her books again, making sure that she exchanged some words of various subjects with each and every person. She fully understood the importance of appreciation and she knew that if she was the customer and not the writer, she would have enjoyed the same few moments of personal attention from a popular novelist.

It was becoming dark outside when finally the last customer in line entered the store. Mrs. Martin, the store manager was about to close the door when an elderly couple arrived. The man, dressed in a black suit and black long overcoat, asked Mrs. Martin, who stood by the entrance, where they could find Chava's book. She glanced at them with curious eyes as the man and the woman, whom she assumed was the elderly man's wife, didn't look like people who would read many romance or even suspense novels. Nevertheless, she led them to the counter where earlier that morning mountains of Chava's books were temporarily stationed. There were only a couple dozen left and the man lifted one of them and paid for it with cash. "Is Ms. Diamond still here to sign this book?" asked the man.

"I believe she is about to leave, but I can check for you," she offered and when the man nodded, she hurried towards the back of the store where the signing table was set up. Chava was talking to Sandy and Angela about a magazine article that was published with pictures of her and text quotations from what she said to the audience during the ill fated Lillian Walker show, when Mrs. Martin cleared her throat to get their attention. "Excuse me Ms. Diamond; there is couple who wish to have your book signed. Should I tell them that you have already left?" she asked.

"I am still here," answered Chava. "Please send them back here."

Mrs. Martin turned around to go back to the front of the store and a few minutes later she returned with the couple. Chava had her back to them, but when she looked at Sandy's face showing a surprised expression, she turned around and her shock was equal to her friend's surprise. "May I help you?" she asked forcing her voice to remain calm while her stomach was cramping up from nervousness.

"I would like you to dedicate this book to our son," said the man and handed the book to Chava. "I am Rabbi Yisrael Ben-Yishan and this is my wife, Sa'ada. I am the father of Avi. We met in Eilat a few months ago and I am hoping that you are able to recall our meeting," he said to Chava.

Chava instead of looking at him, she looked directly at his wife who stood there with her head bowed. "I indeed remember very clearly as that night cost me a great deal of pain in more than one way," she replied. She picked up a pen from the table and wrote in the inside cover. "I am dying to forgive, but I am living to forget, Chava Diamond."

She handed the book back to the Rabbi. "Thank you for coming and enjoy the book," said Chava and was about to turn back toward Angela, when she felt a touch on her arm. She turned around and she was surprised to see that it was Sa'ada, Avi's mother who touched her.

She had a sad look in her eyes as she talked to Chava, but she was unable to understand her as Sa'ada was speaking to her in Hebrew. Before she can tell them that she did not understand what she was saying, Rabbi Ben-Yishan began to translate. "My wife wanted you to know, that we believe that our son, Avi loves you more, than we first thought that he did. He talked great deal to us about you, where you came from, how you made it on your own after your husband left you, and we learned to respect you and like you," Sa'ada stopped talking, and for the first time she looked into Chava's brown eyes with gentleness and pleading. Just then Chava realized that she was looking at a woman who genuinely regretted her behavior towards Chava back in Israel. She also sensed a mother's love and concern for her son, whom she managed to turn into an unhappy man. She reached out and took Chava's hands into hers, and Sa'ada once again began to talk, and the Rabbi translated her words to Chava.

"I am very sorry that I tried to discourage my son from marrying you, and you must forgive me for it. I want my son Avi to be a happy man once again. I realized that it is only you who can make him happy, nobody else," she said and squeezed Chava's hands.

Chava's eyes filled with tears and a moment later so did Sa'ada's. She drew Chava to her chest and hugged her. Although a sharp pain shot through her shoulder, Chava didn't want Avi's mother to let go. She forgave her and she wanted to forget what had taken place between them.

"Where is Avi now?" she asked them.

CHAPTER FORTY-SEVEN

She slowly pressed the card into the hotel room's lock, and when the light turned green, she pushed down the door handle. The door opened quietly, and discreetly. There was quiet inside the hotel room and for a moment Chava thought that perhaps she was alone. Walking deeper inside the large room, she noticed that someone was laying on the top of the bed, fully dressed.

Avi fell asleep after his parents left on their "mysterious mission," as they called it. For months, his sleeping was marred by nightmares that he never experienced before, not even after bloody battles with terrorists or going on clandestine missions. There were things in life that he got used to and brushed them away as they were part of his life, and they were necessary evils to protect his much terrorized country. But what happened between Chava and him was an entirely different story in nature. It was just as torturous as any incident when he had to take a human life.

Avi was never afraid of dying, and he was never afraid of taking chances. It dramatically changed after he first met Chava in Poland, he felt a never experienced feeling of wanting to be with someone so badly that he would rather be dead if he could not have been with that person he loved, and it was Chava.

When his parents arrived to Eilat from Tel Aviv and he told them that he asked Chava to be his wife, his mother Sa'ada, a deeply religious Jewish person was about to be physically ill when she learned that Chava was an American and a divorced woman. Avi, her only son out of three children was the center of her universe. Although Avi's job took him to places, and forced him to do things that she would rather did not think about, having a non religious person and what she called a "used one" in her family, she just simply could not give her blessing to. She talked to Avi almost three straight hours before they all joined Avi's teammates in that hotel's restaurant in Eilat, where Avi was supposed to introduce his "American woman" to them.

Sa'ada was not certain why she forced herself not to like Chava, who was obviously deeply in love with Avi, but she did. She didn't even want to look at

Chava when she joined them at the table. Yes, she did see the hurt and pain in her son's eyes, but she hoped that like other times before, her son would recover quickly and meet someone else, someone who was a Sabra, someone who was born and raised in Israel. And then, when the American woman, Chava told them that she was no longer Jewish, her feelings were justified. During those three long hours while she talked to her son, Sa'ada used threats, curses and whatever she could to talk him out of marrying her.

What seemed even stranger to Sa'ada, that even her Rabbi husband tried to stop the way she behaved towards their son, and the first time in his life the Rabbi failed to stop his wife from giving ill advice to their son. When Sa'ada went to use the restroom, the Rabbi reminded his son that he should follow his true feelings and not what others tried to force upon him.

That night Sa'ada saw her son's real pain for the first time when he stormed into their hotel room and almost tore up the furniture. Although he did not cry, she saw tears in his eyes as he told his shocked parents that Chava lost their baby, and that it was their fault as much as it was his. He yelled into their faces that he would never forgive them, never. What changed Sa'ada's mind? It was the love that she felt for her only son, and the love and the pain that she saw in her son's eyes convinced her that she indeed made a terrible mistake. She desperately wanted to correct what she had done and perhaps salvage what she could possibly find in Chava's heart towards her son.

When Avi returned to Israel after the shooting incident which made the news even in Israel, he went directly to his parent's house outside Tel Aviv in Kfar Saba, and told them that they must help him to get Chava and her love back. It was a challenge that Sa'ada gladly undertook and while she had never flown before, she and her husband, Rabbi Ben-Yishan, traveled half way around the world to help their son and Chava to find each other once again.

Chava slowly made her way to the bed and sat down next to Avi. He was laying on his back with one of his hands under the pillow and the other one was rested on his stomach. Chava bent over him with her eyes closed and inhaled his aftershave, which she knew that no matter where she was or what she was doing; she would never have any difficulty to recall.

Her fingers gently touched his lips and her entire body trembled from the memory of those passionate kisses that they once shared. She pulled her hand back and with the finger she touched his lips, she touched her own.

Avi opened his eyes and it took him a few seconds to register that he was not dreaming, she was actually physically there in his presence. The silence that settled between them spoke louder than any words they could have mastered out loud. Their eyes locked together interchanging memories and guesses about past references of love and the hope of a still existing one.

He pulled his hand from under the pillow and in it was his Glock revolver. Chava was taken aback seeing the gun, but she recalled that there was one always present where Avi stayed. He placed the gun on the nightstand and he reached out for Chava, he pulled her down to him. She didn't protest, as so many times she dreamed about this moment, and she wanted that to happen more than anything, well, almost anything.

Chava laid her head on his chest and he gently stroked her hair. She slowly raised herself and bent over him, gently kissing him for a brief moment as she was taking a sample of the softness of his lips. She did that over and over again until his arms went around her back and he forced her body to turn, to be underneath him.

He wanted to tell her how sorry he was for what he had done, how much it pained him to learn of the loss of their first child, how much he missed her, how much he wanted her emotionally and physically, but most of all, he wanted to tell her that he couldn't go on without her love. Instead, he just looked at her longingly until he could stand it no more.

His lips parted hers and she was so ready for him, that if he had not kissed her in that moment, she would have done it herself. It was impossible to tell where the kisses turned into touching, but soon, pieces of their clothing pealed off one by one in a fast pace. He just couldn't believe it, and he kept on telling himself that he was not dreaming. Her body was just as beautiful and desirable as he remembered, and he wanted her more than he ever wanted anything or anyone.

Chava softly moaned as his lips were moving down on her body while his hands were caressing her. Her hands grabbed the bed sheet when his tongue discovered her again, and she knew that if she had to, she would beg him to take her. Chava was more than ready for him and he knew it, but so was he. Avi entered her with an unforgiving thrust and she gasped, but not from pain, but from the pleasure from becoming one with him once again. She just couldn't help it, she held on to him tightly, pulling Avi down to her to feel him not only inside of her, but to feel his breath on her face and his lips on her lips.

"I love you," he whispered to her. Those were the first words spoken to her by him since Sandy's wedding, and it couldn't have been a more perfect way to initiate a conversation.

"I love you too," she replied between taking deep breaths.

He stopped moving and just looked at her, marveling the woman who took over his heart and occupied his mind the majority of the time. "I will never let you go again," he said and he sealed his promise with a deep kiss.

"You owe me," she said breathing hard.

"I'll pay you back if you tell me what I owe you," he promised.

"You owe me a child," she said and smiled at him. "Or two," she added.

He caressed her hair and the outline of her face. "I believe that I am almost ready to pay you back," he said and laughed. She nodded and pushed his hand down to touch her and he began to move faster. A short time later a smile appeared on Chava's face, but she bit her lips together because that long missed sensation was coming at her with full speed. She cried out Avi's name and he climaxed with her at the same time.

CHAPTER FORTY-EIGHT

O nce in a while Chava would think back to the days when she thought
that love forever eluded her, and that the only joy she would find was
telling stories to readers, stories about her fantasies and wishful thinking, but
destiny had other plans for her.

She found true happiness in the most unexpected circumstances thanks to
her mother's final wishes. As she sat outside on her patio with her baby girl,
Shayna in her arms, who busied herself with nursing while her chubby little
hands holding onto Chava's breast, swollen with milk, she glanced over to her
husband. Avi had their three year old son, Chaim sitting on his lap, happily
accepting the food that his father was giving him.

Avi looked up and he smiled at her and glanced at their baby girl. "I want
to claim that spot back you know," he joked and Chava laughed softly. "You
are making me very happy," he said to Chava and she knew that those words
were truly spoken.

CHAPTER FORTY-NINE

(Summary of Events)

C hava and Avi remained in Sausalito, California, and when their second child Shayna turned two years old, Chava gave birth to twins, a boy and a girl. She continued writing and her books remained successful best sellers, some of them even made it to the big screen, and some of them were turned into mini series on cable networks.

Chava became more popular than ever after her live and suspense filled television appearance on the Lillian Walker's Daily Show. Eventually she was offered her own show on the same network which she gratefully declined. Eventually Lillian Walker was indicted by a grand jury for money laundering, and was sentenced to fifteen years in a federal prison which she could partly thank Chava for. Evidently the FBI became interested in Lillian Walker after Chava's appearance on the show, and the discussion that they had with a representative from the Holocaust Survivors Research Center that was investigating Nazi war criminals. Justice had been served in more ways than one. The tattoo number that caused so much grief and death of many was confirmed to be a pass code number in a bank in Geneva, Switzerland. Investigations began and some of the survivors were found still alive. They also managed to locate some of the relatives of murdered concentration camp victims, and the stolen goods, the ones that could be verified who they belong to were returned to their rightful owners.

Avi was very busy with his new job with an Israeli Security Company whose corporate office was located in San Francisco. Although at times his work required travels to other areas of the country, he made all efforts to spend as much time with his adored family as he could.

One of Avi's sisters also moved to Sausalito and became a nanny to her brother's children, a job that she wanted and loved. Later on when she met a Jewish college student while she was learning English, she got married but continued her work as a nanny.

Sandy and Tomer remained Chava and Avi's closest friends and they also had two children. Very frequently the two families traveled together on vacations and to Israel to visit their spouse's relatives.

Chava's ex-husband, Colonel Matthew Roberts who served two full tours in Iraq was killed in action during his third tour in the war and terror ravaged country. To Chava's surprise; he left everything from his expensive home in San Francisco, including his life insurance policies to Chava. She didn't want any of it and she donated every penny she received from his estate and from the military to various charities around the country.

EPILOG

There was not a single day in her life when Chava did not think about her mother. Just one look at her children, and her husband, Avi, was enough for Chava to trigger childhood memories and the memory of her beloved mother. After she gave birth to their first child, their son Chaim which meant "life" in Hebrew, she began to understand the mystery of her mother's final wishes.

Her mother, Helene's first wish was to be cremated and it took Chava a long time to realize, that it was nothing other than a tactical and a practical move from her mother's part. She wanted to make it easier for Chava to fulfill her two final wishes. Her second wish, that she wanted Chava to take her ashes back to Auschwitz was more symbolic in nature. She wanted to prove that not only that she survived the horrors, the emotional and physical torture she suffered in the camp, but that she was able to leave that place of death not once, but twice and not even her ashes were forced to be spread around the countryside like thousands of others.

Helene's third wish at first seemed simple, as Chava thought that her mother just wanted to have her ashes scattered over the Red Sea as a symbol of getting her freedom from captivity of her bad memories fulfilled at the same location where, according to the Bible Moses also led his people out of bondage through the parted Red Sea.

It took her years to realize that there was a hidden agenda behind her late mother's third wish. Helene wanted her daughter, Chava to discover the truth about her family, to rediscover her abandoned religion, but most of all; she wanted Chava to discover herself. Helene Diamond succeeded.

Made in the USA
Middletown, DE
10 March 2022

62458545R00136